KT-381-540

THE SECRET BENEATH THE VEIL

THE SECRET BENEATH THE VEIL

BY

DANI COLLINS

First published in Great Britain 2016
By Mills & Boon, an imprint of HarperCollins*Publishers*
1 London Bridge Street, London, SE1 9GF

Large Print edition 2017

ISBN: 978-0-263-07049-1

Our policy is to use papers that are natural, renewable and recyclable products and made from wood grown in sustainable forests. The logging and manufacturing processes conform to the legal environmental regulations of the country of origin.

Printed and bound in Great Britain
by CPI Antony Rowe, Chippenham, Wiltshire

To you, Dear Reader,
for loving romance novels as much as I do.
I hope you enjoy this one.

CHAPTER ONE

THE AFTERNOON SUN came straight through the windows, blinding Viveka Brice as she walked down the makeshift aisle of the wedding she was preventing—not that anyone knew that yet.

The interior of the yacht club, situated on this remote yet exclusive island in the Aegean, was all marble and brass, adding more bounces of white light. Coupled with the layers of her veil, she could hardly see and had to reluctantly cling to the arm of her reviled stepfather.

He probably couldn't see any better than she could. Otherwise he would have called her out for ruining his plan. He certainly hadn't noticed she wasn't Trina.

She was getting away with hiding the fact her sister had left the building. It made her stomach both churn with nerves and flutter with excitement.

She squinted, trying to focus past the standing guests and the wedding party arranged before the robed minister. She deliberately avoided looking at the tall, imposing form of the unsuspecting groom, staring instead through the windows and the forest of masts bobbing on the water. Her sister was safe from this forced marriage to a stranger, she reminded herself, trying to calm her racing heart.

Forty minutes ago, Trina had let her father into the room where she was dressing. She'd still been wearing this gown, but hadn't yet put on the veil. She had promised Grigor she would be ready on time while Viveka had kept well out of sight. Grigor didn't even know Viveka was back on the island.

The moment he'd left the room, Viveka had helped Trina out of the gown and Trina had helped her into it. They had hugged hard, then Trina had disappeared down a service elevator and onto the seaplane her true love had chartered. They were making for one of the bigger islands to the north where arrangements were in place to marry them the moment they touched land. Viveka was buying them time by allaying suspicion, letting the ceremony continue as long as possible before she revealed herself and made her own escape.

She searched the horizon again, looking for the flag of the boat she'd hired. It was impossible to spot and that made her even more anxious than the idea of getting onto the perfectly serviceable craft. She hated boats, but she wasn't in the class that could afford private helicopters to take her to and fro. She'd given a sizable chunk of her savings to Stephanos, to help him spirit Trina away in that small plane. Spending the rest on crossing the Aegean in a speedboat was pretty close to her worst nightmare, but the ferry made only one trip per day and had left her here this morning.

She knew which slip the boat was using, though. She'd paid the captain to wait and Stephanos had assured her she could safely leave her bags on board. Once she was exposed, she wouldn't even change. She would seek out that wretched boat, grit her teeth and sail into the sunset, content that she had finally prevailed over Grigor.

Her heart took a list and roll as they reached the top of the aisle, and Grigor handed her icy fingers to Trina's groom, the very daunting Mikolas Petrides.

His touch caused a *zing* of something to go through her. She told herself it was alarm. Nervous tension.

His grip faltered almost imperceptibly. Had he felt that static shock? His fingers shifted to enfold hers, pressing warmth through her whole body. Not comfort. She didn't fool herself into believing he would bother with that. He was even more intimidating in person than in his photos, exactly as Trina had said.

Viveka was taken aback by the quiet force he emanated, all chest and broad shoulders. He was definitely too much masculine energy for Viveka's little sister. He was too much for *her*.

She peeked into his face and found his gaze trying to penetrate the layers of her veil, brows lowered into sharp angles, almost as if he suspected the wrong woman stood before him.

Lord, he was handsome with those long clean-shaven plains below his carved cheekbones and the small cleft in his chin. His eyes were a smoky gray, outlined in black spiky lashes that didn't waver as he looked down his blade of a nose.

We could have blue-eyed children, she had thought when she'd first clicked on his photo. It was one of those silly facts of genetics that had caught her imagination when she had been young enough to believe in perfect matches. To this day it was an attribute she thought made a man more attractive.

She had been tempted to linger over his image and speculate about a future with him, but she'd been on a mission from the moment Trina had tearfully told her she was being sold off in a business merger like sixteenth-century chattel. All Viveka had had to see were the headlines that tagged Trina's groom as the son of a murdered Greek gangster. No *way* would she let her sister marry this man.

Trina had begged Grigor to let her wait until March, when she turned eighteen, and to keep the wedding small and in Greece. That had been as much concession as he'd granted. Trina, legally allowed to marry whomever she wanted as of this morning, had *not* chosen Mikolas Petrides, wealth, power and looks notwithstanding.

Viveka swallowed. The eye contact seemed to be holding despite the ivory organza between them, creating a sense of connection that sent a fresh thrum of nervous energy through her system.

She and Trina both took after their mother in build, but Trina was definitely the darker of the two, with a rounder face and warm, brown eyes, whereas Viveka had these icy blue orbs and natural blond streaks she'd covered with the veil.

Did he know she wasn't Trina? She shielded her eyes with a drop of her lashes.

The shuffle of people sitting and the music halting sent a wash of perspiration over her skin. Could he hear her pulse slamming? Feel her trembles?

It's just a play, she reminded herself. Nothing about this was real or valid. It would be over soon and she could move on with her life.

At one time she had imagined acting for a living. All her early career ambitions had leaned toward starving artist of one kind or another, but she'd had to grow up fast and become more practical once her mother died. She had worked here at this yacht club, lying about her age so they'd hire her, washing dishes and scrubbing floors.

She had wanted to be independent of Grigor

as soon as possible, away from his disparaging remarks that had begun turning into outright abuse. He had helped her along by kicking her out of the house before she'd turned fifteen. He'd kicked her off this island, really. Out of Greece and away from her sister because once he realized she had been working, that she had the means to support herself and wouldn't buckle to his will when he threatened to expel her from his home, he had ensured she was fired and couldn't get work anywhere within his reach.

Trina, just nine, had been the one to whisper, *Go. I'll be okay. You should go.*

Viveka had reached out to her mother's elderly aunt in London. She had known Hildy only from Christmas cards, but the woman had taken her in. It hadn't been ideal. Viveka got through it by dreaming of bringing her sister to live with her there. As recently as a few months ago, she had pictured them as two carefree young women, twenty-three and eighteen, figuring out their futures in the big city—

"I, Mikolas Petrides..."

He had an arresting voice. As he repeated his name and spoke his vows, the velvet-and-steel cadence of his tone held her. He smelled good, like fine clothes and spicy aftershave and something unique and masculine that she knew would imprint on her forever.

She didn't want to remember this for the rest of her life. It was a ceremony that wasn't even supposed to be happening. She was just a placeholder.

Silence made her realize it was her turn.

She cleared her throat and searched for a suitably meek tone. Trina had never been a target for Grigor. Not just because she was his biological daughter, but also because she was on the timid side—probably because her father was such a mean, loudmouthed, sexist bastard in the first place.

Viveka had learned the hard way to be terrified of Grigor. Even in London his cloud of intolerance had hung like a poison cloud, making her careful about when she contacted Trina, never setting Trina against him by confiding her suspicions, always aware he could hurt Viveka through her sister.

She had sworn she wouldn't return to Greece, certainly not with plans that would make Grigor hate her more than he already did, but she was confident he wouldn't do more than yell in front of all these wedding guests. There were media moguls in the assemblage and paparazzi circling the air and water. The risk in coming here was a tall round of embarrassed confusion, nothing more.

She sincerely hoped.

The moment of truth approached. Her voice thinned and cracked, making her vows a credible imitation of Trina's as she spoke fraudulently in her sister's place, nullifying the marriage—and merger—that Grigor wanted so badly. It wasn't anything that could truly balance the loss of her mother, but it was a small retribution. Viveka wore a grim inner smile as she did it.

Her bouquet shook as she handed it off and her fingers felt clumsy and nerveless as she exchanged rings with Mikolas, keeping up the ruse right to the last minute. She wouldn't sign any papers, of course, and she would have to return these rings. Darn, she hadn't thought about that.

Even his hands were compelling, so well shaped and strong, so sure. One of his nails looked... She wasn't sure. Like he'd injured it once. If this were a real wedding, she would know that intimate detail about him.

Silly tears struck behind her eyes. She had the same girlish dreams for a fairy-tale wedding as any woman. She wished this were the beginning of her life with the man she loved. But it wasn't. Nothing about this was legal or real.

Everyone was about to realize that.

"You may kiss the bride."

Mikolas Petrides had agreed to this marriage for one reason only: his grandfather. He wasn't a sentimental man or one who allowed himself to be manipulated. He sure as hell wasn't marrying for love. That word was an immature excuse for sex and didn't exist in the real world.

No, he felt nothing toward his bride. He felt nothing toward anyone, quite by conscious decision.

Even his loyalty to his grandfather was provisional. Pappoús had saved his life. He'd *given* Mikolas this life once their blood connection had been verified. He had recognized Mikolas as his grandson, pulling him from the powerless side of a brutal world to the powerful one.

Mikolas repaid him with duty and legitimacy. His grandfather had been born into a good family during hard times. Erebus Petrides hadn't stayed on the right side of the law as he'd done what he'd seen as necessary to survive. Living a corrupt life had cost the old man his son and Mikolas had been Erebus's second chance at an heir. He had given his grandson full rein with his ill-gotten empire on the condition Mikolas turn it into a legal—yet still lucrative—enterprise.

No small task, but this marriage merger was the final step. To the outside observer, Grigor's world-renowned conglomerate was absorbing a second-tier corporation with a questionable pedigree. In reality, Grigor was being paid well for a company logo. Mikolas would eventually run the entire operation.

Was it irony that his mother had been a laundress? Or appropriate?

Either way, this marriage had been Grigor's condition. He wanted his own blood to inherit his wealth. Mikolas had accepted to make good on his debt to his grandfather. Marriage would work for him in other ways and it was only another type of contract. This ceremony was more elaborate than most business meetings, but it was still just a date to fix signatures upon dotted lines followed by the requisite photo op.

Mikolas had met his bride—a girl, really—twice. She was young and extremely shy. Pretty enough, but no sparks of attraction had flared in him. He'd resigned himself to affairs while she grew up and they got to know one another. *Therein might be another advantage to marriage*, he had been thinking distantly, while he waited for her to walk down the aisle. Other women wouldn't wheedle for marriage if he already wore a ring.

Then her approach had transfixed him. Something happened. *Lust.*

He was never comfortable when things happened outside his control. This was hardly the time or place for a spike of naked hunger for a woman. But it happened.

She arrived before him veiled in a waterfall mist that he should have dismissed as an irritating affectation. For some reason he found the mystery deeply erotic. He recognized her perfume as the same scent she'd worn those other times, but rather than sweet and innocent, it now struck him as womanly and heady.

Her lissome figure wasn't as childish as he'd first judged, either. She moved as though she owned her body, and how had he not noticed before that her eyes were such a startling shade of blue, the kind that sat as a pool of water against a glacier? He could barely see her face, but the intensity of blue couldn't be dimmed by a few scraps of lace.

His heart began to thud with an old, painful beat. *Want.* The real kind. The kind that was more like basic necessity.

A flicker of panic threatened, but he clamped down on the memories of deprivation. Of denial. Terror. Searing pain.

He got what he wanted these days. Always. He was getting *her.*

Satisfaction rolled through him, filling him with anticipation for this pomp and circumstance to end.

The ceremony progressed at a glacial pace. Juvenile eagerness struck him when he was finally able to lift her veil. He didn't celebrate Christmas, yet felt it had arrived early, just for him.

He told himself it was gratification at accomplishing the goal his grandfather had assigned him. With this kiss, the balance sheets would come out of the rinse cycle, clean and pressed like new. Too bad the old man hadn't been well enough to travel here and enjoy this moment himself.

Mikolas revealed his bride's face and froze.

She was beautiful. Her mouth was eye-catching with a lush upper lip and a bashful bottom one tucked beneath it. Her chin was strong and came up a notch in a hint of challenge while her blue, blue irises blinked at him.

This was no girl on the brink of legal age. She was a woman, one who was mature enough to look him straight in the eye without flinching.

She was *not* Trina Stamos.

"Who the hell are you?"

Gasps went through the crowd.

The woman lifted a hand to brush her veil free of his dumbfounded fingers.

Behind her, Grigor shot to his feet with an ugly curse. "What are you doing here? Where's Trina?"

Yes. Where was his bride? Without the right

woman here to speak her vows and sign her name, this marriage—*the merger*—was at a standstill. *No.*

As though she had anticipated Grigor's reaction, the bride zipped behind Mikolas, using him like a shield as the older man bore down on them.

"You little bitch!" Grigor hissed. Trina's father was not as shocked by the switch as he was incensed. He clearly knew this woman. A vein pulsed on his forehead beneath his flushed skin. "Where is she?"

Mikolas put up a hand, warding off the old man from grabbing the woman behind him. He would have his explanation from her before Grigor unleashed his temper.

Or maybe he wouldn't.

Another round of surprised gasps went through the crowd, punctuated by the clack of the fire door and a loud, repetitive ring of its alarm.

His bride had bolted out the emergency exit.

What the *hell*?

CHAPTER TWO

VIVEKA RAN EVERY DAY. She was fit and adrenaline pulsed through her arteries, giving her the ability to move fast and light as she fled Grigor and his fury.

The dress and the heels and the spaces between planks and the floating wharf were another story. *Bloody hell.*

She made it down the swaying ramp in one piece, thanks to the rails on either side, but then she was racing down the unsteady platform between the slips, scanning for the flag of her vessel—

The train of her dress caught. She didn't even see on what. She was yanked back and that was all it took for her to lose her footing completely. *Stupid heels.*

She turned her ankle, stumbled, tried to catch herself, hooked her toe in a pile of coiled rope and threw out an arm to snatch at the rail of the yacht in the slip beside her.

She missed, only crashing into the side of the boat with her shoulder. The impact made her "oof!" Her grasp was too little, too late. She slid sideways and would have screamed, but had the sense to suck in a big breath before she fell.

Cold, murky salt water closed over her.

Don't panic, she told herself, splaying out her limbs and only getting tangled in her dress and veil.

Mom. This was what it must have been like for her on that night far from shore, suddenly finding herself under cold, swirling water, tangled in an evening dress.

Don't panic.

Viveka's eyes stung as she tried to shift the veil enough to see which way the bubbles were going. Her dress hadn't stayed caught. It had come all the way in with her and floated all around her, obscuring her vision, growing heavier. The chill of the water penetrated to her skin. The weight of the dress dragged her down.

She kicked, but the layers of the gown were in

the way. Her spiked heels caught in the fabric. This was futile. She was going to drown within swimming distance to shore. Grigor would stand above her and applaud.

The back of her hand scraped barnacles and her foot touched something. The seabed? Her hand burned where she'd scuffed it, but that told her there was a pillar somewhere here. She tried to scrabble her grip against it, desperately thinking she had never held her breath this long and couldn't hold it any longer.

Don't panic.

She clawed at her veil with her other hand, tried to pull it off her hair. She would never get all these buttons open and the dress off in time to kick herself to the surface—

Don't panic.

The compulsion to gasp for air was growing unstoppable.

A hand grabbed her forearm and tugged her.

Yes, please. Oh, God, please!

Viveka blew out what little air she still had, fighting not to inhale, fighting to kick and help bring herself to the blur of light above her, fighting to reach it…

As she broke through, she gasped in a lungful of life-giving oxygen, panting with exertion, thrusting back her veil to stare at her rescuer.

Mikolas.

He looked murderous.

Her heart lurched.

With a yank, he dragged her toward a diving ramp off the back of a yacht and physically set her hand upon it. She slapped her other bleeding hand onto it, clinging for dear life. Oh, her hand stung. So did her lungs. Her stomach was knotted with shock over what had just happened. She clung to the platform with a death grip as she tried to catch her breath and think clear thoughts.

People were gathering along the slip, trying to see between the boats, calling to others in Greek and English. "There she is!" "He's got her." "They're safe."

Viveka's dress felt like it was made of lead. It continued trying to pull her under, tugged by the wake that set all the boats around them rocking and sucking. She shakily managed to scrape the veil off her hair, ignoring the yank on her scalp as she raked it from her head. She let it float away, not daring to look for Grigor. She'd caught a glimpse of his stocky legs and that was enough. Her heart pounded in reaction.

"What the *hell* is going on?" Mikolas said in that darkly commanding voice. "Where is Trina? Who are you?"

"I'm her sis—" Viveka took a mouthful of water as a swell bashed the boat they clung to. "*Pah.* She didn't want to marry you."

"Then she shouldn't have agreed to." He hauled himself up to sit on the platform.

Oh, yes, it was just that easy.

He was too hard to face with that lethal expression. How did he manage to look so action-star handsome with his white shirt plastered to his muscled shoulders, his coat and tie gone, his hair flattened to his head? It was like staring into the sun.

Viveka looked out to where motorboats had circled to see where the woman in the wedding gown had fallen into the water.

Was that her boat? She wanted to wave, but kept a firm grip on the yacht as she used her free hand to pick at the buttons on her back. She eyed the distance to the red-and-gold boat. She couldn't swim that far in this wretched dress, but if she managed to shed it…?

Mikolas stood and, without asking, bent down to grasp her by the upper arms, pulling her up and out of the water, grunting loud enough that it was insulting. He swore after landing her on her feet beside him. His chest heaved while he glared at her limp, stained gown.

Viveka swayed on her feet, trying to keep her balance as the yacht rocked beneath them. She was still wearing the ridiculously high heels, was still in shock, but for a few seconds she could only stare at Mikolas.

He had saved her life.

No one had gone out of their way to help her like that since her mother was alive. She'd been a pariah to Grigor and a burden on her aunt, mostly fending for herself since her mother's death.

She swallowed, trying to assimilate a deep

and disturbing gratitude. She had grown a thick shell that protected her from disregard, but she didn't know how to deal with kindness. She was moved.

Grigor's voice above her snapped her back to her situation. She had to get away. She yanked at her bodice, tearing open the delicate buttons on her spine and trying to push the clinging fabric down her hips.

She wore only a white lace bra and underpants beneath, but that was basically a bikini. Good enough to swim out to her getaway craft.

To her surprise, Mikolas helped her, rending the gown as if he cursed its existence, leaving it puddled around her feet and sliding into the water. He didn't give her a chance to dive past him, however. He set wide hands on her waist and hefted her upward where bruising hands took hold of her arms—

Grigor.

"Nooo!" she screamed.

That ridiculous woman nearly kicked him in the face as he hefted her off the diving platform to the main deck of the yacht. Grigor was above, taking hold of her to bring her up. What did she think? That he was throwing her back into the sea?

"Noooo!" she cried and struggled, but Grigor pulled her all the way onto the deck where he stood.

She must be crazy, behaving like this.

Mikolas came up the ladder with the impetus of a man taking charge. He hated surprises. *He* controlled what happened to himself. No one else.

At least Grigor hadn't set this up. He'd been tricked as well, or he wouldn't be so furious.

Mikolas was putting that together as he came up to see Grigor shaking the nearly naked woman like a terrier with a rat. Then he slapped her across the face hard enough to send her to her knees.

No stranger to violence, Mikolas still took it like a punch to the throat. It appalled him on a level so deep he reacted on blind instinct, grabbing Grigor's arm and shoving him backward even as the woman threw up her arm as though to block a kick.

Stupid reaction, he thought distantly. It was a one-way ticket to a broken forearm.

But now was not the moment for a tutorial on street fighting.

Grigor found his balance and trained his homicidal gaze on Mikolas.

Mikolas centered his balance with readiness, but in his periphery saw the woman stagger toward the rail. Oh, hell, no. She was not going to ruin his day, then slip away like a siren into the deep.

He turned from Grigor's bitter "You should have let her drown" and provoked a cry of "Put me down!" from the woman as he caught her up against his chest.

She was considerably lighter without the gown, but still a handful of squirming damp skin and slippery muscle as he carried her off the small yacht.

On the pier, people parted and swiveled like gaggles of geese, some dressed in wedding regalia, others obviously tourists and sailors, all babbling in different languages as they took in the commotion.

It was a hundred meters to his own boat and he felt every step, thanks to the pedal of the woman's sharp, silver heels.

"Calm yourself. I've had it with this side-show. You're going to tell me where my bride has gone and why."

CHAPTER THREE

VIVEKA WAS SHAKING right down to her bones. Grigor had hit her, right there in front of the whole world. Well, the way the yacht had been positioned, only Mikolas had probably seen him, but in the back of her mind she was thinking that this was the time to call the police. With all these witnesses, they couldn't ignore her complaint. Not this time.

Actually, they probably could. Her report of assault and her request for a proper investigation into her mother's death had never been heeded. The officers on this island paid rent to Grigor and didn't like to impact their personal lives by carrying out their sworn duties. She had learned that bitter lesson years ago.

And this brute wouldn't let her go to do anything!

He was really strong. He carried her in arms that were so hard with steely muscle it almost hurt to be held by them. She could tell it wasn't worth wasting her energy trying to escape. And he wore a mask of such controlled fury he intimidated her.

She instinctively drew in on herself, stomach churning with reaction while her brain screamed at her to swim out to her hired boat.

"Let me go," she insisted in a more level tone.

Mikolas only bit out orders for ice and bandages to a uniformed man as he carried her up a narrow gangplank, boarding a huge yacht of aerodynamic layers and spaceship-like rigging. The walls were white, the decks teak, the sheer size and luxury of the vessel making it more like a cruise liner than a personal craft.

Greek mafia, she thought, and wriggled harder, signaling that she sincerely wanted him to put her down. *Now.*

Mikolas strode into what had to be the master cabin. She caught only a glimpse of its grand decor before he carried her all the way into a luxurious en suite and started the shower.

"Warm up," he ordered and pointed to the black satin robe on the back of the door. "Then we'll bandage your hand and ice your face while you explain yourself."

He left.

She snorted. *Not likely.*

Folding her arms against icy shivers, she eyed the small porthole that looked into the expanse of open water beyond the marina. She might fit through it, but even as the thought formed, a crewman walked by on the deck outside. She would be discovered before she got through it and in any case, she wasn't up for another swim. Not yet. She was trembling.

Reaction was setting in. She had nearly drowned. Grigor had hit her. He'd do worse if he got his hands on her again. Had he come aboard behind them?

She wanted to cry out of sheer, overwhelmed reaction.

But she wouldn't.

Trina was safe, she reminded herself. Never again did she have to worry about her little sister. Not in the same way, anyway.

The steaming shower looked incredibly inviting. Its gentle hiss beckoned her.

Don't cry, she warned herself, because showers

were her go-to place for letting emotion overcome her, but she couldn't afford to let down her guard. She may yet have to face Grigor again.

Her insides congealed at the thought.

She would need to pull herself together for that, she resolved, and closed the curtain across the porthole before picking herself free of the buckles on her shoes. She stepped into the shower still wearing her bra and undies, then took them off to rinse them and— Oh. She let out a huff of faint laughter as she saw her credit card stuck to her breast.

The chuckle was immediately followed by a stab of concern. Her bags, passport, phone and purse were on the hired boat. Was the captain waiting a short trot down the wharf? Or bobbing out in the harbor, wondering if she'd drowned? Grabbing this credit card and shoving it into her bra had been a last-minute insurance against being stuck without resources if things went horribly wrong, but she hadn't imagined things would go *this* far wrong.

The captain was waiting for her, she assured herself. She would keep her explanations short and sweet to Mikolas and be off. He seemed like a reasonable man.

She choked on another snort of laughter, this one edging toward hysteria.

Then another wave of that odd defenselessness swirled through her. Why had Mikolas saved her? It made her feel like— She didn't know what this feeling was. She never relied on anyone. She'd never been *able* to. Her mother had loved her, but she'd died. Trina had loved her, but she'd been too young and timorous to stand up to Grigor. Aunt Hildy had helped her to some extent, but on a quid-pro-quo basis.

Mikolas was a stranger who had risked his life to preserve hers. She didn't understand it.

It infused her with a sense that she was beholden to him. She hated that feeling. She had had a perfect plan to get Hildy settled, bring Trina to London once she was eighteen and finally start living life on her own terms. Then Grigor had ruined it by promising Trina to this… *criminal*.

A criminal who wasn't averse to fishing a woman out of the sea—something her stepfather hadn't bothered doing with her mother, leaving that task to search and rescue.

She was still trembling, still trying to make sense of it as she dried off with a thick black towel monogrammed with a silver *M.* She stole a peek in his medicine chest, bandaged her hand, used some kind of man-brand moisturizer that didn't have a scent, rinsed with his mouthwash, then untangled her hair with a comb that smelled like his shampoo. She used his hair dryer to dry her underwear and put both back on under his robe.

The robe felt really good, light and cool and slippery against her humid skin.

She felt like his lover wearing something this intimate.

The thought made her blush and a strange wistfulness hit her as she worked off his rings—both the diamond that Trina had given her and the platinum band he'd placed on her finger himself—and set them on the hook meant for facecloths. He was *not* the sort of man she would ever want to marry. He was far too daunting and she needed her independence, but she did secretly long for someone to share her life with.

Someone kind and tender who would make her laugh and maybe bring her flowers sometimes.

Someone who wanted her in his life.

She would *not* grow maudlin about her sister running off with Stephanos, seemingly choosing him over Viveka, leaving her nursing yet another sting of rejection. Her sister was entitled to fall in love.

With a final deep breath, she emerged into the stateroom.

Mikolas was there, wearing a pair of black athletic shorts and towel-dried hair, nothing else. His silhouette was a bleak, masculine statue against the closed black curtains.

The rest of the room was surprisingly spacious for a boat, she noted with a sweeping glance. There was a sitting area with a comfortable-looking sectional facing a big-screen TV. A glass-enclosed office allowed a tinted view of a private deck in the bow. She averted her gaze from the huge bed covered with a black satin spread and came back to the man who watched her with an indecipherable expression.

He held a drink, something clear and neat. Ouzo, she assumed. His gaze snagged briefly on the red mark on her cheek before traversing to her bare feet and coming back to slam into hers.

His expression still simmered with anger, but there was something else that took her breath. A kind of male assessment that signaled he was weighing her as a potential sex partner.

Involuntarily, she did the same thing. How could she not? He was really good-looking. His build was amazing, from those broad, bare shoulders to that muscled chest to those washboard abs and soccer-star legs.

She was not a woman who gawked at men. She considered herself a feminist and figured if it was tasteless for men to gaze at pinup calendars, then women shouldn't objectify men, either, but seriously. *Wow.* He was muscly without being overdeveloped. His skin was toasted a warm brown and that light pattern of hair on his chest looked like it had been sculpted by the loving hand of Mother Nature, not any sort of waxing specialist.

An urge to touch him struck her. Sexual desire wasn't something that normally hit her out of the blue like this, but she found herself growing warm with more than embarrassment. She wondered what it would be like to roam her mouth over his torso, to tongue his nipples and lick his skin. She felt an urge to splay her hands over his muscled waist and explore lower, push aside his waistband and *possess*.

Coils of sexual need tightened in her belly.

Where was the lead-up? The part where she spent ages kissing and nuzzling before she decided maybe she'd like to take things a little further? She never flashed to shoving down a man's pants and stroking him!

But that fantasy hit her along with a deep yearning and a throbbing pinch between her legs.

Was he getting *hard*? The front of his shorts lifted.

She realized where her gaze had fixated and jerked her eyes back to his, shocked with herself and at his blatant reaction.

His expression was arrested, yet filled with consideration and—she caught her breath—yes, that was an invitation. An arrogant *Help yourself.* Along with something predatory. Something that was barely contained. Decision. Carnal hunger.

The air grew so sexually charged, she couldn't find oxygen in it. The rhythm of her breaths changed, becoming subtle pants. Her nipples were stimulated by the shift of the robe against the lace of her bra. She became both wary and meltingly receptive.

This was crazy. She shook her head, as if she could erase all this sexual tension like an app that erased content on her phone if she joggled it back and forth hard enough.

With monumental effort, she jerked her gaze from his and stared blindly at the streak of light between the curtains. She folded her arms in self-protection and kept him in her periphery.

This was really stupid, letting him bring her into his bedroom like this. A single woman who lived in the city knew to be more careful.

"Use the ice," he said with what sounded like a hint of dry laughter in his tone. He nodded toward a side table where an ice pack sat on a small bar towel.

"It's not that bad," she dismissed. She'd had worse. Her lip might be puffed a little at the corner, but it was nothing like the time she'd walked around with a huge black eye, barely able to see out of it, openly telling people that Grigor had struck her. *You shouldn't talk back to him*, her teacher had said, mouth tight, gaze avoiding hers.

Grigor shouldn't have called her a whore and burned all her photos of her mother, she had retorted, but no one had wanted to hear *that*.

Mikolas didn't say anything, only came toward her, making her snap her head around and warn him off with a look.

Putting his glass down, he lifted his phone and clicked, taking a photo of her, surprising her so much she scowled.

"What are you doing?"

"Documenting. I assume Grigor will claim you were hurt falling into the water," he advised with cool detachment.

"You don't want me to try to discredit your business partner? Is that what you're saying? Are you going to take a photo after you leave your own mark on the other side of my face?" It was a dicey move, daring him like that, but she was so *sick* of people protecting *Grigor*. And she needed to know Mikolas's intentions, face them head-on.

Mikolas's stony eyes narrowed. "I don't hit women." His mouth pulled into a smile that was more an expression of lethal power than anything else. "And Grigor has discredited himself." He tilted the phone to indicate the photo. "Which may prove useful."

Viveka's insides tightened as she absorbed how cold-blooded that was.

"I didn't know Grigor had another daughter." Mikolas moved to take up his drink again. "Do you want one?" he asked, glancing toward the small wet bar next to the television. Both were inset against the shiny wood-grain cabinetry.

She shook her head. Better to keep her wits.

"Grigor isn't my father." She always took great satisfaction in that statement. "My mother married him when I was four. She died when I was nine. He doesn't talk about her, either."

Or the boating accident. Her heart clenched like a fist, trying to hang on to her memories of her mother, knotting in fury at the lack of a satisfactory explanation, wanting to beat the truth from Grigor if she had to.

"Do you have a name?" he asked.

"Viveka." The corner of her mouth pulled as

she realized they'd come this far without it. She was practically naked, wearing a robe that had brushed his own skin and surrounded her in the scent of his aftershave. "Brice," she added, not clarifying that most people called her Vivi.

"Viveka," he repeated, like he was trying out the sound. They were speaking English and his thick accent gave an exotic twist to her name as he shaped out the *Vive* and added a short, hard *ka* to the end.

She licked her lips, disturbed by how much she liked the way he said it.

"Why the melodrama, Viveka? I asked your sister if she was agreeable to this marriage. She said yes."

"Do you think she would risk saying no to something Grigor wanted?" She pointed at the ache on her face.

Mikolas's expression grew circumspect as he dropped his gaze into his drink, thumb moving on the glass. It was the only indication his thoughts were restless beneath that rock-face exterior.

"If she wants more time," he began.

"She's marrying someone else," she cut in.

"Right this minute, if all has gone to plan." She glanced for a clock, but didn't see one. "She knew Stephanos at school and he worked on Grigor's estate as a landscaper."

Trina had loved the young man from afar for years, never wanting to tip her hand to Grigor by so much as exchanging more than a shy hello with Stephanos, but she had waxed poetic to Viveka on dozens of occasions. Viveka hadn't believed Stephanos returned the crush until Trina's engagement to Mikolas had been announced.

"When Stephanos heard she was marrying someone else, he asked Trina to elope. He has a job outside of Athens." One that Grigor couldn't drop the ax upon.

"Weeding flower beds?" Mikolas swirled his drink. "She could have kept him on the side after we married, if that's what she wanted."

"Really," Viveka choked.

He shrugged a negligent shoulder. "This marriage is a business transaction, open to negotiation. I would have given her children if she wanted them, or a divorce eventually, if that was her preference. She should have spoken to me."

"Because you're such a reasonable man—who just happens to trade women like stocks and bonds."

"I'm a man who gets what he wants," he said in a soft voice, but it was positively deadly. "I want this merger."

He sounded so merciless her heart skipped in alarm. *Gangster.* She found a falsely pleasant smile.

"I wish you great success in making your dreams come true. Do you mind if I wear this robe to my boat? I can bring it back after I dress or maybe one of your staff could come with me?" She pushed her hand into the pocket and gripped her credit card, feeling the edge dig into her palm. Where was Grigor? she wondered. She had no desire to pass him on the dock and get knocked into the water again—this time unconscious.

Mikolas's expression didn't change. He said nothing, but she had the impression he was laughing at her again.

Something made her look toward the office and the view beyond the bow. The marina was tucked against a very small indent on the island's coastline. The view from shore was mostly an expanse of the Aegean. But the boats weren't passing in front of this craft. They were coming and going on both sides. The slant of sunlight on the water had shifted.

The yacht was moving.

"Are you kidding me?" she screeched.

CHAPTER FOUR

MIKOLAS THREW BACK the last of his ouzo, clenched his teeth against the burn and set aside his glass with a decisive *thunk*. He searched for the void that he usually occupied, but he couldn't find it. He was swirling in a miasma of lascivious need, achingly hard after the way Viveka had stared at his crotch and swallowed like her mouth was watering.

He absently ran a hand across his chest where his nipples were so sharp they pained him and adjusted himself so he wouldn't pop out of his shorts, resisting the urge to soothe the ache with a squeeze of his fist.

His reaction to her was unprecedented. He was an experienced man, had a healthy appetite for sex, but had never reacted so immediately and irrepressibly to any woman.

This lack of command over himself disturbed him. Infuriated him. He was insulted at being thrown over for a gardener and unclear on his next move. Retreat was never an option for him, but he'd left the island to regroup. That smacked of cowardice and he pinned the blame for all of it on this woman.

While she stood there with her hand closed over the lapels of his robe, holding it tight beneath her throat. Acting virginal when she was obviously as wily and experienced as any calculating opportunist he'd ever met.

"Let's negotiate our terms, Viveka." From the moment she had admitted to being Trina's sister he had seen the logical way to rescue this deal. Hell, by turning up in Trina's gown she'd practically announced to him how this would play out.

Of course it was a catch-22. He wasn't sure he wanted such a tempting woman so close to him, but he refused to believe she was anything he couldn't handle.

Viveka only flashed him a disparaging look and spun toward the door.

He didn't bother stopping her. He followed at a laconic pace as she scurried her way out to the stern of the mid-deck. Grasping the rail in one hand, she shaded her eyes with the other, scanning the empty horizon. She quickly threw herself to the port side. Gazing back to the island, which had been left well behind them, she made a distressed noise and glared at him again, expression white.

"Is Grigor on board?"

"Why would he be?"

"I don't know!" Her shoulders relaxed a notch, but she continued to look anxious. "Why did you leave the island?"

"Why would I stay?"

"Why would you take me?" she cried.

"I want to know why you've taken your sister's place."

"You didn't have to leave shore for that!"

"You wanted Grigor present? He seemed to be inflaming things." Grigor hadn't expected his departure, either. Mikolas's phone had already buzzed several times with calls from his would-be business partner.

That had been another reason for Mikolas's departure. If he'd stayed, he might have assaulted Grigor. The white-hot urge had been surprisingly potent and yes, that too had been provoked by this exasperating woman.

It wasn't a desire to protect *her*, Mikolas kept telling himself. His nature demanded he dominate, particularly over bullies and brutes. His personal code of ethics wouldn't allow him to stand by and watch any man batter a woman.

But Grigor's attack on this one had triggered something dark and primal in him, something he didn't care to examine too closely. Since cold-blooded murder was hardly a walk down the straight and narrow that was his grandfather's expectation of him, he'd taken himself out of temptation's reach.

"I had a boat hired! All my things are on it." Viveka pointed at the island. "Take me back!"

Such a bold little thing. Time to let her know who was boss.

"Grigor promised this merger if I married his daughter." He gave her a quick once-over. "His stepdaughter will do."

She threw back her head. "Ba-ha-ha," she near shouted and shrugged out of his robe, dropping it to the deck. "No. 'Bye." Something flashed in her hand as she started to climb over the rail.

She was fine-boned and supple and so easy to take in hand. Perhaps he took more enjoyment than he should in having another reason to touch her. Her skin was smooth and warm, her wrists delicate in his light grip as he calmly forced them behind her back, trapping her between the rail and his body.

She strained to look over her shoulder, muttering, “Oh, you—!” as something fell into the water with a glint of reflected light. “That was my credit card. Thanks a *lot*.”

“Viveka.” He was stimulated by the feel of her naked abdomen against his groin, erection not having subsided much and returning with vigor. Her spiked heels were gone, which was a pity. They’d been sexy as hell, but when it came to rubbing up against a woman, the less clothes the better.

She smelled of his shampoo, he noted, but there was an intriguing underlying scent that was purely hers: green tea and English rain. And that heady scent went directly into his brain, numbing him to everything but thoughts of being inside her.

Women were more subtle than men with their responses, but he read hers as clearly as a billboard. Not just the obvious signs like the way her nipples spiked against the pattern of her see-through bra cups, erotically abrading his chest and provoking thoughts of licking and sucking at them until she squirmed and moaned. A blush stained her cheeks and she licked her lips. There was a bonelessness to her. He could practically feel the way her blood moved through her veins like warm honey. He knew instinctively that opening his mouth against her neck would make her shiver and surrender to him. Her arousal would feed into his and they'd take each other to a new dimension.

Where did that ridiculous notion come from? He was no sappy poet. He tried to shake the idea out of his head, but couldn't rid himself of the certainty that sex with her would be the best he'd ever known. They were practically catching fire from this light friction. His heart was ramping with strength in his chest, his body magnetized to hers.

He was incensed with her, he reminded himself, but he was also intrigued by this unique attunement they had. Logic told him it was dangerous, but the primitive male inside him didn't give a damn. He *wanted* her.

"This is kidnapping. And assault," she said, giving a little struggle against his grip. "I thought you didn't hurt women."

"I don't let them hurt themselves, either. You'll kill yourself jumping into the water out here."

Something flickered in her expression. Her skin was very white compared with her sister's. How had he not noticed that from the very first, veil notwithstanding?

"Stop behaving like a spoiled child," he chided.

She swung an affronted look to him like it was the worst possible insult he could level at her. "How about you stop acting like you own the world?"

"This *is* my world. You walked into it. Don't complain how I run it."

"I'm trying to leave it."

"And I'll let you." Something twisted in his gut, as if that was a lie. A big one. "After you fix the damage you've done."

"How do you suggest I do that?"

"Marry me in your sister's place."

She made a choking noise and gave another wriggle of protest, heel hooking on the lower rung of the rail as if she thought she could lift herself backward over the rail.

All she managed to do was pin herself higher against him. She stilled. Hectic color deepened in her cheekbones.

He smiled, liking what she'd done. Her movement had opened her legs and brought her cleft up to nestle against his shaft. She'd caught the same zing of sexual excitement that her movement had sent through him. He nudged lightly, more of a tease than a threat, and watched a delicate shiver go through her.

It was utterly enthralling. He could only stare at her parted, quivering mouth. He wanted to cover and claim it. He wanted to drag his tongue over every inch of her. Wanted to push at his elastic waistband, press aside that virginal white lace and thrust into the heat that was branding him through the thin layers between them.

He had expected to spend this week frustrated. Now he began to forgive her for this switch of hers. They would do very nicely together. Very. Nicely.

"Let's take this back to my stateroom." His

voice emanated from somewhere deep in his chest, thick with the desire that gripped him.

Her eyes flashed with fear before she said tautly, "To consummate a marriage that won't happen? Did you see how Grigor reacted to me? He'll never let me sub in for Trina. If anything would make him refuse your merger, marrying me would do it."

Mikolas slowly relaxed his grip and stepped back, trailing light fingers over the seams at her hips.

Goose bumps rose all over her, but she ignored it, hoping her knickers weren't showing the dampness that had released at the feel of him pressed against her.

What was *wrong* with her? She didn't even *do* sex. Kissing and petting were about it.

She dipped to pick up the robe and knotted it with annoyance. How could she be this hot when the wind had cooled to unpleasant and the sky was thickening with clouds?

She sent an anxious look at the ever-shrinking island amid the growing whitecaps. It was way too far to swim. Mikolas might have done her a favor taking her out of Grigor's reach, but being at sea thinned her composure like it was being spun out from a spool.

"You're saying if I want Grigor to go through with the merger, I should turn you over to him?" he asked.

"What? *No!*" Such terror slammed into her, her knees nearly buckled. "Why would you even think of doing something like that?"

"The merger is important to me."

"My *life* is important to me." Tears stung her eyes and she had to blink hard to be able to see him. She had a feeling her lips were trembling. Where was the man who had saved her? Right now, Mikolas looked as conscienceless as Grigor.

Crushed to see that indifference, she hid her distress by averting her gaze and swallowed back the lump in her throat.

"This is nothing," she said with as much calm as she could, pointing at her face, trying to reach through to the man who had said he didn't hurt women. "Barely a starting point for him. I'd rather take my chances with the sharks."

"You already have." The flatness of his voice

sent a fresh quake of uncertainty through her center.

What did it say about how dire her situation was that she was searching for ways to reach him? To persuade *this* shark to refrain from offering her giftwrapped to the other one?

"If—if—" She wasn't really going to say this, was she? She briefly hung her head, but what choice did she have? She didn't have to go all the way, just make it good for him, right? She had a little experience with that. A very tiny little bit. He was hard, which meant he was up for it, right? "If you want sex…"

He made a scoffing noise. "*You* want sex. I'll decide if and when I give it to you. There's no leverage in offering it to me."

Sex was a basket of hang-ups for her. Offering herself had been really hard. Now she felt cheap and useless.

She pushed her gaze into the horizon, trying to hide how his denigration carved into her hard-won confidence.

"Go below," he commanded. "I want to make some calls."

She went because she needed to be away from him, needed to lick her wounds and reassess.

A purser showed her into a spacious cabin with a sitting room, a full en suite and a queen bed with plenty of tasseled pillows in green and gold. The cabinetry was polished to showcase the artistic grains in the amber-colored wood and the room was well-appointed with cosmetics, fresh fruit, champagne and flowers.

Her stomach churned too much to even think of eating, but she briefly considered drinking herself into oblivion. Once she noticed the laptop dock, however, she began looking for a device to contact…whom? Aunt Hildy wasn't an option. Her workmates might pick up a coffee or cover for her if she had to run home, but that was the extent of favors she could ask of them.

It didn't matter anyway. There was nothing here. The telephone connected to the galley or the bridge. The television was part of an onboard network that could be controlled by a tablet, but there was no tablet to be found.

At least she came across clothes. Women's, she noted with a cynical snort. Mikolas must have been planning to keep his own paramour on the side after his marriage.

Everything was in Viveka's size, however, and it struck her that this was Trina's trousseau. This was her sister's suite.

Mikolas hadn't expected her sister to share his room? Did that make him more hard-hearted than she judged him? Or less?

Men never dominated her thoughts this way. She never let them make her feel self-conscious and second-guess every word that passed between them. This obsession with Mikolas was a horribly susceptible feeling, like he was important to her when he wasn't.

Except for the fact he held her life in his iron fist.

Thank God she had saved Trina from marrying him. She'd done the right thing taking her sister's place and didn't hesitate to make herself at home among her things, weirdly comforted by a sense of closeness to her as she did.

Pulling on a floral wrap skirt and a peasant blouse—both deliberately light and easily removed if she happened to find herself treading water—Viveka had to admit she was relieved

Mikolas had stopped her from jumping. She *would* rather take her chances with sharks than with Grigor, but she didn't have a death wish. She was trying not to think of her near drowning earlier, but it had scared the hell out of her.

So did the idea of being sent back to Grigor.

Somehow she had to keep a rational head, but after leaving Grigor's oppression and withstanding Aunt Hildy's virulence, Viveka couldn't take being subjugated anymore. That's why she'd come back to help Trina make her own choices. The idea of her sister living in sufferance as part of a ridiculous business deal had made her furious!

Opening the curtains that hid two short, wide portholes stacked upon each other, she searched the horizon for a plan. At least this wasn't like that bouncy little craft she'd dreaded. This monstrosity moved more smoothly and quietly than the ferry. It might even take her to Athens.

That would work, she decided. She would ask Mikolas to drop her on the mainland. She would meet up with Trina, Stephanos could arrange for her things to be delivered, and she would find her way home.

This pair of windows was some sort of extension, she realized, noting the cleverly disguised seam between the upper and lower windows. The top would lift into an awning while the bottom pushed out to become the railing on a short balcony. Before she thought it through, her finger was on the button next to the diagram.

The wall began to crack apart while an alarm went off with a horrible honking blare, scaring her into leaping back and swearing aloud.

Atop that shock came the interior door slamming open.

Mikolas had dressed in suit pants and a crisp white shirt and wore a *terrible* expression.

"I just wanted to see what it did!" Viveka cried, holding up a staying hand.

What a liability she was turning into.

Mikolas moved to stop and reverse the extension of the balcony while he sensed the engines being cut and the yacht slowing. As the wall restored itself, he picked up the phone and instructed his crew to stay the course.

Hanging up, he folded his arms and told himself this rush of pure, sexual excitement each time he looked at Viveka was transitory. It was the product of a busy few weeks when he hadn't made time for women combined with his frustration over today's events. Of course he wanted to let off steam in a very base way.

She delivered a punch simply by standing before him, however. He had to work at keeping his thoughts from conjuring a fantasy of removing that village girl outfit of hers. The wide, drawstring collar where her bra strap peeked was an invitation, the bare calves beneath the hem of her pretty skirt a promise of more silken skin higher up.

Those unpainted toes seemed ridiculously unguarded. So did the rest of her, with her hair tied up like a teenager and her face clean.

Some women used makeup as war paint, others as an invitation. Viveka hadn't used any. She hadn't tried to cover the bruise, and lifted that discolored, belligerent chin of hers in a brave stare that was utterly foolish. She had no idea whom she was dealing with.

Yet something twisted in his chest. He found her nerve entirely too compelling. He wanted to feed that spark of energy and watch it detonate in his hands. He bet she scratched in bed and was dismayingly eager to find out.

Women were *never* a weakness for him. No one was. Nothing. Weakness was abhorrent to him. Helplessness was a place he refused to revisit.

"We'll eat." He swept a hand to where the door was still open and one of the porters hovered.

He sent the man to notify the chef and steered her to the upper aft deck. The curved bench seat allowed them to slide in from either side, shifting cushions until they met in the middle, where they looked out over the water. Here the wind was gentled by the bulk of the vessel. It was early spring so the sun was already setting behind the clouds on the horizon.

She cast a vexed look toward the view. He took it as annoyance that the island was long gone behind them and privately smirked, then realized she was doing it again: pulling all his focus and provoking a reaction in him.

He forced his attention to the porter as he arrived with place settings and water.

"You'll eat seafood?" he said to Viveka as the porter left.

"If you tell me to, of course I will."

A rush of anticipation for the fight went through him. "Save your breath," he told her. "I don't shame."

"How does someone influence you, then? Money?" She affected a lofty tone, but quit fiddling with her silverware and tucked her hands in her lap, turning her head to read him. "Because I would like to go to Athens—as opposed to wherever you think you're taking me."

"I have money," he informed, skipping over what he intended to do next because he was still deciding.

He stretched out his arms so his left hand, no longer wearing the ring she'd put on it, settled behind her shoulder. He'd put the ring in his pocket along with the ones she had worn. Her returning them surprised him. She must have known what they were worth. Why wasn't she trying to use them as leverage? Not that it would work, but he expected a woman in her position to at least try.

He dismissed that puzzle and returned to her question. "If someone wants to influence me, they offer something I want."

"And since I don't have anything you want…?" Little flags of color rose on her cheekbones and she stared out to sea.

He almost smiled, but the tightness of her expression caused him to sober. Had he hurt her with his rejection earlier? He'd been brutal because he wasn't a novice. You didn't enter into any transaction wearing your desires on your sleeve the way she did.

But how could she not be aware that she *was* something he wanted? Did she not feel the same pull he was experiencing?

How did she keep undermining his thoughts this way?

As an opponent she was barely worth noticing. A brief online search had revealed she had no fortune, no influence. Her job was a pedestrian position as data entry clerk for an auto parts chain. Her network of social media contacts was small, which suggested an even smaller circle of real friends.

Mikolas's instinct when attacked was to crush. If Grigor had switched his bride on purpose, he would already be ruined. Mikolas didn't lose to anyone, especially weak adversaries who weren't even big enough to appear on his radar.

Yet Viveka had slipped in like a ninja, taking him unawares. On the face of it, that made her his enemy. He had to treat her with exactly as much detachment as he would any other foe.

But this twist of hunger in his gut demanded an answering response from her. It wasn't just ego. It was craving. A weight on a scale that demanded an equal weight on the other side to balance it out.

The porter returned, poured their wine, and they both sipped. When they were alone again, Mikolas said, "You were right. Grigor wants you."

Viveka paled beneath her already stiff expression. "And you want the merger."

"My grandfather does. I have promised to complete it for him."

She bit her bottom lip so mercilessly it disappeared. "Why?" she demanded. "I mean, why is this merger so important to him?"

"Why does it matter?" he countered.

"Well, what is it you're really trying to accomplish? Surely there are other companies that could give you what you want. Why does it have to be Grigor's?"

She might be impulsive and a complete pain in the backside, but she was perceptive. It *didn't* have to be Grigor's company. He was fully aware of that. However.

"Finding another suitable company would take time we don't have."

"A man with your riches can't buy as much as he needs?" she asked with an ingenuous blink.

She was a like a baby who insisted on trying to catch the tiger's tail and stuff it in her mouth. Not stupid, but cheerfully ignorant of the true danger she was in. He couldn't afford to be lenient.

"My grandfather is ill. I had to call him to tell him the merger has been delayed. That was disappointment he didn't need."

She almost threw an askance look at him, but seemed to read his expression and sobered, getting the message that beneath his civilized exterior lurked a heartless mercenary.

Not that he enjoyed scaring her. He usually treated women like delicate flowers. After sleeping in cold alleys that stank of urine, after being tortured at the hands of degenerate, pitiless men, he'd developed an insatiable appetite for luxury and warmth and the sweet side of life. He especially enjoyed soft kittens who liked to be stroked until they purred next to him in bed.

But if a woman dared to cross him, as with any man, he ensured she understood her mistake and would never dream of doing so again.

"I owe my grandfather a great deal." He waved at their surroundings. "This."

"I presumed it was stolen," she said with a haughty toss of her head.

"No." He was as blunt as a mallet. "The money was made from smuggling profits, but the boat was purchased legally."

She snapped her head around.

He shrugged, not apologizing for what he came from. "For decades, if something crossed the border or the seas for a thousand miles, legal or illegal, my grandfather—and my father when he was alive—received a cut."

He had her attention. She wasn't saucy now. She was wary. Wondering why he was telling her this.

"Desperate men do desperate things. I know

this because I was quite desperate when I began trading on my father's name to survive the streets of Athens."

Their chilled soup arrived. He was hungry, but neither of them moved to pick up their spoons.

"Why were you on the streets?"

"My mother died. Heart failure, or so I was told. I was sent to an orphanage. I hated it." It had been a palace, in retrospect, but he didn't think about that. "I ran away. My mother had told me my father's name. I knew what he was reputed to be. The way my mother had talked, as if his enemies would hunt me down and use me against him if they found me… I thought she was trying to scare me into staying out of trouble. I didn't," he confided drily. "Boys of twelve are not known for their good judgment."

He smoothed his eyebrow where a scar was barely visible, but he could still feel where the tip of a blade had dragged very deliberately across it, opening the skin while a threat of worse—losing his eye—was voiced.

"I watched and learned from other street gangs and mostly stuck to robbing criminals because they don't go to the police. As long as I was faster and smarter, I survived. Threatening my father's wrath worked well in the beginning, but without a television or computer, I missed the news that he had been stabbed. I was caught in my lie."

Her eyes widened. "What happened?"

"As my mother had warned me, my father's enemies showed great interest. They asked me for information I didn't have."

"What do you mean?" she whispered, gaze fixed to his so tightly all he could see was blue. "Like…?"

"Torture. Yes. My father was known to have stockpiled everything from electronics to drugs to cash. But if I had known where any of it was kept, I would have helped myself, wouldn't I? Rather than trying to steal from them? They took their time believing that." He pretended the recollection didn't coat him in cold sweat.

"Oh, my God." She sat back, fingertips covering her faint words, gaze flickering over her shoulder to where his left hand was still behind her.

Ah. She'd noticed his fingernail.

He brought his hand between them, flexed its stiffness into a fist, then splayed it.

"These two fingernails." He pointed, affecting their removal as casual news. "Several bones broken, but it works well enough after several surgeries. I'm naturally left-handed so that was a nuisance, but I'm quite capable with both now, so…"

"Silver lining?" she huffed, voice strained with disbelief. "How did you get away?"

"They weren't getting anywhere with questioning me and hit upon the idea of asking my grandfather to pay a ransom. He had no knowledge of a grandson, though. He was slow to act. He was grieving. Not pleased to have some pile of dung attempting to benefit off his son's name. I had no proof of my claim. My mother was one of many for my father. That was why she left him."

He shrugged. Female companionship had never been a problem for any of the Petrides men. They were good-looking and powerful and money was seductive. Women found *them*.

"Pappoús could have done many things, not least of which was let them finish killing me. He asked for blood tests before he paid the ransom. When I proved to be his son's bastard, he made me his heir. I suddenly had a clean, dry bed, ample food." He nodded at the beautiful concoction before them: a shallow chowder of corn and buttermilk topped with fat, pink prawns and chopped herbs. "I had anything I wanted. A motorcycle in summer, ski trips in winter. Clothes that were tailored to fit my body in any style or color I asked. Gadgets. A yacht. Anything."

He'd also received a disparate education, tutored by his grandfather's accountant in finance. His real estate and investment licenses were more purchased than earned, but he had eventually mastered the skills to benefit from such transactions. Along the way he had developed a talent for managing people, learning by observing his grandfather's methods. Nowadays they had fully qualified, authentically trained staff to handle every matter. Arm-twisting, even the emotional kind he was utilizing right now, was a retired tactic.

But it was useful in this instance. Viveka needed to understand the bigger picture.

Like his grandfather, he needed a test.

"In return for his generosity, I have dedicated myself to ensuring my grandfather's empire operates on the right side of the law. We're mostly there. This merger is a final step. I have committed to making it happen before his health fails him. You can see why I feel I owe him this."

"Why are you being so frank with me?" Her brow crinkled. "Aren't you afraid I'll repeat any of this?"

"No." Much of it was online, if only as legend and conjecture. While Mikolas had pulled many dodgy stunts like mergers that resembled money laundering, he'd never committed actual crimes.

That wasn't why he was so confident, however.

He held her gaze and waited, watching comprehension solidify as she read his expression. She would not betray him, he telegraphed. Ever.

Her lashes quivered and he watched her swallow.

Fear was beginning to take hold in her. He told himself that was good and ignored the churn of self-contempt in his belly. He wasn't like the men who had tormented him.

But he wasn't that different. Not when he casually picked up his wineglass and mentioned,

"I should tell you. Grigor is looking for your sister. You could save yourself by telling him where to find her."

"No!" The word was torn out of her, the look on her face deeply anxious, but not conflicted. "Maybe he never hit her before, but it doesn't mean he wouldn't start now. And this?" She waved at the table and yacht. "She had these trappings all her life and would have given up all of it for a kind word. At least I had memories of our mother. She didn't even have me, thanks to him. So no. *I* would rather go back to Grigor than sell her out to him."

She spoke with brave vehemence, but her eyes grew wet. It wasn't bravado. It was loyalty that would cost her, but she was willing to pay the price.

"I believe you," he pressed with quiet lack of mercy. "That Grigor would resort to violence. The way he spoke when I returned his call—" Mikolas considered himself immune to rabid foaming at the mouth. He knew firsthand how depraved a man could act, but the bloodlust in Grigor's voice had been disturbing. Familiar in a grim, dark way.

And educational. Grigor wasn't upset that his daughter was missing. He was upset the merger had been delayed. He was taking Viveka's involvement very personally and despite all his posturing and hard-nosed negotiating in the lead-up, he was revealing impatience for the merger to complete.

That told Mikolas his very thorough research prior to starting down this road with Grigor may have missed something. It wasn't a complete surprise that Grigor had kept something up his sleeve. Mikolas had chosen Grigor because he hadn't been fastidious about partnering with the Petrides name. Perhaps Grigor had thought the sacrifice to his reputation meant he could withhold certain debts or other liabilities.

It could turn out that Viveka had done Mikolas a favor, giving him this opportunity to review everything one final time before closing. He could, in fact, gain more than he'd lost.

Either way, Grigor's determination to reach new terms and sign quickly put all the power back in Mikolas's court, exactly where he was most comfortable having it.

Now he would establish that same position with Viveka and his world would be set right.

"Even if he finds her, what can he do to her?" she was murmuring, linking her hands together, nail beds white. "She's married to Stephanos. His boss works for a man who owns news outlets. Big ones. Running her to ground would accomplish nothing. No, she's safe." She seemed to be reassuring herself.

"What about you?" He was surprised she wasn't thinking of herself. "He sounded like he would hunt you down no matter where you tried to hide." It was the dead-honest truth.

Dead.

Honest.

"So you might as well turn me over and save him the trouble? And close your precious deal with the devil?" So much fire and resentment sparked off her it was fascinating.

"This deal *is* important to me. Grigor knows Pappoús is unwell, that I'm reluctant to look for another option. He wants me to hand you over, close the deal and walk away with what I want—which is to give my grandfather what he wants."

"And what I want doesn't matter." She was

afraid, he could see it, but she refused to let it overtake her. He had to admire that.

"You got what you wanted," he pointed out. "Your sister is safe from my evil clutches."

"Good," she insisted, but her mouth quivered before she clamped it into a line. One tiny tear leaked out of the corner of her eye.

Poor, steadfast little kitten.

But that depth of loyalty pleased him. She was passing her test.

He reached out to stroke her hair even though it only made her flinch and flash a look of hatred at him.

"Are you enjoying terrorizing me?"

"Please," he scoffed, taking up his glass of wine to swirl and sip, cooling a mouth that was burning with anticipation as he finalized his decision. "I'm treating you like a Fabergé egg."

He ignored the release of tension inside him as what he really wanted moved closer to his grasp.

"Grigor makes an ugly enemy. You understand why I don't want to make him into one of mine," he said.

"Is it starting to grate on your conscience?" she charged. "That he'll beat me to a pulp and throw me into the nearest body of water? I thought you didn't shame."

"I don't. But I need you to see very clearly that the action I'm taking comes at a cost. Which you will repay. I will not be leaving you in Athens, Viveka. You are staying with me."

CHAPTER FIVE

VIVEKA'S VISION GREW grainy and colorless for a moment. She thought she might pass out, which was not like her at all. She was tough as nails, not given to fainting spells like a Victorian maiden.

She had been subtly hyperventilating this whole time Mikolas had been tying his noose around her neck. Now she'd stopped breathing altogether.

Had she heard him right?

He looked like a god, his neat wedding haircut finger-combed to the side, his mouth symmetrical and unwavering after smiting her with his words. His gray eyes were impassive. Just the facts.

"But—" she started to argue, wanting to bring up Aunt Hildy.

He shook his head. "We're not bargaining. Actions have consequences. These are yours."

"You," she choked, trying to grasp what he was saying. "*You* are my consequence?"

"It's me or Grigor. I've already told you that I won't allow you to hurt yourself, so yes. I have chosen your consequence. We should eat. Before it gets warm," he said with a whimsical levity that struck her as bizarre in the middle of this intense, life-altering conversation.

He picked up his spoon, but she only stared at him. Her fingers were icicles, stiff and frozen. All of her muscles had atrophied while her heart was racing. Her mind stumbled around in the last glimmers of the bleeding sun.

"I have a life in London," she managed. "Things to do."

"I'm sure Grigor knows that and has men waiting."

Her panicked mind sprang to Aunt Hildy, but she was out of harm's reach for the moment. Still, "Mikolas—"

"Think, Viveka. Think hard."

She was trying to. She had been searching for alternatives this whole time.

"So you're abandoning the merger?" She hated the way her voice became puny and confused.

"Not at all. But the terms have changed." He was making short work of his soup and waved his spoon. "With your sister as my wife, Grigor would have had considerable influence over me and our combined organization. I was prepared to let him control his side for up to five years and pay him handsomely for his trouble. Now the takeover becomes hostile and I will push him out, take control of everything and leave him very little. I expect he'll be even more angry with you."

"Then don't be so ruthless! Why aggravate him further?"

His answer was a gentle nudge of his bent knuckle under her chin, thumb brushing the tender place at the corner of her mouth.

"He left a mark on my mistress. He needs to be punished."

Her heart stopped. She jerked back. "Mistress!"

"You thought I was keeping you out of the goodness of my heart?"

Her vision did that wobble again, fading in and out. "You said you didn't want sex." Her voice sounded like it was coming from far away.

"I said I would decide if and when I gave it to you. I have decided. Are you not going to eat those?" He had switched to his fork to eat his prawns and now stabbed one from her bowl, hungrily snapping it between his teeth, but his gaze was watchful when it swung up to hers.

"I'm not having sex with you!"

"You've changed your mind?"

"*You* did," she pointed out tartly, wishing she was one of those women who could be casual about sex. She'd been anxious from the get-go, which was probably why it had turned into this massive issue for her. "I'm not something you can buy like a luxury boat with your ill-gotten gains," she pointed out.

"I haven't purchased you." He gave her a frown of insult. "I've earned your loyalty the same way my grandfather earned mine, by saving your life. You will show your gratitude by being whatever I need you to be, wherever I need you to be."

"I'm not going to be *that*! If I understand you correctly, you want to live within the law. Well, pro tip, forcing women to have sex is against the law."

"Sex will be a fringe benefit for both of us."

He was flinty in the face of her sarcasm. "I won't force you and I won't have to."

"Keep. *Dreaming*," she declared.

His fork clattered into his empty bowl and he shifted to face her, one arm behind her, one on the table, bracketing her into a space that enveloped her in masculine energy.

She could have skittered out the far side of the bench, but she held her ground, trying to stare him down.

His gaze fell to her mouth, causing her abdominals to tighten and tremble.

"You're not thinking about it? Wondering? *Dreaming*," he mocked in a voice that jarred because he did *not* sound angry. He sounded amused and knowing. "Let's see, shall we?"

His hand shifted to cup her neck. The caress of his thumb into the hollow at the base of her throat unnerved her. If he'd been forceful, she would have reacted with a slap, but this felt almost tender. She trusted this hand. It had dragged her up to the surface of the water, giving her life.

So she didn't knock that hand away. She didn't hit him in the face as he neared, or pull away to say a hard *No*.

Somehow she got it into her head she would prove he didn't affect her. Maybe she even thought she could return to him that rejection he'd delivered earlier.

Maybe she really did want to know how it would be with him.

Whatever the perverse impulse that possessed her, she sat there and let him draw closer, keeping her mouth set and her gaze as contemptuous as she could make it.

Until his lips touched hers.

If she had expected brutality, she was disappointed. But he wasn't gentle, either.

His hold firmed on her neck as he plundered without hesitation, opening his mouth over hers in a hot, wet branding that caused a burn to explode within her. His tongue stabbed and her lips parted. Delicious swirls of pleasure invaded her belly and lower. Her eyes fluttered closed so she could fully absorb the sensations.

She *had* wondered. Intrigue had held her still for this kiss and she moaned as she basked in it, bones dissolving, muscles weakening.

He kissed her harder, dismantling her attempt to remain detached in a few short, racing heartbeats. He dragged his lips across hers in an erotic crush, the rough-soft texture of his lips like silken velvet.

All her senses came alive to the heat of his chest, the woodsy spice scent on his skin, the salt flavor on his tongue. Her skin grew so sensitized it was painful. She felt vulnerable with longing.

She splayed her free hand against his chest and released a sob of capitulation, no longer just accepting. Participating. Exploring the texture of his tongue, trying to compete with his aggression and consume him with equal fervor.

He pulled back abruptly, the loss of his kiss a cruelty that left her dangling in midair, naked and exposed. His chest moved with harsh breaths that seemed triumphant. The glitter in his eye was superior, asserting that *he* would decide *if* and *when*.

"No force necessary," he said with satisfaction deepening the corners of his mouth.

This was how it had been for her mother, Viveka realized with a crash back to reality. Twenty years ago, Grigor had been handsome and virile, provoking infatuation in a lonely widow. Viveka's earliest memories of being in his house had been ones of walking in on intimate clinches, quickly told to make herself scarce.

As Viveka had matured, she had recognized a similar yearning in herself for a man's loving attention. She understood how desire had been the first means that Grigor had used to control his wife, before encumbering her with a second child, then ultimately showing his ugliest colors to keep her in line.

Sex was a dangerous force that could push a woman down a slippery slope. That was what Viveka had come to believe.

It was doubly perilous when the man in question was so clearly not impacted by their kiss the way she was. Mikolas's indifference hurt, inflicting a loneliness on her that matched those moments in her life that had nearly broken her: losing her mother, being banished from her sister to an aunt who should have loved her, but hadn't.

She had to look away to hide her anguish.

The porter arrived to bring out the next course.

Mikolas didn't even look up from his plate as he said, "What is the name of the man who has your things? I would like to retrieve your passport before Grigor realizes it's under his nose."

Viveka needed to tell him about Aunt Hildy, but didn't trust her voice.

Mikolas said little else through the rest of their meal, only admonishing her to eat, stating at the end of it, "I want to finish the takeover arrangements. You have free run of the yacht unless you show me you need to be confined to your room."

"You seriously think I'll let you keep me like some kind of pirate's doxy?"

"Since I'm about to stage a raid and appoint myself admiral of Grigor's corporate fleet, I can't deny that label, can I? You call yourself whatever you want."

She glared at his back as he walked away.

He left her to her own devices and there must have been something wrong with her because, despite hating Mikolas for his overabundance of confidence, she was viciously glad he was running Grigor through.

At no point should she consider Mikolas her hero, she cautioned herself. She should have known there'd be a cost to his saving her life.

She flashed back to Grigor calling her useless baggage. To Hildy telling her to earn her keep.

She wasn't even finished repaying Hildy! That hardly put her in a position to show "gratitude" to Mikolas, did it?

Oh, she hated when people thought of her as some sort of nuisance. This was why she had been looking forward to settling Hildy and striking out on her own. She could finally prove to herself and the world that she carried her own weight. She was not a lodestone. She wasn't.

A rabbit hole of self-pity beckoned. She avoided it by getting her bearings aboard the aptly named *Inferno*. The top deck was chilly and dark, the early night sky spitting rain into her face as the wind came up. The hot tub looked appealing, steaming and glowing with colored underwater lights. When the porter appeared with towels and a robe, inviting her to use the nearby change room, she was tempted, but explained she was just looking around.

He proceeded to give her a guided tour through the rest of the ship. She didn't know what the official definition for "ship" was, but this behemoth had to qualify. The upper deck held the bridge along with an outdoor bar and lounge at the stern. A spiral staircase in the middle took them down to the interior of the main deck. Along with Mikolas's stateroom and her own, there was a formal dining room for twelve, an elegant lounge with a big-screen television and a baby grand piano. Outside, there was a small lifeboat in the bow, in front of Mikolas's private sundeck, and a huge sunbathing area alongside a pool in the stern.

The extravagance should have filled her with contempt, but instead she was calmed by it, able to pretend this wasn't a boat. It was a seaside hotel. One that happened to be priced well beyond her reach, but *whatever*.

It wasn't as easy to pretend on the lower deck, which was mostly galley, engine room, less extravagant guest and crew quarters. And, oh, yes, another boat, this one a sexy speedboat parked in an internal compartment of the stern.

Her long journey to get to Trina caught up to her at that point. She'd left London the night before and hadn't slept much while traveling. She went back to her suite and changed into a comfortable pair of pajamas—ridiculously pretty ones in peacock-blue silk. Champagne-colored lace edged the bodice and tickled the tops of her bare feet, adding to the feeling of luxuriating in pure femininity.

She hadn't won a prize holiday, she reminded herself, trying not to be affected by all this lavish comfort. A gilded cage was still a prison and she would *not* succumb to Mikolas's blithe expectation that he could "keep" her. He certainly would not *seduce* her with his riches and pampering.

I won't force you and I won't have to.

She flushed anew, recalling their kiss as she curled up on the end of the love seat rather than crawl into bed. She wanted to be awake if he arrived expecting sex. When it came to making love, she was more about fantasy than reality, going only so far with the few men she'd dated. That kiss with Mikolas had shaken her as much as everything else that had happened today.

Better to think about that than her near-drowning, though.

Her thoughts turned for the millionth time to her mother's last moments. Somehow she began imagining her mother was on this boat and they were being tossed about in a storm, but she couldn't find her mother to warn her. It was a dream, she knew it was a dream. She hadn't been on the other boat when her mother was lost, but she could feel the way the waves were battering this one—

Sitting up with a gasp, she sensed they'd hit rough waters. Waves splashed against the glass of her porthole and the boat rocked enough she was rolling on her bed.

How had she wound up in bed?

With a little sob, she threw off the covers and pushed to her feet.

Fear, Aunt Hildy would have said, was no excuse for panic. Viveka did not consider herself a brave person at all, but she had learned to look out for herself because no one else ever had. If this boat was about to capsize, she needed to be on deck wearing a life jacket to have a fighting chance at survival.

Holding the bulkhead as she went into the passageway, she stumbled to the main lounge. The lifeboat was on this deck, she recalled, but in the bow, on the far side of Mikolas's suite. The porter had explained all the safety precautions, which had reassured her at the time. Now all she could think was that it was a stupid place to store life jackets.

Mikolas always slept lightly, but tonight he was on guard for more than old nightmares. He was expecting exactly what happened. The balcony in Viveka's stateroom wasn't the only thing alarmed. When she left her suite, the much more discreet internal security system caused his phone to vibrate.

He acknowledged the signal, then pushed to his feet and adjusted his shorts. That was another reason he'd been restless. He was hard. And he never wore clothes to bed. They were uncomfortable even when they weren't twisted around his erection, but he'd anticipated rising at some point to deal with his guest so he had supposed he should wear something to bed.

He'd expected to find release *with* his guest, but when he'd gone to her room, she'd been fast asleep, curled up on the love seat like a child resisting bedtime, one hand pillowing her cheek. She hadn't stirred when he'd carried her to the bed and tucked her in, leaving him sorely disappointed.

That obvious exhaustion, along with her pale skin and the slight frown between her brows, had plucked a bizarre reaction from him. Something like concern. That bothered him. He was impervious to emotional manipulations, but Viveka was under his skin—and she hadn't even been awake and doing it deliberately.

He sighed with annoyance, moving into his office.

If a woman was going to wake him in the night, it ought to be for better reasons than this.

He had no doubt this private deck in the bow was her destination. He'd watched her talk to his porter extensively about the lifeboat and winch system while he'd sat here working earlier. He wasn't surprised she was attempting to escape. He wasn't even angry. He was disappointed. He hated repeating himself.

But there was an obdurate part of him that enjoyed how she challenged him. Hardly anyone stood up to him anymore.

Plus he was sexually frustrated enough to be pleased she was setting up a midnight confrontation. When he'd kissed her earlier, desire had clawed at his control with such savagery, he'd nearly abandoned one for the other and made love to her right there at the table.

His need to be in command of himself and everyone else had won out in the end. He'd pulled back from the brink, but it had taken more effort than he liked to admit.

"Come on," he muttered, searching for her in the dim glow thrown by the running lights.

This was an addict's reaction, he thought with self-contempt. His brain knew she was lethal, but the way she infused him with a sense of omnipotence was a greater lure. He didn't care that he risked self-destruction. He still wanted her. He was counting the pulse beats until he could feel the rush of her hitting his system.

Where *was* she?

Not overboard again, surely.

The thought sent a disturbing punch into the middle of his chest. He didn't know what had made him throw off his jacket and shoes and dive in after her today. It had been pure instinct. He'd shot out the emergency exit behind her, determined to hear why she had upended his plans, but he hadn't been close enough to stop her tumble into the water.

His heart had jammed when he'd seen her knock into the side of the yacht, worried she was unconscious as she went under.

Pulling her and that whale of a gown to the surface had nearly been more than he could manage. He didn't know what he would have done if the strength of survival hadn't imbued him. Letting go of her hadn't been an option. It wasn't basic human decency that had made him dive into that water, but something far more powerful that refused, absolutely refused, to go back to the surface without her.

Damn it, now he couldn't get that image of her disappearing into the water out of his head. He pushed from his office onto his private deck, where the rain and splashing waves peppered his skin. She wasn't coming down the stairs toward him.

He climbed them, walking along the outer rail of the mid-deck, seeing no sign of her.

Actually, he walked right past her. He spied her when he paused at the door into the bridge, thinking to enter and look for her on the security cameras. Something made him glance back the way he'd come and he spotted the ball of dark clothing and white skin under the life preserver ring.

What the hell?

"Viveka." He retraced his few steps, planting his bare feet carefully on the wet deck. "What are you doing out here?"

She lifted her face. Her hair was plastered in tendrils around her neck and shoulders. Her chin rattled as she stammered, "I n-n-need a l-l-life v-v-vest."

"You're freezing." *He* was cold. He bent to draw her to her feet, but she stubbornly stayed in a knot of trembling muscle, fingers wrapped firmly around the mount for the ring.

What a confounding woman. With a little more force, he started to peel her fingers open.

The boat listed, testing his balance.

Before he could fully right himself, Viveka cried out and nearly knocked him over, rising to throw her arms around his neck, slapping her soaked pajamas into his front.

He swore at the impact, working to stay on his feet.

"Are we going over?"

"No."

He could hardly breathe, she was clinging so tightly to his neck, and shaking so badly he could practically hear her bones rattling. He swore under his breath, putting together all those anxious looks out to the water. This was why she hadn't shown the sense to be terrified of *him* today. She was afraid of boats.

"Come inside." He drew her toward the stairs down to his deck.

She balked. "I don't want to be trapped if we capsize."

"We won't capsize."

She resisted so he picked her up and carried her all the way through his dark office into his stateroom, where he'd left a lamp burning, kicking doors shut along the way.

He sat on the edge of his bed, settling her icy, trembling weight on his lap. "This is only a bit of wind and freighter traffic. We're hitting their wakes. It's not a storm."

There was no heat beneath these soaked pajamas. Even in the dim light, he could see her lips were blue. He ran his hands over her, trying to slick the water out of her pajamas while he rubbed warmth into her skin.

"There doesn't have to be a storm." She was pressing into him, her lips icy against his collarbone, arms still around his neck, relaxing and convulsing in turns. "My mother drowned when it was calm."

"From a boat?" he guessed.

"Grigor took her out." Her voice fractured. "Maybe on purpose to drown her. I don't know, but I think she wanted to leave him. He took her out sailing and said he didn't know till morning that she fell, but he never acted like he cared. He told me to stop crying and take care of Trina."

If this was a trick, it was seriously good acting. The emotion in her voice sent him tumbling into equally disturbing memories buried deep in his subconscious. *Your mother died while you were at school.* The landlord had made the statement without hesitation or regret, casually destroying Mikolas's world with a few simple words. *A woman from child services is coming to get you.*

So much horror had followed, Mikolas barely registered anymore how bad that day had been. He'd shuffled it all into the past once his grandfather had taken him in. The page had been turned and he never leafed back to it.

But suddenly he was stricken with that old grief. He couldn't ignore the way her heart pounded so hard he felt it against his arm across her back. Her skin was clammy, her spine curled tight against life's blows.

His hand unconsciously followed that hard curve, no longer just warming her, but trying to soothe while stealing a long-overdue shred of comfort for himself from someone who understood what he'd suffered.

He recovered just as quickly, shaking off the moment of empathy and rearranging her so she was forced to look up at him.

"I've been honest with you, haven't I?" Perhaps he sounded harsh, but she had cracked something in him. He didn't like the cold wind blowing through him as a result. "I would tell you if we were in danger. We're not."

Viveka believed him. That was the ridiculous part of it. She had no reason to trust him, but why would he be so blunt about everything else and hide the fact they were likely to capsize? If he said they were safe, they were safe.

"I'm still scared," she admitted in a whisper, hating that she was so gutless.

"Think of something else," he chided. The edge of his thumb gave her jaw a little flick, then he dipped his head and kissed her.

She brought up a hand to the side of his face, thinking she shouldn't let this happen again, but his stubble was a fascinating texture against her palm and his lips were blessedly hot, sending runnels of heat through her sluggish blood. Everything in her calmed and warmed.

Then he rocked his mouth to part her lips with the same avid, possessive enjoyment as earlier and cupped her breast and she shuddered under a fresh onslaught of sensations. The rush hurt, it was so powerful, but it was also like that moment when he'd dragged her to the surface. He was dragging her out of her phobia into wonder.

She instinctively angled herself closer, the silk of her pajamas a wet, annoying layer between them as she tried to press herself through his skin.

He grunted and grew harder under her bottom. His arms gathered her in with a confident, sexual possessiveness while his knees splayed wider so she sat deeper against the firm shape of his sex.

Heat rushed into her loins, sharp and powerful. All of her skin burned as blood returned to every inch of her. She didn't mean to let her tongue sweep against his, but his was right there, licking past her lips, and the contact made lightning flash in her belly.

His aggression should have felt threatening, but it felt sexy and flagrant. As the kiss went on, the waves of pleasure became more focused. The way he toyed with her nipple sent thrums of excitement rocking through her.

She gasped for air when he drew back, but she didn't want to stop. Not yet. She lifted her mouth so he returned and kissed her harder. Deeper.

Her breast ached where he massaged it and the pulse between her legs became a hungry throb as he shifted wet silk against the tight point of her nipple.

His hand slid away, pulling the soggy material up from her quivery belly. He flattened his palm there, branding her cold, bare skin. His fingers searched along the edge of her waistband and he lifted his head, ready to slide his hand between her closed thighs.

"Open," he commanded.

Viveka gasped and shot off his lap, stumbling when her knees didn't want to support her. "What—no!"

She covered her throat where her pulse was racing, shocked at herself. He kept turning her into this...*animal*. That's all this was: hormones. Some kind of primal response to the caveman who happened to yank her out of the lion's jaws. The primitive part of her recognized an alpha male who could keep her offspring alive so her body wanted to make some with him.

Mikolas dropped one hand, then the other behind him, leaning on his straight arms, knees wide. His nostrils flared as he eyed her. It was the only sign that her recoil bothered him.

Contractions of desire continued to swirl in her abdomen. That part of her that was supposed to be able to take his shape felt so achy with carnal need she was nearly overwhelmed.

"You said you wouldn't make me," she managed in a shaky little voice.

It was a weak defense and they both knew it.

He cocked one brow in a mocking, *I don't have to*. The way his gaze traveled down her made her afraid for what she looked like, silk clinging to distended nipples and who knew what other telltale reactions.

She pulled the fabric away from her skin and looked to the door.

"You're bothered by your reaction to me. Why? I think it's exciting." The rasp of his arousal-husky voice made her inner muscles pinch with involuntary eagerness. "Come here. I'll hold you all night. You'll feel very safe," he promised, but his mouth quirked with wicked amusement.

She hugged herself. "I don't sleep around. I don't even know you!"

"I prefer it that way," he provided.

"Well, I don't!"

He sighed, rising and making her heart soar with alarmed excitement. It fell as he turned and walked away to the corner of the room.

She had rejected *him*, she reminded herself. This sense of rebuff was completely misplaced.

But he was so appealing with his tall, powerful frame, spine bracketed by supple muscle in the way of a martial artist rather than a gym junkie. The low light turned his skin a dark, burnished bronze and he had a really nice butt in those wet, clinging boxers.

She ought to leave, but she watched him search out three different points before he drew the wall inward like an oversize door. The cabinetry from her stateroom came with it, folding back to become part of his sitting room, creating an archway into her suite.

"I haven't used this yet. It's clever, isn't it?" he remarked.

If she didn't loathe boats so much, she might have agreed. As it was, she could only hug herself, dumbfounded to see they were now sharing a room.

"You'll feel safer like this, yes?"

Not likely!

He didn't seem to expect an answer, just turned to open a drawer. He pawed through, coming up with a pink long-sleeved top in waffle weave and a pair of pink and mint green flannel pajama pants. "Dry off and put these on. Warm up."

She waved at the archway. "Why did you do that?"

"You don't find it comforting?"

Oh, she was not sticking around to be laughed at. She snatched the pajamas from his hand, not daring to look into his face, certain she would see mockery, and made for the bathroom in her own suite. *Infuriating* man.

She would close the wall herself, she decided as she clumsily changed, even though she preferred the idea of him being in the same room with her. He was not a man to be relied on, she reminded herself. If she had learned nothing else in life, it was that she was on her own.

Then she walked out and found a life vest on the foot of her bed. When she glanced toward his room, his lamp was off.

She clutched the cool bulk of the vest to her chest, insides crumpling.

"Thank you, Mikolas," she said toward his darkened room.

A pause, then a weary "Try not to need it."

CHAPTER SIX

VIVEKA WAS SO emotionally spent, she slept late, waking with the life vest still in her crooked arm.

Sitting up with an abrupt return of memory, she noted the sun was streaming in through the uncovered windows of Mikolas's stateroom. The yacht was sailing smoothly and she could swear that was the fresh scent of a light breeze she detected. She swung her feet to the floor and moved into his suite with a blink at the brightness.

He didn't notice her, but she caught her breath at the sight of him. He was lounging on the wing-like extension from his sitting area. It was fronted by what looked like the bulkhead of his suite and fenced on either side by glass panels anchored into thin, stainless steel uprights. The wind blew over him, ruffling his dark hair.

She might have been alarmed by the way the ledge dangled over the water, but he was so relaxed, slouched on a cushioned chair, feet on an ottoman, she could only experience again the pinch of deep attraction.

He had his tablet in one hand, a half-eaten apple in the other and he was mostly naked. Again. All he wore were shorts, these ones a casual pair in checked gray and black even though the morning breeze was quite cool.

Her heart actually panged that she had to keep fighting him. He looked so casually beautiful. It wasn't just about her, though, but Aunt Hildy.

He lifted his head and turned to look at her as though he'd been aware of her the whole time. "Are you afraid to come out here?"

She was terrified, but it had nothing to do with the water and everything to do with how he affected her.

"Why are you allowed to have your balcony open and I got in trouble for it?" she asked, choosing a tone of belligerence over revealing her intimidation, forcing her legs to carry her as far as the opening.

"I had a visitor." He nodded at the deck beside his ottoman.

Her bag.

Stunned, she quickly knelt and rifled through it, coming up with her purse, phone, passport… Everything exactly as it should be. Even her favorite hair clip. She gathered and rolled the mess of her hair in a well-practiced move, weirdly comforted by that tiny shred of normalcy.

When she looked up at him, Mikolas was watching her. He finished his apple with a couple of healthy bites and flipped the core into the water.

"Help yourself." He nodded toward where a sideboard was set up next to the door to his office.

"I'm in time-out? Not allowed out for breakfast?"

No response, but she quickly saw there was more than coffee and a basket of fruit here. The dishes contained traditional favorites she hadn't eaten since leaving Greece nine years ago.

Somehow she'd convinced herself she hated everything about this country, but the moment she saw the *tiganites*, nostalgia closed her throat. A sharp memory of asking her mother if she could cut up her sister's pancakes and pour the *petimezi* came to her. Nothing tasted quite like grape molasses. Her heart panged, while her mouth watered and her stomach contracted with hunger.

"Have you eaten?" she called, hoping he didn't hear the break in her voice. She glanced out to see he didn't have a plate going.

"Óchi akóma." Not yet.

She gave him a large helping of the smoked pork omelet along with pancakes and topped up his coffee, earning a considering look as she served him.

Yes, she was trying to soften him up. A woman had to create advantages where she could with a man like him.

"Efcharistó," he said when she joined him.

"Parakaló." She was trying to act casual, but she had chosen to start with yogurt and thyme honey. The first bite tasted so perfect, was such a burst of early childhood happiness, when her mother had been alive and her sister a living doll she could dress and feed, she had to close her eyes, pressing back tears of homecoming.

Mikolas watched her, reluctantly fascinated by the emotion that drew her cheeks in while she savored her breakfast. Pained joy crinkled her brow. It was sensual and sexy and poignant. It was *yogurt*.

He forced his gaze to his own plate.

Viveka was occupying entirely too much real estate in his brain. It had to stop.

But even as he told himself that, his mind went back to last night. How could it not, with her sitting across from him braless beneath her long-sleeved nightshirt? The soft weight of her breast was still imprinted on his palm, firm and shapely, topped with a sensitive nipple he'd longed to suck.

Instantly he was primed for sex. And damn it, she'd been as fully involved as he had been. He wasn't so arrogant he made assumptions about women's states of interest. He took pains to ensure they were with him every step of the way when he made love to them. She'd been pressing herself into him, returning his kiss, moaning with enjoyment.

Fine, he could accept that she thought they were moving too fast. Obviously she was a bit of a romantic, flying across the continent to help her sister marry her first love. But sex would happen between them. It was inevitable.

When he had opened the passageway between their rooms, however, it hadn't been for sex. He had wanted to ease her anxiety. She had been nothing less than a nuclear bomb from the moment he'd seen her face, but he'd found himself searching out the catch in the wall, giving her access to *his* space, which had never been his habit with any woman.

He didn't understand his actions around her. This morning, he'd actually begun second-guessing his decision to keep her, which wasn't like him at all. Indecision did not make for control in any situation. He certainly couldn't back down because he was *scared.* Of being around a particular *woman.*

Then the news had come through that Grigor was, indeed, hiding debts in two of his subsidiaries. There was no room for equivocating after that. Mikolas had issued a few terse final orders, then notified Grigor of his intention to take over with or without cooperation.

Grigor had been livid.

Given the man's vile remarks, Mikolas was

now as suspicious as Viveka that her stepfather had killed her mother. Viveka would stay with him whether he was comfortable in her presence or not.

Whether she liked it or not. At least until he could be sure Grigor wouldn't harm her.

She opened her dreamy blue eyes and looked like she was coming back from orgasm. Sexual awareness shimmered like waves of desert heat between them.

Yes. Sex was inevitable.

Her gaze began to tangle with his, but she seemed to take herself in hand. She sat taller and cleared her throat, looking out to the water and lifting a determined chin, cheekbones glowing with pink heat.

He mentally sighed, too experienced a fighter not to recognize she was preparing to start one.

"Mikolas." He mentally applauded her take-charge tone. "I *have* to go back to London. My aunt is very old. Quite ill. She needs me."

He absorbed that with a blink. This was a fresh approach at least.

She must have read his skepticism. Her mouth tightened. "I wish I was making it up. I'm not."

If he expected her trust—and he did—he would have to trust her in return, he supposed. "Tell me about her," he invited.

She looked to the clear sky, seeming to struggle a moment.

"There's not much to tell. She's the sister of my grandmother and took me in when Grigor kicked me out, even though she was a spinster who never wanted anything to do with children. She had a career before women really did. Worked in Parliament, but not as an elected official. As a secretary to a string of them. She had some kind of lofty clearance, served coffee to all sorts of royals and diplomats. I think she was in love with a married man," she confided with a wrinkle of her nose.

Definitely a sentimentalist.

She shrugged, murmuring, "I don't have proof. Just a few things she said over the years." She picked up her coffee and cupped her hands around it. "She was always telling me how to behave so men wouldn't think things." She made a face. "I'm sure the sexism in her day was appalling. She was adamant that I be independent, pay my share of rent and groceries, know how to look after myself."

"She didn't take her own advice? Make arrangements for herself?"

"She tried." Her shoulder hitched in a helpless shrug. "Like a lot of people, she lost her retirement savings with the economic crash. For a while she had an income bringing in boarders, but we had to stop that a few years ago and remortgage. She has dementia." Her sigh held the weight of the world. "Strangers in the house upset her. She doesn't recognize me anymore, thinks I'm my mother, or her sister, or an intruder who stole her groceries." She looked into her cooling coffee. "I've begun making arrangements to put her into a nursing home, but the plans aren't finalized."

Viveka knew he was listening intently, thought about leaving it there, where she had stopped with the doctors and the intake staff and with Trina during their video chats. But the mass on her conscience was too great. She'd already told Mikolas about Grigor's abuse. He might actually understand the rest and she really needed it off her chest.

"I *feel* like I'm stealing from her. She worked really hard for her home and deserves to live in it, but she can't take care of herself. I have to run home from work every few hours to make sure she hasn't started a fire or caught a bus to who knows where. I can't afford to stay home with her all day and even if I could…"

She swallowed, reminding herself not to feel resentful, but it still hurt. Not just physically, either. She had tried from Day One to have a familial relationship with her aunt and it had all been for naught.

"She started hitting me. I know she doesn't mean it to be cruel. She's scared. She doesn't understand what's happening to her. But I can't take it."

She couldn't look at him. She already felt like the lowest form of life and he wasn't saying anything. Maybe he was letting her pour out her heart and having a laugh at her for getting smacked by an old lady.

"Living with her was never great. She's always been a difficult, demanding person. I was planning to move out the minute I finished school, but she started to go downhill. I stayed to keep house and make meals and it's come to this."

The little food she'd eaten felt like glue in her stomach. She finished up with the best argument she could muster.

"You said you're loyal to your grandfather for what he gave you. That's how I feel toward her. The only way I can live with removing her from her home is by making sure she goes to a good place. So I have to go back to London and oversee that."

Setting aside her coffee, she hugged herself, staring sightlessly at the horizon, not sure if it was guilt churning her stomach or angst at revealing herself this way.

"Now who is beating you up?" Mikolas challenged.

She swung her head to look at him. "You don't think I owe her? Someone needs to advocate for her."

"Where is she now?"

"I was coming away so I made arrangements with her doctor for her to go into an extended-care facility. It's just for assessment and referral, though. The formal arrangements have to be completed. She can't stay where she is and she can't go home if I'm not there. Her doctor is expecting me for a consult this week."

Mikolas reached for his tablet and tapped to place a call. A moment later, the tablet chimed. Someone answered in German. They had a lengthy conversation that she didn't understand. Mikolas ended with, *"Dankeschön."*

"Who was that?" she asked as he set aside the tablet.

"My grandfather's doctor. He's Swiss. He has excellent connections with private clinics all over Europe. He'll ensure Hildy is taken into a good one."

She snorted. "Neither of us has the kind of funds that will underwrite a private clinic arranged by a posh specialist from Switzerland. I can barely afford the extra fees for the one I'm hoping will take her."

"I'll do this for you, to put your mind at ease."

Her mind blanked for a full ten seconds.

"Mikolas," she finally sputtered. "I *want* to do it. I definitely don't want to be in your debt over it!" She ignored the fact that he had already decided she owed him.

Men expect things when they do you a favor, she heard Hildy saying.

A lurching sensation yanked at her heart, like a curtain being pulled aside on its rungs, exposing her at her deepest level. "What kind of sex do you think you're going to get out of me that would possibly compensate you for something like that? Because I can assure you, I'm not that good! You'll be disappointed."

So disappointed.

Had she just said "you'll"? Like she was a sure thing?

She tightened her arms across herself, refusing to look at him as this confrontation took the direction she had hoped it wouldn't: right into the red-light district of Sexville.

"If that sounds like I just agreed to have sex with you, that's not what I meant," Viveka bit out, voice less strident, but still filled with ire.

Mikolas couldn't think of another woman he'd encountered with such an easily tortured conscience or with such a valiant determination to protect people she cared about while completely disregarding the cost to herself.

She barely seemed real. He was in danger of being *moved* by her depth of loyalty toward her aunt. A jaded part of him had to question whether she was doing exactly what she claimed she wasn't: trying to manipulate him into underwriting the old woman's care, but unlike most women in his sphere, she wasn't offering sex as compensation for making her problems go away.

While he was finding the idea of her coming to his bed motivated by anything other than the same passion that gripped him more intolerable by the second.

"Let us be clear," he said with abrupt decision. "The debt you owe me is the loss of a wife."

She didn't move, but her blue eyes lifted to fix on him, watchful and limitless as the sky.

"My intention was to marry, honeymoon this week, then throw a reception for my new bride, introducing her to a social circle that has been less than welcoming to someone with my pedigree when I only ever had a mistress du jour on my arm."

Being an outsider didn't bother him. He had

conditioned himself not to need approval or acceptance from anyone. He preferred his own company and had his grandfather to talk to if he grew bored with himself.

But ostracism didn't sit well with a nature that demanded to overcome any circumstance. The more he worked at growing the corporation, the more he recognized the importance of networking with the mainstream. Socializing was an annoying way to spend his valuable time, but necessary.

"Curiosity, if nothing else, would have brought people to the party," he continued. "The permanence of my marriage would have set the stage for developing other relationships. You understand? Wives don't form friendships with women they never see again. Husbands don't encourage their wives to invite other men's temporary liaisons for drinks or dinner."

"Because they're afraid their wives will hear about their own liaisons?" she hazarded with an ingenuous blink.

Really, no sense of self-preservation.

"It's a question of investment. No one wants to put time or money into something that lacks a stable future. I was gaining more than Grigor's company by marrying. It was a necessary shift in my image."

Viveka shook her head. "Trina would have been hopeless at what you're talking about. She's sweet and funny, loves to cook and pick flowers for arrangements. You couldn't ask for a kinder ear if you need to vent, but playing the society wife? Making small talk about haute couture and trips to the Maldives? You, with your sledgehammer personality, would have crushed her before she was dressed, let alone an evening trying to find her place in the pecking order of upper-crust hens."

"Sledgehammer," he repeated, then accused facetiously, "Flirt."

She blushed. It was pretty and self-conscious and fueled by this ivory-tusked, sexual awareness they were both pretending to ignore. Her gaze flashed to his, naked and filled with last night's trance-like kiss. Her nipples pricked to life beneath the pink of her shirt. So did the flesh between his legs. The moment became so sexually infused, he almost lost the plot.

That's how he wanted it to be between them: pure reaction. Not installment payments.

He reined himself in with excruciating effort, throat tight and body readied with tension as he continued.

"Circulating with the woman who broke up my wedding is not ideal, but will look better than escorting a rebound after being thrown over. Since you'll be with me until I've neutralized Grigor, we will be able to build that same message of constancy."

"What do you mean about neutralizing Grigor?"

"I spoke to him this morning. He's not pleased with my takeover or the fact you're staying with me. You need some serious protections in place. Did you have your mother's death investigated?"

That seemed to throw her. Her face spasmed with emotion.

"I was only nine when it happened so it was years before I really put it all together and thought he could have done it. I was fourteen when I asked the police to look into it, but they didn't take me seriously. The police on the island are in his pocket. The whole island is and

I don't really blame them. I've learned myself that you play by his rules or lose everything. Probably the only reason he didn't kill me for making a statement was because it would have been awfully suspicious if something happened to me right after my complaint. But stirring up questions was one of the reasons he kicked me out. Why?"

"I will hire a private investigator to see what we can find. If something can be proved and he's put in prison, you'll be out of his reach."

"That could take years!"

"And will make him that much more incensed with you in the short term," he said drily. "But as you say, if he's under suspicion, it wouldn't look good if anything happened to you. I think it will afford you protection in the long term."

"You're going to start an investigation, take care of my aunt and protect me from Grigor and all I have to do is pretend to be your girlfriend." Her voice rang with disbelief. "For how *long*?"

"At least until the merger completes and the investigation shows some results. Play your part well and you might even earn my forgiveness for disrupting my life so thoroughly."

Her laugh was ragged and humorless. "And sex?"

She tossed her head, affecting insouciance, but the small frown between her brows told him she was anxious. That aggravated him. He could think of nothing else but discovering exactly how incendiary they would be together. If she wasn't equally obsessed, he was at a disadvantage.

Not something he ever endured.

With a casual flick of his hand, he proclaimed, "Like today's fine weather, we'll enjoy it because it's there."

Did a little shadow of disappointment pass behind her eyes? What did she expect? Lies about falling in love? They really were at an impasse if she expected that ruse.

Her mouth pursed to disguise what might have been a brief tremble. She pushed to stand. "Yes, well, the almanac is predicting heavy frost. Dress warm." She reached for her bag. "I'm going to my room."

"Leave your passport with me."

She turned back to regard him with what he was starting to think of as her princess look, very haughty and down the nose. "Why?"

"To arrange travel visas."

"To where?"

"Wherever I need you to be."

"Give me a 'for instance.'"

"Asia, eventually, but you wanted to go to Athens, didn't you? There's a party tonight. Do as you're told and I'll let you off the boat to come with me."

Her spine went very straight at that patronizing remark. Her unfettered breasts were not particularly heavy, but magnificent in their shape and firmness and chill-sharpened points. He was going to go out of his mind if he didn't touch her again soon.

As if she read his thoughts, her brows tugged together with conflict. She was no doubt thinking that the return of her purse and arrival in Athens equaled an excellent opportunity to set him in the rearview mirror.

He tensed, waiting out the minutes of her indecision. Oddly, it was not unlike the anticipation of pain. His breath stilled in his lungs, throat tight, as he willed her to do as he said.

Do not make me ask again.

Helplessness flashed in her expression before she ducked her head and drew her passport out of her bag, hand trembling as she held it out to him.

A debilitating rush of relief made his own arm feel like it didn't even belong to him. He reached to take it.

She held on while she held his gaze, incredibly beautiful with that hard-won determination lighting her proud expression. "You *will* make sure Aunt Hildy is properly cared for?"

"You and Pappoús will get along well. He holds me to my promises, too."

She released the passport into his possession, averting her gaze as though she didn't want to acknowledge the significance. Clearing her throat, she took out her phone. "I want to check in with Trina. May I have the WiFi code?"

"The security key is a mix of English and Greek characters." He held out his other hand. "I'll do it for you."

She released a noise of impatient defeat, slapped her phone into his palm and walked away.

CHAPTER SEVEN

MIKOLAS HAD SET himself up in her contacts with a selfie taken on her phone, of him sitting there like a sultan on his yacht, taking ownership of her entire life.

She couldn't stop looking at it. Those smoky eyes of his were practically making love to her, the curve of his wide mouth quirked at the corners in not quite a smile. It was more like, *I know you're naked in the shower right now.* He was so brutally handsome with his chiseled cheekbones and devil-doesn't-give-a-damn nonchalance he made her chest hurt.

Yet he had also forwarded a request from the Swiss doctor for her aunt's details along with a recommendation for one of those beyond-top-notch dementia villages that were completely unattainable for mere mortals. A quick scan of its website told her it was very patient-centric and prided itself on compassion and being ahead of the curve with quality treatment. All that was needed was the name of her aunt's physician to begin Hildy's transfer into the facility's care.

Along with Trina's well-being, a good plan for Aunt Hildy was the one thing Viveka would sell her soul for. It was a sad commentary on her life that it was the only thing pulling her back to London. She had no community there, rarely had time for dating or going out with friends. Her neighbor was nice, but mostly her life had revolved around school, then work and caring for Aunt Hildy. There was no one worrying about her now, when she had been stolen like a concubine by this throwback Spartan warrior.

She sighed, not even able to argue that her job was a career she needed to get back to. One quick email and her position had been snapped up by one of the part-timers who need the hours. She'd be on the bottom rung when she went back. If she went back. She'd accepted that job for its convenience to home, and in the back of her mind, she'd already been planning to make a change once she had Hildy settled.

But Aunt Hildy had faced nothing but challenges all her life and, in her way, she'd been

Viveka's lifeline. The old woman shouldn't have to suffer and wouldn't. Not if Viveka could help it.

And now that Mikolas had spelled out that sex wasn't mandatory…

Oh, she didn't want to think about sex with that man! He already made her feel so unlike herself she could hardly stand it. But she couldn't help wondering what it would be like to lie with him. Something about him got to her, making her blood run like cavalry into sensual battle. Sadly, Viveka had reservations that made the idea of being intimate with him seem not just ill-advised but completely impossible.

So she tried not to think of it and video-called Trina. Her sister was both deliriously joyful and terribly worried when she picked up.

"Where *are* you? Papa is furious." Her eyes were wide. "I'm scared for you, Vivi."

"I'm okay," she prevaricated. "What about you? You've obviously talked to him. Is he likely to come after you?"

"He doesn't believe this was my decision. He blames you for all of it and it sounds—I'm not sure what's going on at his office, but things are off the rails and he thinks it's your fault. I'm so sorry, Vivi."

"That doesn't surprise me," Viveka snorted, hiding how scared the news made her. "Are you and Stephanos happy? Was all of this worth it?"

"So happy! I knew he was my soul mate, but oh, Vivi!" Her sister blushed, growing even more radiant, saying in a self-conscious near-whisper, "Being married is even better than I imagined it would be."

Lovemaking. That's what her little sister was really talking about.

Envy, acute and painful, seared through Viveka. She had always felt left out when women traded stories about men and intimacy. Dating for her had mostly been disastrous. Now even her younger sister was ahead of her on that curve. It made Viveka even more insecure in her sexuality than she already was.

They talked a few more minutes and Viveka was wistful when she ended the call. She was glad Trina was living happily-ever-after. At one time, she'd believed in that fairy tale for herself, but had become more pragmatic over the years, first by watching the nightmare that her mother's romance turned into, then challenged by Aunt Hildy for wanting a man to "complete" her.

She hadn't thought of it that way, exactly. Finding a soul mate was a stretch, true, but why shouldn't she want a companion in life? What was the alternative? Live alone and lonely, like Aunt Hildy? Engage in casual hookups like Mikolas had said he preferred?

She was not built for fair-weather frolics.

Her introspection was interrupted by a call from Hildy's doctor. He was impressed that she was able to get her aunt into that particular clinic and wanted to make arrangements to move her the next morning. He assured Viveka she was doing the right thing.

The die was cast. Not long after, the ship docked and Viveka and Mikolas were whisked into a helicopter. It deposited them on top of *his* building, which was an office tower, but he had a penthouse that took up most of an upper floor.

"I have meetings this afternoon," he told her. "A stylist will be here shortly to help you get ready."

Viveka was typically ready to go out within thirty minutes. That included shampooing and drying her hair. She had never in her life started four hours before an appointment, not even when she had fake-married the man who calmly left her passport on a side table like bait and walked out.

Not that this world was so different from living with Grigor, Viveka thought, lifting her baleful gaze from the temptation of her passport to gaze around Mikolas's private domain. Grigor had been a bully, but he'd lived very well. His island mansion had had all the same accoutrements she found in Mikolas's penthouse: a guest room with a full bath, a well-stocked wine fridge and pantry, a pool on a deck overlooking a stunning view.

None of it put her at ease. She was still nervous. Expectation hung over her. Or rather, the question of what Mikolas expected.

And whether she could deliver.

Not sex, she reminded herself, trying to keep her mind off that. She turned to tormenting herself with anxiety over how well she would perform in the social arena. She wasn't shy, but she wasn't particularly outgoing. She wasn't particularly pretty, either, and she had a feeling every other woman at this party would be gorgeous if Mikolas thought she needed four hours of beautification to bring her up to par.

The stylist's preparation wasn't all shoring up of her looks, however. It was pampering with massage and a mani-pedi, encouragement to doze by the pool while last-minute adjustments were made to her dress, and a final polish on her hair and makeup that gave her more confidence than she expected.

As she eyed herself in the gold cocktail dress, she was floored at how chic she looked. The cowled halter bodice hung low across her modest chest and the snug fabric hugged her hips in a way that flattered her figure without being obvious. The color brought out the lighter strands in her hair and made her skin look like fresh cream.

The stylist had trimmed her mop, then let its natural wave take over, only parting it to the side and adding two little pins so her face was prettily framed while the rest fell away in a shiny waterfall around her shoulders. She applied false eyelashes, but they were just long enough to make her feel extra feminine, not ridiculous.

"I've never known how to make my bottom

lip look as wide as the top," Viveka complained as her lips were painted. The bruise Grigor had left there had faded overnight to unnoticeable.

"Why would you want to?" the woman chided her. "You have a very classic look. Like old Hollywood."

Viveka snorted, but she'd take it.

She had to acknowledge she was delighted with the end result, but became shy when she moved into the lounge to find Mikolas waiting for her.

He took her breath, standing at the window with a drink in his hand. He'd paired his suit with a gray shirt and charcoal tie, ever the dark horse. It was all cut to perfection against his frame. His profile was silhouetted against the glow of the Acropolis in the distance. *Zeus*, she thought, and her knees weakened.

He turned his head and even though he was already quite motionless, she sensed time stopping. Maybe they both held their breath. She certainly did, anxious for kind judgment.

Behind her, the stylist left, leaving more tension as the quiet of the apartment settled with the departure of the lift.

Viveka's eyes dampened. She swallowed to ease the dryness in the back of her throat. "I have no idea how to act in this situation," she confessed.

"A date?" he drawled, drawing in a breath as though coming back to life.

"Is that all it is?" Why did it feel so monumental? "I keep thinking that I'm supposed to act like we're involved, but I don't know much about you."

"Don't you?" His cheek ticked and she had the impression he didn't like how much she did know.

"I guess I know you're the kind of man who saves a stranger's life."

That seemed to surprise him.

She searched his enigmatic gaze, asking softly, "Why did you?" Her voice held all of the turbulent emotions he had provoked with the act.

"It was nothing," he dismissed, looking away to set down his glass.

"Please don't say that." But was it realistic to think her life had meant something to him after one glimpse? No. Her heart squeezed. "It wasn't nothing to me."

"I don't know," he admitted tightly. His eyes moved over her like he was looking for clues. "But I wasn't thinking ahead to this. Saving a person's life shouldn't be contingent on repayment. I just reacted."

Unlike his grandfather, who had wanted to know he was actually getting his grandson before stepping in. *Oh, Mikolas.*

For a moment, the walls between them were gone and the bright, magnetic thing between them tugged. She wanted to move forward and offer comfort. Be whatever he needed her to be.

For one second, he seemed to hover on a tipping point. Then a layer of aloofness fell over him like a cloak.

"I don't think anyone will have trouble believing we're involved when you look at me like that." He smiled, but it was a tad cruel. "If I wasn't finally catching up to someone I've been chasing for a while, I would accept your invitation. But I have other priorities."

She flinched, stunned by the snub.

Fortunately he didn't see it, having turned away to press the call button to bring back the elevator.

She moved on stiff legs to join him, fighting tears of wounded self-worth. Her throat ached. Compassion wasn't a character flaw, she reminded herself. Just because Grigor and Hildy and this *jackass* weren't capable of appreciating what she offered didn't mean she was worthless.

She couldn't help her reaction to him. Maybe if she wasn't such an incurable *virgin*, she'd be able to handle him, she thought furiously, but that's what she was and she hated him for taunting her with it.

She was wallowing so deep in silent offense, she moved automatically, leaving the elevator as the doors opened, barely taking in her surroundings until she heard her worst nightmare say, *"There she is."*

CHAPTER EIGHT

MIKOLAS WAS KICKING himself as the elevator came to a halt.

Viveka had been so beautiful when she had walked into the lounge, his heart had lurched. An unfamiliar lightheartedness had overcome him. It hadn't been the money spent on her appearance. It was the authentic beauty that shone through all the labels and products, the kind that waterfalls and sunsets possessed. You couldn't buy that kind of awe-inspiring magnificence. You couldn't ignore it, either, when it was right in front of you. And when you let yourself appreciate it, it felt almost healing…

He never engaged in rose smelling and sunset gazing. He lived in an armored tank of wealth, emotional distance and superficial relationships. His dates were formalities, a type of foreplay. It wasn't sexism. He invested even less in his dealings with men.

His circle never included people as unguarded as Viveka, with her defensive shyness and yearning for acceptance. Somehow that guilelessness of hers got through his barriers as aggression never would. She'd asked him why he'd saved her life and before he knew it, he was reliving the memory of pleading with everything in him for his grandfather—a stranger at the time—to save *him*.

Erebus hadn't.

Not right away. Not without proof.

Words such as *despair* and *anguish* were not strong enough to describe what came over him when he thought back to it.

She had had an idea what it was, though, without his having to say a word. He had seen more in her eyes than an offer of sex. Empathy, maybe. Whatever it was, it had been something so real, it had scared the hell out of him. He couldn't lie with a woman when his inner psyche was torn open that far. Who knew what else would spill out?

He needed escape and she needed to stay the hell back.

He was so focused on achieving that, he

walked out of the elevator not nearly as aware of his surroundings as he should be.

As they came alongside the security desk, he heard, “There she is,” and turned to see Grigor lunging at Viveka, nearly pulling her off her feet, filthy vitriol spewing over her scream of alarm.

“—think you can investigate me? I’ll show you what murder looks like—”

Reflex took over and Mikolas had broken Grigor’s nose before he knew what he was doing.

Grigor fell to the floor, blood leaking between his clutching fingers. Mikolas bent to grab him by the collar, but his security team rushed in from all directions, pressing Mikolas’s Neanderthal brain back into its cave.

“Call the police,” he bit out, straightening and putting his arm around Viveka. “Make sure you mention his threats against her life.”

He escorted Viveka outside to his waiting limo, afraid, genuinely afraid, of what he would do to the man if he stayed.

As her adrenaline rush faded in the safety of the limo, Viveka went from what felt like a screaming pitch of tension to being a spent match, brittle and thin, charred and cold.

It wasn't just Grigor surprising her like that. It was how crazed he'd seemed. If Mikolas hadn't stepped in… But he had and seeing Grigor on the receiving end of the sickening thud of a fist connecting to flesh wasn't as satisfying as she had always imagined it would be.

She *hated* violence.

She figured Mikolas must feel the same, given his past. Those last minutes as they'd come downstairs kept replaying in her mind. She'd been filled with resentment as they'd left the elevator, hotly thinking that if saving a person's life didn't require repayment, why was he forcing her to go to this stupid party? He said she was under his protection, but it was more like she was under his thumb.

But the minute she was threatened, the very second it had happened, he had leaped in to save her. Again.

It was as ground-shaking as the first time.

Especially when the aftermath had him feeling the bones in his repaired hand like he was checking for fractures. His thick silence made her feel sick.

"Mikolas, I'm sorry," Viveka said in a voice that flaked like dry paint.

She was aware of his head swinging around but couldn't look at him.

"You know I only had Trina's interest at heart when I came to Greece, but it was inconsiderate to you. I didn't appreciate the situation I was putting you in with Grigor—"

"That's enough, Viveka."

She jolted, stung by the graveled tone. It made the blood congeal in her veins and she hunched deeper into her seat, turning her gaze to the window.

"That was my fault." Self-recrimination gave his voice a bitter edge. "We signed papers for the merger today. I made sure he knew why I was squeezing him out. He tried to cheat me."

It was her turn to swing a surprised look at him. He looked like he was barely holding himself in check.

"I wouldn't have discovered it until after I was married to Trina, but your interference gave me a chance to review everything. I wound up getting a lot of concessions beyond our original deal. Things were quite ugly by the end. He was already blaming you so I told him I'd started an investigation. I should have expected something like this. I owe *you* the apology."

She didn't know what to say.

"You helped me by stopping the wedding. Thank you. I hope to hell the investigation puts him in jail," he added tightly.

He was staring at her intently, nostrils flared.

Her mouth trembled. She felt awkward and shy and tried to cover it with a lame attempt at levity. "Between Grigor and Hildy, I've spent most of my life being told I was an albatross of one kind or another. It's refreshing to hear I've had a positive effect for once. I thought for sure you were going to yell at me..." Her voice broke.

She sniffed and tried to catch a tear with a trembling hand before it ruined her makeup.

He swore and before she realized what he was doing, he had her in his lap.

"Did he hurt you? Let me see your arm where he grabbed you," he demanded, his touch incredibly gentle as he lightly explored.

"Don't be sweet to me right now, Mikolas. I'll fall apart."

"You prefer the goon from the lobby?" he growled, making a semihysterical laugh bubble up.

"You're not a goon," she protested, but obeyed the hard arms that closed around her and cuddled into him, numb fingers stealing under the edge of his jacket to warm against his steady heartbeat.

He ran soothing hands over her and let out a breath, tension easing from both of them in small increments.

She was still feeling shaky when they reached the Makricosta Olympus.

"I hate these things," he muttered as he escorted her to the brightly decorated ballroom. "We should have stayed in."

Too late to leave. People were noting their entrance.

"Do you mind if I…?" she asked as she spotted the ladies' room off to the right. She could only imagine how she looked.

A muscle pulsed in his jaw, like he didn't want

her out of his sight, but after one dismayed heartbeat he said, "I'll be at the bar."

Reeling under an onslaught of gratitude and confusion and yearning, she hurried to the powder room and moved directly to the mirror to check her makeup. She felt like a disaster, but had only a couple of smudges to dab away.

"Synchórisi," the woman next to her said, gaze down as she fiddled with the straps on her shimmery black dress. Releasing a distinctly British curse she said, "My Greek is nonexistent. Is there any chance you speak English?"

Viveka straightened from the mirror, taking a breath to gather her composure. "I do."

"Oh, you're upset." The woman was a delicate blonde and her smile turned concerned. "I'm sorry. I shouldn't have bothered you."

"No, I'm fine," she dismissed with a wobbly smile. The woman was doing her a favor, not letting her dwell on all the mixed emotions coursing through her. "Not the bad kind of crying."

"Oh, did he do something nice?" she asked with a pleased grin. "Because husbands really ought to, now and again."

"He's not my husband, but..." Viveka thought

of Mikolas saving her and thanking her for the wedding debacle. Her heart wobbled again and she had to swallow back a fresh rush of emotion. “He did.”

“Good. I’m Clair, by the way.” She offered her free hand to shake while her other hand stayed against her chest, the straps of her halter-style bodice dangling over her slender fingers.

“Viveka. Call me Vivi.” Eyeing the straps, she guessed, “Wardrobe malfunction?”

“The worst! Is there any chance you have a pin?”

“I don’t. Can you tie them?” She circled her finger in the air. “Turn around. Let’s see what happened to the catch.”

They quickly determined the catch was long gone and they were too short to tie.

“I bet a tiepin would hold it. Give me a minute. I’ll ask Mikolas for his,” Viveka offered.

“Good idea, but ask my husband,” Clair said. “Then I won’t have to worry about returning it.”

Viveka chuckled. “Let me guess. Your husband is the man in the suit?” She thumbed toward the ballroom filled with a hundred men wearing ties and jackets.

Clair grinned. "Mine's easy to spot. He's the one with a scar here." She touched her cheek, drawing a vertical line. "Also, he's holding my purse. I needed two hands to keep myself together long enough to get in here or I would have texted him to come help me."

"Got it. I'll be right back."

Mikolas stood with the back of his hand pressed to a scotch on the rocks. So much for behaving mainstream and law-abiding, he thought dourly.

He was watching for Viveka, still worried about her. When she had apologized, he'd been floored, already kicking himself for bringing her downstairs at all. He could be at home making love to her, none of this having happened. Instead, he'd let her be terrorized.

There she was. He tried to catch her eye, but she scanned the room, then made for a small group in the far corner from the band.

Mikolas swore under his breath as she approached his target: Aleksy Dmitriev. The Russian magnate had logistics interests that crossed paths with his own from the Aegean through to the Black Sea. Dmitriev had never once returned Mikolas's calls and it grated. He hated being the petitioner and resented the other man for relegating him to that role.

Mikolas knew why Dmitriev was avoiding him. He was scrupulous about his reputation. He wouldn't risk sullying it by attaching himself to the Petrides name.

While Mikolas knew working with Dmitriev would be another seal of legitimacy for his own organization. That's why he wanted to partner with him.

Dmitriev stared at Viveka like she was from Mars, then handed her his drink. He removed his tiepin, handed it to her, then took back his glass. When she asked him something else, he nodded at a window ledge where a pocketbook sat. Viveka scooped it up and headed back to the ladies' room.

What the *hell*?

Viveka was thankful for the small drama that Clair had provided, but flashed right back to seesaw emotions when she returned to Mikolas's side. He stood out without trying. He wore that look of disinterest that alpha wolves wore with their packs, confident in his superiority so with nothing to prove.

A handful of men in sharp suits had clustered around him. They all wore bored-looking women on their arms.

Mikolas interrupted the conversation when she arrived. He took her hand and made a point of introducing her.

She smiled, but the man who'd been speaking was quick to dismiss her and continue what he was saying. He struck her as the toady type who sucked up to powerful men in hopes of catching scraps. The way the women were held like dogs on a leash was very telling, too.

Viveka let her gaze stray to the other groups, seeing the dynamic was very different in Clair's circle, where she was nodding at whoever was speaking, smiling and fully engaged in the conversation. Her husband was looking their way and she pressed a brief smile onto her mouth.

Nothing.

Mikolas had been right about invisible barriers.

"This must be your new bride if the merger has gone through," one of the other men broke in to say, frowning with confusion as he jumped his gaze between her and Mikolas.

I have a name, Viveka wanted to remind the man, but apparently on this side of the room, she was a "this."

"No," Mikolas replied, offering no further explanation.

Viveka wanted to roll her eyes. It was basic playground etiquette to act friendly if you wanted to be included in the games. That was what he wanted, wasn't it? Was this what he had meant when he had said it was her task to change how he was viewed?

"I stopped the wedding," she blurted. "He was supposed to marry my sister, but..." She cleared her throat as she looked up at Mikolas, laughing inwardly at the ridiculous claim she was about to make. "I fell head over heels. You weren't far behind me, were you?"

Mikolas wore much the same incredulous expression he had when he'd lifted her veil.

"Your sister can't be happy about that," one of the women said, perking up for the first time.

"She's fine with it," Viveka assured with a wave. "She'd be the first to say you should follow your heart, wouldn't she?" she prodded Mikolas, highly entertained with her embellishment on the truth. *Laugh with me*, she entreated.

"Let's dance." His grip on her hand moved to her elbow and he turned her toward the floor. As he took her in his arms seconds later, he said, "I cannot believe you just said that."

"Oh, come on. You said we should appear long-term. Now they think we're in love and by the way, your friends are a pile of sexist jerks."

"I don't have friends," he growled. "Those are people whose names I know."

His touch on her seemed to crackle and spark, making her feel sensitized all over. At the same time, she thought she heard something in his tone that was a warning.

Dancing with him was easy. They moved really well together right out of the gate. She let herself become immersed in the moment, where the music transmitted through them, making them move in unison. He held her in his strong arms and the closeness was deliciously stimulating. Her heart fluttered and she feared she really would tumble into deep feelings for him.

"They should call it heels over head," she said,

trying to break the spell. “We’re head over heels right now. It means you’re upright.”

He halted their dance, started to say something, but off to her right, Clair said, “Vivi. Let me introduce you properly. My husband, Aleksy Dmitriev.”

Mikolas pulled himself back from a suffocating place where his emotions had knotted up. She’d been joking with all that talk of love, he knew she had, but even having a falsehood put out there to those vultures had made him uncomfortable.

He had been pleased to feel nothing for Trina. He would have introduced her as his wife and the presumption of affection might have been made, but it wouldn’t have been true. It certainly wouldn’t have been something that could be used to prey on his psyche, not deep down where his soul kept well out of the light.

Viveka was different. Her blasé claim of love between them was an overstatement and he ought to be able to dismiss it. But as much as he wanted to feel nothing toward her, he couldn’t.

Everything he'd done since meeting her proved to himself that he felt *something.*

He tried to ignore how disarmed that made him feel, concentrating instead on finding himself face-to-face with the man who'd been evading him for two years.

Dmitriev looked seriously peeved, mouth flat and the scar on his face standing out white.

It's the Viveka effect, Mikolas wanted to drawl.

Dmitriev nodded a stiff acknowledgment to Viveka's warm smile.

"Did you think you were being robbed?" Viveka teased him.

"It crossed my mind." Dmitriev lifted a cool gaze to Mikolas. *When I realized she was with you*, he seemed to say.

Mikolas kept a poker face as Viveka finished the introduction, but deep down he waved a flag of triumph over Dmitriev being forced to come to him.

It was only an introduction, he reminded himself. A hook. There was no reeling in this kind of fish without a fight.

"We have to get back to the children," Clair

was saying. "But I wanted to thank you again for your help."

"My pleasure. I hope we'll run into each other in future," Viveka said. Mikolas had to give her credit. She was a natural at this role.

"Perhaps you can add us to your donor list," Mikolas said. *I do my homework*, he told Dmitriev with a flick of his gaze. Clair ran a foundation that benefited orphanages across Europe. Mikolas had been waiting for the right opportunity to use this particular door. He had no scruples about walking through it as Viveka's plus one.

"May I?" Clair brightened. "I would love that!"

Mikolas brought out one of his cards and a pen, scrawling Viveka's details on the back, mentally noting he should have some cards of her own printed.

"I'd give you one of mine, but I'm out," Clair said, showing hands that were empty of all but a diamond and platinum wedding band. "I've been talking up my fund-raising dinner in Paris all night—oh! Would you happen to be going there at the end of next month? I could put you on that list, too."

"Please do. I'm sure we can make room," Mikolas said smoothly. *We, our, us.* It was a foreign language to him, but surprisingly easy to pick up.

"I'm being shameless, aren't I?" Clair said to her husband, dipping her chin while lifting eyes filled with playful culpability.

The granite in Dmitriev's face eased to what might pass for affection, but he sounded sincere as he contradicted her. "You're passionate. It's one of your many appealing qualities. Don't apologize for it."

He produced one of his own cards and stole the pen Mikolas still held, wordlessly offering both to his wife.

I see what you're doing, Dmitriev said with a level stare at Mikolas while Clair wrote. Dmitriev was of similar height and build to Mikolas. He was probably the only man in the room whom Mikolas would instinctively respect without testing the man first. He emanated the same air of self-governance that Mikolas enjoyed and had more than demonstrated he couldn't be manipulated into doing anything he didn't want to do.

He provoked all of Mikolas's instincts to dominate, which made getting this man's contact details that much more significant.

But even though he wasn't happy to be giving up his direct number, it was clear by Dmitriev's hard look that it was a choice he made consciously and deliberately—for his wife.

Mikolas might have lost a few notches of regard for the man if his hand hadn't still been throbbing from connecting with Grigor's jaw. Which he'd done for Viveka.

It was an uncomfortable moment of realizing it didn't matter how insulated a man believed himself to be. A woman—one for whom he'd gone heels over head—could completely undermine him.

Which was why Mikolas firmed himself against letting Viveka become anything more than the sexual infatuation she was. The only reason he was bent out of shape was because they hadn't had sex yet, he told himself. Once he'd had her, and anticipation was no longer clouding his brain, he'd be fine.

"That was what we came for," he said, after the couple had departed. He indicated the card

Viveka was about to drop into her pocketbook. "We can leave now, too."

Mikolas made a face at the card the doorman handed him on their way in, explaining he was supposed to call the police in the morning to make a statement. They didn't speak until they were in the penthouse.

"I've wanted Dmitriev's private number for a while. You did well tonight," he told her as he moved to pour two glasses at the bar.

"It didn't feel like I did anything," she murmured, quietly glowing under his praise. She yearned for approval more than most people did, having been treated as an annoyance for most of her early years.

"It's easy for you. You don't mind talking to people," he remarked, setting aside the bottle and picking up the glasses to come across and offer hers. "Do you take yours with water?"

"I haven't had ouzo in years," she murmured, trying to hide her reaction to him by inhaling the licorice aroma off the alcohol. "I shouldn't have had it when I did. I was far too young. *Yiamas*."

Mikolas threw most of his back in one go, eyes never leaving hers.

"What, um…?" Oh, this man easily emptied her brain. "You, um, don't like talking to people? You said you hated those sorts of parties."

"I do," he dismissed.

"Why?"

"Many reasons." He shrugged, moving to set aside his glass. "My grandfather had a lot to hide when I first came to live with him. I was too young to be confident in my own opinions and didn't trust anyone with details about myself. As an adult, I'm surrounded by people who are so superficial, crying about ridiculous little trials, I can't summon any interest in whatever it is they're saying."

"Should I be complimented that you talk to me?" she teased.

"I keep trying not to." Even that was delivered with self-deprecation tilting his mouth.

Her heart panged. She longed to know everything about him.

His gaze fixed on her collarbone. He reached out to take her hair back from her shoulder.

"You've had one sparkle of glitter here all night," he said, fingertip grazing the spot.

It was a tiny touch, an inconsequential remark, but it devastated her. Her insides trembled and she went very still, her entire being focused on the way he ever so lightly tried to coax the fleck off her skin.

Behind him, the lamps cast amber reflections against the black windows. The pool glowed a ghostly blue on the deck beyond. It made radiance seem to emanate from him, but maybe that was her foolish, dampening eyes.

Painful yearning rose in her. It was familiar, yet held a searing twist. For a long time she had wanted a man in her life. She wanted a confidant, someone she could kiss and touch and sleep beside. She wanted intimacy, physical and emotional.

She had never expected this kind of corporeal desire. She hadn't believed it existed, definitely hadn't known it could overwhelm her like this.

How could she feel so attracted and needy toward a man who was so ambivalent toward her? It was excruciating.

But when he took her glass and set it aside,

she didn't resist. She kept holding his gaze as his hands came up to frame her face. And waited.

His gaze lowered to her lips.

They felt like they plumped with anticipation.

She looked at his mouth, not thinking about anything except how much she wanted his kiss. His lips were so beautifully shaped, full, but undeniably masculine. The tip of his tongue wet them, then he lowered his head, came closer.

The first brush of his damp lips against hers made her shudder in release of tension while tightening with anticipation. She gasped in surrender as his hands whispered down to warm her upper arms, then grazed over the fabric of her dress.

Then his mouth opened wider on hers and it was like a straight shot of ouzo, burning down her center and warming her through, making her drunk. Long, dragging kisses made her more and more lethargic by degrees, until he drew back and she realized her hand was at the back of his head, the other curled into the fabric of his shirt beneath his jacket.

He released her long enough to shrug out of

his jacket, loosened his tie, then pulled her close again.

Her head felt too heavy for her neck, easily falling into the fingers that combed through her hair and splayed against her scalp. He kissed her again, harder this time, revealing the depth of passion in him. The aggression. It was scary in the way thunder and high winds and landslides were both terrifying and awe-inspiring. She clung to him, moaning in submission. Not just to him, but to her own desire.

They shuffled their feet closer, sealing themselves one against the other, trying to press through clothing and skin so their cells would weave into a single being.

The thrust of his aroused flesh pressed into her stomach and a wrench of conflict went through her. This moment was too perfect. It felt too good to be held like this, to ruin it with humiliating confessions about her defect and entreaties for special treatment. She felt too much toward him, not least gratitude and wonder and a regard that was tied to his compliments and his protection and his hand dragging her to the surface of the water before he'd even known her name.

She ached to share something with him, had since almost the first moment she'd seen him. *Be careful*, she told herself. Sex was powerful. She was already very susceptible to him.

But she couldn't make herself stop touching him. Her hands strayed to feel his shape, tracing him through his pants. It was a bold move for her, but she was entranced. Curious and enthralled. There was a part of her that desperately wanted to know she could please a man, *this* man in particular.

His breath hissed in and his whole body hardened. He gathered his muscles as if he was preparing to dip and lift her against his chest.

She drew back.

His arms twitched in protest, but he let her look at where his erection pressed against the front of his suit pants. He was really aroused. She licked her lips, not superconfident in what she wanted to do, but she wanted to do it.

She unbuckled his belt.

His hands searched under the fall of her hair. His touch ran down her spine, releasing the back of her dress.

As the cool air swirled from her waist around

to her belly, her stomach fluttered with nerves. She swallowed, aware of her breasts as her bodice loosened and shifted against her bare nipples. She shivered as his fingertips stroked her bare back. Her hands shook as she pulled his shirt free and clumsily opened his buttons, then spread the edges wide so she could admire his chest.

Pressing her face to his taut skin, she rubbed back and forth and back again, absorbing the feel of him with her brow and lips, drawing in his scent, too moved to smile when he said something in a tight voice and slid his palm under her dress to brand her bottom with his hot palm.

Her mouth opened of its own accord, painting a wet path to his nipple. She explored the shape with her tongue, earned another tight curse, then hit the other one with a draw of her mouth. Foreplay and foreshadowing, she thought with a private smile.

"Bedroom," he growled, bringing his hands out of her dress and setting them on her waist, thumbs against her hip bones as he pressed her back a step.

Dazed at how her own arousal was climbing,

Viveka smiled, pleased to see the glitter in his eyes and the flush on his cheeks. It increased her tentative confidence. She placed her hands on his chest and let her gaze stray past him to the armchair, silently urging him toward it.

Mikolas let her have her way out of sheer fascination. He refused to call it weakness, even though he was definitely under a spell of some kind. He had known there was a sensual woman inside Viveka screaming to get out. He hadn't expected this, though.

It wasn't manipulation, either. There were no sly smiles or knowing looks as she slid to her knees between his, kissing his neck, stroking down his front so his abdominals contracted under her tickling fingertips. She was focused and enthralled, timid but genuinely excited. It was erotic to be wanted like this. Beyond exciting.

As she finished opening his pants, his brain shorted out. He was vaguely aware of lifting his hips so she could better expose him. The sob of want that left her was the kind of siren call that had been the downfall of ancient seamen. He nearly exploded on the spot.

He was thick and aching, so hot he wanted to rip his clothes from his body, but he was transfixed. He gripped the armrest in his aching hand and the back of the chair over his shoulder with the other, trying to hold on to his control.

He shouldn't let her do this, he thought distantly. His discipline was in shreds. But therein lay her power. He couldn't make himself stop her. That was the naked truth.

She took him in hand, her touch light, her pale hands pretty against the dark strain of his flesh. He was so hard he thought he'd break, so aroused he couldn't breathe, and so captivated, he could only hold still and watch through slitted eyes as her head dipped.

He groaned aloud as her hair slid against his exposed skin and her wet mouth took him in, narrowing his world to the tip of his sex. It was the most exquisite sensation, nearly undoing him between one breath and the next. She kept up the tender, lascivious act until he was panting, barely able to speak.

"I can't hold back," he managed to grit out.

Slowly her head lifted, pupils huge as pansies in the dim light, mouth swollen and shiny like he'd been kissing her for hours.

"I don't want you to." Her hot breath teased his wet flesh, tightening all his nerve endings, pulling him to a point that ended where her tongue flicked out and stole what little remained of his willpower.

He gave himself up to her. This was for both of them, he told himself. He would have staying power after this. He'd make it good for her, as good as this. Nothing could be better, but at least this good—

The universe exploded and he shouted his release to the ceiling.

CHAPTER NINE

VIVEKA HUGGED THE front of her gaping dress to her breasts and could barely meet her own glassy eyes in the mirror. She was flushed and aroused and deeply self-conscious. She couldn't believe what she'd just done, but she had no regrets. She had enjoyed giving Mikolas pleasure. It had been extraordinary.

She had needed that for herself. She wasn't a failure in the bedroom after all. Okay, the lounge, she allowed with a smirk.

Her hand trembled as she removed the pins from her hair, pride quickly giving way to sexual frustration and embarrassment. Even a hint of desolation. If she wasn't such a freak, if she wasn't afraid she'd lose herself completely, they could have found release together.

Being selfless was satisfying in other ways, though. He might be thanking her for breaking up the wedding and saving him a few bucks, but she was deeply grateful for the way he had acknowledged her as worth saving, worth protecting.

The bathroom door that she'd swung almost closed pushed open, making her heart catch.

Mikolas took up a lazy pose that made carnal hunger clench mercilessly in her middle. The flesh that was hot with yearning squeezed and ached.

His open shirt hung off his shoulders, framing the light pattern of hair that ran down from his breastbone. His unfastened pants gaped low across his hips, revealing the narrow line of hair from his navel. His eyelids were heavy, disguising his thoughts, but his voice was gritty enough to make her shiver.

"You're taking too long."

The words were a sensual punch, flushing her with eager heat. At the same time, alarm bells—anxious clangs of performance anxiety—went off within her, cooling her ardor.

"For?" She knew what he meant, but she'd taken care of his need. They were done. Weren't they? If she'd ever had sex before, she wouldn't be so unsure.

"Finishing what you started."

"You did finish. You can't—" Was he growing hard again? It looked like his boxers were straining against the open fly of his pants.

She read. She knew basic biology. She knew he'd climaxed, so how was that happening? Was she really so incapable of gratifying a man that even oral sex failed to do the job?

"You can't… Men don't…again. Can they?" She trailed off, blushing and hating that his first real smile came at the expense of her inexperience.

"I'll last longer this time," he promised drily. "But I don't want to wait. Get your butt in that bed, or I'll have you here, bent over the sink."

Oh, she was never going to be that spontaneous. Ever. And for a first time? While he talked about lasting a *long* time?

"No." She hitched the shoulder of her dress and reached behind herself to close it. "You finished. We're done." Her face was on fire, but inside she was growing cold.

He straightened off the doorjamb. "What?"

"I don't want to have sex." Not entirely true. She longed to understand the mystique behind the act, but his talk of sink-bending only told her how far apart they were in experience. The more she thought about it, the more she went into a state of panic. Not him. Not tonight when she was already an emotional mess.

She struggled to close her zip, then crossed her arms, taking a step backward even though he hadn't moved toward her.

He frowned. "You don't want sex?"

Was he deaf?

"No," she assured him. Her back came up against the towel rail, which was horribly uncomfortable. She waved toward the door he was blocking. "You can go."

He didn't move, only folded his own arms and rocked back on his heels. "Explain this to me. And use small words, because I don't understand what happened between the lounge and here."

"Nothing happened." She couldn't stand that he was making her wallow in her inadequacy. "You…I mean, I *thought* I gave you what you wanted. If you thought—"

He didn't even want her. Not really. He would decide *if* and *when*, she recalled.

Good luck with that, champ. Her body made

that decision for everyone involved, no matter what her head said.

Do not cry. Oh, she hated her body right now. Her stupid, dumb body that had made her life go so far sideways she didn't even understand how she was standing here having this awful conversation.

"Can you just go?" She glared at him for making this so hard for her, but her eyes stung. She bet they were red and pathetic looking. If he made her tell him, and he laughed—*"Please?"*

He stayed there one more long moment, searching her gaze, before slowly moving back, taking the door with him, closing it as he left. The click sounded horribly final.

Viveka stepped forward and turned the lock, not because she was afraid he'd come in looking for sex, but afraid he'd come in and catch her crying.

With a wrench of her hand, she started the shower.

Mikolas was sitting in the dark, nursing an ouzo, when he heard Viveka's door open.

He'd closed it himself an hour ago, when he'd

gone in to check on her and found her on the guest bed, hair wrapped in a towel, one of his monogramed robes swallowing her in black silk. She'd been fast asleep, her very excellent legs bare to midthigh, a crumpled tissue in her lax grip. Several more had been balled up around her.

Rather than easing his mind, rather than answering any of the million questions crowding his thoughts, the sight had caused the turmoil inside him to expand, spinning in fresh and awful directions. Was he such a bad judge of a woman's needs? Why did he feel as though he'd taken advantage of her? She had pressed him into this very chair. She had opened his pants. She had gone down and told him to let go.

He'd been high as a kite when he had tracked her into her bathroom, certain he'd find her naked and waiting for him. Every red blood cell he possessed had been keening with anticipation.

It hadn't gone that way at all.

She'd felt threatened.

He was a strong, dominant man. He knew that and tried to take his aggressive nature down a notch in the bedroom. He knew what it was like to be brutalized by someone bigger and more powerful. He would never do that to the smaller and weaker.

He kept having flashes of slender, delicate Viveka looking anxious as she noticed he was still hard. He thought about her fear of Grigor. A libido-killing dread had been tying his stomach in knots ever since.

He couldn't bear the idea of her being abused that way. He'd punched Grigor tonight, but he wished he had killed him. There was still time, he kept thinking. He wasn't so far removed from his bloodline that he didn't know how to make a man disappear.

He listened to Viveka's bare feet approach, thinking he couldn't blame her for trying to sneak out on him.

She paused as she arrived at the end of the hall, obviously noticing his shadowed figure. She had changed into pajamas and clipped up her hair. She tucked a stray wisp behind her ear.

"I'm hungry. Do you want toast?" She didn't wait for his response, charging past him through to the kitchen.

He unbent and slowly made his way into the kitchen behind her.

She had turned on the light over the stove and kept her back to him as she filled the kettle at the sink. After she set the switch to Boil, she went to the freezer and found a frozen loaf of sliced bread.

Still keeping her back to him, she broke off four slices and set them in the toaster.

"Viveka."

Her slender back flinched at the sound of his voice.

So did he. The things he was thinking were piercing his heart. He'd been bleeding internally since the likeliest explanation had struck him hours ago. When someone reacted that defensively against sexual contact, the explanation seemed really obvious.

"When you said Grigor abused you…" He wasn't a coward, but he didn't want to speak it. Didn't want to hear it. "Did he…?" His voice failed him.

Viveka really wished he hadn't still been up. In her perfect world, she never would have had to face him again, but as the significance of his broken question struck her, she realized she couldn't avoid telling him.

She buried her face in her hands. "No. That's not it. Not at all."

She *really* didn't want to face him.

But she had to.

Shoulders sagging, she turned and wilted against the cupboards behind her. Her hands stayed against her stinging cheeks.

"Please don't laugh." That's what the one other man she'd told had done. She'd felt so raw it was no wonder she hadn't been able to go all the way with him, either.

She dared a peek at Mikolas. He'd closed a couple of buttons, but his shirt hung loose over his pants. His hair was ruffled, as though his fingers had gone through it a few times. His jaw was shadowed with stubble and he looked tired. Troubled.

"I won't laugh." He hadn't slept, even though it was past two in the morning. For some reason that flipped her heart.

"I wasn't a very happy teenager, obviously," she began. "I did what a lot of disheartened young girls do. I looked for a boy to save me. There was a nice one who didn't have much, but he had a kind heart. I can't say I loved him, not even puppy love, but I liked him. We started seeing each other on the sly, behind Grigor's back. After a while it seemed like the time to, you know, have sex."

The toaster made a few pinging, crackling noises and the kettle was beginning to hiss. She chewed her lip, fully grown and many years past it, but still chagrined.

"I mean, fourteen is criminally young, I realize that. And not having any really passionate feelings for him… It's not a wonder it didn't work."

"Didn't work," he repeated, like he was testing words he didn't know.

She clenched her eyes shut. "He didn't fit. It hurt too much and I made him stop. Please don't laugh," she rushed to add.

"I'm not laughing." His voice was low and grave. "You're telling me you're a virgin? You never tried again?"

"Oh, I did," she said to the ceiling, insides scraped hollow.

She moved around looking for the tea and butter, trying to escape how acutely humiliating this was.

"My life was a mess for quite a while, though. Grigor found out I'd been seeing the boy and that I'd gone to the police about Mum. He kicked me out and I moved to London. *That* was a culture shock. The weather, the city. Aunt Hildy had all these rules. It wasn't until I finished my A levels and was working that I started dating again. There was a guy from work. He was very smooth. I realize now he was a player, but I was quite taken in."

The toast popped and she buttered it, taking her time, spreading right to the edges.

"He laughed when I told him why I was nervous." She scraped the knife in careful licks across the surface of the toast. "He was so determined to be The One. We fooled around a little, but he was always putting this pressure on me to go all the way. I *wanted* to have sex. It's supposed to be great, right?"

Pressure arrived behind her eyes again. She couldn't look at him, but she listened, waiting for his confirmation that yes, all the sex he'd had with his multitude of lovers had been fantastic.

Silence.

"Finally I said we could try, but it really hurt. He said it was supposed to and didn't want to stop. I lost my temper and threw him out. We haven't spoken since."

"Do you still work with him?"

"No. Old job. Long gone." The toast was buttered before her on two plates, but she couldn't bring herself to turn and see his reaction.

She was all cried out, but familiar, hopeless angst cloaked her. She just wanted to be like most people and have sex and like it.

"Are you laughing?" Her voice was thready and filled with the embarrassed anguish she couldn't disguise.

"Not at all." His voice sounded like he was talking from very far away. "I'm thinking that not in a thousand years would I have guessed that. Nothing you do fits with the way other people behave. It didn't make sense that you would give me pleasure and not want anything for yourself. You respond to me. I couldn't imagine why you didn't want sex."

"I *do* want sex," she said, flailing a frustrated hand. "I just don't want it to *hurt*." She finally turned and set his plate of toast on the island, avoiding his gaze.

The kettle boiled, giving her breathing space as she moved to make the tea. When she sat down, she went around the far end of the island and took the farthest stool from where he stood ignoring the toast and tea she'd made for him.

She couldn't make herself take a bite. Her body was hot and cold, her emotions swinging from hope to despair to worry.

"You're afraid I wouldn't stop if we tried." His voice was solemn as he promised, "I would, you know. At any point."

A tentative hope moved through her, but she shook her head. "I don't want to be a project." Her spoon clinked lightly as she stirred the sugar into her tea. "I can't face another humiliating attempt. And yes, I've been to a doctor. There's nothing wrong. I'm just…unusually…" She sighed hopelessly. "Can we stop talking about this?"

He only pushed his hands into his pockets. "I wasn't trying to talk you into anything. Not tonight. Unless you want to," he said in a wry mutter, combing distracted fingers through his hair.

"I wouldn't say no. You're not a project, Viveka. I want you rather badly."

"Do you?" She scoffed in a strained voice, reminding him, "You said *you* would decide if and when. That *I* was the only one who wanted sex. I can't help the way I react to you, you know. I might have tried with you tonight if I'd thought it would go well, but..."

Tears came into her eyes. It was silly. She was seriously dehydrated from her crying jags earlier. There shouldn't be a drop of moisture left in her.

"I wanted you to like it," she said, heart raw. "I wanted to know I could, you know, *satisfy* a man, but no. I didn't even get that right. You were still hard and—"

He muttered something under his breath and said, "Are you really that oblivious? You *did* satisfy me. You leveled me. Blew my mind. Reset the bar. I don't have words for how good that was." He sounded aggrieved as he waved toward the lounge. "My desire for you is so strong I was aroused all over again just thinking about doing the same to you. *That's* why I was hard again."

If he didn't look so uncomfortable admitting that, she might have disbelieved him.

"When we were on the yacht, you said you thought it was exciting that I respond to you." Her chest ached as she tried to figure him out. "If the attraction is just as strong for you, why don't you want me to know? Why do you keep—I mean, before we went out tonight, you acted as if you could take it or leave it. It's *not* the same for you, Mikolas. That's why I don't think it would work."

"I never like to be at a disadvantage, Viveka. We had been talking about some difficult things. I needed space."

"But if we're equal in feeling *this* way…? Attracted, I mean, why don't you want me to know that?"

"That's not an advantage, is it?"

His words, that attitude of prevailing without mercy, scraped her down to the bones.

"You'll have to tell me sometime what that's like," she said, dabbing at a crumb and pressing it between her tight lips. "Having the advantage, I mean. Not something I've ever had the pleasure of experiencing. Not something I should want to go to bed with, frankly. So *why do I*?"

He did laugh then, but it was ironic, completely lacking any humor.

"For what it's worth, I feel the same." He walked out, leaving his toast and tea untouched.

Mikolas was trying hard to ignore the way Viveka Brice had turned his life into an amusement park. One minute it was a fun house of distorted mirrors, the next a roller coaster that ratcheted his tension only to throw him down a steep valley and around a corner he hadn't seen.

Home, he kept thinking. It was basic animal instinct. Once he was grounded in his own cave, with the safety of the familiar around him, all the ways that she'd shaken up his world would settle. He would be firmly in control again.

Of course he had to keep his balance in the dizzying teacup of her trim figure appearing in a pair of hip-hugging jeans and a completely asexual T-shirt paired with the doe-eyed wariness that had crushed his chest last night.

He couldn't say he was relieved to hear the details of her sexual misadventures. The idea of her lying naked with other men grated, but at least she hadn't been scarred by the horrifying brutality he'd begun to imagine.

On the other hand, when she had finally opened up, the nakedness in her expression had been difficult to witness. She was tough and brave and earnest and too damned sensitive. Her insecurity had reached into him in a way that antagonism couldn't. The bizarre protectiveness she already inspired in him had flared up, prompting him to assuage her fears, reassure her. He had wound up revealing himself in a way that left him mistrustful and feeling like he'd left a flank unguarded.

Not a comfortable feeling at all.

He hadn't been able to sleep. Much of it had been the ache in his body, craving release in hers. He yearned to *show* her how it could be between them. At the same time, his mind wouldn't stop turning over and over with everything that had happened since she had marched into his life. At what point would she quit pulling the rug out from under him?

"Are you taking me back in time? What is

that?" She was looking out the window of the helicopter.

He leaned to see. They were approaching the mansion and the ruins built into the cliff below it.

"That is the tower where you will be imprisoned for the rest of your life." *There* was a solution, he thought.

"Don't quit your day job for comedy."

Her quick rejoinder made humor tug at the corner of his mouth. He was learning she used jokes as a defense, similar to how he was quick to pull rank and impose his control over every situation. The fact she was being cheeky now, when he was in her space, told him she was shoring up her walls against him. That niggled, but wasn't it what he wanted? Distance? Barriers?

"The Venetians built it." He gazed at her clean face so close to his, her naked lips. She smelled like tea and roses and woman. He wanted to eat her alive. "See where the stairs have been worn away by the waves?"

Viveka couldn't take in anything as she felt the warmth off the side of his face and caught the smell of his aftershave. She held herself very still, trying not to react to his closeness, but her lips tingled, longing to graze his jaw and find his mouth. Lock with him in a deep kiss.

"We preserved the ruins as best we could. Given the fortune we spent, we were allowed to build above it."

She forced her gaze to the view, instantly enchanted. What little girl hadn't dreamed of being spirited away to an island castle like in a fairy tale?

The modern mansion at the top of the cliff drew her eye unerringly. The view was never-ending in all directions and the ultracontemporary design was unique and fascinating, sprawling in odd angles that were still perfectly balanced. It was neither imposing nor frivolous. It was solid and sophisticated. Dare she say elegant?

She noticed something on the roof. "Are those solar panels?"

"*Naí*. We also have a field of wind turbines. You can't see them from here. We're planning a tidal generator, too. We only have to finalize the location."

"How ecologically responsible of you." She

turned her face and they were practically nose to cheekbone.

He sat back and straightened his cuff.

"I like to be self-sufficient." A tick played at the corner of his mouth.

Under no one's power but his own. She was seeing that pattern very clearly. Should she tell him it made him predictable? she wondered with private humor.

A few minutes later, she followed him into an interior she hadn't expected despite all she'd seen so far of the way he lived. The entrance should have struck her as over the top, with its smooth marble columns and split staircase that went up to a landing overlooking, she was sure, the entire universe.

The design remained spare and masculine, however, the colors subtle and golden in the midday light. Ivory marble and black wrought iron along with accents of Hellenic blue made the place feel much warmer than she expected. As they climbed the stairs, thick fog-gray carpet muffled their steps.

The landing looked to the western horizon.

Viveka paused, experiencing a strange sensation that she was looking back toward a life that was just a blur of memory, no longer hers. Oddly, the idea slid into her heart not like a blade that cut her off from her past, but more like something that caught and anchored her here, tugging her from a sea of turbulence to pin her to this stronghold.

She rubbed her arms at the preternatural shiver that chased up her entire body, catching Mikolas's gaze as he waited for her to follow him up another level.

The uppermost floor was fronted by a lounge that was surrounded by walls of glass shaded by an overhang to keep out the heat. They were at the very top of the world here. That's how it felt. Like she'd arrived at Mount Olympus, where the gods resided.

There was a hot tub on the veranda along with lounge chairs and a small dining area. She stayed inside, glancing around the open-plan space of a breakfast nook, a sitting area with a fireplace and an imposing desk with two flat monitors with a printer on a cabinet behind it, obviously Mikolas's home office.

As she continued exploring, she heard Mikolas

speaking, saying her name. She followed to an open door where a uniformed young man came out. He saw her, nodded and introduced himself as Titus, then disappeared toward the stairs.

She peered into the room. It was Trina's boudoir. Had to be. There were fresh flowers, unlit candles beside the bucket of iced champagne, crystal glasses, a peignoir set draped across the foot of the white bed, and a box of chocolates on a side table. The exterior walls were made entirely out of glass and faced east, which pleased her. She liked waking to sun.

Don't love it, she cautioned herself, but it was hard not to be charmed.

"Oh, good grief," she gasped as Mikolas opened a door to what she had assumed was a powder room. It was actually a small warehouse of prêt-à-porter.

"Did you buy all of Paris for her?" She plucked at the cuff of a one-sleeved evening gown in silver-embroidered lavender. The back wall was covered in shoes. "I hate to tell you this, but my foot is a full size bigger than Trina's."

"One of your first tasks will be to go through all of this so the seamstress can alter where necessary. The shoes can be exchanged." He shrugged one shoulder negligently.

The closet was huge, but way too small with both of them in it.

She tried to disguise her self-consciousness by picking up a shoe. When she saw the designer name, she gently rubbed the shoe on her shirt to erase her fingerprint from the patent leather and carefully replaced it.

"Change for lunch with my grandfather. But don't take too long."

"Where are you going?" she asked, poking her head out to watch him cross to a pair of double doors on the other side of her room, not back to the main part of the penthouse.

"My room." He opened one of the double doors as he reached it, revealing what she thought at first was a private sitting room, but that white daybed had a towel rolled up on the foot of it.

Drawn by curiosity, she crossed to follow him into the bathroom. Except it was more like a high-end spa. There was an enormous round tub set in a bow of glass that arched outward so the illusion for the bather was a soak in midair.

"Wow." She slowly spun to take in the extravagance, awestruck when she noted the small forest that grew in a rock garden under a skylight. A path of stones led through it to a shower *area* against the back wall. Nozzles were set into the alcove of tiled walls, ready to spray from every level and direction, including raining from the ceiling.

She clapped her hand over her mouth, laughing.

The masculine side of the room was a double sink and mirror designed along the black-and-white simplistic lines Mikolas seemed to prefer, bracketed by a discreet door to a private toilet stall that also gave access to his bedroom. Her side was a reflection of his, with one sink removed to make way for a makeup bench and a vanity of drawers already filled with unopened cosmetics.

"You live like this," she murmured, closing the drawer.

"So do you. Now."

Temporarily, she reminded herself, but it was still like trying to grasp the expanse of the universe. Too much to comprehend.

A white robe that matched the black ones she'd

already worn hung on a hook. She flipped the lapel enough to see the monogram, expecting a T and finding an M. She sputtered out another laugh. He was so predictably possessive!

"Can you be ready in twenty minutes?"

"Of course," she said faintly. "Unless I get lost in the forest on the way back to my room."

My room. Freudian slip. She dropped her gaze to the mosaic in the floor, then walked through her water closet to her room.

It was only as she stood debating a pleated skirt versus a sleeveless floral print dress that the significance of that shared bathroom struck her: he could walk in on her naked. Anytime.

CHAPTER TEN

VIVEKA WASN'T SURE what she expected Mikolas's grandfather to look like. A mafia don from an old American movie? Or like many of the other retired Greek men who sat outside village *kafenions*, maybe wearing a flat cap and a checked shirt, face lined by sun and a hard life in the vineyard or at sea?

Erebus Petrides was the consummate old-world gentleman. He wore a suit as he shared a drink with them before they dined. He had a bushy white mustache and excellent posture despite his stocky weight and the cane he used to walk. He and Mikolas didn't look much alike, but they definitely had the same hammered silver eyes and their voices were two keys of a similar strong, commanding timbre.

Erebus spoke English, but preferred Greek, stretching her to recall a vocabulary she hadn't tested in nine years—something he gently reproached her over. It was a pleasant meal that could have been any "Meet the Parents" occasion as they politely got to know each other. She had to keep reminding herself that the charismatic old man was actually a notorious criminal.

"He seems very nice," she said after Erebus had retired for an afternoon rest.

Mikolas was showing her around the rest of the house. They'd come out to the pool deck where a cabana was set up like a sheikh's tent off to the side and the Ionian Sea gleamed into the horizon.

Mikolas didn't respond and she glanced up to see his mouth give a cynical twitch.

"No?" she prompted, surprised.

"He wouldn't have saved me if I hadn't proven to be his grandson."

Her heart skipped and veered as she absorbed that none of this would have happened. She wouldn't be here and neither would he. They never would have met. *What would have become of that orphaned boy?*

"Do you wish that your mother had told your father about you?"

"She may have. My father was no saint," he

said with disparagement. "And there is no point wishing for anything to be different. Accept what is, Viveka. I learned that long ago."

It wasn't anything she didn't see in a pop philosophy meme on her newsfeed every day, but she always resisted that fatalistic view. She took a few steps away from him as though to distance herself from his pessimism.

"If I accepted what I was given, I would still be listening to Grigor call me ugly and useless." She didn't realize her hands became tight fists, or that he had come up behind her, until his warm grip gently forced her to bend her elbow as he lifted her hand.

He looked at her white knuckles poking like sharp teeth. His thumb stroked along that bumpy line.

"You've reminded me of something. Come." He smoothly inserted his thumb to open her fist and kept her hand as he tugged her into the house.

"Where?"

He only pulled her along through the kitchen and down the service stairs into a cool room where he turned on the lights to reveal a gym.

Perhaps the original plans had drawn it up as a wine cellar, but it was as much a professional gym as any that pushed memberships every January. Bike, tread, elliptical. Every type of weight equipment, a heavy bag hanging in the corner, skipping ropes dangling from a hook and padded mats on the floor. It was chilly and silent and smelled faintly of leather and air freshener.

"You'll meet me here every morning at six," he told her.

"Pah," she hooted. "Not likely."

"Say that again and I'll make it five."

"You're serious?" She made a face, silently telling him what she thought of that. "For heaven's sake, why? I do cardio most days, but I prefer to work out in the evening."

"I'm going to teach you to throw a punch. This—" he lifted the hand he still held and reshaped it into a fist again "—can do better. And this—" he touched under her chin, lifting her face and letting his thumb tag the spot on her lip where Grigor's mark had been "—won't happen again. Not without your opponent discovering very quickly that he has picked a fight with the wrong woman."

She had been trying to pretend she wasn't vitally aware of her hand in his. Now he was touching her face, looking into her eyes, standing too close.

Somehow she had thought that giving him pleasure would release some of this sexual tension between them. Now everything they'd confessed made it so much worse. The pull was so much *deeper*. He knew things about her. Intensely personal things.

She drew away, breaking all contact, trying to keep a grip on herself as she took in what he was saying.

"You keep surprising me. I thought you were a hardened…" She cut him a glance of apology. "Criminal. You're actually quite nice, aren't you? Wanting to teach me how to defend myself."

"Everyone who surrounds me is a strength, not a liability. That's all this is."

"Liability." The label winded her, making her look away. It was familiar, but she had hoped there was a growing regard between them. But no. He might be attracted to her sexually, last night might have changed her forever, but she was still that thing he was saddled with.

"Right. Whatever you need me to be, wherever." She fought not to let her smarting show, but from her throat to her navel she burned.

"Do you like feeling helpless?" he demanded.

"No," she choked. This feeling of being at *his* mercy was excruciating.

"Then be here at six prepared to work."

What had he been thinking? Mikolas asked himself the next morning. This was hell.

Viveka showed up in a pair of clinging purple pants that ended below her knees. The spandex was shiny enough to accent every dip and curve of her trim thighs. Her pink T-shirt came off after they'd warmed up with cardio, revealing the unique landscape of her abdomen. Now she wore only a snug blue sports bra that flattened her modest breasts and showed off her creamy shoulders and chest and flat midriff.

He was so distracted by lust, he would get his lights blacked out for sure.

He would deserve it. And he couldn't even make a pass to slake it. He'd told two of his guards who had come in to use the gym that they could stay. They were spotting each other, grunting over the weights, while Mikolas put his hands on Viveka to adjust her stance and coached her through stepping into a punch. She smelled like shampoo and woman sweat. Like they'd been petting each other into acute arousal.

"You're holding back because you're afraid you'll hurt yourself," he told her when she struck his palm. He stopped her to correct her wrist position and traced up the soft skin of her forearm. "Humans have evolved the bone structure in here to withstand the impact of a punch."

"My bones aren't as big as yours," she protested. "I *will* hurt myself in a real fight. Especially if I don't have this." She held up her arm to indicate where he'd wrapped her hands to protect them.

"You might even break your hand," he told her frankly. "But that's better than losing your life, isn't it? I want you on the heavy bag twice a day for half an hour. Get used to how it feels to connect so you won't hesitate when it counts. Learn to use your left with as much power as the right."

Her brow wrinkled with concentration as she

went back to jabbing into his palms. She was taking this seriously, at least.

That earnestness worried him, though. It would be just like her to take it to heart that *she* should protect *him*. He'd blurted out that remark about liability last night because he hadn't wanted to admit that her inability to protect herself had been eating at him from the moment he'd seen Grigor throw her around on the deck of a stranger's yacht.

He'd hurt her feelings, of course. She'd made enough mentions of Grigor's disparagement and her aunt's indifference that he understood Viveka had been made to feel like a burden and was very sensitive to it. That heart of hers was so easily bruised!

The more time he spent with her, the more he could see how utterly wrong they were for each other. He could wind up hurting her quite deeply.

I do want sex. I just don't want it to hurt.

Her jab was off-center, glancing off his palm so she stumbled into him.

"Sorry. I'm getting tired," she said breathlessly.

"I wasn't paying attention," he allowed, helping her find her feet.

Damn it, if he didn't keep his guard up, they were both going to get hurt.

Viveka was still shaking from the most intense workout of her life. Her arms felt like rubber and she needed the seamstress's help to dress as they worked through the gowns in her closet. She would have consigned Mikolas firmly to hell for this morning's punishment, but then his grandfather's physiotherapist arrived on Mikolas's instruction to offer her a massage.

"He said you would need one every day for at least a week."

Viveka had collapsed on the table, groaned with bliss and went without prompting back to the gym that afternoon to spend another half hour on the wretched heavy bag.

"You'll get used to it," Mikolas said without pity at dinner, when she could barely lift her fork.

"Surely that's not necessary, is it?" Erebus admonished Mikolas, once his grandson had explained why Viveka was so done in.

"She wants to learn. Don't you?" Mikolas's tone dared her to contradict him, but he wasn't demanding she agree with him in front of his grandfather. He was insisting on honesty.

"I do," she admitted with a weighted sigh, even though the very last thing she ever wanted was to engage in a fistfight. She couldn't help wondering if Grigor would have been as quick to hit her if she'd ever hit him back, though. She'd never had the nerve, fearing she'd only make things worse.

Mikolas's treatment of her in the gym, as dispassionate as it had been, had also been heartening. He seemed to have every confidence in her ability to defend herself if she only practiced. That was an incredibly compelling thought. Empowering.

It made her grateful to him all over again. And yes, deep down, it made her want to make him proud. To show him what she was capable of. Show herself.

Of course, the other side of that desire to be plucky and capable was a churning knowledge that she was being a coward when it came to sex. She wanted to be proficient in that arena, too.

The music was on low when they came into the lounge of his penthouse later, the fire glowing and a bottle of wine and glasses waiting. Beyond the windows, stars sparkled in the velvet black sky and moonlight glittered on the sea.

Had he planned this? To seduce her?

Did she want to be seduced?

She sighed a little, not sure what she wanted anymore.

"Sore?" he asked, moving to pour the wine.

"Hmm? Oh, it's not that bad. The massage helped. No, I was just thinking that I'm stuck in a holding pattern."

He lifted his brows with inquiry.

"I thought once Hildy was sorted, I would begin taking my life in hand. Trina was supposed to come live with me. I had some plan that we would rent a flat and take online quizzes, choose a career and register for classes…" She had been looking forward to that, but her sister's life had skewed off from hers and she didn't even have the worry of Hildy any longer. "Instead, my future is a blank page."

On Petrides letterhead, she thought wryly.

"I'll figure it out," she assured herself. "Eventually. I won't be here forever, right?"

That knowledge was the clincher. If it had

taken her twenty-three years to find a man who stirred her physically, how long would it take to find another?

She looked over to him.

Whatever was in her face made him set down the bottle, corkscrew angled into the unpopped cork.

"I keep telling myself to give you time." His voice was low and heavy, almost defeated. "But bringing you into my bed is all I can think about. Will you let me? I just want to touch you. Kiss you. Give you what you gave me."

Her belly clenched in anticipation. She couldn't imagine being *that* uninhibited, but she couldn't imagine *not* going to bed with him. She wanted him *so much* and she honestly didn't know how to resist any longer.

Surrender happened with one shaken, "Yes."

He kind of jolted, like he hadn't expected that. Then he came across and took her face in his two hands, covering her lips with his hot, hungry mouth. They kissed like lovers. Like people who had been separated by time and distance and deep misunderstanding. She curled her arms around his neck and he broke away long enough to scoop her up against his chest, then kissed her again as he carried her to his bedroom.

She waited for misgivings and none struck. Her fingers went into his hair as she kissed him back.

He came down on the mattress with her and she opened her eyes only long enough to catch an impression of monochromatic shades lit by the bluish half-moon. The carpet was white, the furniture silver-gray, the bedspread black.

Then Mikolas tucked her beneath him and stroked without hurry from her shoulder, down her rib cage, past her waist and along her hip.

"You can—" she started to say, but he brushed another kiss over her lips, lazy and giving and thorough.

"Don't worry," he murmured and kissed her again. "I just want to touch you." Another soft, sweet, lingering kiss. "I'll stop if you tell me to." Kissing and kissing and kissing.

It was delicious and tender and not the least bit threatening with his heavy hand only making slow, restless circles where her hip met her waist.

She wanted more. She wanted sex. It wasn't like the other times she'd wanted sex. Then it had been something between an obligation and a frustrating goal she was determined to achieve.

This was nothing like that. She wanted *him*. She wanted to share her body with Mikolas, feel him inside her, feel close to him.

Make love to me, she begged him with her lips, and ran her hands over him in a silent message of encouragement. When she rolled and tried to open the zip on her dress, he made a ragged noise and found it for her, dragging it down. He lifted away to draw her sleeve off her arm, exposing her bra. One efficient flick of his fingers and the bra was loose.

With reverence, he eased the strap down her arm, dislodging the cup so her breast thrust round and white, nipple turgid with wanton need.

Insecurity didn't have time to strike. He lowered his head and tongued lightly, cupped with a warm hand, then with another groan of appreciation, opened his mouth in a hot branding, letting her get used to the delicate suction before pulling a little harder.

Her toes curled. She wanted to speak, to tell him this was good, that he wouldn't have to stop, but sensation rocked her, coiling in her abdomen, making her loins weep with need. When his hand stroked to rub her bottom, she dragged at her skirt herself, earning a noise of approval as she drew the ruffled fabric out of the way.

He teased her, tracing patterns on her bare thighs, lifting his head to kiss her again and give her his tongue as he made her wait and wait.

"Mikolas," she gasped.

"This?" He brought his hand to the juncture of her thighs and settled his palm there, letting her get used to the sensation. The intimacy. "I want that, too," he breathed against her mouth.

She bit back a cry of pure joy as the weight of his hand covered her, hot and confident. He rocked slowly, increasing the pressure in increments, inciting her to crook her knee so she was open to his touch. Eyes closed, she let herself bask in this wonderful feeling, tension climbing.

When he lifted his hand, she caught her breath in loss, opening her eyes.

He was watching her while his fingertips traced the edge of her knickers, then began to draw them down her thighs.

The friction of lace against her sensitized skin

made her shiver. As the coolness of the room struck her damp, eager flesh, she became starkly aware of how her clothing was askew, her breast exposed, her sex pouted and needy, her body trembling with ridiculously high desire.

For a moment anxiety struck. She wanted to rush past this moment, rush through the hard part, have done with this interminable impasse. She lifted her hips so he could finish skimming them away, but when he came down beside her again, he only combed her hair back from her face.

"I just want to feel you. I'll be gentle," he promised, and kissed her lightly.

Yes, she almost screamed.

Embarrassment ought to be killing her, but arousal was pulsing in her like an electrical current. And when he cradled her against him this way, she felt very safe.

They kissed and his hand covered her again. This time she was naked. The sensation was so acute she jolted under his touch.

"Just feel," he cajoled softly. "Tell me what you like. Is that good?"

He did things then that were gorgeous and

honeyed. She knew how her body worked, but she had never felt this turned on. She didn't let herself think, just floated in the deep currents of pleasure he swirled through her.

"Like that?" He kept up the magical play, making tension coil through her so she moaned beneath his kiss, encouraging him. Yes, like that. Exactly like that.

He pressed one finger into her.

She gasped.

"Okay?" he breathed against her cheek.

She clasped him with her inner muscles, loving the sensation even though it felt very snug. She was so aroused, so close, she covered his hand with her own and pressed. She rocked her hips as he made love to her with his hand and shattered into a million pieces, cries muffled by his smothering kiss.

CHAPTER ELEVEN

THEY WERE GOING to kill each other.

Mikolas was fully clothed and if she shaped him through his pants right now, he would explode.

But oh, she was amazing. He licked at her panting lips, wanting to smile at the way she clung to his mouth with her own, but weakly. She was still shivering with the aftershocks of her beautiful, stunning orgasm.

He caressed her very, very gently, coaxing her to remain aroused. He wanted to do that to her again. Taste her. Drown in her.

She made a noise and kissed him back with more response, restless hands picking at his shirt, looking for the buttons.

He broke them open with a couple of yanks, then shrugged it off and discarded it, too hot for clothes. On fire for her.

She pulled her other arm free of her dress and

held up her arms for him to come back. Soft curves, velvety skin. He loved the feel of her against his bare chest and biceps. Delicate, but spry. So warm, smelling of rain and tea and the drugging scent of sexual fulfillment.

Her smooth hands traced over his torso and back, making him groan at how good it felt on skin that was taut and sensitized. She tasted like nectarines, he thought, opening his mouth on the swell of her breast. He tongued her nipple, more aggressive than he had been the first time.

She arched for more.

He was going too fast, he cautioned himself, but he wanted to consume her. He wanted her dress out of the way, he wanted her hands everywhere on him—

She arched to strip the garment down.

He slid down the bed as he whisked the dress away, pressing his lips to her quivering belly, blowing softly on the fine hairs of her mound, laughing with delight at finally being here. He was so filled with desire his heart was slamming, pulse reverberating through his entire body.

“Mikolas,” she breathed.

Her fingers were in his hair like she was petting a wolf, tugging hard enough to force him to lift his head before he'd barely nuzzled her.

"Make love to me."

A lightning rod of lust went through him. He steeled himself to maintain his control when all he wanted was to push her legs apart and rise over her.

"I am." He was going to make her scream with release.

"I mean really." Her hand moved to cradle his jaw, her touch light against the clenched muscle in his cheek. Entreaty filled her eyes. "Please."

She had come into his life to destroy him in the most subversive yet effective way possible.

He could barely move, but he drew back, coming up on an elbow, trying to hold on to what shreds of gentlemanly conduct he possessed.

"Do you ever do what's expected of you?"

"You don't want to?" The appalled humiliation that crept into her tone scared the hell out of him.

"Of course I *want* to." He spoke too harshly. He was barely hanging on to rational thought over here.

She tensed, wary.

He set his hand on her navel, breathed, tried to

find something that passed for civilized behavior, but found only the thief he had once been. His hand stole lower, unable to help himself. His thumb detoured along her cleft, finding her slick and ready. Need pearled into one place that made her gasp raggedly when he found it, circling and teasing.

Her thighs relaxed open. She arched to his touch. "Please," she begged. "I want to know how it feels."

He was only human, not a superhero. He pulled away, hearing her catch back a noise of injury.

Her breath caught in the next instant as she saw he was rising to open his pants. He stripped in jerky, uncoordinated movements, watching her swallow and bite her bottom lip. He made himself take his time retrieving the condom so she had lots of opportunity to change her mind.

"I'll stop if you want me to," he promised as he covered himself, then settled over her. He would. He didn't know how, but he would.

Please don't make me stop.

It would really happen this time. Viveka's nerves sizzled as Mikolas covered her. He was such a big person compared with her. He *loomed.* She skimmed her fingertips over his broad shoulders and was starkly aware of how much space his hips and thighs took up as he settled without hesitation between her own.

She tensed, nervous.

He kissed her in abbreviated catches of her mouth that didn't quite satisfy before he pulled away, then did it again.

She made a noise of impatience and wiggled beneath him. "I want—"

"Me, too," he growled against her mouth. Then he lifted to trace himself against her folds. "You're sure?" he murmured, looking down to where they touched.

So sure. "Yes," she breathed.

He positioned himself and pressed.

It hurt. So much. She fought her instinctive tension, tried to make herself relax, tried not to resist, but the sting became more and more intense. He seemed huge. Tears came into her eyes. She couldn't hold back a throaty noise of anxiety.

He stilled, shuddering. The sting subsided a little.

“Viveka.” His voice was ragged. “That’s just the tip—” He hung his head against her shoulder, forehead damp with perspiration, big body shaking.

“Don’t stop.” She caught her foot behind his thigh and tried to press him forward.

“*Glykia mou*, I don’t want to hurt you.” He lifted his face and wore a tortured expression.

“That’s why it’s okay if you do.” Her mouth quivered, barely able to form words. It still hurt, but she didn’t care. “I trust you. Please don’t make me do this with someone else.”

He bit out a string of confounded curses, looking into the shadows for a moment. Then he met her gaze and carefully pressed again.

She couldn’t help flinching. Tensing. The stretch hurt a lot. He paused again, looked at her with as much frustration as she felt.

“Don’t try to be gentle. Just do it,” she told him.

He wavered, then made a tight noise of angst, covered her mouth, gathered himself and thrust deep.

She arched at the flash of pain, crying out into his mouth.

They both stayed motionless for a few hissing breaths.

Slowly the pain eased to a tolerable sting. She moved her lips against his and he kissed her gently. Sweetly.

"Do you hate me?" His voice was thick, his brow tense as he set it against hers. His expression was strained.

He didn't move, letting her get used to the feel of a man inside her for the first time. And he held her in such protective arms, her eyes grew wet from the complete opposite of pain: happiness.

She returned his healing kiss with one that was a little more inciting.

"No," she answered, smiling shakily, feeling intensely close to him. She let her arms settle across his back and traced the indent of his spine, enjoying the way he reacted with a shiver.

"Want to stop?" he asked.

"No." Her voice was barely there. Tentatively she moved a little, settling herself more comfortably beneath him. "I'm not sure I want you to move at all," she admitted wryly. "Ever."

His breath released on a jagged chuckle. "You are going to be the death of me."

Very carefully, he shifted so he was angled on his elbow, then he made a gentling noise and touched where they were joined.

"You feel so good," he crooned in Greek, gently soothing and stimulating as he murmured compliments. "I thought nothing could be better than the way you took me apart with your mouth, but this feels incredible. You're so perfect, Viveka. So lovely."

The noise that escaped her then was pure pleasure. He was leading her down the road of stirred desire to real excitement. It felt strange to have him lodged inside her while her arousal intensified. Part of her wanted him to move, but she was still wary of the pain and this felt so good. The way he stretched her accentuated the sensations. She grew taut and deeply aroused. Restless and—

"Oh, Mikolas. Please. Oh—" A powerful climax rocked her. Her sheath clenched and shivered around his hard shape with such power she could hardly breath. Stars imploded behind her eyes and she clung to him, crying out with ecstasy. It was beautiful and selfish and heavenly.

As the spasms faded, he began to pull away. The friction felt good, except sharp. She wasn't sure she could take that in a prolonged way, but then he was gone from her body and she was bereft.

"You didn't, did you?" She reached to find his thick shaft, so hard and hot, obviously unsatisfied.

He folded his hand over hers and pumped into her fist. Two, three times, then he pressed a harsh groan into her shoulder, mouth opening so his teeth sat against her skin, not quite biting while he shuddered and pulsed against her palm.

Shocked, but pleased, she continued to pleasure him until he relaxed and released her. He removed the condom with a practiced twist, then rolled away and sat up to discard it. Before he came back, he dragged the covers down and pulled her with him as he slid under them.

"Why did you do that?" she asked as he molded her to his front, stomach to stomach.

"So we won't be cold while we sleep." He adjusted the edge of the sheet away from her face.

"You know what I mean." She pinched his chest, unable to lie still when it felt so good to rub her naked legs against his and nuzzle his collarbone with her lips.

"Learn to speak plainly when we're in bed," he ordered.

"Or what?" She was giddy, so happy with being his lover she felt like the sun was lodged inside her.

"Or I may not give you what you want."

They were both silent a moment, bodies quieting.

"You did," she said softly, adjusting her head against his shoulder. "Thank you."

He didn't say anything, but his hand moved thoughtfully in her hair.

A frozen spike of insecurity pierced her. "Did *you* like it?"

He snorted. "I have just finessed my way through initiating a particularly delicate virgin. My ego is so enormous right now, it's a wonder you fit in the bed."

Viveka woke to an empty bed, couldn't find Mikolas in the penthouse, realized she was late for the gym and decided she was entitled to a bath. She was climbing out of it, a thick white towel loosely clutched around her middle, when he strolled in wearing his gym shorts and nothing else.

"Lazy," he stated, pausing to give her a long, appreciative look.

"Seriously?" Before that bath, she had ached *everywhere.*

His mouth twitched and he came closer, gaze skimming down her front. "Sore?"

She shrugged a shoulder, instantly so shy she nearly couldn't bear it. The things they'd done!

She blushed, aware that her gaze was coveting the hard planes of his body, and instantly wanted to be close to him. Touch, feel, kiss…more.

She wasn't sure how to issue the invitation across the expanse of the spa-like bathroom, but he wasn't the novice she was. He took the last few laconic steps to reach her, spiky lashes lowering as he stared at her mouth. When his head dipped, she lifted her chin to meet his kiss. Her free hand found his stubbled cheek while her other kept her towel in place.

"Mmm…" she murmured, liking the way he didn't rush, but kissed her slowly and thoroughly.

He drew back and tried taking the towel in his two hands.

She hesitated.

"I only want a peek," he cajoled.

"It's daylight," she argued.

"Exactly."

If she had feared that having sex would weaken her will around him, the fear was justified. She wanted to please him. She wanted to offer her whole self and plead with him to cherish her. Her fingers relaxed under the knowledge she was giving up more than control of a towel.

As he opened it, however, and took a long eyeful of her sucked-in stomach and thrust-out breasts, she saw desire grip him with the same lack of mercy it showed her. He swallowed, body hardening, jaw clenched like he was under some kind of deep stress.

"I was only going to kiss you," he said, lifting lust-filled eyes to hers. "But if you—"

"I do," she assured him.

He let the towel drop and she met him mid-way, moaning with acquiescence as he pressed her onto the daybed. Her inhibitions about the daylight quickly burned up as his stubble slid down her neck to her breast where he sucked and made her writhe. When he slid even lower, scraping her stomach then her thighs as he knelt on the floor, she threw her arm across her eyes and let him do whatever he wanted.

Because it was what she wanted. Oh, that felt exquisite.

"Don't stop," she pleaded when he lifted his head.

"Can you take me?" he growled, scraping his teeth with mock threat along her inner thigh.

She nodded, little echoes of wariness threatening, but she couldn't take her eyes off his form as he rose and moved to the mirror over his sink, found a condom and covered himself.

When he came back and stood over her, she stayed exactly as he'd left her, splayed weakly with desire, like some harem girl offered for his pleasure.

His hands flexed like he was struggling against some kind of internal pain.

"Mikolas," she pleaded, holding out her arms.

He made a noise of agony and came down over

her, heavy and confident, thighs pressing hers wide as he positioned himself. "I don't want to hurt you." His hand tangled in her hair. "But I want you so damned much. Stop me if it hurts."

"It's okay," she told him, not caring about the burn as she arched, inviting him to press all the way in. It hurt, but his first careful thrusts felt good at the same time. The friction of him moving inside her made the connection that much more intense. She rose to the brink very quickly, climaxing with a sudden gasp, clinging to him, shocked at her reaction.

He shuddered, lips pressed into her neck, and hurried to finish with her, groaning fulfillment against her skin.

She was disappointed when he carefully disengaged and sat up, his back to her.

She started to protest that it was okay, holding him in her didn't hurt anymore, but she was distracted by the marks on his back. They were pocked scars that were visible only because the light was so bright. She'd seen his back on the yacht, but in lamplight she hadn't noticed the scars. They weren't raised, but there were more than a dozen.

"What happened to your back?" she asked, puzzled.

Mikolas rose and walked first to his side of the room, where he scanned around his sinks, then went across to her vanity, where he found the remote for the shower.

"We should set some ground rules," he said.

"Leave the remote on your side?" she guessed as she rose. She walked past her discarded towel for her white robe, wondering why she bothered when she was thinking of joining him in the shower. She wanted to touch him, to close this distance that had arisen so abruptly between them.

"That," he agreed. "And we'll only be together for a short time. Call me your lover if you want to, but do not expect us to fall in love. Keep your expectations low."

She fell back a step as she tied her robe, giving it a firm yank like the action could tie off the wound he'd just inflicted.

But what did she think they were doing? Like fine weather, they were enjoying each other because they were here. That was all.

“I wasn’t fishing for a marriage proposal,” she defended.

“So long as we’re clear.” He aimed the remote and started the shower jets.

Scanning his stiff shoulders, she said, “Is this because I asked about your back? I’m sorry if that was too personal, but I’ve told you some really personal things about me.”

“Talk to me about whatever you want. If I don’t want to tell you something, I won’t.” He spoke with aloof confidence, but his expression faltered briefly, mouth quirking with self-deprecation.

Because he had already shared more than made him comfortable?

“There’s nothing wrong with being friends, is there?”

He glanced at her, his expression patient, but resolute.

“You don’t have friends,” she recalled from the other night, thinking, *I can see why.* “What’s wrong with friendship? Don’t you want someone you can confide in? Share jokes with?”

His rebuff was making her feel like a houseguest who had to be tolerated. Surely they were past that! He'd just enjoyed *her* hospitality, hadn't he?

"They're cigar burns," he said abruptly, rattling the remote control onto the space behind the sink. "I have more on the bottoms of my feet. My captors used to make me scream so my grandfather could hear it over the phone. *There was more than one call.* Is that the sort of confiding you're looking for, Viveka?" he challenged with antagonism.

"Mikolas." Her breath stung like acid against the back of her throat. She unconsciously clutched the robe across her shattered heart.

"That's why I don't want to share more than our bodies. There's nothing else worth sharing."

Mikolas had been hard on Viveka this morning, he knew that. But he'd been the victim of forces greater than himself once before and already felt too powerless around her. The way she had infiltrated his life, the changes he was making for her, were unprecedented.

Earlier that day, he had risen while she slept and spent the morning sparring, trying to work his libido into exhaustion. She had to be sore. He wasn't an animal.

But one glance at her rising from the bath and all his command over himself had evaporated. At one point, he'd been quite sure he was prepared to beg.

Begging was futile. He *knew* that.

But so was thinking he could treat Viveka like every other woman he'd slept with. Many of them had asked about his back. He'd always lied, claiming chicken pox had caused the scars. For some reason, he didn't want to lie to Viveka.

When he had finally blurted out the ugly truth, he'd seen something in her expression that he outwardly rejected, but inwardly craved: agony on his behalf. Sadness for that dark time that had stolen his innocence and left him with even bigger scars that no one would ever see.

Damn it, he was self-aware enough to know he used denial as a coping strategy, but there was no point in raking over the coals of what had been done to him. Nothing would change it. Viveka wanted a jocular companion to share opinions and anecdotes with. He was never going to be that person. There was too much gravity and anger in him.

So he had schooled her on what to expect, and it left him sullen through the rest of the day.

She wasn't much better. In another woman, he would have called her subdued mood passive-aggressive, but he already knew how sensitive Viveka was under all that bravado. His churlish behavior had tamped down her natural cheerfulness. That made him feel even more disgusted with himself.

Then his grandfather asked her to play backgammon and she brightened, disappearing for a couple of hours, coming back to the penthouse only to change for the gym.

Why did that annoy him? He wanted her to be self-sufficient and not look to him to keep her amused. Later that evening, however, when he found her plumping cushions in the lounge, he had to ask, "What are you doing?"

"Tidying up." She carried a teacup and plate to the dumbwaiter and left it there.

"I pay people to do that."

"I carry my weight," she said neutrally.

He pushed his hands into his pockets, watching her click on a lamp and turn off the overhead light, then lift a houseplant—honest to God, she checked a plant to see if it needed water rather than look at him.

"You're angry with me for what I said this morning."

"I'm not." She sounded truthful and folded her arms defensively, but she finally turned and gave him her attention. "I just never wanted to be in this position again."

The bruised look in her eye made him feel like a heel.

"What position?" he asked warily.

"Being forced on someone who doesn't really want me around." Her tight smile came up, brave, but fatalistic.

"It's not like that," he ground out. "I told you I want you." Admitting it still made him feel like he was being hung by his feet over a ledge.

"Physically," she clarified.

Before the talons of a deeper truth had finished digging into his chest, she looked down, voice so low he almost didn't hear her.

"So do I. That's what worries me," she continued.

"What do you mean?"

She hugged herself, shrugging. Troubled. "Not something worth sharing," she mumbled.

Share, he wanted to demand, but that would be hypocritical. Regret and apology buzzed around him like biting mosquitoes, annoying him.

It had taken him years to come to this point of being completely sure in himself. A few days with this woman, and he was second-guessing everything he was or had or did.

"Can we just go to bed?" Her doe eyes were so vulnerable, it took a moment for him to comprehend what she was saying. He had thought they were fighting.

"Yes," he growled, opening his arms. "Come here."

She pressed into him, her lips touching his throat. He sighed as the turmoil inside him subsided.

Every night, they made love until Viveka didn't even remember falling asleep, but she always woke alone.

Was it personal? she couldn't help wondering. Did Mikolas not see anything in her to like? Or was he simply that removed from the normal needs of humanity that he genuinely didn't want any closer connections? Did he realize his behavior was hurtful? Did he know and not *care*?

Whenever she had dreamed of being in an intimate relationship with a man, it had been intimacy across the board, not this heart-wrenching openness during sex and a deliberate distance outside of it. Was she saying too much? *Asking* too much?

She became hypersensitive to every word she spoke, trying to refrain from getting too personal. The constant weighing and worrying was exhausting.

It was harder when they traveled. At least with his grandfather at the table, the conversation flowed more naturally. As Mikolas dragged her to various events across Europe, she had to find ways to talk to him without putting herself out there too much.

"I might go to the art gallery while you're in meetings this morning. Unless you want to come? I could wait until this afternoon," was a typical, neutral approach. She loved spending time with him, but couldn't say *that*.

"I can make myself available after lunch."

"It's an exhibition of children's art," she clarified. "Is that something you'd want to see?" Now she felt like she was prying. Her belly clenched as she awaited rejection.

He shrugged, indifferent. "Art galleries aren't something I typically do, but if you want to see it, I'll take you."

Which made her feel like she was imposing on his time, but he was already tapping it into his schedule. Later he paced around the place, not saying much, while she held back asking what he thought. She wanted to tell him about her early aspirations and point to what she liked and ask if he'd ever messed around with finger paints as a child.

She actually found herself speaking more freely to strangers over cocktails than she did with him. He always listened intently, but she didn't know if that was for show or what. If he had interest in her thoughts or ambitions, she kept thinking, he would ask her himself, but he never did.

Tonight she was revealing her old fascination with art history and Greek mythology. It felt good to open up, so she shared a little more than she normally would.

"I actually won an award," she confided with a wrinkle of her nose. "It was just a little thing for a watercolor I painted at school. I was convinced I'd become a world-famous artist," she joked. "I've always wanted to take a degree in art, but there's never been the right time."

It was small talk. They were nice people, owners of a hotel chain whom she'd met more than once.

Deep down, she was congratulating herself on performing well at these events, remembering the names of children and occasionally going on shopping dates. Tonight she had found herself genuinely interested in Adara Makricosta's plans for her hotels. That's how her own career goals had come up. Adara Makricosta was the CEO of a family-owned chain and had asked Viveka about her own work.

Viveka sidestepped the admission she was merely a mistress whose job it was to create this warming trend Mikolas was enjoying among the world's most rich and powerful.

"Why didn't you tell me that before?" Mikolas asked when Adara and Gideon had moved on. "About wanting to study art," he prompted when she only looked at him blankly.

Viveka's heart lurched and she almost blurted out, *Because you wouldn't care.* She swallowed. "It's not practical. I thought about taking evening classes around my day job, but I always had Hildy to look after. And I knew once I was in this position, looking to my own future, I would need to devote myself to a proper career, not dabble in something that will never pay the bills."

She ought to be thinking harder about that, not using up all her brain space trying to second-guess the man in front of her.

"You don't have bills now. Sign up for something," he said breezily.

"Where? To what end?" Her throat tightened. "We're constantly on the move and I don't know how long I'll be with you. No. There's no point." It would hurt to see that phoenix of a dream rise up from the ashes only to fly away.

Or was he implying she would be with him for the long term?

She did the unthinkable and searched his expression for some sign that he had feelings for her. That they had a future.

He receded behind a remote mask, horribly quiet for the rest of the night and even while they traveled back to Greece, adding an extra layer of tension to their trip.

Viveka was still smarting over Mikolas's behavior when she woke in his bed the next morning. They were sleeping late after arriving in the wee hours. She stayed motionless, naked in the spoon of his body, not wanting to move and wake him. She often fell asleep in his arms, but she never woke in them. This was a rare moment of closeness.

It was the counterfeit currency that all women—like mother like daughter—too often took in place of real regard.

Because, no matter how distanced she felt from Mikolas during the day, in bed she felt so integral to him it was a type of agony to be anywhere else. When he made love to her, it felt like love. His kisses and caresses were generous, his compliments extravagant. She warmed and tingled just thinking about how good it felt to join with him, but it wasn't just physical pleasure for her. Lying with him, naked and intimate, was emotionally fulfilling.

She was falling for him.

His breathing changed. He hardened against her backside and she bit her lip, heartened by the lazy stroke of his hand and the noise of contentment he made, like he was pleased to wake with her against him.

Such happiness brimmed in her, she couldn't help but wriggle her butt into his hardness, inviting the only affection he seemed to accept, wanting to hold on to this moment of harmony.

His mouth opened on her shoulder and his hand drifted down her belly into the juncture of her thighs. He made a satisfied noise when he found her wet and ready.

She gasped, stimulated by his lazy touch. She stretched her arm to the night table, then handed a condom over her shoulder as she nestled back against him, eager and needy. He adjusted her position and a moment later thrust in, sighing a hot breath against her neck, setting kisses against her nape that were warm and soft. Caring. Surely he cared?

She took him so easily now. It was nothing but pleasure, so much pleasure. She hadn't known her body could be like this: buttery and welcoming. It was almost too good. She was so far ahead of him, having been thinking about this while he slept against her, she soared over the top in moments. She cried out, panting and damp with sweat, overcome and floating, speechless in her orgasmic bliss.

"Greedy," he said in a gritty morning voice, rubbing his mouth against her skin, inhaling and calling her beautiful in Greek. Exquisite. Telling her how much he enjoyed being inside her. How good she made him feel.

He came up on his elbow so he could thrust with more power. His hand went between her legs again, ensuring her pleasure as he moved with more aggression.

She didn't mind his vigor. She was so slick, still so aroused, she reveled in the slap of his hips into her backside, hand knotting in the bottom sheet to brace herself to receive him, making noises close to desperation as she felt a fresh pinnacle hover within reach.

"Don't hold back," he ground out. "Come with me. *Now*."

He pounded into her, the most unrestrained he'd ever been. She cried out as her excitement peaked. An intense climax rolled through her, leaving her shattered and quaking in ecstasy.

He convulsed with equal strength, arms caging her, hoarse shout hot against her cheek. He jerked as she clenched, continuing to push deep so she was hit by wave after wave of aftershocks while he thrust firmly into her, like he was implanting his essence into her core.

As the sensual storm battered them, he remained pressed over her, crushing her beneath his heavy body. Finally, the crisis began to subside and he exhaled raggedly as he slid flat, his one arm under her neck bending so he could cradle her into his front. They were coated in perspiration. It adhered her back to his front and she could feel his heart still pounding unsteadily against her shoulder blade. Their legs were tangled, their bodies still joined, their breaths slowing to level.

It was the most beautifully imperfect moment

of her life. She loved him. Endlessly and completely. But he didn't love her back.

Mikolas had visited hell. Then his grandfather had accepted him and he had returned to the real world, where there were good days and bad days. Now he'd found what looked like heaven and he didn't trust it. Not one little bit.

But he couldn't turn away from it—*from her*—either.

Not without feeling as though he was peeling away his own skin, leaving him raw and vulnerable. He was a molting crab, losing his shell every night and rebuilding it every day.

This morning was the most profound deconstruction yet. He always tried to leave before Viveka woke so he wouldn't start his day impacted by her effect on him, but the sweet way she'd rubbed herself into his groin had undone him. She had gone from a tentative virgin to a sensual goddess capable of stripping him down to nothing but pure sensation.

How could he resist that? How could he not let her press him into service and give himself up to the joy of possessing her. It had been all he could do to hold back so she came with him. Because she owned him. Between the sheets, she completely owned him. Right now, all he wanted in life was to stay in this bed, with her body replete against his, her fingertips drawing light patterns on the back of his hand.

Don't *want*.

He made himself roll away and sit up, to prove himself master over whatever this thing was that threatened him in a way nothing else could.

She stayed inside him, though. In his body as an intoxicant, and in his head as an unwavering awareness. And because he was so attuned to her, he heard the barely discernible noise she made as he pushed to stand. It was a sniff. A lash. A cat-o'-nine-tails that scored through his thick skin into his soul.

He swung around and saw only the bow of her back, still curled on her side where he'd left her. He dropped his knee into the mattress and caught her shoulder, flattening her so he could see her face.

She gasped in surprise, lifting a hand to quickly try to wipe away the tears that stood in her eyes. Self-conscious agony flashed in her expression before she turned her face to hide it.

His heart fell through the earth.

"I thought you were with me." He spoke through numb lips, horrified with himself. He could have sworn she had been as passionately excited as he was. He had felt her slickness, the ripples of her orgasm. Was he kidding himself with how well he thought he knew her?

"You have to tell me if I'm being too rough," he insisted, his usual command buried in a choke of self-reproach.

"It's not that." Her expression spasmed with dismay. She pushed the back of her wrist across her eye, then brushed his hand off her shoulder so she could roll away and sit up. "I used to be so afraid of sex. Now I like it."

She rubbed her hands up and down her arms, the delicacy of her frame striking like a hammer between his eyes. Her nude body pimpled at the chill as she rose.

"I'm grateful," she claimed, turning to offer him a smile, but her lashes were still matted. "Take a bow. Let me know what I owe you."

Those weren't tears of gratitude.

His heart lurched as he found himself right back in that moment where he had impulsively told her to pursue her interests and she had searched for reassurance that she would be with him for the long haul.

I don't know how long I'll be with you.

It had struck him at that moment that at some point she would leave and he hadn't been able to face it. He skipped past it now, only saying her name.

"Viveka." It hurt his throat. "I told you to keep your expectations low," he reminded, and felt like a coward, especially when her smile died.

She looked at him with betrayal, like he'd smacked her.

"Don't," he bit out.

"Don't what? Don't like it?"

"Don't be hurt." He couldn't bear the idea that he was hurting her. "Don't feel *grateful*."

She made a choking noise. "Don't tell me what to feel. That is where you control what I feel." She pointed at the rumpled sheets he knelt upon, then tapped her chest and said on a burst of passion, "In here? This is mine. I'll feel whatever the hell I want."

Her blue eyes glowed with angry defiance, but something else ravaged her. Something sweet and powerful and pure that shot like an arrow to pierce his breastbone and sting his heart. He didn't try to put a name to it. He was afraid to, especially when he saw shadows of hopelessness dim her gaze before she looked away.

"I'm not confusing sex with love, if that's what you're worried about." She moved to the chair and pulled on his shirt from the night before, shooting her arms into it and folding the front across her stomach. She was hunched as though bracing for body blows. "My mother made that mistake." Her voice was scuffed and desolate. "I won't. I know the difference."

Why did that make him clench his fist in despair? He ought to be reassured.

He almost told her this wasn't just sex. When he walked into a room with her hand in his, he was so proud it was criminal. When she dropped little tidbits about her life before she met him, he was fascinated. When she looked dejected like that, his armored heart creaked and rose on quivering legs, anxious to show valor in her name.

Instead he stood, saying, "I'll send an email

today. To ask how the investigation is coming along. On your mother," he clarified, when she turned a blank look on him.

She snorted, sounding disillusioned as she muttered, "Thanks."

"Your head is not in the game today," Erebus said, dragging Viveka's mind to the *távli* board, where he was placing one of his checkers on top of hers.

Were they at *plakoto* already? Until a few weeks ago, she hadn't played since she and Trina were girls, but the rules and strategies had come back to her very quickly. She sat down with Erebus at least once a day if she was home.

"Jet lag," she murmured, earning a *tsk*.

"We don't lie to each other in this house, *poulaki mou*."

Viveka was growing fond of the old man. He was very well-read, kept up on world politics and had a wry sense of humor. At the same time, he was interested in *her*. He called her "my little birdie" and always had something nice to say. Today it had been, *"I wish you weren't leaving for Paris. I miss you when you're traveling."*

She'd never had a decent father figure in her life and knew it was crazy to see this former criminal in that light, but he was also sweetly protective of her. It was endearing.

So she didn't want to offend him by stating that his grandson was tearing her into little pieces.

"I wonder sometimes what Mikolas was like as a child," she prevaricated.

She and Erebus had talked a little about her aunt and he'd shared a few stories from his earliest years. She was deeply curious how such a kind-seeming man could have broken the law and fathered an infamous criminal, but thought it better not to ask.

He nodded thoughtfully, gesturing for her to shake the cup with the dice and take her turn.

She did and set the cup within his reach, but he was staring across the water from their perch outside his private sitting room. In a few weeks it would be too hot to sit out here, but it was balmy and pleasant today. A light breeze moved beneath the awning, carrying his favorite *kantada* folk music with it.

"Pour us an ouzo," he finally said, two papery fingers directing her to the interior of his apartment.

"I'll get in trouble. You're only supposed to have one before dinner."

"I won't tell if you don't," he said, making her smile.

He came in behind her as she filled the small glasses. He took his and canted his head for her to follow him.

She did, slowly pacing with him as he shuffled his cane across his lounge and into his bedroom. There he sat with a heavy sigh into a chair near the window. He picked up the double photo frame on the side table and held it out to her.

She accepted it and took her time studying the black-and-white photo of the young woman on the one side, the boy and girl sitting on a rock at a beach in the other. They were perhaps nine and five.

"Your wife?" she guessed. "And Mikolas's father?"

"Yes. And my daughter. She was… Men always say they want sons, but a daughter is life and light. A way for your wife to live on. Daughters are love in its purest form."

"That's a beautiful thing to say." She wished she knew more about her own father than a few barely recollected facts from her mother. He'd been English and had dropped out of school to work in radio. He'd married her mother because she was pregnant and died from a rare virus that had got into his heart.

She sat on the foot of Erebus's bed, facing him. "Mikolas told me you lost your daughter when she was young. I'm sorry."

He nodded, taking back the frame and looking at it again. "My wife, too. She was beautiful. She looked at me the way you look at Mikolas. I miss that."

Viveka looked into her drink.

"I failed them," Erebus continued grimly. "It was a difficult time in our country's history. Fear of communism, martial law, censorship, persecution. I was young and passionate, courting arrest with my protests. I left to hide on this island, never thinking they would go after my wife."

His cloudy gray eyes couldn't disguise his stricken grief.

"The way my son told me, my daughter was crying, trying to cling to their mother as the military police dragged her away for questioning. They knocked her to the ground. Her ear started bleeding. She never came to. Brain injury, perhaps. I'll never know. My wife died in custody, but not before my son saw her beaten unconscious for trying to go back to our daughter."

Viveka could only cover her mouth, holding back a cry of protest.

"By the time I was reunited with him, my son was twisted beyond repair. I was warped, too. The law? How could I have regard for it? What I did then, bribes, theft, smuggling… None of that sits on my conscience with any great weight. But what my son turned into…"

He cleared his throat and set the photo frame back in its place. His hands shook and he took a long time to speak again.

"My son lost his humanity. The things he did… I couldn't make him stop, couldn't bring him back from that. It was no surprise to me that he was killed so violently. It was the way he lived. When he died I mourned him, but I also mourned what should have been. I was forced to face my many mistakes. The things I had done caused me to outlive my children. I hated the man I had become."

His pain was tangible. Viveka ached for him.

"Into this came a ransom demand. A street rat was claiming to be my grandson. Some of my son's rivals had him."

Her heart clenched. She was listening intently, but was certain she wouldn't be able to bear hearing this.

"You want to know what Mikolas was like as a child? So do I. He came to me as an empty shell. Eyes this big." He made a circle with his finger and thumb. "Thin. Brittle. His hand was crushed, some of his fingernails gone. Three of his teeth gone. He was *broken*." He paused, lined face working to control deep pain, then he admitted, "I think he hoped I would kill him."

She bit her lip, eyes hot and wet, a burn of anguish like a pike spreading from her throat to the pit of her stomach.

"He said that if the blood test hadn't been positive, you wouldn't have helped him." She couldn't keep the accusation, the blame, out of her voice.

"I honestly can't say what I would have done," Erebus admitted, eyes rheumy. "Looking back from the end of my life, I want to believe my conscience would have demanded I help him regardless, but I wasn't much of a man at the time. They showed me a picture and he looked a little like my son, but..."

His head hung heavy with regret.

"He begged me to believe he was telling the truth, to accept him. I took too long." He took a healthy sip of his ouzo.

She'd forgotten she was holding one herself. She sipped, thinking how forsaken Mikolas must have felt. No wonder he was so impermeable.

"He thinks I want him to redeem the Petrides name, but *I* need redemption. To some extent I have it," Erebus allowed with deep emotion. "I'm proud of all he's accomplished. He's a good man. He told me why he brought you here. He did the right thing."

She suppressed a snort. Mikolas's reasons for keeping her and her reasons for staying were so fraught and complex, she didn't see any way to call them wholly right or wrong.

"He has never recovered his heart, though. All the things he has done? It hasn't been for me. He has built this fortress around himself for good reason. He trusts no one, relies on no one."

"Cares about no one," she murmured despondently.

"Is that what puts that hopeless expression on your face, *poulaki mou*?"

She knocked back her drink, giving a little shiver as the sweet heat spread from her tongue to the tips of her limbs. Shaking back her hair, she braced herself and said, "He'll never love me, will he?"

Erebus didn't bother to hide the sadness in his eyes. Because they didn't lie to each other.

Slowly the glow of hope inside her guttered and doused.

"We should go back to our game," he said.

CHAPTER TWELVE

MIKOLAS GLANCED UP as Viveka came out of the elevator. She never used it unless she was coming from the gym, but today she was dressed in the clothes she'd worn to lunch.

She staggered and he shot to his feet, stepping around his desk to hurry toward her. "Are you all right?"

"Fine." She set a hand on the wall, holding up the other to forestall him. "I just forgot that ouzo sneaks up on you like this."

"You've been *drinking*?"

"With your grandfather. Don't get mad. It was his idea, but I'm going to need a nap before dinner. That's what he was doing when I left him."

"This is what you two get up to over backgammon?" He took her arm, planning to help her to her room.

"Not usually, no." Her hand came to his chest. She didn't move, just stared at her hand on his chest, mouth grave, brow wearing a faint pleat. "We were talking."

That sounded ominous. She glanced up and anguish edged the blue of her irises.

Instinctively, he swallowed. His hand unconsciously tightened on her elbow, but he took a half step back from her. "What were you talking about?"

"He loves you, you know." Her mouth quivered, the corners pulling down. "He wishes you could forgive him."

He flinched, dropping his hand from her arm.

"He understands why you can't. Even if you did reach out to him, I don't think he would forgive himself. It's just…sad. He doesn't know how to reach you and—" She rolled to lean her shoulders against the wall, swallowing. "You won't let anyone in, ever, will you? Is this really all you want, Mikolas? Things? Sex without love?"

He swore silently, lifting his gaze to the ceiling, hands bunching into fists, fighting a wave of helplessness.

"I lied to you," he admitted when he trusted his voice. "That first day we met, I said my grandfather gave me anything I wanted." He lowered his gaze to her searching one. “I didn’t want any of those things I asked for.”

He had her whole attention.

“It was my test for him.” He saw now the gifts had been his grandfather’s attempts to earn his trust, but then it had been a game. A deadly, terrifying one. “I asked him for things I didn’t care about, to see if he would get them for me. I never told him what I really wanted. I never told anyone.”

He looked at his palm, rubbed one of the smooth patches where it had been held against a hot kettle, leaving shiny scar tissue.

“I never tell anyone. Physical torture is inhuman, but psychological torture…” His hand began shaking.

“Mikolas.” Her hand came into his. He started to pull away, but his fingers closed over hers involuntarily, holding on, letting her keep him from sinking into the dark memories.

His voice felt like it belonged to someone else. “They would ask me, ‘Do you want water?’ ‘Do you want the bathroom?’ ‘Do you want us to stop?’ Of course I said yes. They never gave me what I wanted.”

Her hand squeezed his and her small body came into the hollow of his front, warm and anxious to soothe, arms going around his stiff frame.

He set his hands on her shoulders, resisting her offer of comfort even though it was all he wanted, ever. He resisted *because* it was what he wanted beyond anything.

"I can't—I'm not trying to hurt him. But if I trust him, if I let him mean too much to me, then what? He's not in a position to be my savior again. He's a weakness to be used against me. I can't leave myself open to that. Can you understand that?"

Her arms around him loosened. For a moment her forehead rested in the center of his chest, then she pressed herself away.

"I do." She took a deep, shaken breath. "I'm going to lie down."

He watched her walk away while two tiny, damp stains on his shirt front stayed cold against his skin.

"Vivi!" Clair exclaimed as she approached with her husband, Aleksy.

Viveka found a real smile for the first time

all night. In days, really. Things between her and Mikolas were more poignantly strained than ever. She loved him so much and understood now that he was never going to let himself love her.

"How's the dress?" Viveka teased, rallying out of despondency for her hostess.

"I've taken to carrying a mending kit." Clair ruefully jiggled her pocketbook.

"I've been looking forward to seeing you again," Viveka said sincerely. "I've had a chance to read up on your foundation. I'm floored by all you do! And I have an idea for a fund-raiser that might work for you."

Mikolas watched Viveka brighten for the first time in days. Her smile caused a pang in his chest that was more of a gong. He wanted to draw that warmth and light of hers against the echoing discord inside him, finally settling it.

"I saw a children's art exhibit when we were in New York. I was impressed by how sophisticated some of it was. It made me think, what if some of your orphans painted pieces for an auction? Here, let me show you." She reached into her purse for her phone, pausing to listen to something Clair was saying about another event they had tried.

Beside him, Aleksy snorted.

Mikolas dragged his gaze off Viveka, lifting a cool brow of inquiry. He had let things progress naturally between the women, not pursuing things on the business front, willing to be patient rather than rush fences and topple his opportunity with the standoffish Russian.

"I find it funny," Aleksy explained. "You went to all this trouble to get my attention, and now you'd rather listen to her than speak to me. I made time in my schedule for you tomorrow morning, if you can tear yourself away…?"

Mikolas bristled at the supercilious look on the other man's face.

Aleksy only lifted his brows, not intimidated by Mikolas's dark glare.

"When we met in Athens, I wondered what the hell you were doing with her. What *she* was doing with *you*. But…" Aleksy's expression grew self-deprecating. "It happens to the best of us, doesn't it?"

Mikolas saw how he had neatly painted himself into a corner. He could dismiss having any regard for Viveka and undo all her good work in getting him this far, or he could suffer the assumption that he had a profound weakness: *her*.

Before he had to act, Viveka said, "Oh, my God," and looked up from her phone. Her eyes were like dinner plates. "Trina has been trying to reach me. Grigor had a heart attack. He's dead."

Mikolas and Viveka left the party amid expressions of sympathy from Clair and Aleksy.

Viveka murmured a distracted "thank you," but they were words that sat on air, empty of meaning. She was in shock. Numb. She wasn't *glad* Grigor was dead. Her sister was too torn up about the loss when she rang her, expressing regret and sorrow that a better relationship with her father would never manifest. Viveka wouldn't wish any sort of pain on her little sister, but she felt nothing herself.

She didn't even experience guilt when Mikolas surmised that Grigor had been under a lot of stress due to the inquiries Mikolas had ordered. He hadn't had much to report the other day, but ended a fresh call to the investigator as they returned to the hotel.

"The police on the island were starting to talk. They could see that silence looked like incompetence at best, bribery and collusion at worst. Charges were sounding likely for your mother's murder and more. My investigator is preparing a report, but without a proper court case, you'll probably never have the absolute truth on how she died. I'm sorry."

She nodded, accepting that. It was enough to know Grigor had died knowing he hadn't got away with his crimes.

"Trina will need me." It felt like she was stating the obvious, but it was the only concrete thought in her head. "I need to book a flight."

"I've already messaged my pilot. He's doing his preflight right now. We'll be in the air as soon as you're ready."

She paused in gathering the things that had been unpacked into drawers for her.

"Didn't I hear Aleksy say something about holding an appointment for you tomorrow?" She looked at the clothes she'd brought to Paris. "Not one thing suitable for a funeral," she murmured. “Would Trina understand if I wore that red gown, do you think?” She pointed across the room to the open closet.

No response from Mikolas.

She turned her head.

He looked like he was trying to drill into her head with his silvery eyes. “I can rebook with Aleksy.”

So careful. So watchful. His remark about coming with her penetrated.

“Do you need to talk to Trina?” she asked, trying to think through the pall of details and decisions that would have to be made. “Because she inherits? Does his dying affect the merger?”

Something she couldn’t interpret flickered across his expression. “There will be things to discuss, yes, but they can wait until she’s dealt with immediate concerns.”

“I wonder if he even kept her in his will,” she murmured, setting out something comfortable to travel in, then pulling off her earrings. Gathering her hair, she moved to silently request he unlatch the sapphire necklace he’d given her this evening. “Trina told me he blamed me for everything, not her, so I hope he didn’t disinherit her.

Who else would he leave his wealth to? Charity? Ba-ha-ha. Not."

The necklace slithered away and she fetched the velvet box, handing it to him along with the earrings, then wormed her way out of her gown.

"Trina better be a rich woman, after everything he put her through. It doesn't seem real." She knew she was babbling. She was processing aloud, maybe because she was afraid of what *would* be said if she wasn't already doing the talking. "I've never been able to trust the times when I've thought I was rid of him. Even after I was living with Hildy, things would come up with Trina and I'd realize he was still a specter in my life. I was so sure the wedding was going to be *it*. Snip, snip, snip."

She made little scissors with her fingers, cutting ties to her stepfather, then bounced her butt into the seat of her jeans and zipped. Her push-up bra was overkill, but she pulled a T-shirt over it, not bothering to change into a different one.

"Now it's really here. He's dead. No longer able to wreck my life."

She made herself face him. Face *it*. The truth she had been avoiding.

"I'm finally safe from him."

Which meant Mikolas had no reason to keep her.

Mikolas was a quick study, always had been. He had seen the light of the train coming at him from the end of the tunnel the moment her lips had shaped the words, *He's dead*.

He had watched her pack and change and had listened to her walk herself to the platform and he still wasn't ready when her pale, pale face tilted up to his to say goodbye.

I can rebook with Aleksy. That was as close as he could come to stating that he was willing to continue their affair. He wasn't offering her solace. She wasn't upset beyond concern for her sister. God knew she didn't need *him*. He had deliberately stifled that expectation in her.

She looked down so all he could see of her expression was her pleated brow. "If you could give me some time to work out how to manage things with Aunt Hildy—"

He turned away, instantly pissed off. *So* pissed off. But he was unable to blame anyone but himself. He was the one who had fought letting ties form between them. He'd called what they had chemistry, sexual infatuation, protection.

"We're square," he growled. "Don't worry about it."

"Hardly. I'll get her house on the market as soon as I can—"

"I have what I wanted," he insisted, while a voice in his head asked, *Do you?* "I'm in," he continued doggedly. "None of the contacts I've made can turn their backs on me now."

"Mikolas—" She lowered to the padded bench in front of the vanity, inwardly quailing. *Don't humiliate yourself*, she thought, but stumbled forward like a love-drunk fool. "I care for you." Her voice thickened. "A lot." She had to clear her throat and swallow. Blink. Her fingers were a tangled mess against her knees. "If you would prefer we stay together…just say it. I know that's hard for you, but…" She warily lifted her gaze.

He was a statue, hands fisted in his pockets, immobile. Unmoved.

Her heart sank. "I can't make an assumption. I would feel like I'm still something you took on. I have to be something…" *You want.* Her mouth wouldn't form the words. This was hopeless. She could see it.

Mikolas's fists were so tight he thought his bones would crack. The shell around his heart was brittle as an egg's, threatening to crack.

"It's never going to work between us," he said, speaking as gently as he could, trying so hard not to bruise her. "You want things that I don't. Things I can't give you." He was trying to be *decent*, but he knew each word was a splash of acid. He felt the blisters forming in his soul. "It's better to end it here."

It happens to the best of us.

What about the worst? What about the ones who pushed it away before they knew what they were refusing?

What about the ones who were afraid because it meant succumbing to something bigger than themselves? Because it meant handing someone, *everyone*, the power to hurt him?

The room seemed to dim and quiet.

She nodded wordlessly, lashes low. Her gorgeous, kissable mouth pursed in melancholy.

And when she was gone, he wondered why, if the threat of Grigor was gone, he was still so worried about her. If he feared so badly that she would hurt him, why was her absence complete agony?

If all he had wanted from her was a damned business contact, why did he blow off his appointment with Aleksy the next morning and sit in a Paris hotel room all day, staring at sapphire jewelry he'd bought because the blue stones matched her eyes, willing his phone to ring?

"You're required to declare funds over ten thousand euros," the male customs agent in London said to Viveka as they entered a room that was like something off a police procedural drama. There was a plain metal table, two chairs, a wastebasket and a camera mounted in the ceiling. If there was a two-way mirror, she couldn't see it, but she felt observed all the same.

And exhausted. The charter from the island after Grigor's funeral had been delayed by weather, forcing her to miss her flight out of Athens. They had rebooked her, but on a crisscross path of whichever flight left soonest in the general direction of London. She hadn't eaten or slept and was positively miserable.

"I forgot I had it," she said flatly.

"You forgot you're carrying twenty-five thousand euros?"

"I was going to put it in the bank in Athens, but I had already missed my connection. I just wanted to get home."

He looked skeptical. "How did you come by this amount of cash?"

"My sister gave it to me. For my aunt."

His brows tilted in a way that said, *Right.*

She sighed. "It's a long story."

"I have time."

She didn't. She felt like she was going to pass out. "Can I use the loo?"

"No." Someone knocked and the agent accepted a file, glancing over the contents before looking at her with more interest. "Tell me about Mikolas Petrides."

"Why?" Her heart tripped just hearing his name. Instantly she was plunged into despair at having broken off with him. When she had left Paris, she had told herself her feelings toward Mikolas were tied up in his protecting her from

Grigor, but as the miles between them piled up, she kept thinking of other things: how he'd saved her life. How he'd brought her a life jacket, and said all the right things that night in Athens. How he'd taught her to fight. And make love.

Tears came into her eyes, but now was not the time.

"It looks like you've been traveling with him," the agent said. "That's an infamous family to truck with."

"The money has nothing to do with him!" That was a small lie. Once Viveka had spilled to her sister how she had come to be Mikolas's mistress, Trina had gone straight to her father's safe and emptied it of the cash Grigor had kept there.

Use this for Hildy. She's my aunt, too. I don't want you in his debt.

Viveka had balked, secretly wanting the tie to Mikolas. Trina had accused her of suffering from Stockholm syndrome. Her sister had matured a lot with her marriage and the death of Grigor. She had actually invited Viveka to live with them, but Viveka didn't want to be in that house, on that island, with newlyweds being tested by Trina's reversal of fortunes, since Grigor had indeed left Trina a considerable amount of money. Truth be told, Trina and Stephanos had a lot to work through.

So did Viveka. The two weeks with her sister had been enormously rejuvenating, but now it was time to finally, truly, take the wheel on her own life.

"Look." She sounded as ragged as she felt. "My half sister came into some money through the death of her father. My aunt is in a private facility. It's expensive. My sister was trying to help. That's all."

"Are you sure you didn't steal the money from Petrides? Because your flight path looks like a rabbit trying to outrun a fox."

"He wouldn't care if I did," she muttered, thinking about how generous he'd always been.

The agent's brows went up.

"I'm kidding! Don't involve him." All that work on his part—a lifetime of building himself into the head of a legitimate enterprise—and she was going to tumble it with one stupid quip? *Nice job, Viveka.*

"Tell me about your relationship with him."

"What do you mean?"

"You slept with him?"

"Yes. And no," she rushed on, guessing what he was going to say next. "Not for twenty-five thousand euros."

"Why did you break it off?"

"Reasons."

"Don't be smart, Ms. Brice. I'm your only friend right now. What was the problem? A lover's tiff? And you helped yourself to a little money for a fresh start?"

"There was no tiff." He didn't love her. That was the tiff. He would never love her and *she loved him so much*. "I'm telling you, the money has nothing to do with him. *I* have nothing to do with him. Not anymore."

She was going to cry now, and completely humiliate herself.

Mikolas was standing at the head of a boardroom table when his phone vibrated.

Viveka's picture flashed onto the screen. It was a photo he'd taken stealthily one day when creeping up on her playing backgammon with his grandfather. He'd perfectly caught her expression as she'd made a strong play, excited triumph brightening her face.

"Where's Vivi?" his grandfather had asked when Mikolas returned from Paris without her.

"Gone."

Pappoús had been stunned. Visibly heartbroken, which had concerned Mikolas. He hadn't considered how Viveka's leaving would affect his grandfather.

Pappoús had been devastated for another reason. "Another broken heart on my conscience," he'd said with tears in his eyes.

"It's not your fault." *He* was the one who had forced her to stay with him. He'd seduced her and tried not to lead her on, but she'd been hurt all the same. "She liked you," he tried to mollify. "If anything, you gave her some of what I couldn't."

"No," his grandfather had said with deep emotion. "If I hadn't left you suffering, you would not be so damaged. You would be able to love her as she's meant to be loved."

The words stung, but they weren't meant to be cruel. The truth hurt.

"You have never forgiven me and I wouldn't

deserve it if you did," Pappoús went on. "I allowed your father to become a monster. He gave you nothing but a name that put you through hell. That is my fault." His shaking fist struck his chest.

He was so white and anguished, Mikolas tensed, worried his grandfather would put himself into cardiac arrest.

"I wasn't a fit man to take you in, not when you needed someone to heal you," Pappoús declared. "My love came too late and isn't enough. You don't trust it. So you've rejected her. She doesn't deserve that pain and it comes back to me. It's my fault she's suffering."

Mikolas had wanted to argue that what Viveka felt toward him wasn't real love, but if anyone knew how to love, it was her. She loved her sister to the ends of the earth. She experienced every nuance of life at a level that was far deeper than he ever let himself feel.

"She'll find love," Mikolas had growled, and was instantly uncomfortable with the idea of another man holding her at night, making her believe in forever. He hated the invisible man who would make her smile in ways he never had, because she finally felt loved in return.

"Vivi is resilient," his grandfather agreed with poignant pride.

She was very resilient.

When Mikolas had received the final report on Grigor's responsibility for her mother's death, he had been humbled. The report had compiled dozens of reports of assault and other wrongdoings across the island, but it was the unearthed statement made by Viveka that had destroyed him.

How much difference was there between one man pulling his tooth and another bruising a girl's eye? Mikolas had lost his fingernails. Viveka had lost her *mother*. He had been deliberately humiliated, forced to beg for air and water—death even—until his DNA had saved him. She had made her way to a relative who hadn't wanted her and had kept enough of a conscience to care for the woman through a tragic decline.

Viveka would find love because, despite all she had endured, she was *willing* to love.

She wasn't a coward, ducking and weaving,

running and hiding, staying in Paris, saying, *It's better that it ends here.*

It wasn't better. It was torment. Deprivation gnawed relentlessly at him.

But the moment her face flashed on his phone, respite arrived.

"I have to take this," Mikolas said to his board, voice and hand trembling. He slid his thumb to answer, dizzy with how just anticipating the sound of her voice eased his suffering. "Yes?"

"I thought I should warn you," she said with remorse. "I've kind of been arrested."

"Arrested." He was aware of everyone stopping their murmuring to stare. Of all the things he might have expected, that was the very last. But that was Viveka. "Are you okay? Where are you? What happened?"

Old instincts flickered, reminding him he was revealing too much, but in this moment he didn't care about himself. He was too concerned for her.

"I'm fine." Her voice was strained. "It's a long story and Trina is trying to find me a lawyer, but they keep bringing up your name. I didn't want to blindside you if it winds up in the papers or something. You've worked so hard to get everything just so. I hate to cast shadows. I'm really sorry, Mikolas."

Only Viveka would call to forewarn him and ask nothing for herself. How in the world had he ever felt so threatened by this woman?

"Where are you?" he repeated with more insistence. "I'll have a lawyer there within the hour."

CHAPTER THIRTEEN

MIKOLAS'S LAWYER LEFT Viveka at Mikolas's London flat, since it was around the corner from his own. She was on her very last nerve and it was two in the morning. She didn't try to get a taxi to her aunt's house. She didn't have the key and would have to ask the neighbor for one tomorrow.

So she prevailed upon Mikolas *again* and didn't bother trying to find bedding for his guest room. She threw a huge pity party for herself in the shower, crying until she couldn't stand, then she folded Mikolas's black robe into a firm hug around her and crawled into his bed with a box of tissues that she dabbed against her leaking eyes.

Sleep was her blessed escape from feeling like she'd only alienated him further with this stupid questioning. The customs agents were hanging on to the money for forty-eight hours, because they could, but the lawyer seemed to think they'd give it up after that. She really didn't care, she was just so exhausted and dejected and she missed Mikolas so bad…

A weight came onto the mattress beside her and a warm hand cupped the side of her neck. The lamp came on as a man's voice said, "Viveka."

She jerked awake, sitting up in shock.

"Shh, it's okay," he soothed. "It's just me. I was trying not to scare you."

She clutched her hand across her heart. "What are you doing here?"

His image impacted her. Not just his natural sex appeal in a rumpled shirt and open collar. Not just his stubbled cheeks and bruised eyes. There was such tenderness in his gaze, her fragile composure threatened to crumple.

"Your lawyer said you were in Barcelona." She had protested against Mikolas sending the lawyer, insisting she was just informing him as a courtesy, but he'd got most of the story out of her before her time on the telephone had run out.

"I was." His hooded lids lowered to disguise what he was thinking and his tongue touched his lip. “And I’m sorry to wake you, but I didn’t want to scare you if I crawled in beside you.”

She followed his gaze to the crushed tissues littering the bed and hated herself for being so obvious. “I was being lazy about making up the other bed. I’ll go—”

“No. We need to talk. I don’t want to wait.” He tucked her hair back from her cheek, behind her ear. “Vivi.”

“Why did you just call me that?” She searched his gaze, her brow pulled into a wrinkle of uncertainty, her pretty bottom lip pinched by her teeth.

“Because I want to. I have wanted to. For a long time.” It wasn’t nearly so unsettling to admit that as he’d feared. He had expected letting her into his heart would be terrifying. Instead, it was like coming home. “Everyone else does.”

A tentative hope lit her expression. “Since when do you want to be like everyone else?”

He acknowledged that with a flick of his brow, but the tiny flame in his chest grew bigger and warmer.

"Since when do I tell you or anyone what I want? Is that what you're really wondering?" He wanted so badly to hold her. Gather all that healing warmth she radiated against him and close up the final gaps in his soul. He made himself give her what she needed first. "I want *you*, Vivi. Not just for sex, but for things I can't even articulate. That scares me to say, but I want you to know it."

She sucked in a breath and covered her mouth with both hands.

This can't be real, Viveka thought, blinking her gritty eyes. She pinched herself and he let out a husk of a laugh, immediately trying to erase the sting with a gentle rub of his thumb.

His hand stayed on her arm. His gaze lifted to her face while a deeply tender glow in his eyes went all the way through her to her soul.

"I was terrified that if I let myself care for you, someone would use that against me. So what did I do? I pushed you away and inflicted the pain on myself. I was right to fear how much it would hurt if you were out of my reach. It's unbearable."

"Oh, Mikolas." Her mouth trembled. "You inflicted it on both of us. I want to be with you. If you want me, I'm right here."

He gathered her up, unable to help himself. For a long time he held her, just absorbing the beauty of having her against him. He was aware of a tickling trickle on his cheek and dipped his head to dry his cheek against her hair.

"Thank you for saying you want me," she said. Her slender arms tightened until she pressed the breath from his lungs. "It's enough, you know." She lifted her red eyes to regard him. "I won't ask you to say you love me. But I should have said it myself before I left Paris. I've been sorry that I didn't. I was trying to protect myself from being more hurt than I was. It didn't work," she said ruefully. "I love you so much."

"You're too generous." He cupped her cheek, wiping away her tear track with the pad of his thumb, humbled. "I want your love, Vivi. I will pay any price for that. Don't let me be a coward. Make me give you what you need. Make me say it and mean it."

"You're not a coward." Fresh tears of empathy

welled in her eyes, seeping into all those cracks and fissures around his heart, widening them so there was more room for her to come in.

"I was afraid to tell you I was coming," he admitted. "I was afraid you wouldn't be here if you knew. That you wouldn't let me try to convince you to stay with me."

Viveka's heart was pattering so fast she could hardly breathe. "You only have to ask," she reminded.

"Ask." Mikolas smoothed her hair back from her face, gazing at her, humbly offering his heart as a flawed human being. "I can't insult you by asking you to *stay* with me. I must ask you the big question. Will you be my wife?"

Viveka's heart staggered and lurched. "Are you serious?"

"Of course I'm serious!" He was offended, but wound up chuckling. "I will have the right woman under the veil this time, too. Actually," he added with a light kiss on her nose, "I did the first time. I just didn't know it yet."

Tears of happiness filled her eyes. She threw her arms around his neck, needing to kiss him then. To hold him and *love* him. "Yes. Of course I'll marry you!"

Their kiss was a poignant, tender reunion, making all of her ache. The physical sparks between them were stronger than ever, but the moment was so much more than that, imbued with trust and openness. It was expansive and scary and uncharted.

Beautiful.

"I want to make love to you," he said, dragging his mouth to her neck. "*Love*, Vivi. I want to wake next to you and make the best of every day we are given together."

"Me, too," she assured him with a catch of joy in her voice. "I love you."

EPILOGUE

"PAPA, I'M COLD."

Viveka heard the words from her studio. She was in the middle of a still life of Callia's toys for the advanced painting class she'd been accepted into. Three years of sketching and pastels, oils and watercolors, and she was starting to think she wasn't half bad. Her husband was always quick to praise, of course, but he was shamelessly biased.

She wiped the paint off her fingers before she picked up the small pink jumper her daughter had left there on the floor. When she came into the lounge, however, she saw that it was superfluous. Mikolas was already turning from his desk to scoop their three-year-old into his lap.

Callia stood on his thigh to curl her arms around his neck before bending her knees and snuggling into his chest, light brown curls tucked trustingly against his shoulder. "I love you," she told him in her high, doll-like voice.

"I love you, too," Mikolas said with the deep timbre of sincerity that absolutely undid Viveka every time she heard it.

"I love Leo, too," she said in a poignant little tone, mentioning her cousin, Trina's newborn son. She had cried when they'd had to come home. She looked up at Mikolas. "Do you love Leo?"

"He spit up on my new shirt," Mikolas reminded drily, then magnanimously added, "But yes, I do."

Callia giggled, then began turning it into a game. "Do you love Theítsa Trina?"

"I've grown very fond of her, yes."

"Do you love Theíos Stephanos?"

"I consider him a good friend."

"Did you love Pappoús?" She pointed at the photo on his desk.

"I did love him, very much."

Callia didn't remember her great-grandfather, but he had held her swaddled form, saying to Viveka, *She has your eyes*, and proclaiming Mikolas to be a very lucky man.

Mikolas had agreed wholeheartedly.

Losing Erebus had been hard for him. For both of them, really. Fortunately, they'd had a newborn to distract them. Falling pregnant had been a complete surprise to both of them, but the shock had quickly turned to excitement and they were so enamored with family life, they were talking of expanding it even more.

"Do you love Mama?" Callia asked.

Mikolas's head came up and he looked across at Viveka, telling her he'd been aware of her the whole time. His love for her shone like a beacon across the space between them.

"My love for your mother is the strongest thing in me."

* * * * *

If you enjoyed this story, check out these other great reads from Dani Collins

BOUGHT BY HER ITALIAN BOSS

THE CONSEQUENCE HE MUST CLAIM

THE MARRIAGE HE MUST KEEP

VOWS OF REVENGE

SEDUCED INTO THE GREEK'S WORLD

Available now!

MILLS & BOON®

Large Print – January 2017

To Blackmail a Di Sione
Rachael Thomas

A Ring for Vincenzo's Heir
Jennie Lucas

Demetriou Demands His Child
Kate Hewitt

Trapped by Vialli's Vows
Chantelle Shaw

The Sheikh's Baby Scandal
Carol Marinelli

Defying the Billionaire's Command
Michelle Conder

The Secret Beneath the Veil
Dani Collins

Stepping into the Prince's World
Marion Lennox

Unveiling the Bridesmaid
Jessica Gilmore

The CEO's Surprise Family
Teresa Carpenter

The Billionaire from Her Past
Leah Ashton

MILLS & BOON®

Large Print – February 2017

The Return of the Di Sione Wife
Caitlin Crews

Baby of His Revenge
Jennie Lucas

The Spaniard's Pregnant Bride
Maisey Yates

A Cinderella for the Greek
Julia James

Married for the Tycoon's Empire
Abby Green

Indebted to Moreno
Kate Walker

A Deal with Alejandro
Maya Blake

A Mistletoe Kiss with the Boss
Susan Meier

A Countess for Christmas
Christy McKellen

Her Festive Baby Bombshell
Jennifer Faye

The Unexpected Holiday Gift
Sophie Pembroke

TAMING THE LAST ACOSTA

TAMING THE LAST ACOSTA

BY

SUSAN STEPHENS

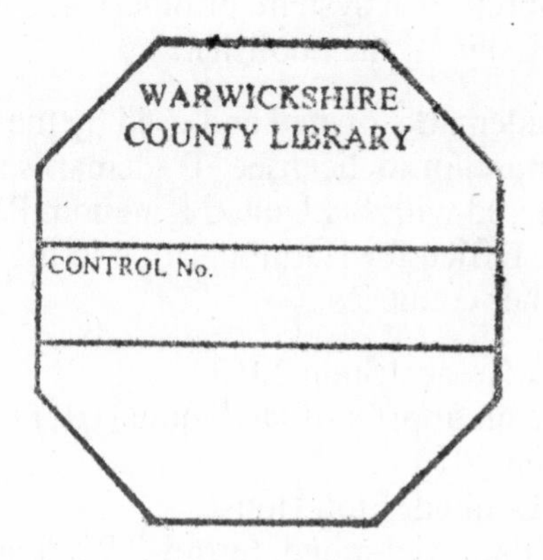

All the characters in this book have no existence outside the imagination of the author, and have no relation whatsoever to anyone bearing the same name or names. They are not even distantly inspired by any individual known or unknown to the author, and all the incidents are pure invention.

First published in Great Britain 2013
by Mills & Boon, an imprint of Harlequin (UK) Limited.
Large Print edition 2013
Harlequin (UK) Limited, Eton House,
18-24 Paradise Road, Richmond, Surrey TW9 1SR

ISBN: 978 0 263 23205 9

Harlequin (UK) policy is to use papers that are natural, renewable and recyclable products and made from wood grown in sustainable forests. The logging and manufacturing process conform to the legal environmental regulations of the country of origin.

Printed and bound in Great Britain
by CPI Antony Rowe, Chippenham, Wiltshire

For Joanne, who holds my hand
when I'm in the dentist's chair.

CHAPTER ONE

TWO PEOPLE IN the glittering wedding marquee appeared distanced from the celebrations. One was a photojournalist, known as Romy Winner, for whom detachment was part of her job. Kruz Acosta, the brother of the groom, had no excuse. With his wild dark looks, barely mellowed by formal wedding attire, Romily—who preferred to call herself no-nonsense Romy—thought Kruz perfectly suited to the harsh, unforgiving pampas in Argentina where this wedding was taking place.

Trying to slip deeper into the shadows, she stole some more shots of him. Immune to feeling when she was working, this time she felt excitement grip her. Not just because every photo editor in the world would pay a fortune to get their hands on her shots of Kruz Acosta, the most elusive of the notorious Acosta brothers, but because Kruz stirred her in some dark, atavistic way, involving a violently raised heartbeat and a lot of ill-timed appreciation below the belt.

Perhaps it was his air of menace, or maybe it was his hard-edged warrior look, but whatever it was she was enjoying it.

All four Acosta brothers were big, powerful men, but rumours abounded where Kruz was concerned, which made him all the more intriguing. A veteran of Special Forces, educated in both Europe and America, Kruz was believed to work for two governments now, though no one really knew anything about him other than his success in business and his prowess on the polo field.

She was getting to know him through her camera lens at this wedding of Kruz's older brother, Nacho, to his beautiful blind bride, Grace. What she had learned so far was less than reassuring: Kruz missed nothing. She ducked out of sight as he scanned the sumptuously decorated wedding venue, no doubt looking for unwanted visitors like her.

It was time to forget Kruz Acosta and concentrate on work, Romy told herself sternly, even if he *was* compelling viewing to someone who made her living out of stand-out shots. It would take more than a froth of tulle and a family reunion to soften Kruz Acosta, Romy guessed, as she ran off another series of images she knew Ronald, her editor at *ROCK!*, would happily give his eye teeth for.

Just one or two more and then she'd make herself scarce…

Maybe sooner rather than later, Romy concluded as Kruz glanced her way. This job would have been a pleasure if she'd had an official press pass, but *ROCK!* was considered a scandal sheet by many, so no one from *ROCK!* had received an invitation to the wedding. Romy was attending on secret business for the bride, on the understanding that she could use some of the shots for other purposes.

Romy's fame as a photographer had reached Grace through Holly Acosta, one of Romy's colleagues at *ROCK!* The three women had been having secret meetings over the past few months, culminating in Grace declaring that she would trust no one but Romy to make a photographic record of her wedding for her husband, Nacho, and for any children they might have. Inspired by the blind bride's courage, Romy had agreed. Grace was fast becoming a friend rather than just another client, and this was a chance in a million for Romy to see the Acostas at play—though she doubted Kruz would be as accommodating as the bride if he caught her.

So he mustn't catch her, Romy determined, shivering with awareness as she focused her lens on the one man in the marquee her camera loved above all others. He had a special sort of energy that seemed to reach her across the crowded tent, and the menace he threw out was alarming. The more shots she took of him, the more she couldn't imagine that much got in his way. It was easy to picture Kruz as a rebellious youth who had gone on to win medals for gallantry in the Special Forces. All the bespoke tailoring in the world couldn't hide the fact that Kruz Acosta was a weapon in disguise. He now ran a formidably successful security company, which placed him firmly in charge of security at this wedding.

A flush of alarm scorched her as Kruz's gaze swept over her like a searchlight and moved on. He must have seen her. The question was: would he do anything about it? She hadn't come halfway across the world in order to return home to London empty-handed.

Or to let down the bride, Romy concluded as she moved deeper into the crowd. This commission for Grace was more of a sacred charge than a job, and she had no intention of being distracted by one of the most alarming-looking men it had ever been her pleasure to photograph. Running off a blizzard of shots, she realised Kruz couldn't have stood in starker contrast to the bride. Grace's gentle beauty had never seemed more pronounced than at this moment, when she was standing beneath a flower-bedecked canopy between her husband and Kruz.

Romy drew a swift breath when the man in question stared straight at her. Lowering her camera, she glanced around, searching for a better hiding place, but shadows were in short supply in the brilliantly lit tent. One of the few things Grace could still detect after a virus had stolen her sight was light, so the dress code for the wedding was 'sparkle' and every corner of the giant marquee was floodlit by fabulous Venetian chandeliers.

Mingling with the guests, Romy kept her head down. The crowd was moving towards the receiving line, where all the Acostas were standing. There was a murmur of anticipation in the queue—and no wonder. The Acostas were an incredibly good-looking family. Nacho, the oldest brother, was clearly besotted by his beautiful new bride, while the sparks flying between Diego and his wedding planner wife Maxie could have ignited a fire. The supremely cool Ruiz Acosta clearly couldn't wait to get his firebrand wife, Romy's friend and colleague Holly, into bed, judging by the looks they were exchanging, while Lucia Acosta, the only girl in this family of four outrageously good-looking brothers, was flirting with her husband Luke Forster, the ridiculously photogenic American polo player.

Which left Kruz...

The only unmarried brother. So what? Her camera loved him, but that didn't mean *she* had to like him—though she would take full advantage of his distraction as he greeted his guests.

Those scars... That grim expression... She snapped away, knowing that everything about Kruz Acosta should put her off, but instead she was spellbound.

From a safe distance, Romy amended sensibly, as a pulse of arousal ripped through her.

And then he really did surprise her. As Kruz turned to say something to the bride his expression softened momentarily. That was the money shot, as it was known in the trade. It was the type of unexpected photograph that Romy was so good at capturing and had built her reputation on.

She was so busy congratulating herself she almost missed Kruz swinging round to stare at her again. Now she knew how a rabbit trapped in headlights felt. When he moved she moved too. Grabbing her kitbag, she stowed the camera. Her hands were trembling as panic mounted inside her. She hurried towards the exit, knowing this was unlike her. She was a seasoned pro, not some cub reporter—a thick skin came with the job. And why such breathless excitement at the thought of being chased by him? She was hardly an innocent abroad where men were concerned.

Because Kruz was the stuff of heated erotic dreams and her body liked the idea of being chased by him. Next question.

Before she made herself scarce there were a few more shots she wanted to take for Grace. Squeezing herself into a small gap behind a pillar, she took some close-ups of flowers and trimmings—richly scented white roses and lush fat peonies in softest pink, secured with white satin ribbon and tiny silver bells. The ceiling was draped like a Bedouin tent, white and silver chiffon lavishly decorated with scented flowers, crystal beads and fiery diamanté. Though Grace couldn't see these details the wedding planner had ensured she would enjoy a scent sensation, while Romy was equally determined to make a photographic record of the day with detailed descriptions in Braille alongside each image.

'Hello, Romy.'

She nearly jumped out of her skin, but it was only a famous celebrity touching her arm, in the hope of a photograph. Romy's editor at *ROCK!* loved those shots, so she had to make time for it. Shots like these brought in the money Romy so badly needed, though what she really longed to do was to tell the story of ordinary people in extraordinary situations through her photographs. One day she'd do that, she vowed stepping forward to take the shot, leaving herself dangerously exposed.

The queue of guests at the receiving line was thinning as people moved on to their tables for the wedding feast, and an icy warning was trickling down her spine before she even had a chance to say goodbye to the celebrity. She didn't need to check to know she was being watched. She usually managed to blend in with the crowd, with or without an official press pass, but there was nothing usual in any situation when Kruz Acosta was in town.

As soon as the celebrity moved on she found another hiding place behind some elaborate table decorations. From here she could observe Kruz to her heart's content. She settled down to enjoy the play of muscle beneath his tailored jacket and imagined him stripped to the buff.

Nice...

The only downside was Grace had mentioned that although Kruz felt at home on the pampas he was going to open an office in London—'Just around the corner from *ROCK!*,' Grace had said, as if it were a good thing.

Now she'd seen him, Romy was sure Kruz Acosta was nothing but trouble.

But attractive... He was off-the-scale *hot*.

But she wasn't here to play make-believe with one of the lead characters at this wedding. She had got what she needed and she was out of here.

Glancing over her shoulder, she noticed that Kruz was no longer in the receiving line.

So where the hell was he?

She scanned the marquee, but there was no sign of Kruz anywhere. There were quite a few exits from the tent—he could have used any one of them. She wasn't going to take any chances, and would head straight for the press coach to send off her copy. Thank goodness Holly had given her a key.

The press coach wasn't too far. She could see its twinkling lights. She quickened her step, fixing her gaze on them, feeling that same sense of being hunted—though why was she worried? She could look after herself. Growing up small and plain had ruled out girlie pursuits, so she had taken up kick-boxing instead. Anyone who thought they could take her camera was in for a big surprise.

He had recognised the girl heading towards the exit. There was no chance he would let her get away. Having signed off the press passes personally, he knew Romy Winner didn't appear on any of them.

Romy Winner was said to be ruthless in pursuit of a story, but she was no more ruthless than he was. Her work was reputed to be cutting-edge and insightful—he'd even heard it said that as a photojournalist Romy Winner had no equal—but that didn't excuse her trespass here.

She had disappointed him, Kruz reflected as he closed in on her. Renowned for lodging herself in the most ingenious of nooks, he might have expected to find Ms Winner hanging from the roof trusses, or masquerading as a waitress, rather than skulking in the shadows like some rent-a-punk oddity, with her pale face, thin body, huge kohl-ringed eyes and that coal-black, gel-spiked, red-tipped hair, for all the wedding guests to stare at and comment on.

So Romy could catch guests off-guard and snap away at her leisure?

Maybe she wasn't so dumb after all. She must have captured some great shots. He was impressed by her cunning, but far less impressed by Señorita Winner's brazen attempt to gate-crash his brother's wedding. He would make her pay. He just hadn't decided what currency he was accepting today. That would depend on his mood when he caught up with her.

Romy hurried on into the darkness. She couldn't shake the feeling she was being followed, though she doubted it was Kruz. Surely he had more important things to do?

Crunching her way along a cinder path, she reasoned that with all the Acosta siblings having been raised by Nacho, after their parents had been killed in a flood, Kruz had enjoyed no softening influence from a mother—which accounted for the air of danger surrounding him. It was no more than that. Her overworked imagination could take a rest. Pausing at a crossroads, she picked up the lights and followed them. She couldn't afford to lose her nerve now. She had to get her copy away. The money Romy earned from her photographs kept her mother well cared for in the nursing home where she had lived since Romy's father had beaten her half to death.

When Romy had first become a photojournalist it hadn't taken her long to realise that pretty pictures earned pennies, while sensational images sold almost as well as sex. Her success in the field had been forged in stone on the day she was told that her mother would need full-time care for the rest of her life. From that day on Romy had been determined that her mother would have the best of care and Romy would provide it for her.

A gust of wind sweeping down from the Andes made her shudder violently. She wondered if she had ever felt more out of place than she did now. She lived in London, amidst constant bustle and noise. Here in the shadow of a gigantic mountain range everything turned sinister at night and her chest tightened as she quickened her step. The ghostly shape of the wedding tent was far behind her now, and ahead was just a vast emptiness, dotted with faint lights from the *hacienda.* There were no landmarks on the pampas and no stars to guide her. The Acosta brothers were giants amongst men, and the land they came from was on the same impressive scale. There were no boundaries here, there was only space, and the Acostas owned most of it.

Rounding a corner, she caught sight of the press coach again and began to jog. Her breath hitched in her throat as she stopped to listen. Was that a twig snapping behind her? Her heart was hammering so violently it was hard to tell. Focusing her gaze on the press coach, with its halo of aerials and satellite dishes, she fumbled for the key, wanting to have it ready in her hand—and cried out with shock as a man's hand seized her wrist.

His other hand snatched hold of her camera. Reacting purely on instinct, she launched a stinging roundhouse kick—only to have her ankle captured in an iron grip.

'Good, but not good enough,' Kruz Acosta ground out.

Rammed up hard against the motorcoach, with

Kruz's head in her face, it was hard for Romy to disagree. In the unforgiving flesh, Kruz made the evidence of her camera lens seem pallid and insubstantial. He was hard like rock, and so close she could see the flecks of gold in his fierce black eyes, as well as the cynical twist on his mouth. While their gazes were locked he brought her camera strap down, inch by taunting inch, until finally he removed it from her arm and placed it on the ground behind him.

'No,' he said softly when she glanced at it.

She still made a lunge, which he countered effortlessly. Flipping her to the ground, he stood back. Rolling away, she sprang up, assuming a defensive position with her hands clenched into angry fists, and demanded that he give it up.

Kruz Acosta merely raised a brow.

'I said—'

'I heard what you said,' he said quietly.

He was even more devastating at short range. She rubbed her arm as she stared balefully. He hadn't hurt her. He had branded her with his touch.

A shocked cry sprang from her lips when he seized hold of her again. His reach was phenomenal. His grip like steel. He made no allowance for the fact that she was half his size, so now every inch of her was rammed up tight against him, and when she fought him he just laughed, saying, 'Is that all you've got?'

She staggered as Kruz thrust her away. She felt humiliated as well as angry. Now he'd had a chance to take a better look at her he wasn't impressed. And why would he be?

'How does a member of the paparazzi get in here?'

Kruz was playing with her, she suspected. 'I'm not paparazzi. I'm on the staff at *ROCK!*'

'My apologies.' He made her a mocking bow. 'So you're a fully paid-up member of the paparazzi. With your own executive office, I presume?'

'I have a very nice office, as it happens,' she lied. He was making her feel hot and self-conscious. She was used to being in control. It was going too far to say that amongst photojournalists she was accorded a certain respect, but she certainly wasn't used to being talked down to by men.

'So as well as being an infamous photojournalist *and* an executive at *ROCK!* magazine,' Kruz mocked, 'I now discover that the infamous Romy Winner is an expert kick-boxer.'

Her cheeks flushed red. Not so expert, since he'd blocked her first move.

'I suppose kick-boxing is a useful skill when it comes to gate-crashing events you haven't been invited to?' Kruz suggested.

'It's one of my interests—and just as well with men like you around—'

'Men like me?' he said, holding her angry stare. 'Perhaps you and I should get on the mat in the gym sometime.'

'Over my dead body,' she fired back.

His look suggested he expected her to blink, or flinch, or even lower her gaze in submission. She did none of those things, though she did find herself staring at his lips. Kruz had the most amazing mouth—hard, yet sensual—and she couldn't help wondering what it would feel like to be kissed by him, though she had a pretty good idea…

An idea that was ridiculous! It wouldn't happen this side of hell. Kruz was one of the beautiful people—the type she liked to look at through her lens much as a wildlife photographer might observe a tiger, without having the slightest intention of touching it. Instead of drooling over him like some lovesick teenager it was time to put him straight.

'Kick-boxing is great for fending off unwanted advances—'

'Don't flatter yourself, Romy.'

Kruz's eyes had turned cold and she shivered involuntarily. There was no chance of getting her camera back now. He was good, economical with his movements, and he was fast.

Who knew what he was like as a lover...?

Thankfully she would never find out. All that mattered now was getting her camera back.

Darting round him, she tried to snatch it—and was totally unprepared for Kruz whipping the leather jacket from her shoulders. Underneath it she was wearing a simple white vest. No bra. She hardly needed one. Her cheeks fired up when he took full inventory of her chest. She could imagine the kind of breasts Kruz liked, and perversely wished she had big bouncing breasts to thrust in his face—if only to make a better job of showing her contempt than her embarrassingly desperate nipples were doing right now, poking through her flimsy top to signal their sheer, agonising frustration.

'Still want to take me on?' he drawled provocatively.

'I'm sure I could make some sort of dent in your

ego,' she countered, crossing her arms over her chest. She circled round him. 'All I want is my property back.' She glanced at the camera, lying just a tantalising distance away.

'So what's on this camera that you're so keen for me not to see?' He picked it up. 'You can collect it in the morning, when I've had a chance to evaluate your photographs.'

'It's my work, and *I* need to edit it—'

'Your unauthorised work,' he corrected her.

There was no point trying to reason with this man. Action was the only option.

One moment she was diving for the camera, and the next Kruz had tumbled her to the ground.

'Now, what shall I do with you?' he murmured, his warm, minty breath brushing her face.

With Kruz pinning her to the ground, one powerful thigh planted either side of her body, her options were limited—until he yanked her onto a soft bed of grass at the side of the cinder path. Then they became boundless. The grass felt like damp ribbons beneath her skin, and she could smell the rising sap where she had crushed it. Overlaying that was the heat of a powerful, highly sexed, highly aroused man.

She should try to escape. She should put up

some sort of token struggle, at least. She should remember her martial arts training and search for a weakness in Kruz to exploit.

She did none of those things. And as for that potential weakness—as it turned out it was one they shared.

As she reached up to push him away Kruz swooped down. Ravishing her mouth was a purposeful exercise, and one at which he excelled. For a moment she was too stunned to do anything, and then the sensation of being possessed, entered, controlled and plundered, even if it was only her mouth, by a man with whom she had been having fantasy sex for quite a few hours, sent her wild with excitement. She even groaned a complaint when he pulled away, and was relieved to find it was only to remove his jacket.

For such a big man Kruz went about his business with purpose and speed. His natural athleticism, she supposed, feeling her body heat, pulse and melt at the thought of being thoroughly pleasured by him. Growing up with a pillow over her head to shut out the violence at home had left her a stranger to romance and tenderness. Given a choice, she preferred to observe life through her camera lens, but when an opportunity for pleasure presented itself she seized it, enjoyed it, and moved on. She wasn't about to turn down *this* opportunity.

Pleasure with no curb or reason? Pleasure without thought of consequence?

Correct, she informed her inner critic firmly. Even the leisurely way Kruz was folding his jacket and putting it aside was like foreplay. He was so sexy. His powerful body was sexy—his hands were sexy—the wide spread of his shoulders was sexy—his shadowy face was sexy.

Kruz's confidence in her unquestioning acceptance of everything that was about to happen was so damn sexy she could lose control right now.

A life spent living vicariously through a camera lens was ultimately unsatisfactory, while this unexpected encounter was proving to be anything but. A rush of lust and longing gripped her as he held her stare. The look they exchanged spoke about need and fulfilment. It was explicit and potent. She broke the moment of stillness. Ripping off his shirt, she sent buttons flying everywhere. Yanking the fabric from the waistband of his pants, she tossed it away, exclaiming with happy shock as bespoke tailoring yielded to hard, tanned flesh. This was everything she had ever dreamed of and more. Liberally embellished with tattoos and scars, Kruz's torso was outstanding. She could hardly breathe for excitement when he found the button on her jeans and quickly dealt with it. He quickly got them down. In comparison, her own fingers felt fat and useless as she struggled with the buckle on his belt.

'Let me help you.'

Kruz held her gaze with a mocking look as he made this suggestion. It was all the aphrodisiac she needed. She cried out with excitement when his thumbs slipped beneath the elastic on her flimsy briefs to ease them down her hips. His big hands blazed a trail of fire everywhere they touched. She couldn't bear the wait when he paused to protect them both, but it was a badly needed wake-up call. The fact that this man had thought of it before she had went some way to reminding her how far she'd travelled from the safe shores she called home.

Her body overruled the last-minute qualms. Her body was one hundred per cent in favour of what was coming. Even her tiny breasts felt swollen and heavy, while her nipples were cheekily pert and obscenely hard, and the carnal pulse throbbing insistently between her legs demanded satisfaction.

Kruz had awakened such an appetite inside her she wouldn't be human if she didn't want to discover what sex could be like with someone who really knew what he was doing. She was about to find out. When Kruz stretched his length against her she could feel his huge erection, heavy and hard against her leg. And that look in his eyes—that slumberous, confident look. It told her exactly what he intended to do with her and just how much she was going to enjoy it. And, in case she was in any doubt, he now spelled out his intentions in a few succinct words.

She gasped with excitement. With hardly any experience of dating, and even less of foreplay, she was happy to hear that nothing was about to change.

CHAPTER TWO

SHE EXCLAIMED WITH shock when Kruz eased inside her. She was ready. That wasn't the problem. Kruz was the problem. He was huge.

Built to scale.

She should have known.

Her breath came in short, shocked whimpers, pain and pleasure combined. It was a relief when he took his time and didn't rush her. She began to relax.

This was good... Yes, better than good...

Releasing the shaking breath from her lungs, she silently thanked him for giving her the chance to explore such incredible sensation at her leisure. Leisure? The brief plateau lasted no more than a few seconds, then she was clambering all over him as a force swept them into a world where moving deeper, harder, rougher, fast and furious, was more than an imperative: it was essential to life.

'You okay?' Kruz asked, coming down briefly

to register concern as she screamed wildly and let go.

It seemed for ever before she could answer him, and then she wasn't sure she said anything that made sense.

'A little better, at least?' he suggested with amusement when she quietened.

'Not that much better,' she argued, blatantly asking for more.

Taking his weight on his arms, Kruz stared down at her.

It didn't get much better than this, Romy registered groggily, lost in pleasure the instant he began to move. She loved his hard, confident mouth. She loved the feeling of being full and ready to be sated. She even loved her grassy bed, complete with night sounds: cicadas chirruping and an owl somewhere in the distance hooting softly. Kruz's clean, musky scent was in her nostrils, and when she turned her head, groaning in extremes of pleasure, her bed of grass added a piquant tang to an already intoxicating mix. She was floating on sensation, hardly daring to move in case she fell too soon. She didn't want it to end, but Kruz was too experienced and made it really hard to hold on. Moving persuasively from side to side, he pushed her little by little, closer to the edge.

'Good?' he said, staring down, mocking her with his confident smile.

'Very good,' she managed on a shaking breath.

And then he did something that lifted her onto an even higher plane of sensation. Slowly withdrawing, he left her trembling and uncertain, before slowly thrusting into her again. Whatever she had imagined before was eclipsed by this intensity of feeling. It was like the first time all over again, except now she was so much more receptive and aroused. She couldn't hold back, and shrieked as she fell, shouting his name as powerful spasms gripped her.

When she finally relaxed what she realised was her pincer grip on Kruz's arms, she realised she had probably bruised him. He was holding her just as firmly, but with more care. She loved his firm grip on her buttocks, his slightly callused hands rough on her soft skin.

'I can't,' she protested as he began to move again . 'I truly can't.'

'There's no such word as *can't*,' he whispered.

Incredibly, he was right. It didn't seem possible that she had anything left, but when Kruz stared deep into her eyes it was as if he was instructing her that she must give herself up to sensation. There was no reason to disobey and she tumbled promptly, laughing and crying with surprise as she fell again.

It turned out to be just the start of her lessons in advanced lovemaking. Pressing her knees back, Kruz stared down. Now she discovered that she loved to watch him watching her. Lifting herself up, she folded her arms behind her head so she had a better view. Nothing existed outside this extreme pleasure. Kruz had placed himself at her disposal, and to reward him she pressed her legs as wide as they would go. He demanded all her concentration as he worked steadily and effectively on the task in hand.

'You really should try holding on once in a while,' he said, smiling against her mouth.

'Why?' she whispered back.

'Try it and you'll find out,' he said.

'Will you teach me?' Her heart drummed at the thought.

'Perhaps,' Kruz murmured.

He wasn't joking, Romy discovered as Kruz led her through a lengthy session of tease and withdraw until her body was screaming for release.

'Greedy girl,' he murmured with approval. 'Again?' he suggested, when finally he allowed her to let go.

Bracing her hands against his chest, she smiled into his eyes. For a hectic hook-up this was turning into a lengthy encounter, and she hadn't got a single complaint. Kruz was addictive. The pleasure he conjured was amazing. But—

'What?' he said as she turned her head away from him.

'Nothing.' She dismissed the niggle hiding deep in her subconscious.

'You think too much,' he said.

'Agreed,' she replied, dragging in a fast breath as he began to move again.

Kruz didn't need to ask if she wanted more; the answer was obvious to both of them. Gripping his iron buttocks, she urged him on as he set up a drugging beat. Tightening her legs around his waist, she moved with him—harder—faster—giving as good as she got, and through it all Kruz maintained eye contact, which was probably the biggest turn-on of all, because he could see where she was so quickly going. Holding her firmly in place, he kept her in position beneath him, and when the storm rose he judged each thrust to perfection. Pushing her knees apart, he made sure they both had an excellent view, and now even he was unable to hold on, and roared with pleasure as he gave in to violent release.

She went with him, falling gratefully into a vortex of sensation from which there was no escape. It was only when she came to that she realised fantasy had in no way prepared her for reality—her fantasies were wholly selfish, and Kruz had woken something inside her that made her care for him just a little bit. It was a shame he didn't feel the same. Now he was sated she sensed a core of ice growing around him. It frightened her, because she was feeling emotional for the first time with a man. And now he was pulling back—emotionally, physically.

No wonder that niggle of unease had gripped her, Romy reflected. She was playing well out of her league. As if to prove this, Kruz was already on his feet, pulling on his clothes. He buckled his belt as if it were just another day at the office. She might have laughed under other circumstances when he was forced to tug the edges of his shirt together where she had ripped the buttons off. He did no more than hide the evidence of her desperation beneath his tie. How could he be so chillingly unfazed by all this? Her unease grew at the thought that what had just happened between them had made a dangerously strong impression on her, while it appeared to have washed over Kruz.

And why not? What happened was freely given and freely taken by both of you.

'Are you okay?' he said, glancing down when she remained immobile.

'Of course I am,' she said in a casual tone. Inwardly she was screaming. Was she really so stupid she had imagined she would come out of something like this unscathed?

Even inward reasoning didn't help—she was still waiting for him to say something encouraging. How pathetic was that? She had never felt like this before, and had no way of dealing with the feelings, so, gathering up her clothes, she lost herself in mundane matters—shaking the grass off her jacket, pulling on her jeans, sorting her hair out, then smoothing her hands over her face, hoping that by the time she removed them she would appear cool and detached.

Wrong. She felt as if she'd come out the wrong end of a spin dry.

Her thoughts turned at last to her camera. It was

still lying on the bank, temptingly close. She had learned her lesson where lunging for it was concerned, but felt confident that Kruz would give it to her now. It was the least he could do.

Fortunately Kruz appeared to be oblivious both to her and to her camera. He was on the phone, telling his security operatives that he was patrolling the grounds.

She eased her neck, as if that would ease the other aches, most of which had taken up residence in her heart.

Hadn't she learned anything from the past? Had Kruz made her forget her father's rages and her mother's dependency on a violent man?

Kruz hadn't been in any way violent towards her—but he was strong, commanding, and detached from emotion. All the things she had learned to avoid.

She was safe in that, unlike her mother, she had learned to avoid the pitfalls of attachment by switching off her emotions. In that she wasn't so dissimilar from Kruz. This was just a brief interlude of fun for both of them and now it was over. Neither of them was capable of love.

Love?

He swung round as she made a wry sound. Love

was a long road to nowhere, with a punch in the teeth at the end. So, yes, if she was in any doubt at all about the protocol between two strangers who'd just had sex on a grassy bank, she'd go with cool and detached every time.

'Right,' he said, ending the call, 'I need to get back.'

'Of course,' she said off-handedly. 'But I'd like my camera first.'

He frowned, as if they were two strangers at odds with each other. 'You've had your fun and now you're on your way,' he said.

She'd asked for that, Romy concluded. 'Well, I'm not going anywhere without it,' she said stubbornly. It was true. The camera was more than a tool of her trade, it was a fifth limb. It was an extension of her body, of her mind. It was the only way she knew how to make the money she needed to support herself and her mother.

'I've told you already. You'll get it back when I've checked it,' he said coldly, hoisting the camera over his shoulder.

'You're my censor now?' she said, chasing after him. 'I don't think so.'

The look Kruz gave her made her stomach clench with alarm.

'You can sleep in the bunkhouse,' he said, 'along with the rest of the press crew. Pick up your camera in the morning from my staff.'

She blinked. He'd said it as if they hadn't touched each other, pleasured each other.

They'd had sex and that was all.

Except for the slap in the face she got from realising that he saw it as no reason to give up her camera. 'By morning it will be too late—I need it now.'

'For what?' he said.

'I have to edit the photographs and then catch the news desk.' It was a lie of desperation, but she would do anything to recover her camera. 'There is another reason,' she added, waiting for a thunderclap to strike her down. This idea had only just occurred to her. 'I need to work on the shots I'm donating to your charity.'

As if he'd guessed, Kruz's eyes narrowed. 'The Acosta charity?'

'Yes.' She had a lot of shots in the can, Romy reasoned, quickly running through them in her mind. She had more than enough to pay for her mother's care and to keep herself off the breadline. She had taken a lot of shots specifically for

Grace's album, and he couldn't have those, but there were more—plenty more.

Had she bought herself a reprieve? Romy wondered as she stared at Kruz. 'I've identified a good opportunity for the charity,' she said, as the germ of an idea sprouted wings.

'Tell me,' Kruz said impatiently.

'My editor at *ROCK!* is thinking about making a feature on the Acostas and your charity.' Or at least she would make sure he was thinking about it by the time she got back. 'Think of how that would raise the charity's profile,' she said, dangling a carrot she hoped no Acosta in his right mind could refuse.

'So why didn't Grace or Holly tell me about this?' Kruz probed, staring at her keenly. 'If either of them had mentioned it I would have made sure you were issued with an official pass.'

'I *am* here on a mission for Grace,' Romy admitted, 'which is how I got in. Grace asked me not to say anything, and I haven't. It's crucial that Nacho doesn't learn about Grace's special surprise. I hope you'll respect that.' Kruz remained silent as she went on. 'I'm sure Grace and Holly were just too wrapped up in the wedding to remember to tell you,' she said, not wanting to get either of her friends into trouble.

Kruz paused. And now she could only wait.

'I suppose Grace could confirm this if I asked her?'

'If you feel like interrogating a bride on her wedding day, I'm sure she would.'

One ebony brow lifted. Whether Kruz believed her or not, for the moment she had him firmly in check.

'The solution to this,' he remarked, 'is that *I* take a look at the shots and *I* decide.'

As he strode away she ran after him. Dodging in front of him, she forced him to stop.

He studied Romy's elfin features with a practised eye. He interpreted the nervous hand running distractedly through her disordered hair. The camera meant everything to her, and if there was one thing that could really throw Ms Winner he had it swinging from his shoulder now. She was terrified he was going to disappear with her camera. She worked with it every day. It was her family, her income stream, her life. He almost felt sorry for her, and then stamped the feeling out. What was Romy Winner to *him?*

Actually, she was a lot more than he wanted

her to be. She had got to him in a way he hadn't quite fathomed yet. 'Is there some reason why I shouldn't see these shots?' he asked, teasing her by lifting the camera to Romy's eye level.

'None whatsoever,' she said firmly, but her face softened in response to his mocking expression and she almost smiled.

Testing Romy was fun, he discovered, and fun and he were strangers. With such a jaundiced palette as his, any novelty was a prize. But he wouldn't taunt her any longer. He wasn't a bully, and wouldn't intentionally try to increase that look of concern in her eyes. 'Shall we?' he invited, glancing at the press coach.

She eyed him suspiciously, perhaps wondering if she was being set up. She knew there was nothing she could do about it, if that were the case. She strode ahead of him, head down, mouth set in a stubborn line, no doubt planning her next move. And then she really did throw him.

'So, what have you got to hide?' she asked him, swinging round at the door

'Me?' he demanded.

Tilting her head to one side, she studied his face. 'People with something to hide are generally wary of me and my camera, so I wondered what *you* had to hide…'

'You think that's why I confiscated it?'

'Maybe,' she said, not flinching from his stare.

That direct look of hers asked a lot of questions about a man who could have such prolonged and spectacular sex with a woman he didn't know. It was a look that suggested Romy was asking herself the same question.

'Are you worried that I might have taken some compromising pictures of you?' she said. There was a tug of humour at one corner of her mouth.

'Worried?' He shook his head. But the truth was he had never been so reckless with a woman. He sure as hell wouldn't be so reckless again.

'Kruz?' she prompted.

His name sounded soft on her lips. That had to be a first. He smiled. 'What?'

'Just checking you know I'm still here.'

He gave her a wry look and felt a surge of heat when she tossed one back. He wasn't an animal. He was still capable of feeling. His brother Nacho had made him believe that when Kruz had been discharged from the army hospital. It was Nacho who had persuaded him to channel his particular talents into a security company, saying Kruz must need and feel and care before he could really start living again. Nacho was right. The more he looked at Romy, the more human he felt.

Did Kruz *have* to stare at her lips like that? Here she was, trying to forget her body was still thrilling from his touch, and he wasn't making it easy. She was a professional woman, trying to persuade herself she would soon get over tonight—yet all he had to do was look at her for her to long for him to take hold of her and draw her into an embrace that was neither sexual nor mocking. She had never wanted to share and trust and rest awhile quite so badly.

And she wasn't about to fall into that trap now.

'Shall we take a look?'

She looked at Kruz and frowned.

'The pictures?' he prompted, and she realised that he had not only removed the key to the press coach from her hand, but had opened the door and was holding it for her.

That yearning feeling inside...?

It wasn't helpful. Women who felt the urge to nurture men would end up like her mother: battered, withdrawn, and helpless in a nursing home.

She led the way into the coach. Her manner

was cold. They were both cold, and that suited her fine.

Romy's mood now was a slap in the face to him after what they'd experienced together, but he had to concede she was only as detached as he was. He was just surprised, he supposed, that those much vaunted attributes of tenderness and sensitivity, which women were supposed to possess in abundance, appeared to have bypassed her completely. He should be pleased about that, but he wasn't. He was offended. Romy was the first woman who hadn't clung to him possessively after sex. And bizarrely, for the first time in his life, some primitive part of him had wanted her to.

'Are you coming in?' she said, when he stood at the entrance at the top of the steps.

His senses surged as he brushed past her. However unlikely it seemed to him, this whip-thin fighting girl stirred him like no other. He wanted more. So did she, judging by than quick intake of breath. He could feel her sexual hunger in the energy firing between them. But Romy wanted more that he could give her. He wanted more of Romy, but all he wanted was sex.

CHAPTER THREE

SHE MADE HER way down the aisle towards the area at the rear of the coach set aside for desks and equipment. Her small, slender shape, dressed all in black, quickly became part of the shadows.

'I know there's a light switch in here somewhere,' she said.

Her voice was a little shaky now the door was closed, and the tension rocketed between them. He could feel her anticipation as she waited for his next move. He could taste it in the air. He could detect her arousal. He was a hunter through and through.

'Here,' he said, pressing a switch that illuminated the coach and set some unseen power source humming.

'Thank you,' she said, with her back to him as she sat down at a desk.

'You'll need this,' he said, handing over the camera.

She thanked him and hugged it to her as if it contained gold bars rather than her shots.

He had more time than he needed while she logged on. He used it to reflect on what had happened over the past hour or so. Ejecting Romy from the wedding feast should have been straightforward. She should have been on her way to Buenos Aires by now, then back to London. Instead his head was still full of her, and his body still wanted her. He could still hear her moaning and writhing beneath him and feel her beneath his hands. He could still taste her on his mouth, and he could remember the smell of her soap-fresh skin. He smiled in the shadows, remembering her attacking him, that tiny frame surprisingly strong, yet so undeniably feminine. Why did Romy Winner hide herself away behind the lens of a camera?

A blaze of colour hit the screen as she began to work. What he saw answered his question. Romy Winner was quite simply a genius with a camera. Images assailed his senses. The scenery was incredible, the wildlife exotic. Her pictures of the Criolla ponies were extraordinary. She had captured some amusing shots of the wedding guests, but nothing cruel, though she *had* caught out some of the most pompous in less than flattering moments. She'd taken a lot of pictures of the staff too, and it was those shots that really told a story.

Perhaps because more expression could be shown on faces that hadn't been stitched into place, he reflected dryly as Romy continued to sort and select her images.

She'd made him smile. Another first, he mused as she turned to him.

'Well?' she said. 'Do you like what you see?'

'I like them,' he confirmed. 'Show me what else you've got.'

'There's about a thousand more.'

'I'm in no hurry.' For maybe the first time in his life.

'Why don't you pull up a chair?' she suggested. 'Just let me know if there any images you don't feel are suitable for the charity.'

'So I'm your editor now?' he remarked, with some amusement after her earlier comment about censorship.

'No,' she said mildly. 'You're a client I want to please.'

He inclined his head in acknowledgement of this. He could think of a million ways she could please him. When she turned back to her work he thought the nape of her neck extremely vulnerable and appealing, just for starters. He considered dropping a kiss on the peachy flesh, and then decided no. Once he'd tasted her…

'What do you think of these?' she said, distracting him.

'Grace is very beautiful,' he said as he stared at Romy's shots of the bride. He could see that his new sister-in-law was exquisite, like some beautifully fashioned piece of china. But did Grace move him? Did she make his blood race? He admired Grace as he might admire some priceless *objet d'art*, but it was Romy who heated his blood.

'She is beautiful, isn't she?' Romy agreed, with a warmth in her voice he had never noticed before. She certainly didn't use that voice when she spoke to him.

And why should he care?

Because for the first time in his life he found himself missing the attentions of a woman, and perhaps because he was still stung, after Romy's enthusiastic response to their lovemaking, that she wasn't telling him how she thrilled and throbbed, and all the other things his partners were usually at such pains to tell him. Had Romy Winner simply feasted on him and moved on? If she had, it would be the first time any woman had turned the tables on him.

'This is the sort of shot my editor loves,' she said as she brought a picture of him up on the screen.

'Why is that?'

'Because you're so elusive,' she explained. 'You're hardly ever photographed. I'll make a lot from this,' she added with a pleased note in her voice.

Was he nothing but a commodity?

'Though what I'd *like* to do,' she explained, 'is give it to the charity. So, much as I'd like to make some money out of you, you can have this one *gratis*.'

As she turned to him he felt like laughing. She was so honest, he felt…uncomfortable. 'Thank you,' he said with a guarded expression. 'If you've just taken a couple of shots of me you can keep the rest. '

'What makes you think I'd want to take more than one?'

Youch.

What, indeed? He shrugged and even managed to smile at that.

Romy Winner intrigued him. He had grown up with women telling him he was the best and that they couldn't get enough of him. He'd grown up fighting for approval as the youngest of four highly skilled, highly intelligent brothers. When he couldn't beat Nacho as a youth he had turned to darker pursuits—in which, naturally, he had excelled—until Nacho had finally knocked some sense into him. Then Harvard had beckoned, encouraging him to stretch what Nacho referred to as the most important muscle in his body: the brain. After college he had found the ideal outlet for his energy and tirelessly competitive nature in the army.

'There,' Romy said, jolting him back from these musings. 'You're finished.'

'I wouldn't be too sure of that,' he said, leaning in close to study her edited version. He noticed again how lithe and strong she was, and how easy it would be to pull her into his arms.

'I have a deadline,' she said, getting back to work.

'Go right ahead.' He settled back to watch her.

The huge press coach was closing in on her, and all the tiny hairs on the back of her neck were standing erect at the thought of Kruz just a short distance away. She could hear him breathing. She could smell his warm, sexy scent. Some very interesting clenching of her interior muscles suggested she was going to have to concentrate really hard if she was going to get any work done.

'Could you pass me that kitbag?' she said, without risking turning round. She needed a new memory card and didn't want to brush past him.

Her breath hitched as their fingers touched and that touch wiped all sensible thought from her head. All she could think about now was what they had done and what they could do again.

Work!

She pulled herself back to attention with difficulty, but even as she worked she dreamed, while her body throbbed and yearned, setting up a nagging ache that distracted her.

'Shall I put this other memory card in the pocket for you?' Kruz suggested.

She realised then that she had clenched her hand over it. 'Yes—thank you.'

His fingers were firm as they brushed hers again, and that set up more distracting twinges and delicious little aftershocks. Would she ever be able to live normally again?

Not if she kept remembering what Kruz had done—and so expertly.

Her mind was in turmoil. Every nerve-ending

in her body felt as if it had been jangled. And all he'd done was brush her hand!

Somehow she got through to the end of the editing process and was ready to show him what she'd got. She ran through the images, giving a commentary like one stranger informing another about this work, and even while Kruz seemed genuinely interested and even impressed she felt his aloofness. Perhaps he thought she was a heartless bitch after enjoying him so fully and so vigorously. Perhaps he thought she took *what* she wanted *when* she wanted. Perhaps he was right. Perhaps they deserved each other.

So why this yearning ache inside her?

Because she wanted things she couldn't have, Romy reasoned, bringing up a group photograph of the Acostas on the screen. They were such a tight-knit family…

'Are you sure you want to give me all these shots?'

'Concerned, Kruz?' she said, staring at him wryly. 'Don't worry about me. I've kept more than enough shots back.'

'I'd better see the ones you're giving me again.'

'Okay. No problem.' She ran through them again, just for the dangerous pleasure of having

Kruz lean in close. She had never felt like this before—so aware, alert and aroused. It was like being hunted by the hunter she would most like to be caught by.

'These are excellent,' Kruz commented. 'I'm sure Grace can only be thrilled when she hears the reaction of people to these photographs.'

'Thank you. I hope so,' she said, concentrating on the screen. Grace's wedding was the first romantic project she had worked on. Romy was better known as a scandal queen. And that was one of the more polite epithets she'd heard tossed her way.

'This one I can't take,' Kruz insisted when she flashed up another image on the screen. 'You have to make *some* money,' he reminded her.

Was this a test? Was he paying her off? Or was that her insecurity speaking? He might just be making a kindly gesture, and she maybe should let him.

She shook her head. 'I can't sell this one,' she said quietly. 'I want you to have it.'

The picture in question showed Kruz sharing a smile with his sister, Lucia. It was a rare and special moment between siblings, and it belonged to them alone—not the general public. It was a moment in time that told a story about Nacho's success at bringing up his brothers and sister while he was still very young. They would see that when they studied it, just as she had. She wouldn't dream of selling something like that.

'Frame it and you'll always have a reminder of what a wonderful family you have.'

Why was she doing this for him? Kruz wondered suspiciously. He eased his shoulders restlessly, realising that Romy had stirred feelings in him he hadn't experienced since his parents were alive. He stared at her, trying to work out why. She was fierce and passionate one moment, aloof and withdrawn the next. He might even call her cold. He couldn't pretend he understood her, but he'd like to—and that was definitely a first.

'Thank you,' he said, accepting the gift. 'I appreciate it.'

'I'll make a copy for Lucia as well,' she offered, getting back to work.

'I know my sister will appreciate that.' After Lucia had picked herself off the floor because he'd given her a gift outside of her birthday or Christmas.

The tension between them had subsided with this return to business. He was Romy's client and she was his photographer—an excellent photographer. Her photographs revealed so much about other people, while the woman behind the lens guarded her inner self like a sphinx.

DAMN. She was going to cry if she didn't stop looking at images of Grace and Nacho. So that was what love looked like…

'Shall we move on?' she said briskly, because Kruz seemed in no hurry to bring the viewing session to an end. She was deeply affected by some of the shots she had captured of the bridal couple, and that wasn't helpful right now. Since she was a child she had felt the need to protect her inner self. Drawing a big, thick safety curtain around herself rather than staring at an impossible dream on the screen would be her action of choice right now.

'That was a heavy sigh,' Kruz commented.

She shrugged, neither wanting nor able to confide in him. 'I just need to do a little more work,' she said. 'That's if you'll let me stay to do it?' she added, turning to face him, knowing it could only be a matter of minutes before they went their separate ways.

This was the moment she had been dreading

and yet she needed him to go, Romy realised. Staring at those photographs of Grace and Nacho had only underlined the fact that her own life was going nowhere.

'Here,' she said, handing over the memory stick. 'These are for you and for the charity. You *will* keep that special shot?' she said, her chest tightening at the thought that Kruz might think nothing of it.

'So I can stare at myself?' he suggested, slanting her a half-smile.

'So you can look at your family,' she corrected him, 'and feel their love.'

Did he *have* to stare at her so intently? She wished he wouldn't. It made her uncomfortable. She didn't know what Kruz expected from her.

'What?' she said, when he continued to stare.

'I never took you for an emotional woman,' he said.

'Because I'm not,' she countered, but her breath caught in her throat, calling her a liar. The French called this a *coup de foudre*—a thunderbolt. She had no explanation for the longing inside her except to say Kruz had turned her life inside out. It made no sense. They hardly knew each other outside of sex. They didn't know if they could trust each other, and they had no shared history. They had everything to learn about each other and no time to do so. And why would Kruz *want* to know more about her?

They could be friends, maybe...

Friends? She almost laughed out loud at this naïve suggestion from a subconscious that hadn't learned much in her twenty-four years of life. Romy Winner and Kruz Acosta? Ms Frost and Señor Ice? Taking time out to get to know each other? To *really* get to know each other? The idea was so preposterous she wasn't going to waste another second on it. She'd settle for maintaining a truce between them long enough for her to leave Argentina in one piece with her camera.

'Thanks for this,' Kruz said, angling his stubble-shaded chin as he slipped the memory stick into his pocket.

She felt lost when he turned to go—something else she would have to get used to. She had to get over him. She'd leave love at first sight to those who believed in it. As far as she was concerned love at first sight was a load of bull. Lust at first sight, maybe. Lack of self-control, certainly.

Her throat squeezed tight when he reached the door and turned to look at her.

'How are you planning to get back to England, Romy?'

'The same way I arrived, I guess,' she said wryly.

'Did you bring much luggage with you?'

'Just the essentials.' She glanced at her kitbag, where everything she'd brought to Argentina was stashed. 'Why do you ask?'

'My jet's flying to London tomorrow and there are still a few spare places, if you're stuck.'

Did he mean stuck as in unprepared? Did he think she was so irresponsible? Maybe he thought she was an opportunist who seized the moment and thought nothing more about it?

'I bought a return ticket,' she said, just short of tongue in cheek. 'But thanks for the offer.'

Kruz shrugged, but as he was about to go through the door he paused. 'You're passing up the chance to take some exclusive shots of the young royals—'

'So be it,' she said. 'I wouldn't dream of intruding on their privacy.'

'Romy Winner passing up a scoop?'

'What you're suggesting sounds more like a cheap thrill for an amateur,' she retorted, stung by his poor opinion of her. 'When celebrities or royals are out in public it's a different matter.'

Kruz made a calming motion with his hands.

'I *am* calm,' she said, raging with frustration at the thought that they had shared so much yet knew so little about each other. Kruz had tagged her with the label paparazzi the first moment he'd caught sight of her—as someone who would do anything it took to get her shots. Even have sex with Kruz Acosta, presumably, if that was what was required.

'Romy—'

'What?' she flashed defensively.

'You seem…angry?' Kruz suggested dryly.

She huffed, as if she didn't care what he thought, but even so her gaze was drawn to his mouth. 'I just wonder what type of photographer you think I am,' she said, shaking her head.

'A very good one, from what I've seen today, Señorita Winner,' Kruz said softly, completely disarming her.

'*Gracias*,' she said, firming her jaw as they stared at each other.

And now Kruz should leave. And she should stay where she was—at the back of the coach, as far away from him as possible, with a desk, a chair and most of the coach seats between them.

She waited for him to go, to close the door behind him and bring this madness to an end.

He didn't go.

Leaning over the driver's seat, Kruz hit the master switch and the lights dimmed, and then he walked down the aisle towards her.

CHAPTER FOUR

THEY COLLIDED SOMEWHERE in the middle and there was a tangle of arms and moans and tongues and heated breathing.

She kicked off her boots as Kruz slipped his fingers beneath the waistband of her jeans. The button sprang free and the zipper was down, the fabric skimming over her hips like silk, so that now she was wearing only her jacket, the white vest and her ridiculously insubstantial briefs. Kruz ripped them off. Somehow the fact that she was partly clothed made what was happening even more erotic. There was only one area that needed attention and they both knew it.

Her breathing had grown frantic, and it became even more hectic when she heard foil rip. She was working hectically on Kruz's belt and could feel his erection pressing thick and hard against her hand. She gasped with relief as she released him. She was getting better at this, she registered dazedly, though her brain was still scrambled and she was gasping for breath. Kruz, on the other hand, was breathing steadily, like a man who knew exactly where he was going and how to get there. His control turned her on. He was a rock-solid promise of release and satisfaction, delivered in the most efficient way

'Wrap your legs around me, Romy,' he commanded as he lifted her.

Kruz's movements were measured and certain, while she was a wild, feverish mess. She did as he said, and as she clung to him he whipped his hand across the desk, clearing a space for her. She groaned with anticipation as he moved between her legs. The sensation was building to an incredible pitch. She cried out encouragement as he positioned her, his rough hands firm on her buttocks just the way she liked them. Pressing her knees back, he stared into her eyes. Pleasure guaranteed, she thought, reaching up to lace her fingers through his hair, binding him to her.

This time...this one last time. And then never again.

She was so ready for him, so hungry. As Kruz sank deep, shock, pleasure, relief, eagerness, all combined to help her reach the goal. Thrusting firmly, he seemed to feel the same urgency, but then he found his control and began to tease her. Withdrawing slowly, he entered her again in the way she loved. The sensation was incredible and she couldn't hold on. She fell violently, noisily, conscious only of her own pleasure until the waves had subsided a little, when she was finally able to remember that this was for both of them. Tightening her muscles, she left Kruz in no doubt that she wasn't a silent partner but a full participant.

He smiled into her eyes and pressed her back against the desk. Wherever she took him he took her one level higher. Pinning her hands above her head, he held her hips firmly in place with his other hand as he took her hard and fast. There was no finesse and only one required outcome, and understanding the power she had over him excited her. Grabbing his arms, she rocked with him, welcoming each thrust as Kruz encouraged her in his own language. Within moments she was flying high in a galaxy composed entirely of light, with only Kruz's strong embrace to keep her safe.

It was afterwards that was awkward, Romy realised as she pulled on her jeans. When they were together they were as close as two people could be—trusting, caring, encouraging, pleasuring.

But now they were apart all that evaporated, disappeared almost immediately. Kruz had already sorted out his clothes and was heading for the door. They could have been two strangers who, having fallen to earth, had landed in a place neither of them recognised.

'The seat on the jet is still available if you need it,' he said, pausing at the door.

She worked harder than ever to appear nonchalant. If she looked at Kruz, really looked at him, she would want him to stay and might even say so.

'I won't be stuck,' she said, assuming an air of confidence. 'But thanks again for the offer. And don't forget I'm only an e-mail away if you ever need any more shots from the wedding.'

'And only round the corner when I get to London,' he said opening the door.

What the hell...? She pretended not to understand. Say anything at all and her cool façade would shatter into a million pieces. When tears threatened she bit them back. She wasn't going to ask Kruz if they would meet up in London. This wasn't a date. It was a heated encounter in the press coach. And now it was nothing.

'I'll put the lights on for you,' he said, killing her yearning for one last meaningful look from Kruz.

'That would be great. Thank you.' She was proud of herself for saying this without expression. She was proud of remaining cool and detached. 'I've got quite a bit of work left to do.'

'I'll leave you to it, then,' he said. 'It's been a pleasure, Romy.'

Her head shot up. Was he mocking her?

Kruz was mocking both of them, Romy realised, seeing the tug at one corner of his mouth.

'Me too,' she called casually. After all, this was just another day in the life of a South American playboy. It didn't matter how much her heart ached because Kruz had gone, leaving her with just the flickering images of him on a computer screen for company.

Glancing back, he saw Romy through the window of the coach. She was poring over the monitor screen as if nothing had happened. She certainly wasn't watching him go. She was no clinging vine. It irked him. His male ego had taken a severe hit. He was used to women trying to pin him down, asking him when they'd meet again—if he'd call them—could they have his number? Romy didn't seem remotely bothered.

The wedding party was still in full swing as he

approached the marquee. He rounded up his team, heard their reports and supervised the change-over for the next shift. All of these were measurable activities, which were a blessed relief after his encounter with the impossible-to-classify woman he'd left working in the press coach.

The woman he still wanted

Yeah, that one, he thought.

The noise coming from the marquee was boisterous, joyous, celebratory. Shadows flitted to and fro across the gently billowing tent, silhouettes jouncing crazily from side to side as the music rose and fell.

And Romy was on her own in the press coach.

So what? She was safe there. He'd get someone to check up on her later.

Stopping dead in his tracks, he swung round to look back the way he'd come. He'd send one of the men to make sure she made it to the bunk-house safely.

Really?

Okay, so maybe he'd do that himself.

Romy shot up. Hearing a sound in the darkness, she was instantly awake. Reaching for the light on the nightstand, she switched it on. And breathed a sigh of relief.

'Sorry if I woke you,' the other girl said, stumbling over the end of the bed as she tried to kick off her shoes, unzip her dress and tumble onto the bed all at the same time. 'Jane Harlot, foreign correspondent for *Frenzy* magazine—pleased to meet you.'

'Romy Winner for *ROCK!*'

Jane stretched out a hand and missed completely. 'Brilliant—I love your pictures. Harlot's not my real name,' Jane managed, before slamming a hand over her mouth. 'Sorry—too much to drink. Never could resist a challenge, even when it comes from a group of old men who look as if they have pickled their bodies in alcohol to preserve them.'

'Here, let me help you,' Romy offered, recognising a disaster in the making. Swinging her legs over the side of the bed, she quickly unzipped her new roomie's dress. 'Did you have a good time?'

'Too good,' Jane confessed, shimmying out of the red silk clingy number. 'Those gauchos really know how to drink. But they're chivalrous too. One of them insisted on accompanying me to the press coach and actually waited outside while I sent my copy so he could escort me back here.'

'He waited for you outside the press coach?'

'Of course outside,' Jane said, laughing. 'He was about ninety. And, anyway, it didn't take me long to send my stuff. What I write is basically a comic strip. You know the sort of thing—scandal, slebs, stinking rich people. I only got a look-in because my dad used to work with one of the reporters who got an official invitation and he brought me in as his assistant.'

Looking alarmed at this point, Jane waved a hand, keeping the other hand firmly clamped over her mouth.

Jane had landed a big scoop, and Romy was hardly in a position to criticise the other girl's methods. This wasn't a profession for shrinking violets. The Acostas had nothing to worry about, but some of their guests definitely did, she reflected, remembering those prominent personalities she had noticed attending the wedding with the wrong partner.

'Are you sure you're okay?' she asked with concern as Jane got up and staggered in the general direction of the bathroom.

'Fine…I'll sleep it off on the plane going home.

The gauchos said their boss has places going spare on his private jet tomorrow, so I'll be travelling with the young royals, no less. And I'll be collected from here and taken to the airstrip in a limo. I'll be in the lap of luxury one minute and my crummy old office the next.'

'That's great—enjoy it while you can,' Romy called out, trying to convince herself that this was a good thing, that she was in fact *Saint* Romy and thoroughly thrilled for Jane, and didn't mind at all that the man she'd had sex with hadn't even bothered to see her back to the bunkhouse safely.

He stayed on post until the lights went out in the bunkhouse and he was satisfied Romy was safely tucked up in bed. Pulling away from the fence-post, it occurred to him that against the odds his caring instinct seemed to have survived. But before he could read too much into that he factored his security business into the mix. Plus he had a sister. Before Lucia had got together with Luke he had always hoped someone would keep an eye on her when he wasn't around. Why should he be any different where a girl like Romy was concerned?

* * *

London. Monday morning. The office. Grey skies. Cold. Bleak. Dark-clad people racing back and forth across the rainswept street outside her window, heads down, shoulders hunched against the bitter wind.

It might as well be raining inside, Romy thought, shivering convulsively in her tiny cupboard of an office. It was so cold.

She was cold inside and out, Romy reflected, hugging herself. She was back at work, which normally she loved, but today she couldn't settle, because all she could think about was Kruz. And what was the point in that? She should do something worthwhile to make her forget him.

Something like *this*, Romy thought some time later, poring over the finished version of Grace Acosta's wedding journal. She had added a Braille commentary beside each photograph, so that Grace could explain each picture as she shared the journal. Romy had worried about the space the Braille might take up at first but, putting herself in Grace's place, had known it was the right thing to do.

Sitting back, she smiled. She had been looking forward to this moment for so long—the moment when she could hand over the finished journal to Grace. She wasn't completely freelance yet, though this tiny office at *ROCK!* had housed many notable freelance photographers at the start of their careers and Romy dreamed of following in their footsteps. She hoped this first, really important commission for Grace would be the key to helping her on her way, and that she could make a business out of telling stories with pictures instead of pandering to the insatiable appetite for scandal. Maybe she could tell real stories about real people with her photographs—family celebrations, local news, romance—

Romance?

Yes. Romance, Romy thought, setting her mouth in a stubborn line.

Excuse me for asking the obvious, but what exactly do you know about romance?

As her inner critic didn't seem to know when to be quiet, she answered firmly: *In the absence of romance in my own life, my mind is a blank sheet upon which I will be able to record the happy moments in other people's lives.*

Gathering up her work, Romy headed for the editing suite run by the magazine's reining emperor of visuals: Ronald Smith. *ROCK!* relied on photographs for impact, which made the editor one of the most influential people in the building.

'Ronald,' Romy said, acknowledging her boss as she walked into his hushed and perfumed sanctum.

'Well? What have you got for me, princess?' Ronald demanded, lowering his *faux*-tortoiseshell of-the-moment spectacles down his surgically enhanced nose.

'Some images to blow your socks off,' she said mildly.

'Show me,' Ronald ordered.

Romy stalled as she arranged her images on the viewing table. There was no variety. Why hadn't she seen that before?

Possibly because she had given the best images to Kruz?

Ronald was understandably disappointed. 'This seems to be a series of shots of the waiting staff,' he said, raising his head to pin her with a questioning stare.

'They had the most interesting faces.'

'I hope our readers agree,' Ronald said wearily, returning to studying the images Romy had set out for him. 'It seems to me you've creamed off the best shots for yourself, and that's not like you, Romy.'

A rising sense of dread hit her as Ronald removed his glasses to pinch the bridge of his nose. She needed this job. She needed the financial security and she hated letting Ronald down.

'I can't believe,' he began, 'that I send you to Argentina and you return with nothing more than half a dozen shots I can use—and not one of them of the newly married couple in the bridal suite.'

Romy huffed with frustration. Ronald really had gone too far this time. 'What did you expect? Was I supposed to swing in through their window on a vine?'

'You do whatever it takes,' he insisted. 'You do what you're famous for, Romy.'

Intruding where she wasn't wanted? Was that to be her mark on history?

'It was you who assured me you had an in to this wedding,' Ronald went on. 'When *ROCK!* was refused representation at the ceremony I felt confident that you would capture something special for us. I can't believe you've let us down. I wouldn't have given you time off for this adventure if I had known you would return with precisely nothing. You're not freelance yet, Romy,' he said, echoing her own troubled thoughts. 'But the way you're heading you'll be freelancing sooner than you want to be.'

She was only as good as her last assignment, and Ronald wouldn't forget this. She had to try and make things right. 'I must have missed something,' she said, her brain racing to find a solution. 'Let me go back and check my computer again—'

'I think you better had,' Ronald agreed. 'But not now. You look all in.'

Sympathy from Ronald was the last thing she had expected and guilty tears stung her eyes. She didn't deserve Ronald's concern. 'You're right,' she said, pulling herself together. 'Jet-lag has wiped me out. I should have waited until tomorrow. I'm sorry I've wasted your time.'

'You haven't wasted my time,' Ronald insisted. 'You just haven't shown me anything commercial—anything I can use.'

'I'm confident I can get hold of some more shots. Just give me chance to look. I don't want to disappoint you.'

'It would be the first time that you have,' Romy's editor pointed out. 'But first I want you to promise that you'll leave early today and try to get some rest.'

'I will,' she said, feeling worse than ever when she saw the expression on Ronald's face.

Actually, she did feel a bit under the weather. And to put the cap on her day she had grown a nice crop of spots. 'I won't let you down,' she said, turning at the door.

'Oh, I almost forgot,' Ronald said, glancing up from the viewing table. 'There's someone waiting for you in your office.'

Some hopeful intern, Romy guessed, no doubt waiting in breathless anticipation for a few words of encouragement from the once notorious and now about to be sacked Romy Winner. She pinned a smile to her face. No matter that she felt like a wrung-out rag and her only specialism today was projecting misery and failure, she would find those words of encouragement whatever it took.

Hurrying along the corridors of power on the fifth floor, she headed for the elevators and her lowly cupboard in the basement. She could spare Ronald some shots from Grace's folder. Crisis averted. She just had to sort them out. She should have sorted them out long before now.

But she hadn't because her head was full of Kruz.

'Thank you,' she muttered as her inner voice

stated the obvious. Actually, the real reason was because she was still jet-lagged. She hadn't travelled home in a luxurious private jet but in cattle class, with her knees on her chin in an aging commercial plane.

And whose fault was that?

'Oh, shut up,' Romy said out loud, to the consternation of her fellow travellers in the elevator.

The steel doors slid open on a different world. Gone were the cutting edge bleached oak floors of the executive level, the pale ecru paint, the state-of-the-art lighting specifically designed to draw attention to the carefully hung covers of *ROCK!* In the place of artwork, on this lowly, worker bee level was a spaghetti tangle of exposed pipework that had nothing to do with minimalist design and everything to do with neglect. A narrow avenue of peeling paint, graffiti and lino led to the door of her trash tip of a cupboard.

Stop! Breathe deeply. Pin smile to face. Open door to greet lowly, hopeful intern—

Or not!

'Language, Romy,' Kruz cautioned.

Had she said a bad word? Had she even spoken? 'Sorry,' she said with an awkward gesture. 'I'm just surprised to see you.' *To put it mildly.*

It took her a moment to rejig her thoughts. She had been wearing her most encouraging smile, anticipating an intern waiting eagerly where she had once stood, hoping for a word of encouragement to send her on her way. Romy had been lucky enough to get that word, and had been determined that whoever wanted to see her today would receive some encouragement too. She doubted Kruz needed any.

So forget the encouraging word.

Okay, then.

Standing by the chipped and shabby table that passed for her desk, Kruz Acosta, in all his business-suited magnificence, accessorised with a stone-faced stare and an over-abundance of muscle, was toying with some discarded images she had printed out, scrunched up and had been meaning to toss.

They were all of him.

CHAPTER FIVE

OKAY, SHE COULD handle this. She had to handle this. Whatever Kruz was here for *it wasn't her.*

She had to make sure he didn't leave with the impression that he had intimidated her.

And how was she going to achieve that with her heart racing off the scale?

She was going to remain calm, hold her head up high and meet him on equal ground.

'I like your office, Romy,' he murmured, in the sexy, faintly mocking voice she remembered only too well. 'Do all the executives at *ROCK!* get quite so much space?'

'Okay, okay,' she said, closing this down before he could get started. 'So space is at a premium in the city.'

The smile crept from Kruz's mouth to his eyes, which had a corresponding effect on her own expression. That was half the trouble—it was hard to remain angry with him for long. She guessed

Kruz probably had the top floor of a skyscraper to himself, with a helipad as the cherry on top.

'What can I do for you, Kruz?' she said, proud of how cool she sounded.

So many things. Which was why he'd decided to call by. His office was just around the corner. And he'd needed to…to take a look at some more photographs, he remembered, jolting his mind back into gear.

'Those shots you gave me for the charity,' he said, producing the memory stick Romy had given him back in Argentina.

'What about them?' she said.

She had backed herself into the furthest corner of the room, with the desk between them like a shield. In a room as small as this he could still reach her, but he was content just to look at her. She smelled so good, so young and fresh, and she looked great. 'The shots you gave me are fantastic,' he admitted. 'So much so I'd like to see what else you've got.'

'Oh,' she said.

Was she blinking with relief? Romy could act nonchalant all she liked, but he had a sister and he knew all about acting. He took in her working outfit—the clinging leggings, flat fur boots, the long tee—and as she approached the desk and sat down he concluded that she didn't need to try hard to look great. Romy Winner was one hell of a woman. Was she ready for him now? he wondered as she bit down on her lip.

'We've decided the charity should have a calendar,' he said, 'and we thought you could help. What you've given me so far are mostly people shots, which are great—but there are too many celebrities. And the royals… Great shots, but they're not what we need.'

'What do you want?' she said.

'Those character studies of people who've worked on the *estancia* for most of their lives. Group shots used to be taken in the old days, as well as individual portraits, and that's a tradition I'd like to revive. You make everyone look like members of the same family, which is how I've always seen it.'

'Team Acosta?' she suggested, the shadow of a smile creeping onto her lips.

'Exactly,' he agreed. He was glad he didn't have to spell it out to her. On reflection, he didn't have to spell anything out for Romy. She *got* him.

'What about scenery, wildlife—that sort of thing?' she said, turning to her screen.

'Perfect. I think we're going to make one hell of a calendar,' he enthused as she brought up some amazing images.

Hallelujah! She could hardly believe her luck. This was incredible. She wouldn't lose her job after all. Of course a charity would want vistas and wildlife images, while Ronald wanted all the shots Kruz wanted to discard. She hadn't been thinking straight in Argentina—*for some reason*—and had loaded pictures into files without thinking things through.

'So you don't mind if I have the people shots back?' she confirmed, wondering if it was possible to overdose on Kruz's drugging scent.

'Not at all,' he said, in the low, sexy drawl that made her wish she'd bothered to put some make-up on this morning, gelled her hair and covered her spots.

'You look tired, Romy,' he added as she started loading images onto a clean memory stick. 'You don't have to do this now. I can come back later.'

'Better you stay so you're sure you get what you want,' she said.

'Okay, I will,' he said, hiding his wry smile. 'Thanks for doing this at such short notice.'

She couldn't deny she was puzzled. He was

happy to stay? Either Kruz wanted this calendar really badly, or he was…what? Checking up on her? Checking her out?

Not the latter, Romy concluded. Kruz could have anyone he wanted, and London was chock-a-block full of beautiful women. Hard luck for her, when she still wanted him and felt connected to him in a way she couldn't explain.

Fact: what happened in the press coach is history. Get used to it.

With a sigh she lifted her shoulders and dropped them again in response to her oh, so sensible inner voice. Wiping a hand across her forehead, she wondered if it was hot in here.

'Are you okay?' Kruz asked with concern.

No. She felt faint. Another first. 'Of course,' she said brightly, getting back to her work.

The tiny room was buzzing with Kruz's energy, she thought—which was the only reason her head was spinning. She stopped to take a swig of water from the plastic bottle on her desk, but she still didn't feel that great.

'Will you excuse me for a moment?' she said shakily, blundering to her feet.

She didn't wait to hear Kruz's answer. Rushing

from the desk, she just made it to the rest room in time to be heartily sick.

It was just a reaction at having her underground bunker invaded by Kruz Acosta, Romy reasoned as she studied the green sheen on her face. Swilling her face with cold water, she took a drink and several deep breaths before heading back to her room—and she only did that when she was absolutely certain that the brief moment of weakness had been and gone.

He was worried about Romy. She looked pale.

'No… No, I'm fine,' she said when he asked her if she was all right as she breezed back into the room. 'Must have been something I ate. Sorry. You don't need to hear that.'

He shrugged. 'I was brought up on a farm. I'm not as rarefied as you seem to think.'

'Not rarefied at all,' she said, flashing him a glance that jolted him back to a grassy bank and a blue-black sky.

'It's hot in here,' he observed. No wonder she felt faint. Opening the door, he stuck a chair in the way. Not that it did much good. The basement air was stale. He hated the claustrophobic surroundings.

'Why don't you sit and relax while I do this?' she suggested, without turning from the screen.

'It won't take long, will it?'

She shook her head.

'Then I'll stand, thank you.'

In the tiny room that meant he was standing close behind her. He was close enough to watch Romy's neck flush as pink as her cheeks.

With arousal? With awareness of him?

He doubted it was a response to the images she was bringing up on the screen.

He felt a matching surge of interest. Even under the harsh strip-light Romy's skin looked as temptingly soft as a peach. And her birdwing-black hair, which she hadn't bothered to gel today, was enticingly thick and silky. A cluster of fat, glossy curls caressed her neck and softened her un-made-up face…

She was lovely.

She felt better, so there was no reason for this raised heartbeat apart from Kruz. Normally she could lose herself in work, but not today. He was such a presence in the small, dingy room—such a presence in her life. Shaking her head, she gave a wry smile.

'Is something amusing you?' he said.

'No,' she said, leaning closer to the screen, as if the answer to her amusement lay there. There was nothing amusing about her thoughts. She should be ashamed, not smiling asininely as it occurred to her that she had never seen Kruz close up in the light other than through her camera. Of course she knew to her cost that close up he was an incredible force. She was feeling something of that now. She could liken it to being close to a soft-pawed predator, never being quite sure when it would pounce and somehow—insanely—longing for that moment.

'There. All done,' she said in a brisk tone, swinging round to face him.

It was a shock to find him staring at her as if his thoughts hadn't all been of business. Confusion flooded her. Confusion wasn't something she was familiar with—except when Kruz was around. The expression in his eyes didn't help her to regain her composure. Kruz had the most incredible eyes. They were dark and compelling, and he had the longest eyelashes she'd ever seen.

'These are excellent,' he said, distracting her. 'When you've copied them to a memory stick you'll keep copies on your computer, I presume?'

'Yes, of course,' she said, struggling to put her

mind in gear and match him with her business plan going forward. 'They're all in a file, so if you want more, or you lose them, just ask me.' *For anything,* she thought.

'And you can supply whatever I need?'

She hesitated before answering, and turning back to the screen flicked through the images one more time. 'Are you pleased?'

'I'm very pleased,' Kruz confirmed.

Even now he'd pulled back he couldn't get that far away, and he was close enough to make her ears tingle. She kept her gaze on the monitor, not trusting herself to look round. This was not Romy Winner, thick-skinned photojournalist, but someone who felt as self-conscious as a teenager on her first date. But she wasn't a kid, and this wasn't a date. This was the man she'd had sex with after knowing him for around half an hour. When thousands of miles divided them she could just about live with that, but when Kruz was here in her office—

'Your compositions are really good, Romy.'

She exhaled shakily, wondering if it was only she who could feel the electricity between them.

'These shots are perfect for the calendar,' he

went on, apparently immune to all the things she was feeling.

She logged off, wanting him to go now, so her wounded heart would get half a chance to heal.

'And on behalf of the family,' Kruz was saying. 'I'm asking you to handle this project for us.'

She swung round. Wiping a hand across her face, she wondered what she'd missed.

'That's if you've got time?' Kruz said, seemingly faintly amused as he stared down at her. 'And don't worry—my office is just around the corner, so I'll be your liaison in London.'

Don't worry?

Her heart was thundering as he went on.

'I'd like to see a mock-up of the calendar when you've completed it. I don't foresee any problems, just so long as you remember that quality is all-important when it comes to the Acosta charity.'

Her head was reeling. Was she hearing straight? The Acosta family was giving her the break she had longed for? She couldn't think straight for all the emotion bursting inside her. She had to concentrate really hard to take in everything Kruz was telling her. A commission for the Acosta family? What better start could she have?

Something that didn't potentially tie her in to Kruz?

She mustn't think about that now. She just had to say yes before she lost it completely.

'No,' she blurted, as the consequences of seeing Kruz again and again and again sank in. 'I'd love to do it, but—'

'But what?' he said with surprise.

Answering his question meant looking into that amazing face. And she could do that. But to keep on seeing Kruz day after day, knowing she meant nothing to him… That would be too demoralising even to contemplate. 'I'd love to do it,' she said honestly, feeling her spirit sag as she began to destroy her chances of doing so, 'but I don't have time. I'm really sorry, Kruz, but I'm just too tied up here—'

'Enjoying the security that comes with working for one of the top magazines?' he interrupted, glancing round. 'I can see it would take guts to take time out from *this.*'

She wasn't in the mood for his mockery.

'No worries,' he said, smiling faintly as he moved towards the door. 'I'll just tell Grace you can't find the time to do it.'

'Grace?' she said.

'Grace is our new patron. It was Grace who suggested I approach you—but I'm sure there are plenty of other photographers who can do the job.'

Ouch!

'Wait—'

Kruz paused with his hand on the door. She remembered those hands from the grassy bank and from the press coach, and she remembered what they were capable of. Shivering with longing, she folded her arms around her waist and hugged herself tight.

'Well?' Kruz prompted. 'What am I going to say to Grace? Do you have a message for her, Romy?'

How could she let Grace down? Grace was trying to help her. They had had a long talk when Romy had first arrived in Argentina. Grace had been so easy to talk to that Romy had found herself pouring out her hopes and dreams for the future. She had never done that with anyone before, but somehow her words came easily when she was with Grace. Maybe Grace's gentle nature had allowed her to lower her guard for once.

'I'll do it,' she said quietly.

'Good,' Kruz confirmed, as if he had known she would all along.

She should be imagining her relief when he

closed the door behind him rather than wishing he would stay so they could discuss this some more—so she could keep him here until they shared more than just memories of hot sex on someone else's wedding day.

'Romy? You don't seem as pleased about this work as I expected you to be.'

She flushed as Kruz's gaze skimmed over her body. 'Of course I'm pleased.'

'So I can tell Grace you'll do this for her?'

'I'd rather tell her myself.'

Kruz's powerful shoulders eased in a shrug. 'As you wish.'

There was still nothing for her on that stony face, but she was hardly known for shows of emotion herself. Like Kruz, she preferred to be the one in control. A further idea chilled her as they locked stares. Romy's control came from childhood, when showing emotion would only have made things worse for her mother. When her father was in one of his rages she'd just had to wait quietly until he was out of the way before she could go to look after her mother, or he'd go for her too, and then she'd be in no state to help. Control was just as important to Kruz, which prompted the question: what dark secret was he hiding?

Romy worked off her passions at the gym in the kick-boxing ring, where she found the discipline integral to martial arts steadying. Maybe Kruz found the same. His instinctive and measured response to her roundhouse kick pointed to someone for whom keeping his feelings in check was a way of life.

The only time she had lost it was in Argentina, Romy reflected, when something inside her had snapped. *The Kruz effect?* All those years of training and learning how to govern her emotions had been lost in one passionate encounter.

She covered this disturbing thought with the blandest of questions. 'Is that everything?'

'For now.'

Ice meets ice—today. In Argentina they had been on fire for each other. But theirs was a business relationship now, Romy reminded herself as Kruz prepared to leave. She had to stop thinking about being crushed against his hard body, the minty taste of his sexy mouth, or the sweet, nagging ache that had decided to lodge itself for the duration of his visit at the apex of her thighs. If he knew about that she'd be in real trouble.

'It's been good to see you again,' she said, as if to test her conviction that she was capable of keeping up this cool act.

'Romy,' Kruz said, acknowledging her with a dip of his head and just the slightest glint of humour in his eyes.

The Acosta brothers weren't exactly known for being monks. Kruz was simply being polite and friendly. 'It will be good to be in regular contact with Grace,' she said, moving off her chair to show him out.

'Talking of which…' He paused outside her door.

'Yes?' She tried to appear nonchalant, but she felt faint again.

'We're holding a benefit on Saturday night for the charity, at one of the London hotels. Grace will be there, and I thought it would be a great opportunity for you two to get together and for you to meet my family so you can understand what the charity means to us. That's if you're interested?' he said wryly.

She stared into Kruz's eyes, trying to work out his motive for asking her. Was it purely business, or something else…?

His weary sigh jolted her back to the present.

'When you're ready?' he prompted, staring pointedly at his watch.

'Saturday…?'

'Yes or no?'

He said it with about as much enthusiasm as if he were booking the local plumber to sort out a blocked drain. 'Thank you,' she said formally. 'As you say, it's too good a chance to miss—seeing Grace and the rest of your family.'

'I'm glad to hear it. There may be more work coming your way if the calendar is a success. A newsletter, for example.'

'That's a great idea. Shall I bring my camera?'

'Leave it behind this time,' Kruz suggested, his dark glance flickering over her as he named the hotel where they were to meet.

She couldn't pretend not to be impressed.

'Dress up,' he said.

She gave him a look that said no one told her what to wear. But on this occasion it wasn't about her. This was for Grace. She still felt a bit mulish—if only because Kruz was the type of man she guessed liked his women served up fancy, with all the trimmings. Elusive as he was, she'd seen a couple of shots of him with society beauties, and though he had looked bored on each occasion the girls had been immaculately groomed. But, in fairness to the women, the only time she'd seen Kruz animated was in the throes of passion.

'Something funny?' he said.

'I'll wear my best party dress,' she promised him with a straight face.

'Saturday,' he said, straightening up to his full imposing height. 'I'll pick you up your place at eight.'

Her eyes widened. She had thought he'd meet her at the hotel. Was she Kruz's *date?*

No, stupid. He's just making sure you don't change your mind and let The Family down.

'That's fine by me,' she confirmed. 'Before you go I'll jot my address down for you.'

He almost cracked a smile. 'Have you forgotten what business I'm in?'

Okay, Señor Control-Freak-Security-Supremo. Point taken.

Her address was no secret anyway, Romy reasoned, telling herself to calm down. 'Eight o' clock,' she said, holding Kruz's mocking stare in a steady beam.

'Until Saturday, Romy.'

'Kruz.'

She only realised when she'd closed the door

behind him and her legs almost gave way that she was shaking. Leaning back against the peeling paintwork, she waited until Kruz's footsteps had died away and there was nothing to disrupt the silence apart from the hum of the fluorescent light.

This was ridiculous, she told herself some time later. She was being everything she had sworn never to be. She had allowed herself to become a victim of her own overstretched heart.

There was only one cure for this, Romy decided, and she would find it when she worked out her frustrations in the ring at the gym tonight. Meanwhile she would lose herself in work. Maybe tonight she would be better giving the punch-bag a workout rather than taking on a sparring partner. She didn't trust herself with a living, breathing opponent in her present mood. And she needed the gym. She needed to rebalance her confidence levels before Saturday. She wanted to feel her strength and rejoice in it—her strength of will, in particular. She had to remember that she was strong and successful and independent and safe—and she planned to keep it that way. She especially had to remember that on Saturday.

Saturday!

What the hell was she going to wear?

CHAPTER SIX

'LOOKING HOT,' ONE of the guys said in passing, throwing a wry smile her way as Romy finished her final set of blows on the punch-bag.

The bag must have taken worse in its time, but it had surely never taken a longer or more fearsomely sustained attack from a small angry woman with more frustration to burn off than she could handle. Romy nodded her head in acknowledgement of the praise. This gym wasn't a place for designer-clad bunnies to scope each other out. This was a serious working gym, where many of the individuals went on to have successful careers in their chosen sport.

'What's eating you, Romy?' demanded the grizzled old coach who ran the place, showing more insight into Romy's bruised and battered psyche than her fellow athlete as Romy rested, panting, with her still gloved hands braced on her knees. 'Man trouble?'

You know me too well, she thought, though

she denied it. 'You know me, Charlie,' she said, straightening up. 'Have camera, will travel. No man gets in the way of that.'

'I bet that camera's cosy to snuggle up to on a cold night,' Charlie murmured in an undertone as he moved on to oversee the action in another part of his kingdom.

What did Charlie know? What did *anyone* know? Romy scowled as she caught sight of herself in one of the gym's full-length mirrors. What man in his right mind would want a sweating firebrand with more energy than sense? *Kruz wouldn't.* With her bandaged hands, bitten nails, boy's shorts and clinging, unflattering vest, she looked about as appealing as a wet Sunday. She probably smelled great too. Taking a step back, she nodded her thanks as another athlete offered to help her with the gloves.

'Looking fierce,' he said.

'Ain't that the truth?' Romy murmured. She was a proper princess, complete with grubby sweatband holding her electro-static hair off her surly, sweaty face.

He saw her the moment he walked into the gym. Or rather something drew his stare to her. She felt him too. Even with her back turned he saw a quiver of awareness ripple down her spine. And now she was swinging slowly round, as if she had to confirm her hunch was correct.

We have to stop meeting like this, he thought as they stared at each other. He nodded curtly. Romy nodded back. Yet again rather than looking at him, like other women, Romy Winner was staring at him as if she was trying to psych him out before they entered the ring.

That could be arranged too, he reflected.

They were still giving each other the hard stare when the elderly owner of the gym came up to him. 'Hey, Charlie.' He turned, throwing his towel round his neck so he could extend a hand to greet an old friend warmly.

'You've spotted our lady champion, I see,' Charlie commented.

Kruz turned back to stare at Romy. 'I've seen her.'

Romy had finished her routine. He was about to start his. She looked terrific. It would be rude not to speak to her.

Oh... Argh! What the...?

Romy blenched. For goodness' sake, how could

anyone look *that* good? Kruz was ridiculously handsome. And what the hell was he doing in *her* gym? Wasn't there somewhere billionaire health freaks could hang out together and leave lesser mortals alone to feel good about themselves a few times a week?

Even with the unforgiving lights of the workmanlike sports hall blazing down on him Kruz looked hot. Tall, tanned and broader than the other men sharing his space, he drew attention like nothing else. And he was coming over—oh, *good.* Even a warrior woman needed to shower occasionally, and Kruz was as fresh as a daisy.

Gym kit suited him, she decided as he advanced. With his confident stroll and those scars and tattoos showing beneath his skimpy top he was a fine sight. She wanted him all over again. If she'd never met him before she'd want him. And, inconveniently, she wanted him twice as much as she ever had. A quick glance around reassured Romy that she wasn't the only one staring. She couldn't blame the gym members for that. Muscles bunched beneath his ripped and faded top, and the casual training pants hung off his hips. Silently, she whimpered.

And Kruz didn't walk, he prowled, Romy reflected, holding her ground as he closed the distance between them. His pace was unhurried but remorseless and, brave as she was, she felt her throat dry—it was about the only part of her that was.

'We meet again,' he said with some amusement, stopping tantalisingly within touching distance.

'I didn't expect it to be so soon,' she said offhandedly, reaching for a towel just as someone else picked it up.

'Here—have this. I can always grab another.'

'I couldn't possibly—'

Kruz tossed his towel around her neck. Taking the edges, she wrapped it round her shoulders like a cloak. It still held his warmth.

'So you're really serious about the gym?' he said.

'I like to break sweat,' she agreed, shooting him a level stare as if daring him to find fault with that. 'Why haven't I seen you here before?' she said as an afterthought. 'You slumming it?'

'Please,' Kruz murmured. 'My office is only round the corner.'

'And you don't have a gym?' she said, opening her eyes wide with mock surprise.

'It's under construction,' he said, giving her the cynical look he was so good at.

'I'm impressed,' she said.

'You should be.'

If only that crease in his cheek wasn't so attractive. 'Maybe I'll come and take a look at it when it's finished.'

'I might hold you to that.'

Please. 'I'm very busy,' she said dryly, still holding the dark, compelling stare. 'I have a very demanding private client.'

Kruz's eyes narrowed as he held her gaze. 'I hope I know him.'

'I think you do. So, how do you know Charlie?' she said, seizing on the first thing that came to mind to break the stare-off between them.

'Charlie's an old friend,' Kruz explained, pulling back.

'Were you both in the army?' she asked on a hunch.

'Same regiment,' Kruz confirmed, but then he went quiet and the smile died in his eyes. 'I'd better get started,' he said.

'And I'd better go take my shower,' she agreed as they parted.

'Don't miss the fun,' Charlie called after her.

'What fun?'

'Don't miss Kruz in the ring.'

She turned to look at him.

'Why don't you come in the ring with me?' Kruz suggested. 'You could be my second.'

'Sorry. I don't do second.'

He laughed. 'Or you could fight me,' he suggested.

'Do I look stupid? Don't answer that,' she said quickly, holding up her hands as Kruz shot her a look.

This was actually turning out better than she had thought when she'd first seen Kruz walk into the gym. They were sparring in good way—verbally teasing each other—and she liked that. It made her feel warm inside.

Charlie caught up with her on the way to the changing rooms. 'Don't be too hard on him, Romy.'

'Who are we talking about? Kruz?'

'You know who we're talking about,' the old pro said, glancing around to make sure they weren't being overheard. 'Believe me, Romy, you have no idea what that man's been through.'

'No, I don't,' she agreed. 'I don't know anything about him. Why would I?'

Did Charlie know anything? Had Kruz said something? Her antennae were twitching on full alert.

'You should know what he's done for his friends,' Charlie went on, speaking out of the corner of his mouth. 'The lives he's saved—the things he's seen.'

The guarded expression left her face. This was the longest speech she had ever heard Charlie make. There was no doubt in her mind Charlie was sincere, and she felt reassured that Kruz hadn't said anything about their encounter to him.

'I don't think Kruz wants anyone to go easy on him,' she said thoughtfully, 'but I'll certainly bear in mind what you've said.'

Charlie shook his head in mock disapproval. 'You're a hard woman, Romy Winner. You two deserve each other.'

'Now, that's something I have to disagree with,' Romy said, lightening up. 'You just don't know your clientele, Charlie. Shame on you.' She smiled as she gave Charlie a wink.

'I know them better than you think,' Charlie muttered beneath his breath as Romy shouldered her way into the women's changing room. 'Go take that shower, then join me ringside,' he called after her.

Romy rushed through her shower, emptying a whole bottle of shower gel over her glowing body before lathering her hair with a half a bottle of shampoo. The white tiled floor in the utilitarian shower block was like a skating rink by the time she had finished. Thank goodness her hair was short, she reflected, frantically towelling down. She didn't want to miss a second of this bout. She stared at herself in the mirror. Make-up? Her eyes were bright enough with excitement and her cheeks were flushed. Tugging on her leggings, her flat boots and grey hoodie, she swung her gym bag on to her shoulder and went to join the crowd assembling around the ring at the far end of the gym.

The scent of clean sweat mingled with anticipation came to greet her. This was her sort of party.

'Quite a crowd,' she remarked to Charlie, feeling her heart lurch as Kruz vaulted the ropes into the ring. When he turned to look at her, her heart went crazy. Naked to the waist, Kruz was so hot her body couldn't wait to remind her about getting up close and personal with him. She pressed her thighs together, willing the feeling to subside.

No such luck. As Kruz turned his back and she saw his muscles flex the pulse only grew stronger.

'It's not often we get two champions in the ring—even here at my gym,' Charlie said, his scratchy voice tense with anticipation.

The other kick-boxer was a visitor from the north of England called Heath Stamp. He'd been a bad boy too, according to rumour, and Romy knew him by reputation as a formidable fighter. But Heath was nothing compared to Kruz in her eyes. Kruz's hard, bronzed body gleamed with energy beneath the lights. He was a man in the peak of health, just approaching his prime.

A man with the potential to happily service a harem of women.

'Stop,' she said out loud, in the hope of silencing her inner voice.

'Did you say something, Romy?' Charlie enquired politely, cupping his ear.

'No—just a reminder to myself,' she said dryly.

'There's no one else the champ can spar with,' Charlie confided, without allowing his attention to be deflected for a second from the ring.

'Lucky Kruz came along, then.'

'I'm talking about Kruz,' Charlie rebuked her.

'Kruz is the champ. I should know. I trained him in the army.'

She turned to stare at the rapt face of the elderly man standing next to her. He knew more about Kruz than she did. And he would be reluctant to part with a single shred of information unless it was general info like Kruz's exploits in the gym. What *was* it with Charlie today? She'd never seen him so animated. She'd never seen such fierce loyalty in his eyes or heard it in his voice. It made her want to know all those things Kruz kept secret—for he did keep secrets. Of that much she was certain.

So some men were as complex as women, Romy reasoned, telling herself not to make a big deal out of it as the referee brought the two combatants together in the centre of the ring. Kruz was entitled to his privacy as much as she was, and he was lucky to have a loyal friend like Charlie.

As the bout got under way and the onlookers started cheering Romy only had eyes for one man. The skill level was intense, but there was something about Kruz that transcended skill and made him a master. Being a fighter herself, she suspected that he was holding back. She wondered about this, knowing Kruz could have ended the match in Round One if he had wanted to. Instead he chose to see it through until his opponent began to flag, when Kruz called a halt. Proclaiming the match a draw, he bumped the glove of his opponent, raising Heath Stamp's arm high in the air before the referee could say a word about it.

'That's one of the benefits of having a special attachment to this gym,' Kruz explained, laughing when she pulled him up on it as he vaulted the ropes to land at her side.

'A special attachment?' she probed.

'I used to own it,' he revealed casually, his voice muffled as he rubbed his face on a towel.

'You used to own this gym?'

'That's right,' Kruz confirmed, pulling the towel down.

She glanced round, frowning. Charlie was busy consoling the other fighter. She'd known Charlie for a number of years and had always assumed *he* owned the gym. 'I had no idea you were in the leisure industry,' she said, turning back to Kruz.

'Amongst other things.' Grabbing a water bottle from his second, Kruz drank deeply before pouring the rest over his head. 'I own a lot of gyms, Romy.'

'News to me.'

'My apologies,' he said with a wry look. 'I'll make sure my PA puts you on my "needs to know" list right away.'

'See that you do,' she said, with a mock-fierce stare. Were they getting on? Were they *really* getting on?

'So, what are you doing next?' Kruz asked her.

'Going home.'

'What about food?'

'What about it? I'm not hungry.'

'Surely you're over your sickness now?'

'Yes, of course I am.' Actually, she *had* felt queasy again earlier on.

'Hang on while I take a shower,' he said. 'I'll see you in Reception in ten.'

'But—'

That was all she had time for before Kruz headed off. Raking her short hair with frustration, she was left to watch him run the gauntlet of admirers on his way to the men's changing room. Why did he want to eat with her? Or was food not on the menu? Her heart lurched alarmingly at the thought that it might not be. She wasn't about to fall into ever-ready mode. Just because she enjoyed sex with a certain man it did *not* mean Kruz had a supply on tap.

In all probability he just wanted to talk about the charity project, her sensible self reassured her.

And if he didn't want to chat...?

They'd be in a café somewhere. What was the worst that could happen?

They'd leave the food and run?

Clearly the bout had put Kruz in a good mood, Romy concluded as he came through the inner doors into the reception area.

'Ready to go?' he said, holding the door for her.

So far so good. Brownie points for good manners duly awarded.

'There's a place just around the corner,' he said, 'where we can get something to eat.'

'I know it.' He was referring to the café they all called the Greasy Spoon—though nothing could be further from the truth. True enough, it was a no-nonsense feeding station, with bright lights, Formica tables, hard chairs, but there was a really good cook on the grill who served up high-quality ingredients for impatient athletes with colossal appetites.

They found a table in the window. There wasn't much of a view as it was all steamed up. The air-conditioning was an open door at the back of the kitchen.

'Okay here?' Kruz said when they were settled.

'Fine. Thank you.' She refused to be overawed by him—but that wasn't easy when her mind insisted on undressing him.

She was working for the Acosta family now, Romy reminded herself, and she had to concentrate on that. It was just a bit odd, having had the most amazing sex with this man and having to pretend they had not. Kruz seemed to have forgotten all about it—or maybe it was just one more appetite to slake, she reflected as the waitress came to take their order.

'Do you mind if I take a photo of you?' she said, pulling out her phone.

'Why?' Kruz said suspiciously.

'Why the phone? I don't have my camera.'

'Why the photograph?'

'Because you look half human—because this is a great setting—because everyone thinks of the Acostas as rarefied beings who live on a different planet to them. I just want to show people that you do normal things too.'

'Steak and chips?' Kruz suggested wryly, tugging off his heavy jacket.

'Steak and chips,' she agreed, returning his smile. Oh, boy, how that smile of his heated her up. 'You'd better not be laughing at me,' she warned, running off a series of shots.

'Let me see,' he said, holding out his hand for her phone.

'Me first,' she argued. *Wow.* She blew out a slow, controlled breath as she studied the shot. Kruz's thick, slightly too long hair waved and gleamed like mahogany beneath the lights. The way it caught on his sideburns and stubble was…

'Romy?' he said

'Not yet,' she teased. 'You'll have to wait for the newsletter.' *To see those powerful shoulders clad in the softest air-force blue cashmere and those well-packed worn and faded jeans...*

'Romy?' Kruz said, sounding concerned when she went off into her own little dreamworld.

Snap! Snap!

'There. That should do it,' she said, passing the phone across the table.

'Not bad,' Kruz admitted grudgingly. 'You've reminded me I need to shave.'

'Glad to be of service,' she said, blushing furiously half a beat later. Being that type of service was not what she meant, she assured herself sternly as Kruz pushed the phone back to her side of the table.

Fortunately their food arrived, letting her off the hook. She had ordered a Caesar salad with prawn, while Kruz had ordered steak and fries. Both meals were huge. And every bit as delicious as expected.

'This is a great place,' she said, tucking in. As Kruz murmured agreement she made the mistake of glancing at his mouth. Fork suspended, she stared until she realised he was looking at her mouth too. 'Yours good?' she murmured distractedly. Kruz had a really sexy mouth. And an Olympian appetite, she registered as he called for a side of mushrooms, onion rings and a salad to add to his order.

'Something wrong with your meal, Romy?'

'No. It's delicious.' She stared intently at her salad, determined not to be distracted by him again.

Food was a great ice-breaker. It oiled the wheels of conversation better than anything she knew. 'So, tell me more about Charlie's gym. I've been going there for years and I had no idea you used to own it.'

Kruz frowned. 'What do you want to know?'

'I always thought Charlie owned it. Not that it matters,' she said.

'He does own it.' And, when she continued to urge him on with a look of interest, Kruz offered cryptically, 'Things change over time, Romy.'

'Right.' The conversation seemed to have gone the same way as their empty plates. 'Charlie never stopped talking about you,' she said to open it up again. 'He admires you so much, Kruz.'

Personal comments were definitely a no-no, she concluded as Kruz gave her a flat black look. 'Do you want coffee?' He was already reaching for his wallet. This down-time was over.

'No. I'm fine. Let me get this.'

For once in her life she managed not to fumble and got out a couple of twenties to hand to the waitress before Kruz had a chance to disagree.

He did not look pleased. 'You should not have done that,' he said.

'Why not? Because you're rich and I'm not?'

'Don't be so touchy, Romy.'

She was touchy? 'I'm not touchy,' she protested, standing up. 'Aren't you the guy who's taking me to some swish event on Saturday?' She shrugged. 'The least I can do is buy you dinner.'

'You will be a guest of the family on Saturday,' he said.

Heaven forfend she should mistake it for a date.

'And where Charlie's concerned I'd prefer you don't say anything about the gym to him,' Kruz added. 'That man is not and never has been in my debt. If anything, I'm in his.'

She hadn't anticipated such a speech, and wondered what lay behind it—especially in light of Charlie's words about Kruz. *The plot thickens,* she thought. But as it showed no sign of being solved any time soon she followed Kruz to the door.

'Until Saturday,' he said, barely turning to look at her as he spoke.

Someone was touchy when it came to questions about his past. 'I'll meet you at the hotel,' she said briskly, deciding she really did not want him at her place. She was surprised when he didn't argue.

She watched Kruz thread his way through the congested traffic with easy grace—talking of which, for Grace's sake she would find something other than sweats or leggings to wear on Saturday night. She wanted to do the family proud. She didn't want to stand out for all the wrong reasons. Khalifa's department store was on her way home, so she had no excuse.

In the sale she picked out an understated column of deep blue silk that came somewhere just above her knees. It was quite flattering. The rich blue made her hair seem shinier and brought out the colour of her eyes. No gel or red tips on Saturday, she thought, viewing herself in the mirror. She normally dressed to please herself, but she didn't want to let Grace down. And, okay, maybe she *did* want strut her stuff just a little bit in front of Kruz. This was one occasion when being 'wiry', as Charlie frequently and so unflatteringly referred to her, was actually an advantage. The sale stuff was all in tiny sizes. She even tried on a pair of killer heels—samples, the salesgirl told her.

'That's why they're in the sale,' the girl explained. 'You're the first person who can get her feet into them. They're size Tinkerbell.'

Romy slanted her a smile. 'Tinkerbell suits me fine. I always did like to create a bit of mayhem.'

They both laughed as they took Romy's haul to the till.

'You'll have men flocking,' the girl told her as she rang up Romy's purchases.

'Yeah, right.' And the one man she would like to come flocking would be totally unmoved. 'Thanks for all your help,' Romy said, flashing a goodbye smile as she picked up the bag.

CHAPTER SEVEN

SOMETHING PROPELLED HIM to his feet. Romy had just entered the sumptuously dressed ballroom. He might have known. Animal instinct had driven him to his feet, he acknowledged wryly as that same instinct transferred to his groin. Romy had taken his hint to dress for the occasion, expanding his thoughts as to what she might wear beyond his wildest dreams. Hunger pounded in his eyes as her slanting navy blue gaze found his. Nothing could have prepared him for this level of transformation, or for the way she made him feel. He acted nonchalant as she began to weave her way through the other guests, heading for their table, but with that short blue-black hair, elfin face and the understated silk dress she was easily the most desirable woman in the room.

'Kruz...'

'Romy,' he murmured as she drew to a halt in front of him.

'Allow me introduce you around,' he said, eventually remembering his manners.

His family smiled at Romy and then glanced at him. He was careful to remain stonily impassive. His PA had arranged the place cards so that Romy was seated on the opposite side of the table to him, where he could observe her without the need to engage her in conversation. He had thought he would prefer it that way, but when he saw the way his hot-blooded brothers reacted to her he wasn't so sure.

It was only when it came to the pudding course and Grace suggested they should all change places that he could breathe easily again.

'So,' he said, settling down in the chair next to Romy, 'what did you and Grace decide about the charity?' The two women hadn't stopped talking all evening and had made an arresting sight, Grace with her refined blond beauty and Romy the cute little gamine at her side.

'We discussed the possibility of a regular newsletter, with lots of photographs to show what we do.'

'We?' he queried.

'Do you want me to own this or not?' Romy parried with a shrewd stare.

'Of course I do. It's important to me that everyone involved feels fully committed to the project.' Surprisingly, he found Romy's business persona incredibly sexy. 'That's how I've found employees like it in the past.'

'I'm not your employee. I work for myself, Kruz.'

'Of course you do,' he said, holding her gaze until her cheeks pinked up.

She was all business now—talking about anything but personal matters. That was what he expected of Romy in this new guise, but it didn't mean he had to like it.

'We also talked about a range of greetings cards to complement the calendar—Kruz, are you listening to me?'

'It sounds as if you and Grace have made a good start,' he said, leaning back in his chair.

The urge to sit with Romy and monopolise her conversation wasn't so much a case of being polite as a hunting imperative. His brothers were still sitting annoyingly close to her, though in fairness she didn't seem to notice them.

She was so aroused she was finding it embarrassing. Her cheeks were flushed and she didn't even dare to look down to see if her ever-ready nipples were trying to thrust their way through the flimsy silk. She couldn't breathe properly while she was sitting this close to Kruz—she couldn't think. She could only feel. And there was a lot of feeling going on. Her lips felt full, her eyes felt sultry. Her breasts felt heavy. And her nipples were outrageously erect. *There.* She knew she shouldn't have looked. Her breathing was super-fast, and she felt swollen and needy and—

'More wine, madam?'

'No, thank you,' she managed to squeak out. She'd hardly touched the first glass. Who needed stimulus when Kruz Acosta was sitting next to her?

'Would you like to dance?'

She gaped at the question and Kruz raised a brow.

'It's quite a simple question,' he pointed out, 'and all you have to say is yes or no.'

For once in her life she couldn't say anything at all. The table was emptying around them. Everyone was on their feet, dirty-dancing to a heady South American beat. The dance floor was packed. Kruz was only being polite, she reasoned. And she could hardly refuse him without appearing rude.

'Okay,' she said, trying for off-hand as she left the table.

There was only one problem here—her legs felt like jelly and sensation had gathered where it shouldn't, rivalling the music with a compelling pulse. Worse, Kruz was staring knowingly into her eyes. He didn't need to say a word. She was already remembering a grassy bank beneath a night sky in Argentina and a press coach rocking. His touch on her back was all the more frustrating for being light. They had around six inches of dance floor to play in and Kruz seemed determined they would use only half those inches. Pressed up hard against him, she was left wondering if she could lose control right here, right now. The way sensation was mounting inside her made that seem not only possible but extremely probable.

'Are you all right, Romy?' Kruz asked.

She heard the strand of amusement in his voice. He knew, damn him! 'Depends what you mean by all right?' she said.

Somehow she managed to get through the rest of the dance without incident, and neither of them spoke a word on their way back to the table. The palm of Kruz's hand felt warm on her back, and maybe that soothed her into a dream state, for the next thing she knew he had led her on past the table, through the exit and on towards the elevators.

They stood without explanation, movement or speech as the small, luxuriously upholstered cabin rose swiftly towards one of the higher floors. She didn't mean to stare at it, but there was a cosy-looking banquette built into one side of the restricted space. She guessed it was a thoughtful gesture by the hotel for some of its older guests. Generously padded and upholstered in crimson velvet, the banquette was exerting a strangely hypnotic effect on her—that and the mirror on the opposite side.

She sucked in a swift, shocked breath as Kruz stopped the elevator between floors.

'No…' she breathed.

'Too much of a cliché?' he suggested, with that wicked grin she loved curving his mouth.

They came together like a force of nature. It took all he'd got to hold Romy off long enough for him to protect them both. Remembering the last time, when she had wrenched the shirt from his pants, he kept her hands pinned above her head as he kissed her, pressing her hard against the wall. She tasted fresh and clean and young and perfect—all the things he was not. His stubble scraped her as he buried his face in her neck and her lips were already bruised. Inhaling deeply, he kissed her below the ear for the sheer pleasure of feeling tremors course through her body. His hands moved quickly to cup the sweet remembered swell of her buttocks.

This was everything he remembered, only better. Her skin was silky-smooth. His rough hands were full of her. In spite of being so tiny she had curves in all the right places and she fitted him perfectly. Lodging one thigh between her legs, he moved her dress up to her waist and brought her lacy underwear down. 'Wrap your legs around me, Romy,' he ordered, positioning her on the very edge of the banquette.

Pressing her knees back, he stared down as he tested that she was ready. This was the first time he had seen her—really seen her—and she was more than ready. Those tremors had travelled due south and were gripping her insistently now.

'Oh, please,' she gasped, holding her thighs wide for him.

She alternated her pleas to him with glances in the mirror, where he knew the sight of him ready and more than willing to do what both of them needed so badly really turned her on. He obliged by running the tip of his straining erection against her. She panted and mewled as she tried to thrust her hips towards him to capture more. He had her in a firm grasp, and though he was equally hungry it pleased him to make her wait.

'What do you want?' he murmured against her mouth, teasing her with his tongue.

He should have known Romy Winner would tell him, in no uncertain language. With a laugh he sank deep, and rested a moment while she uttered a series of panting cries.

'Good?' he enquired softly.

Her answer was to groan as she threw her head back. Withdrawing slowly, he sank again—slowly and to the hilt on this occasion. Some time during that steady assault she turned again to look into the mirror. He did too.

'More,' she whispered, her stare fixed on their reflection.

A couple of firm thrusts and she was there, shrieking as the spasms gripped her, almost bouncing her off the banquette. The mirror was great for some things, but when it came to this only staring into Romy's eyes did it for him. But even that wasn't enough for them. It wasn't nearly enough, he concluded as Romy clung to him, her inner muscles clenching violently around him. Picking her up, he maintained a steady rhythm as he pressed her back against the wall.

'More,' he agreed, thrusting into her to a steady beat.

'Again,' she demanded, falling almost immediately.

'You're very greedy,' he observed with satisfaction, taking care to sustain her enjoyment for as long as she could take it.

'Your turn now,' she managed fiercely.

'If you insist,' he murmured, determined to bring her with him.

Romy was a challenge no man could resist and he had not the slightest intention of trying. She was hypersensitive and ultra-needy. She was a willing mate and when he was badly in need of someone who could halfway keep up. Romy could more than keep up.

This was special. This was amazing. Kruz was so considerate, so caring. And she had thought the worst of him. She had badly misjudged him, Romy decided as Kruz steadied her on her feet when they had taken their fill of each other. For now.

'Okay?' he murmured.

Pulling her dress down, she nodded. Feeling increasingly self-conscious, she rescued her briefs and pulled them on.

'I'll take you upstairs to freshen up,' Kruz reassured her as she glanced at her hair in the mirror and grimaced.

Kruz was misunderstood, she decided, leaning on him. Yes, he was hard, but only because he'd had to be. But he could be caring too—under the right circumstances.

'Thanks,' she said, feeling the blush of approval spreading to her ears. 'I'd appreciate a bit of tidy-up before I return to the ballroom.'

She had a reputation for being a hard nut too, but not with Kruz…never with Kruz, she mused, staring up at him through the soft filter of after-glow. Maybe after all this time her heart was alive again. Maybe she was actually learning to trust someone…

They exited the elevator and she quickly realised that the Acostas had taken over the whole floor. There were security guards standing ready to open doors for them, but what she presumed must be Kruz's suite turned out to be an office.

'The bathroom's over there,' he said briskly,

pointing in the direction as his attention was claimed by a pretty blond woman who was keen to show him something on her screen.

This wasn't embarrassing, Romy thought as people shot covert glances as her as she made her way between the line of desks.

And if she would insist on playing with fire...

Locking herself in the bathroom, she took a deep, steadying breath. When would she ever learn that this was nothing more than sex for Kruz, and that she was nothing more than a feeding station for him? And it was too late to worry about what anyone thought.

Running the shower, she stripped off. Stepping under the steaming water felt like soothing balm. She would wash every trace of Kruz Acosta away and harden her resolve towards him as she did so. But nothing helped to ease the ache inside her. It wasn't sexual frustration eating away at her now. It was something far worse. It was as if a seed had been planted the first time they met, and that seed had not only survived but had grown into love.

Love?

Love. What else would you call this certain feeling? And no wonder she had fallen so hard, Romy reasoned, cutting herself some slack as she stepped out of the shower. Kruz was a force of nature. She'd never met anyone like him before.

She was a grown woman who should have known better than to fall for the charms of a man like Kruz—a man who was in no way going to fall at her feet just because she willed it so.

And maybe this grown woman should have checked that there was a towel in the bathroom before she took a shower?

Romy stared around the smart bathroom in disbelief. There was a hand-dryer and that was it. Of course… The hotel had let this as an office, not a bedroom with *en-suite* bathroom. Wasn't that great? How much better could things get?

'Are you ready to go yet?' Kruz bellowed as he hammered on the door.

Fantastic. So now she was the centre of attention of everyone in the office as they waited for her to come out of the bathroom.

'Almost,' she called out brightly, in her most businesslike voice.

Almost? She was standing naked, shivering and dripping all over the floor.

'Couple of minutes,' she added optimistically.

Angling her body beneath a grudging stream of barely warm air wasn't going so well. But there was a grunt from the other side of the door, and retreating footsteps, which she took for a reprieve. Giving up, she called it a day. Slipping on her dress, she ran tense fingers through her mercifully short hair and realised that would have to do. Now all that was left was the walk of shame. Drawing a deep breath, she tilted her chin and opened the door.

Everyone in the office made a point of looking away. *Oh...* She swayed as a wave of faintness washed over her. This was ridiculous. She had never fainted in her life.

'Are you all right, Romy?' Kruz was at her side in an instant with a supporting arm around her shoulders. 'Sit here,' he said, guiding her to a chair when all she longed for was to leave the curious glances far behind. 'I'll get you a glass of water.'

It was a relief when the buzz in the office started up again. She tried to reason away her moment of frailty. She'd hardly drunk anything at the dinner. Had she eaten something earlier that had disagreed with her?

'I'm fine, honestly,' she insisted as Kruz handed her a plastic cup.

'You're clearly not fine,' he argued firmly, 'and I'm going to call you a cab to take you home.'

'But—'

'In fact, I'm going to take you home,' he amended. 'I can't risk you fainting on the doorstep.'

He was going to take her to the tiny terrace she shared with three other girls in a rundown part of town?

Things really couldn't get any better, could they?

She didn't want Kruz to see where she lived. Her aim was one day to live in a tranquil, picturesque area of London by the canal, but for now it was enough to have a roof over her head. She didn't want to start explaining all this to Kruz, or to reveal where her money went. Her mother's privacy was sacrosanct.

She expected Kruz to frown when he saw where she lived. He had just turned his big off-roader into the 'no-go zone', as some of the cabbies called the area surrounding Romy's lodgings. She sometimes had to let them drop her off a couple of streets away, where it was safer for them, and she'd walk the rest of the way home. She wasn't worried about it. She could look after herself. This might look bad to Kruz, but it was home for her as it was for a lot of people.

'What are you doing living here, Romy?'

Here we go. 'Something wrong with it?' she challenged.

Kruz didn't answer. He didn't need to. His face said it all—which was too bad for him. She didn't have to explain herself. She didn't want Kruz Acosta—or anyone else, for that matter—feeling sorry for her. This was something she had chosen to do—*had* to do—took pride in doing. If she couldn't look after her family, what was left?

Stopping the car, Kruz prepared to get out.

'No,' she said. 'I'm fine from here. We're right outside the front door.'

'I'm seeing you in,' he said, and before she could argue with this he was out of the car and slamming the door behind him. Opening her door, he stood waiting. 'This isn't up for discussion,' he growled when she hesitated.

Was anything where Kruz was concerned?

CHAPTER EIGHT

ROMY HAD GOT to him when no one else could.

So why Romy Winner?

Good question, Kruz reflected as he turned the wheel to leave the street where Romy lived. As he joined the wide, brilliantly lit road that led back to the glitter of Park Lane, one of London's classiest addresses, he thought about his office back at the hotel and wondered why he hadn't asked one of his staff to drive her home.

Because Romy was his responsibility. Why make any more of it?

Because seeing her safely through her front door had been vital for him.

Finding out where she lived had been quite a shock. He might have expected her to live in a bohemian area, or even an area on the up, but in the backstreets of a nowhere riddled with crime…?

He was more worried than ever about her now. In spite of Romy's protestations she had still looked pale and faint to him. The kick-ass girl had seemed vulnerable suddenly. The pint-sized warrior wasn't as tough as she thought she was. Which made him feel like a klutz for seducing her in the elevator—even if, to be fair, he had been as much seduced as seducer.

Forgetting sex—*if he could for a moment*—why did Romy live on the wrong side of the tracks when she must make plenty of money? She was one of the most successful photojournalists of her generation. So what was she doing with all the money she earned?

And now, in spite of all his good intentions, as he drew the off-roader to a halt outside the hotel's grandiose pillared entrance, all he could think about was Romy, and how she had left him hungry for more.

She was a free spirit, like him, so why not?

Handing over his keys to the hotel valet, he reasoned that neither of them was interested in emotional ties, but seeing Romy on a more regular basis, as Grace had suggested, would certainly add a little spice to his time in London. His senses went on the rampage at this thought. If Romy hadn't been under par this evening he wouldn't be coming back here on his own now.

* * *

She was sick on Monday morning. Violently, sickeningly sick. Crawling back into bed, she pulled the covers over her head and closed her eyes, willing the nausea to go away. She had cleaned her teeth and swilled with mouthwash, but she could still taste bile in her throat.

Thank goodness her housemates had both had early starts that morning, Romy reflected, crawling out of bed some time later. She couldn't make it into work. Not yet, at least. Curling up on the battered sofa in front of the radiator, still in her dressing gown, she groaned as she nursed a cup of mint tea, which was all she could stomach after the latest in a series of hectic trips to the bathroom.

She couldn't be... She absolutely couldn't be—

She wouldn't even think the word. She refused to voice it. She could not be pregnant. Kruz had always used protection.

She had obviously eaten something that disagreed with her. She must have. She had that same light-headed, bilious feeling that came after eating dodgy food.

Dodgy food at one of London's leading hotels? How likely was that? The Greasy Spoon was fa-

mously beyond reproach, and she was Mrs Disinfectant in the kitchen...

Well, *something* had made her feel this way, Romy argued stubbornly as she crunched without enthusiasm on a piece of dry toast.

A glance at the clock reminded her that she didn't have time to sit around feeling sorry for herself; she had a photoshoot with the young star of a reality show this morning, and the greedy maw of *ROCK!* magazine's picture section, infamously steered by Ronald the Remorseless, wouldn't wait.

Neither would the latest invoice for her mother's nursing care, Romy reflected with concern as she left the house. She had already planned her day around a visit to the nursing home, where she checked regularly on all those things her mother was no longer able to sort out for herself. She had no time to fret. She just had to get on and stop worrying about the improbability of two people who had undergone the same emotional bypass coming together to form a new life.

But...

Okay, so there was a chemist just shy of the *ROCK!* office block.

Dragging in the scent of clean and bright air,

Romy assured herself that her visit to the chemist was essential to life, as she needed to stock up on cold and flu remedies. There was quite a lot of that about at the moment. Grabbing a basket, she absentmindedly popped in a pack of handwipes, a box of tissues, some hairgrips—which she never used—and a torch.

Well, you never know.

Making her way to the counter, she hovered in front of the *'Do you Think you Could be Pregnant?'* section, hoping someone else might push in front of her. Finally palming a pregnancy test, with a look on her face which she hoped suggested that she was very kindly doing it for a friend, she glanced around to make sure there was no one she knew in the shop before approaching the counter. As she reached for her purse the pharmacist came over to help.

'Do you have a quick-fire cure for a stomach upset?' Romy enquired brightly, pushing her purchases towards the woman, with the telltale blue and white box well hidden beneath the other packages.

'Nausea?' the pharmacist asked pleasantly. 'You're not pregnant, are you?' she added, filleting the pile to extract the box containing the pregnancy test with all the sleight of hand of a Pick-up-Sticks champion.

'Of course not.' Romy laughed a little too loudly.

'Are you sure?' The woman's gaze was kind and steady, but her glance did keep slipping to the blue and white packet, which had somehow slithered its way to centre stage. 'I have to know before I can give you any medication…'

'Oh, that's just for a friend,' Romy said, feeling her cheeks blaze.

Meanwhile the queue behind her was growing, and several people were coughing loudly, or tutting.

'I think we'd better err on the side of caution,' the helpful young pharmacist said, reaching behind her to pick up some more packages. 'There are several brands of pregnancy test—'

'I'll take all of them,' Romy blurted.

'And will you come back for the nausea remedy?' the woman called after her. 'There are some that pregnant women can take—'

Then let those pregnant women take them, Romy thought, gasping with relief as she shut the door of the shop behind her. How ridiculous was this? She didn't even have the courage to buy what she wanted from a chemist now.

'Someone's waiting for you in your office,' the receptionist told her as she walked back into the building.

Not Kruz. Not now. 'Who?' she said warily.

'Kruz Acosta,' the girl said brightly. 'He was here a couple of days ago, wasn't he? Aren't you the lucky one?'

'I certainly am,' Romy agreed darkly. Girding her loins, she headed for the basement.

'Weren't you with him the other night?' someone else chipped in when she stepped into the crowded elevator. 'Great shot of you on the front page of the *West End Chronicle,* Romy,' someone else chirruped. 'In fact, both you and Kruz look amazing…'

General giggling greeted this.

'Can I see?' She leaned over the shoulder of the first girl to look at the newspaper she was holding.

OMG!

'Oh, that was just a charity thing I attended,' she explained off-handedly, feeling sicker than ever now she'd seen the shot of her and Kruz, slipping not as discreetly as they had thought into the elevator. Kruz's hand on her back and the expression on her face as she stared up at him both told a very eloquent story. And now there was the type of tension in the lift that suggested the slightest comment from anyone and all the girls would burst out laughing. The banner headline hardly helped: *'Are You Ready for Your Close-Up, Ms Winner?'*

Was that libellous? Romy wondered.

Better not to make a fuss, she concluded, reading on.

> 'Who doesn't envy Romy Winner her close encounter with elusive billionaire bad-boy Kruz Acosta? Kruz, the only unmarried brother of the four notorious polo-playing Acostas brothers—'

Groaning, she leaned her head against the back of the lift. She didn't need to read any more to know this was almost certainly the reason Kruz was here to see her now. He must hold her wholly responsible for the press coverage. He probably thought she'd set it up. But it took two to tango, Romy reminded herself as she got out of the elevator and strode purposefully towards her cubby-hole.

Breath left her lungs in a rush when she opened

the door. Would she *ever* get used to the sight of this man? 'Kruz, I'm—'

'Fantastic!' he exclaimed vigorously. 'How are you this morning, Señorita Winner? Better, I hope?'

'Er…' *Maybe pregnant...maybe not.* 'Good. Thank you,' she said firmly, as if she had to convince herself.

Slipping off her coat, she hung it on the back of the office door. Careful not to touch Kruz, she sidled round the desk. Dumping her bag on the floor at her side, she sat in her swivel chair, relieved to have a tangible barrier between them. Kruz was in jeans, a heavy jacket with the collar pulled up and workmanlike boots—a truly pleasing sight. Especially first thing in the morning…

And last thing at night.

And every other time of day.

Waving to the only other chair in the room—a hard-backed rickety number—she invited him to sit down too. And almost passed out when he was forced to swoop down and move her bag. It was one of those tote things that didn't fasten at the top, and all her purchases were bulging out—including a certain blue and white packet.

'I didn't want to knock your bag over,' he explained, frowning when he saw her expression. 'Still not feeling great?'

Clearly blue and white packets held no significance for a man. 'No…I'm fine,' she said.

'Good,' Kruz said, seeming unconvinced. 'I'm very pleased to hear it.'

So why were his lips still pressed in a frown?

And why was she staring at his mouth?

Suddenly super-conscious of her own lips, and how it felt to be kissed by Kruz, she dragged her gaze away. And then remembered the scratch of his stubble on her skin. The marks probably still showed—and she had been too distracted by hormonal stuff this morning to remember to cover them. So everyone had seen them. Double great.

'What can I do for you?' she said.

'You haven't read the article yet?' Kruz queried with surprise.

He made it impossible for her to ignore the scandal sheet as he laid it out on her desk. 'I like the way you went after publicity,' he said.

Was that a glint in his wicked black eyes? She put on a serious act. 'Good,' she said smoothly. 'That's good…'

'The article starts with the usual nonsense about you and me,' he reported, leaning over her desk to point to the relevant passage, 'but then it goes on to devote valuable column inches to the charity.' He looked up, his amused dark eyes plumbing deep. 'I'd like to compliment you on having a colleague standing by.'

'You think I *staged* this?' she exclaimed, mortified that Kruz should imagine she would go to such lengths.

'Well, didn't you?' he said.

There was a touch of hardness in his expression now, and she was acutely conscious of the pregnancy test peeping out of her bag, mocking her desire to finish this embarrassing interview and find out whether she was pregnant or not. There was also a chance that if Kruz caught sight of the test he might think she had set *him* up too. Sick of all the deception, she decided to come clean.

'I'm not sure how that photograph happened,' she admitted, 'other than to say there are always photojournalists on the look-out for a story—especially at big hotels when there's an important event on. I'm afraid I can't claim any credit for it…' She held Kruz's long, considering stare.

'Well, however it happened,' he said, 'it's done the charity no harm at all. So, well done. Hits on our website have rocketed and donations are flooding in.'

'That *is* great news,' she agreed.

'And funny?' he said.

Perhaps it was hormones making want to giggle. She'd heard it said that Romy Winner would stop at nothing to get a story. She had certainly put her back into it this time.

'So you're not offended by the headline?' she said, reverting to business again.

'It amused me,' Kruz confessed.

Well, that wasn't quite what she'd been hoping for. 'Me too,' she said, as if fun in a lift were all part of the job. 'It's all part of the job,' she said out loud, as if to convince herself it were true.

'Great job,' Kruz murmured, cocking his head with the hint of a smile on his mouth.

'Yes,' she said.

'On the strength of the publicity you've generated so far, I'm going to take you to lunch to discuss further strategy.'

Ah. 'Further strategy?' She frowned. 'Lunch at nine-thirty in the morning?'

She was going to visit her mother later. It was the highlight of her day and one she wouldn't miss for the world. It was also something she couldn't share with Kruz.

'We'll meet at one,' he said, turning for the door.

'No. I can't—'

'You have to eat and so do I,' he said.

'I've got a photoshoot,' she remembered with relief. 'And then—' And then she had finished for the day.

'And then you eat,' Kruz said firmly.

'And then I've got personal business.'

'We'll make it supper, then,' he conceded.

By which time she would know. Vivid images of losing control in the elevator flashed into her head—a telling reminder that she had enjoyed sex with Kruz not once, but many times. And it only took one time for a condom to fail.

They exchanged a few more thoughts and comments about the way forward for the charity, and then Kruz left her to plunge into a day where nothing went smoothly other than Romy's visit to her mother. That was like soothing balm after dealing with a spoiled brat who had screamed for ten types of soda and sweets with all the green ones taken out before she would even consider posing for the camera.

What a day of contrasts it had been, she reflected later. When she held her mother's soft, limp hand everything fell into place, and she gained a sense of perspective, but then it was all quickly lost when she thought about Kruz and the possibility of being pregnant.

He studied the report on Romy with interest. She was certainly good at keeping secrets. But then so was he. At least this explained why Romy lived where she did, and why she worked all hours—often forgetting to eat, according to his sources. Romy was an only child whose father had died in jail after the man had left her mother a living corpse after his final violent attack. Romy was her mother's sole provider, and had been lucky to come out of that house alive.

No wonder she was a loner. The violence she had witnessed as a child should have put her off men for life, but it certainly went some way to explaining why Romy snatched at physical relief whilst shunning anything deeper. There had been brief relationships, but nothing significant. He guessed her ability to trust hovered around zero. Which made *him* the last partner on earth for her—not that he was thinking of making his relationship with Romy anything more than it already was. His capacity for offering a woman more than physical relief was also zero.

They made a good pair, he reflected, flinging the document aside, but it wasn't a good pairing in the way Romy wanted it to be. He'd seen how she looked at him, and for the first time in his life he wished he had something to offer. But he had learned long ago it was only possible to survive, to achieve and to develop, to do any of those things, if emotion was put aside. It was far better, in his opinion, to feel nothing and move forward than look back, remember and break.

CHAPTER NINE

WHAT A CRAZY day. Up. Down. And all points in between. And it wasn't over yet. The blue and white packet was still sitting where she had left it on the bathroom shelf, and after that she had supper with Kruz to look forward to—and no way of knowing how it would go.

But her meeting with Kruz would be on neutral territory, Romy reminded herself as she soaped down in the tiny shower stall back at the house she shared with the other girls. She would be in public with him. What was the worst that could happen?

The reporter from the scandal sheet might track them down again?

Kruz had seemed to find that amusing. So why hadn't she?

The thought that Kruz meant so much to her and she didn't mean a thing to him hurt. She'd never been in this position before. She'd always been able to control her feelings. She certainly didn't waste them. She cared for her mother, and for her friends, but where men were concerned—there were no men. And now of all the men in the world she'd had to fall for Kruz Acosta, who had never pretended to be anything more than an entertaining companion with special skills—a man who treated sex like food. He needed it. He enjoyed it. But that didn't mean he remembered it beyond the last meal.

While *she* remembered every detail of what he'd said and how he'd said it, how he'd looked at her, how he'd touched her, and how he'd made her feel. It wasn't just sex for the sake of a quick fix for her. It was meaningful. And it had left her defences in tatters.

More fool her.

She was not going slinky tonight, Romy decided in the bedroom. She was going to wear her off-duty uniform of blue jeans, warm sweater and a floppy scarf draped around her neck.

Glancing at her reflection in the mirror, she was satisfied there was nothing provocative about her appearance that Kruz could possibly misinterpret. She looked as if she was going for supper with a friend, which in some ways she was, but first she had something to do—and the sooner she got it over and done with the sooner she would know.

She already knew.

He stood up and felt a thrill as Romy walked into the steak bar. She looked amazing. She always did to him.

'Romy,' he said curtly, hiding those thoughts. 'Good to see you. Please sit down. We've got a lot I'd like to get through tonight, as I'm going to be away for a while. Before I go I need to be sure we're both singing from the same hymn sheet. Red wine or white?'

She looked at him blankly.

'It's a simple question. Red or white?'

'Er—orange juice, please.'

'Whatever you like.' He let it go. Whatever was eating Romy, it couldn't be allowed to get in the way of their discussion tonight. There was a lot he wanted to set straight—like the budgets that she had to work to.

The waiter handed Romy a menu and she began to study it, while he studied her. After reading the report on Romy he understood a lot more about her. He saw the gentleness she hid so well behind the steel, and the capacity for caring above and beyond anything he could ever have imagined. He jerked his gaze away abruptly. He needed this upcoming trip. He needed space from this woman. No one distracted him like Romy, and he had a busy life—polo, the Acosta family interests, *his* business interests. He had no time to spare for a woman.

To make the break he had arranged a tour of his offices worldwide, with a grudge match with Nero Caracas at the end of it to ease any remaining frustration. A battle between his own Band of Brothers polo team and Nero's Assassins would be more than enough to put his life back in focus, he concluded as Romy laid down the menu and stared at him.

'You're going away?' she said.

'Yes,' he confirmed briskly. 'So, if you're ready to order, let's get back to the agenda. We've got a lot to get through tonight.'

The food was good. He ate well.

Romy picked at her meal and seemed preoccupied.

'Do I?' she said when he asked her about it.

She gave a thin smile to the waiter as she accepted a dessert menu. She'd hardly eaten anything.

'Coffee and ice cream?' he suggested when the waiter returned to take their order. 'They make the best of both here. The ice cream's home-made on the premises—fresh cream and raw eggs.'

She blinked. 'Neither, thank you. I think I've got everything I need here,' she said, collecting up her things as if she couldn't wait to go.

'I'll call for the bill.' This was not the ending to the night he had envisaged. Yes, he needed space from Romy—but on his own terms, and to a time-table that suited him.

Business and pleasure don't mix, he reflected wryly as she left the table, heading for the door. When would he ever learn? But, however many miles he put between them, something told him he would never be far enough away from Romy to put her out of his head.

She guessed shock had made her sick this time. It must be shock. It was only ten o'clock in the evening and she had just brought up every scrap of her picked-over meal. Shock at Kruz going away—just like that, without a word of warning. No explanation at all.

And why would he tell her?

She was nothing to him, Romy realised, shivering as she pulled the patchwork throw off her bed to wrap around her shaking shoulders. She was simply a photographer the Acostas had tasked with providing images for their charitable activities—a photographer who had lost her moral compass on a grassy bank, a press coach and in an elevator. *Classy.* So why hadn't she spoken out tonight? Why hadn't she said something to Kruz? There had been more than one opportunity for her to be straight with him.

About this most important of topics she had to be brutally honest with herself first. This wasn't a business matter she could lightly discuss with Kruz, or even a concern she had about working for the charity. This was a child—a life. This was a new life depending on her to make the right call.

Swivelling her laptop round, she studied the shots she'd taken of Kruz. Not one of them showed a flicker of tenderness or humour. He was a hard, driven man. How would he take the news? She couldn't just blurt out, *You're going to be a daddy,* and expect him to cheer. She wouldn't do that, anyway. The fact that she was having Kruz's baby was so big, so life-changing for both of them, so precious and tender to her, she would choose her moment. She only wished things could be different between them—but wishing didn't make things happen. Actions made things happen, and right now she needed to make money more than she ever had.

As she flicked through the saleable images she hadn't yet offered on the open market, she realised there were plenty—which was a relief. And there were also several elevator shots on the net to hold interest. Thank goodness no one had been around for the grassy bank…

She studied the close-ups of her and Kruz as they had been about to get into the elevator and smiled wryly. They made a cool couple.

And now the cool couple were going to have a baby.

He ground his jaw with impatience as his sister-in-law gave him a hard time. He'd stopped over at the *estancia* in Argentina and appreciated the space. He was no closer to sorting out his feelings for Romy and would have liked more time to do so. The irony of having so many forceful women in one family had not escaped him. Glancing at his wristwatch, he toyed with the idea of inventing a meeting so he had an excuse to end the call.

'Are you still there, Kruz?'

'I'm still here, Grace,' he confirmed. 'But I have pressing engagements.'

'Well, make sure you fit Romy into them,' Grace insisted, in no way deterred.

'I might have to go away again. Can't you liaise with her?'

'And choose which photographs we want to use?'

He swore beneath his breath. 'Forgive me, Grace, but you're in London and I'm not right now.'

'I'll liaise with Romy on one condition,' his wily sister-in-law agreed.

'And that is?' he demanded.

'You see her again and sort things out between you.'

'Can't do that, Grace. Thousands of miles between us,' he pointed out.

'So send for her,' Grace said, as if this were normal practise rather than dramatic in the extreme. 'I've heard the way your voice changes when you talk about Romy. What are you afraid of, Kruz?'

'Me? Afraid?' he scoffed.

'Even men like Nacho have hang-ups—before he met me, that is,' his sister-in-law amended with warmth and humour in her voice. 'Don't let your hang-ups spoil things for you, Kruz. At least speak to her. Promise me?'

He hummed and hawed, and then agreed. What was all the rush about? Romy could just as easily have got in touch with *him*.

Maybe there were reasons?

What reasons?

Maybe her mother was ill. If that were the case he would be concerned for her. Romy's care of her mother was exemplary, according to his investigations. He hadn't thought to ask about her. Grace was right. The least he could do was call Romy and find out.

'Kruz?'

She had to stop hugging the phone as if it were a lifeline. She had to stop analysing every microsecond of his all too impersonal greeting. She had to accept the fact that Kruz was calling her because he wanted to meet for an update on the progress she was making with the banners, posters and flyers for the upcoming charity polo match. She had to get real so she could do the job she was being paid to do. This might all be extra to her work for *ROCK!*, but she had no intention of short-changing either the magazine or the Acosta family. She believed in the Acosta charity and she was going to give it everything she'd got.

'Of course we can meet—no, there's no reason why not.' Except her heart was acting up. It was one thing being on the other end of a phone to Kruz, but being in the same room as him, which was what he seemed to be suggesting…

'Can you pack and come tomorrow?'

'Come where?'

'To the *estancia*, of course.'

Shock coursed through her. 'You're calling me from Argentina? When you said you were going away I had no idea you were going to Argentina.'

'Does that make a difference?' Kruz demanded. 'I'll send the jet—what's your problem, Romy?'

You. 'Kruz, I work—'

'You gave me to understand you were almost self-employed now and could please yourself.'

'Sort of…'

'Sort of?' he queried. 'Are you or aren't you? If your boss at *ROCK!* acts up, check to see if you've got some holiday owing. Just take time off and get out here.'

So speaks the wealthy man, Romy thought, flicking quickly through the diary in her mind.

'Romy?' Kruz prompted impatiently. 'Is there a reason why you can't come here tomorrow?'

Pregnant women were allowed to travel, weren't they? 'No,' she said bluntly. 'There's no reason why I can't travel.'

'See you tomorrow.'

She stared at the dead receiver in her hand. To be in Argentina tomorrow might sound perfectly normal to a jet-setting polo player, but even to a newshound like Romy it sounded reckless. And it gave her no chance to prepare her story, she realised, staring at an e-mail from Kruz containing her travel details that had already flashed up on her screen. Not that she needed a story, Romy reassured herself as she scanned the arrangements he had made for her to board his private jet. She would just tell him the truth. Yes, they had used protection, but a condom must have failed.

Sitting back, she tried to regret what had happened—was happening—and couldn't. How could she regret the tiny life inside her? Mapping her stomach with her hands, she realised that all she regretted was wasting her feelings on Kruz—a man who walked in and out of her life at will, leaving her as isolated as she had ever been.

Like countless other women who had to make do and mend with what life had dealt them.

She would just have to make do and mend *this,* Romy concluded.

Having lost patience with her maudlin meanderings, she tapped out a brief and businesslike reply to Kruz's e-mail. She didn't have to sleep with him. She could resist him. It was just a matter of being sensible. The main thing was to do a good job for the charity and leave Argentina with her pride intact. She would find the right moment to tell Kruz about the baby. They were two civilised human beings and would work it out. She would be on that flight tomorrow, she would finish the job Grace had given her, and then she would decide the way ahead as she always had. Just as she had protected her mother for as long as she could, she would now protect her unborn child. And if that meant facing up to Kruz and telling him how things were going to be from here on in, then that was exactly what she was going to do.

The flight was uneventful. In fact it was soothing compared to what awaited her, Romy suspected, resting back. She tried to soothe herself further by reflecting on all the good things that had happened. She had worked hard to establish herself as a freelance alongside her magazine work, and her photographs had featured in some of the glossies as the product of someone who was more than just a member of the paparazzi. One of her staunchest supporters had turned out to be Ronald, who had made her cry—baby-head, she realised—when he'd said that he believed in her talent and expected her to go far.

Well, she was going far now, Romy reflected, blowing out a long, thoughtful breath as she considered the journey ahead of her. And as to what lay on the other side of that flight… She could only guess that this pampering on a private jet, with freshly squeezed orange juice on tap, designer food and cream kidskin seats large enough to curl up and snooze on, would be the calm before the storm.

Tracing the curve of her stomach protectively as the jet circled before swooping down to land on the Acostas' private landing strip, Romy felt her heart bump when she spotted the *hacienda*, surrounded by endless miles of green with the mountains beyond. The scenery in this part of Argentina was ravishingly beautiful, and the *hacienda* nestled in its grassy frame in such a favoured spot. Bathed in sunlight, the old stone had turned a glinting shade of molten bronze. The pampas was only a wilderness to those who couldn't see the beauty in miles of fertile grass, or to those with no appreciation of the varied wildlife and birdlife that called this place home.

She craned her neck to catch a glimpse of thundering waterfalls crashing down from the Andes and lazy rivers moving like glittering ribbons towards the sea. It made her smile to see how many horses were grazing on the pampas, and her heart thrilled at the sight of the *gauchos* working amongst the herds of Criolla ponies. They were no more than tiny dots as the jet came in to land, and the ponies soon scattered when they heard the engines. She wondered if Kruz was among the riders chasing them…

She was pleased to be back.

The realisation surprised her. She must be mad, knowing what lay ahead of her, Romy concluded as the seatbelt sign flashed on, but against all that was logical this felt like coming home.

After flying overnight, she stepped out of the plane into dry heat on a beautifully sunny day. The sky was bright blue and decorated with clouds that looked like cotton wool balls. The scent of grass and blossom was strong, though it was spoiled a little by the tang of aviation fuel. Slipping on her sunglasses, Romy determined that nothing was going to spoil her enjoyment of this visit. This was a fabulous country, with fabulous people, and she couldn't wait to start taking pictures.

There was a *gaucho* standing next to a powerful-looking truck, which he had parked on the grass verge to one side of the airstrip, but there was no sign of Kruz. She should be relieved about that. It would give her time to settle in, Romy reasoned as the weather-beaten *gaucho* came to greet her. He introduced himself as Alessandro, explaining that Kruz was away from the *estancia.*

Would Kruz be away for a long time? Romy wondered, not liking to ask. Anyway, it was good to know that he wasn't crowding her. *But she missed him.*

Hard luck, she thought wryly as the elderly ranch-hand pointed away across the vast sea of grass. Ah, so Kruz wasn't *staying* away—he was out riding on the pampas. Her heart lifted, but then she reasoned that he must have seen the jet coming into land, yet wouldn't put himself out to come and meet her.

That was good, she told herself firmly. No pressure.

No caring, either.

She stood back as Alessandro took charge of her luggage. 'You mustn't lift anything in your condition,' he said.

She blushed furiously. Was her pregnancy so obvious? She was wearing jeans with a broad elastic panel at the front, and over the top of them a baggy T-shirt *and* a fashionable waterfall cardigan, which the salesgirl had assured Romy was guaranteed to hide her small bump. *Wrong,* Romy concluded. If Alessandro could tell she was pregnant, there would be no hiding the fact from Kruz.

Perhaps people were just super tuned-in to nature out here on the pampas, she reflected as Alessandro opened the door of the cab for her and stood back. Climbing in, she sat down. Breathing a sigh of relief as the elderly *gaucho* closed the door, she took a moment to compose herself. The interlude was short-lived. As she turned to smile at Alessandro when he climbed into the driver's seat at her side her heart lurched at the sight of Kruz, riding flat out across the pampas towards them.

It struck her as odd that she had never seen such

a renowned horseman riding before, but then they actually knew very little about what made each other tick. At this distance Kruz was little more than a dark shadow, moving like an arrow towards her, but it was as if her heart had told her eyes to look for him and here he was. Her spirits rose as she watched him draw closer. Surely a man who was so at one with nature would be thrilled at the prospect of bringing new life into the world?

So why did she feel so apprehensive?

She should be apprehensive, Romy concluded, nursing her bump. This baby meant everything to her, and she would fight for the right to keep her child with her whatever a powerful man like Kruz Acosta had to say about it, but she couldn't imagine he would make things easy for her.

'And now we wait,' Alessandro said, settling back as he turned off the engine.

He had promised himself he would stay out of Romy's way until the evening, giving her a chance to settle in. He wanted her know she wasn't at the top of his list of priorities for the day. Which clearly explained why he was riding across the pampas now, with his sexual radar on red alert. No one excited him like Romy. No one intrigued him as she did. Life was boring without her, he had discovered. Other women were pallid and far too eager to please him. He had missed Romy's fiery temperament—amongst other things—and the way she never shirked from taking him on.

Reining in, he allowed his stallion to approach the truck at a high-stepping trot. Halting, he dismounted. His senses were already inflamed at the sight of her, sitting in the truck. The moment the jet had appeared in the sky, circling overhead, he had turned for home, knowing an end to his physical ache was at last in sight.

Striding over to the truck, he forgot all his good intentions about remaining cool and threw open the passenger door. 'Romy—'

'Kruz,' she said, seeming to shrink back in her seat.

This was not the reception he had anticipated. And why was she hugging herself like that? 'I'll see you at the house,' he said, speaking to Alessandro. Slamming the passenger door, he slapped the side of the truck and went back to his horse.

He could wait, he told himself as he cantered back to the *hacienda.* The house was empty. He had given the housekeepers the day off. He wanted the space to do with as he liked—to do with Romy as he liked.

He stabled the horse before returning to the house. He found Romy in the kitchen, where Alessandro was pouring her a cold drink. The old man was fussing over her like a mother hen. He had never seen that before.

'Romy is perfectly capable of looking after herself,' he said, tugging off his bandana to wipe the dust of riding from his face.

As Alessandro grunted he took another look at Romy, who was seated at the kitchen table, side on to him. She seemed small—smaller than he remembered—but her jaw was set as if for battle. So be it. After his shower he would be more than happy to accommodate her.

'Journey uncomfortable?' he guessed, knowing how restless *he* became if he was caged in for too enough.

'Not at all,' she said coolly, still without turning to face him.

'I'm going to take a shower,' he said, thinking her rude, 'and then I'll brief you on the photographs Grace wants you to take.'

'Romy needs to rest first.'

He stared at Alessandro. The old man had

never spoken to him like that before—had never danced attendance on a woman in all the years he'd known him.

'I'd love a shower too,' Romy said, springing up.

'Fine. See you later at supper,' he snapped, mouthing, *What?* as Alessandro gave him a sharp look. And then, to his amazement, his elderly second-in-command took hold of Romy's bags and led the way out of the kitchen and up the stairs. 'Maria has prepared the front room overlooking the corral,' he yelled after them.

Neither one of them replied.

'What the hell is going on?' he demanded, the moment Alessandro returned.

'You had better ask Señorita Winner that question,' his old *compadre* told him, heading for the door.

'You know—*you* tell me.'

The old *gaucho* answered this with a shrug as he went out through the door.

She shouldn't have left the door to her bedroom open, Romy realised, stirring sleepily. It wasn't wide open, but it was open enough to appear inviting. She had meant to close it, but had fallen asleep on the bed after her shower. Jet-lag and baby-body, she supposed. She needed a siesta these days.

She needed more than that. Holly Acosta had warned her about this phase of pregnancy…hormones running riot…the 'sex-mad phase', Holly had dubbed it, Romy remembered, clutching her pillow as she tried to forget.

Maybe she had left the door open on purpose, Romy concluded as Kruz, still damp from his shower and clad only in a towel, strolled into the room. Maybe she had deluded herself that they could have one last hurrah and then she would tell him. But she had not expected this surge of feeling as her body warmed in greeting. She had not expected Kruz simply to walk into the room expecting sex, or that she would feel quite so ready to oblige him. What had happened to all those bold resolutions about remaining chaste until she had told him about the baby?

She didn't speak. She didn't need to. She just made room for him on the bed. She was well covered in a sheet—which was more than could be said for Kruz. Her throat felt as if it was tied in knots when the towel he had tucked around his waist dropped to the floor.

Settling down on the bed, he kept some tantalising, teasing space between them, while she covered the evidence of her pregnancy with the bedding. Resting on one elbow, he stared into her eyes, and at that moment she would have done anything for him.

Anything.

He toyed with her hair, teasing her with the delay, while she turned her face to brush her lips along his hand. Remembered pleasure was a strong driver—the strongest. She wanted him. She couldn't hide it. She didn't want to. Her body had more needs now than ever before.

'You've put on weight, Romy,' he murmured, suckling on her breasts. 'Don't,' he complained when she tried to stop him, nervous that Kruz might take his interest lower. 'The added weight suits you. I meant it as a compliment.'

Kruz was in a hurry—which was good. She wasn't even sure he noticed the distinct swell of her belly on his way to his destination. She was all sensation…all want and need…with only one goal in mind. She wasn't even sure whether Kruz pressed her legs apart or whether she opened them for him. She only knew that she was resting back on a soft bank of pillows while he held her thighs apart. And when he bent to his task he was so good… Lacing her fingers through his hair, she decided he was a master of seduction—not that she needed much persuasion. He was so skilled. His tongue… His hands… His understanding of her needs and responses was so acute, so knowing, so—

He paused to protect them both. She thought about telling him then, but it would have been ridiculous, and anyway the hunger was raging inside her now. She wanted him. He wanted her. It was a need so deep, so primal, that nothing could stop them now. She groaned as he sank deep. This was so good—it felt so right. Kruz set up a rhythm, which she followed immediately, mirroring his moves, but with more fire, more need, more urgency.

'That's right—come for me, baby.'

She didn't need any encouragement and fell blindly, violently, triumphantly, with screaming, keening, groaning relief. And Kruz kissed her all the while, his strong arms holding her safe as she tumbled fast and hard. His firm mouth softened to whisper of encouragement as he made sure she enjoyed every second of it before he even thought of taking his own pleasure. When he did it raised her erotic temperature again. Just seeing him enjoying her was enough to do that. The pleasure was never-ending, and as wave after wave after wave of almost unbearable sensation washed over her it was Kruz who kept her safe to abandon herself to this unbelievable union of body and soul.

Sensation and emotion combined had to be the most powerful force any human being could tap into, she thought, still groaning with pleasure as she slowly came down. Clinging to Kruz, nestling against his powerful body, left her experiencing feelings so strong, so beautiful, she could hardly believe they were real. She smiled as she kissed him, moving to his shoulders, to his chest, to his neck. After such brutally enjoyable pleasure this was a rare tender moment to treasure. A life-changing moment, she thought as Kruz continued to tend to her needs.

'Romy?'

She sensed the change in him immediately.

'What?' she murmured. But she already knew, and felt a chill run through her when Kruz lifted his head. The look in his eyes told her everything she needed to know. They were black with fury.

'When were you planning to tell me?' he said.

CHAPTER TEN

SHE HAD EVERY reason to hate the condemnation in Kruz's black stare. She loved her child already. Yes, cool, hard, emotionless Romy Winner had turned into a soft, blobby cocoon overnight. But still with warrior tendencies, she realised as she wriggled up the bed. If he wanted a fight she was ready.

Two of them had made this baby, and their child was a precious life she was prepared to defend with her own life. She surprised herself with how immediately her priorities could change. She wasn't alone any more. It would never be just about her again. She was a mother. In hindsight, she had been mad to think Kruz wouldn't notice she was pregnant. The swell of her belly was small, but growing bigger every day, as if the child they'd made together was as proud and strong as its parents.

She was happy to admit her guilt. She *was* guilty of backing away at the first hurdle and not telling Kruz right away. Allowing him to find out like this way was a terrible thing to do. It had been seeing him and forgetting everything in the moment…

'Are you ashamed of the baby?' he said. Springing into a sitting position, he loomed over her, a terrifying powerhouse of suppressed outrage.

Before her mouth had a chance to form words he detached himself from her arms and swung off the bed. Striding across the room, he closed the door on the bathroom and she heard him run the shower. He was shocked and she was frantic. Her mind refused to cooperate and tell her what to do next. She'd really messed up, and now she would be caught in the whirlwind.

He'd been away, she reasoned as she listened to Kruz in the bathroom.

There was the telephone. There was the internet. There was always a way of getting hold of someone. She just hadn't tried.

They didn't have that kind of relationship.

What *did* they have?

She hadn't been prepared for pregnancy because she'd had no reason to suppose she was in line to make a baby.

You had sex, didn't you?

The brutal truth. They'd had sex vigorously and often. Two casual acquaintances coming together for no other purpose than mindless pleasure until the charity gave them a common aim. They had enjoyed each other greedily and thoughtlessly, with only a mind to that pleasure. Maybe Kruz thought she was going to hit him with a paternity suit. Holly had explained to her once that the Acostas were so close and kept the world at bay because massive wealth brought massive risk. They found it hard to trust anyone, because most people had an agenda.

'Kruz—'

She flinched as the door opened and quickly wrapped the sheet around her. Yet again she was wasting time thinking when she should be doing. She should have got dressed and then she could face him as an equal, rather than having to try and tug the sheet from the bottom of the bed so she could retain what little dignity was left to her.

'No— Wait—' Kruz had pulled on his jeans and top and was heading for the door. Somehow she managed to yank the sheet free and stumble towards him. 'Please—I realise this must be a terrible shock for you, but we really have to talk.'

'A *shock*?' he said icily, staring down at her hand on his arm.

She recoiled from him. Suddenly Kruz's arm felt like the arm of a stranger, while she felt like a hysterical woman accosting someone she didn't know.

She tried again—calmly this time. 'Please… We must talk.'

'*Now* we need to talk?' he said mildly.

She had hurt him. But it was so much more than that. Kruz was shocked—felled by the enormity of what she'd been keeping from him. His brain was scrambled. She could tell he needed space. 'Please…' she said gently, trying to appeal to a softer side of him.

'No,' he rapped, pulling away. 'No,' he said again, shaking her off. 'You can't just hit me with this and expect me to produce a ready-made plan.'

She didn't expect anything from him, but she couldn't just let him turn his back and walk away. Moving in front of him, she leaned against the door. 'Well, that's up to you. I can't stop you leaving.'

Kruz's icy expression assured her this was the case.

'I don't want anything from you,' she said, trying to subdue the tremor in her voice. 'I know a baby isn't a good enough reason for us to stay together in some sort of mismatched hook-up—'

'I wasn't aware we were *planning* to hook up,' he cut in with a quiet intensity that really scared her.

She moved away from the door. What else could she do? She felt dead inside. She should have told him long before now, but Kruz's reaction to finding out had completely thrown her. They were both responsible for a new life, but he seemed determined to shut that fact out. She would have to speak to him through lawyers when she got back to England, and somehow she would have to complete her work for the charity while she was here in Argentina—with or without Kruz Acosta's co-operation.

Needing isolation and time to think, she hurried to the bathroom and shut the door—just in time to hear Kruz close the outer door behind him.

No! No! No! This could not be happening. He micro-managed every aspect of his life to make sure something unexpected could never blindside him. So how? Why now?

Why ever?

With no answers that made sense he stalked in the direction of the stables.

A child? *His* child? His baby?

His mind was filled with wonder. But having a child was unthinkable for him. It was a gift he could never accept. He couldn't share his nightmares—not with Romy and much less with an innocent child. Who knew what he was capable of?

In the army they'd said there were three kinds of soldiers: those who were trained to kill and couldn't bring themselves to do it; those who were trained to kill and enjoyed it; and those who were trained to kill and did so because it was their duty. They did that duty on auto-pilot, without allowing themselves to think. He had always thought that last type of soldier was the most dangerous and the most damned, because they had only one choice. That was to live their lives after the army refusing to remember, refusing to feel, refusing to face what they'd done. He was that soldier.

There was only one option open to him. He would allow Romy to complete her work here and then he would send her back. He would provide for the child and for Romy. He would write a detailed list of everything she must have and then he would hand that list over to his PA.

From the first night he had woken screaming he had vowed never to inflict his nightmares on anyone. The things he'd witnessed—the things he'd done—none of that was remotely acceptable to him in the clear light of peace. He was damned for all time. He had been claimed by the dark side, which was the best reason he knew to keep himself aloof from decent people. He could not allow himself to feel anything for Romy, or for their child—not unless he wanted to damage them both. The best, the *only* thing he could do to protect them was to step out of Romy's life.

The mechanical function of tacking up his stallion soothed him and set his decision in stone. The great beast and he would share the wild danger of a gallop across the pampas. They both needed to break free, to run, to seize life without thought or plan for what might lay ahead.

He rode as far as the river and then kicked his booted feet out of the stirrups. Throwing the reins over the stallion's head, he dismounted. All he could see wherever he looked was Romy, and all he could hear was her voice. The apprehension and concern in her eyes was as clear now as if she were standing in front of him. She was frightened she wasn't ready for a baby. *He* would never be ready. His family, who tolerated him, knew more than most people did about him, was enough.

Tipping his face to the sun, he realised this was the first time he had ever backed away from any challenge. He normally met each one head-on. But this tiny unborn child had stopped him dead in his tracks without a road map or a solution. He didn't question the fact that the child was his. The little he knew about Romy gave him absolute trust in what she told him. Whistling up his stallion, he sprang into the saddle and turned for home.

She packed her case and then left the *hacienda* to take the shots she needed for Grace. She knelt and waited silently on the riverbank for what felt like hours for the flocks of birds feeding close by to wheel and soar like ribbons in the sky. She could only marvel at their beauty. It gave her a sort of peace which she hoped would transmit to the baby.

There was no perfect world, Romy concluded. There were only perfect moments like this, populated by imperfect human beings like herself and Kruz, who were just trying to make the best of their journey through life. It was no use wishing she could share this majestic beauty with their child. She would never be invited to Argentina. She might never see the snow-capped Andes and smell the lush green grass again, but her photographs would remind her of the wild land the father of her child inhabited.

Hoisting her kitbag onto her shoulder, she started back to the *hacienda.* She had barely reached the courtyard when she saw Kruz riding towards her. She loved him. It was that simple. Turning in the opposite direction, she kept her head down and walked rapidly away. She wasn't ready for this.

Would she ever be ready for this?

She stopped and changed direction, following him round to the stables, where she found him dismounting. Without acknowledging her presence, he led the stallion past her.

He had been calm, Kruz realised. The ride had calmed him. But seeing Romy again had shaken him to the core. He wanted her—and more than in just a sexual way. He wanted to put his arm around her and share her worries and excitement, to see where the road took them. But Romy's life wasn't an experiment he could dip into. He might not be able to shake the feeling that they belonged together, but the only safe thing for Romy was to put her out of his life.

'Kruz...'

He lifted the saddle onto the fence and started taking his horse's bridle off.

'How could I go to bed with you, knowing I was pregnant,' she said, 'and yet say nothing?'

Her voice, soft and shaking slightly, touched him somewhere deep. He turned to find her frowning. 'Don't beat yourself up about it,' he said without expression. 'What's done is done.'

'And cannot be undone,' she whispered as the stallion turned a reproachful gaze on him. 'Not that I...'

As her voice faded his gaze slipped to her stomach, where the swell of pregnancy was quite evident on her slender frame. In his rutting madness he had chosen not to see it. He felt guilty now.

The stallion whickered and nuzzled him imperatively, searching for a mint. He found one and the stallion took it delicately from his hand. Clicking his tongue, he tried to move the great beast on, but his horse wasn't going anywhere. As of this moment, one small girl with her chin jutting out had half a ton of horseflesh bending to her will.

'He needs feeding,' he said without emotion as he waited for Romy to move aside.

'I have needs too,' she said, but her soft heart

put the horse first, and so she moved, allowing him to lead the stallion to his stable.

'Are you going to make me wait as I made you wait?' she said as she watched him settle the horse.

He was checking its hooves, but lifted his head to look at her.

'Okay, I get it—you're not so petty,' she said. 'But we do have to talk some time, Kruz.'

He returned to what he'd been doing without a word.

She waited by the stable door, watching Kruz looking after his big Criolla. What she wouldn't do for a moment of that studied care…

So what are you standing around for?

'Can I—'

'Can you what?' he said, still keenly aware of her, apparently, even though he had his back turned to her.

'Can I come in and give him a mint?' she asked.

The few seconds' pause felt like an hour.

'Hold your hand out flat,' he said at last.

She took the mint, careful not to touch Kruz more than she had to. Her heart thundered as he stood back. There was nothing between her and the enormous horse that just stood motionless, staring at her unblinking. Her throat felt dry, and her heart was thundering, but then, as if a decision had been made, the stallion's head dropped and its velvet lips tickled her palm. Surprised by its gentleness, she stroked its muzzle. The prickle of whiskers made her smile, and she went on to stroke its sleek, shiny neck. The warmth was soothing, and the contact between them made her relax.

'You're a beauty, aren't you?' she whispered.

Conscious that Kruz was watching her, she stood back and let him take over. He made the horse quiver with pleasure as he groomed it with long, rhythmical strokes. She envied the connection between them.

She waited until Kruz straightened up before saying, 'Can we talk?'

'You're *asking* me?' he said, brushing past her to put the tack away.

His voice was still cold, and she felt as if she had blinked and opened her eyes to find the last few minutes had been a dream and now it was back to harsh reality. But her pregnancy wasn't something she could put to one side. Now it was out in the open she had to see this through, and so she followed Kruz to the tackroom and closed the door behind them. He swung around and, leaning back against the wall, with a face that was set and unfriendly, waited for her to speak.

'I would have told you sooner, if—'

'If you hadn't been climbing all over me?' he suggested in a chilly tone.

She lifted her chin. 'I didn't notice you taking a back seat at the time.'

'So when were you going to tell me that you're pregnant?'

'You seem more concerned about my faults than our child. There were so many times when I wanted to tell you—'

'But your needs were just too great?' he said, regarding her with a face she didn't recognize—a face that was closed off to any possibility of understanding between them.

'I remember my need being as great as yours,' she said. 'Anyway, I don't want to argue with you about this, Kruz. I want to discuss what has happened while we've got the chance. For God's sake, Kruz—what's wrong with you? Anyone would think you were trying to drive me away—taking *your* child with me.'

'You'll stay here until I tell you to go,' he said, snatching hold of her arm.

'Let me go,' she cried furiously.

'There's nowhere for you to go—there's just thousands of miles of nothing out there .'

'I'm leaving Argentina.'

'And then what?' he demanded.

'And then I'll make a life for me and our baby—the baby you don't care to acknowledge.'

Was that a flicker of something human in his eyes? Had she got through to him at last? His grip had relaxed on her arm.

It was a feint of which any fighter would be proud. Kruz was still hot from his ride, still unshaven and dusty, and when his mouth crashed down on hers she knew she should fight him off, but instead she battled to keep him close.

'It's that easy, isn't it?' he snarled, thrusting her away. '*You're* that easy.'

She confronted him angrily. 'You shouldn't have kissed me. You shouldn't have doubted me.' She paused a beat and shook her head. 'And I should have told you sooner than I did.'

'You kissed me back,' he said, turning for the door.

Yes, she had. And she would kiss him again, Romy realised as heat, hope and longing surged inside her. What did that make her? Deluded?

'Where are you going?' she demanded as Kruz opened the door. 'We have to talk this through.'

'I'm done talking, Romy.'

Moving ahead of him, she pressed herself against the door like a barricade. 'I'm just as scared as you are,' she admitted.

'You? Scared?' he said.

'We didn't plan this, Kruz, but however unready we are to become parents, we're no different than thousands of other couples. Whether we're ready or not, in less than a year our lives will be turned upside down by a baby.'

'*Your* life, maybe,' he snapped.

His eyes were so cold…his face was so closed off to her. 'Kruz—'

'I need time to think,' he said sharply.

'No,' she fired back. 'We need to talk about this now.'

Pressing against the door, she refused to move. She was going to say what she had to say and then she would leave Argentina for good.

'There's nothing for you to think about,' she said firmly. 'The baby and I don't need you—and we certainly don't want your money. When I get back to England I'll speak to my lawyers and make sure you have fair access to our child. But that's it. Don't think for one moment that I can't provide everything a baby needs and more.'

The blood drained from his face. He was furious, but Kruz contained his feelings, which made him seem all the more threatening. Her hands flew to cradle her stomach. She was right to feel apprehensive. She had no lawyers, while Kruz probably had a whole team waiting on him. And she had to find somewhere decent to live. For all her brave talk she was in no way ready to welcome a baby into the world yet.

'Do you mind?' he said coldly, staring behind her at the door.

Standing aside, she let him go. What else could she do? She had no more cards to play. If Kruz didn't want any part in the life of his child then she wasn't going to beg. She couldn't pretend it didn't hurt to think he could just brush her off like this. She understood that he guarded his privacy fiercely, but the birth of a baby was a life-changing event for both of them.

But this was day one of her life as a single mother, so she had to get over it. With the lease about to run out on her rented house, she couldn't afford to be downhearted. Her priority was to find somewhere to live. So what if she couldn't afford the area she loved? She maybe never would be able to afford it. She could still find somewhere safe and respectable. She would work all hours to make that happen.

She waited in the shadowy warmth of the tack-room, breathing in the pleasant aroma of saddle soap and horse until she was sure Kruz was long gone, and then she walked out into the brilliant sunlight of the yard to find the big stallion still watching her, with his head resting over the stable door.

'I've made a mess of everything, haven't I?' she said, tugging gently on his forelock. She smoothed the palm of her hand along his pricked ears until he tossed his head and trumpeted. She imagined he was part of the herd who were still out there somewhere on the pampas.

Biting back tears, she glanced towards the *hacienda.* Kruz would be showering down after his ride, she guessed. He would be washing away the dust of the day and, judging by his reaction to her news, he would be washing away all thoughts of Romy and their baby along with it.

CHAPTER ELEVEN

HE'D SLEPT ON it, and now he knew what he was going to do. Towelling down after his shower the next morning, he could see things clearly. Romy's news had stunned him. How could it not, considering his care where contraception was concerned? It shouldn't have happened, but now it *had* happened he would take control.

Tugging on a fresh pair of jeans and a clean top, he raked his thick dark hair into some semblance of order. The future of this baby was non-negotiable. He would not be a part-time parent. He knew the effect it had had on him when his parents had been killed. It wasn't Nacho's fault that Kruz had run wild, but he did believe that a child needed both its parents. Romy could have her freedom, and they would live independent lives, but she must move here to Argentina.

The internet was amazing, Romy concluded as she settled into her narrow seat on the commercial jet. She'd used it to sell the images she didn't need to keep back for the Acosta charity, or for Grace, and had then used the proceeds to book her flight home. Alessandro had insisted on driving her to the airport and carrying her luggage as far as the check-in desk. He was a lovely man, sensitive enough not to ply her with questions. She didn't care that she wasn't flying home in style in a private jet. The staff in the cabin were polite and helpful, and before long she would be back in London on the brink of a new life.

As soon as she had taken the last shot she needed and made plans to leave Argentina she had known there would be no going back. This was the right decision—for her and for her child. She didn't need a man to help her raise her baby. She was strong and self-sufficient, she had her health, and she could earn enough money for both their needs. One thing was certain—she didn't need Kruz Acosta.

Really?

She had panicked to begin with, Romy reasoned as the big, wide jet soared high into the air. But making the break from Kruz was just what she needed. It was a major kick-start to the rest of her life. He was the one losing out if he didn't want to be part of this. She was fine with it. She could live man-free, as she had before.

Reaching for the headphones, she scrolled through the channels until she found a film she could lose herself in—or at least attempt to tune out the voice of her inner critic, who said that by turning her back on Kruz and leaving Argentina without telling him Romy had done the wrong thing yet again.

'Señorita Romily has gone,' Alessandro told him.

'What the hell do you mean, she's gone?' he demanded as Alessandro got out of the pick-up truck.

'She flew back to England this morning,' his elderly friend informed him, stretching his limbs. 'I just got back from taking her to the airport.' Alessandro levelled a challenging look at Kruz that said, *And what are you going to do about it?*

They didn't make men tame and accepting on the pampas, Kruz reflected as he met Alessandro's unflinching stare. 'She went back to England to *that* house?' he snarled, beside himself with fury.

Alessandro's shoulders lifted in a shrug. 'I don't know where she was going, exactly. "Back home" is all she told me. She talked of a lovely area by a canal in London while we were driving to the airport. She said I would love it, and that even so close to a city like London it was possible to find quiet places that are both picturesque and safe. She told me about the waterside cafés and the English pubs, and said there are plenty of places to push a pram.'

'She was stringing you along,' Kruz snapped impatiently. 'She guessed you wouldn't take her to the airport if you knew the truth about where she lived.' And when Alessandro flinched with concern at the thought that he might have led Romy into danger, Kruz lashed out with words as an injured wolf might howl in the night as the only way to express its agony. 'She lives in a terrible place, Alessandro. Even with all the operatives in my employ I cannot guarantee her safety there.'

'Then follow her,' his wise old friend advised.

Kruz shook his head, stubborn pride still ruling him. Romy was having his baby and she had left Argentina without telling him. Twisting the knife in the wound, his old friend Alessandro had helped Romy on her way. 'Why?' he demanded tensely, turning a blazing stare on his old friend's face. 'Why have you chosen to help her?

'I think you know why,' Alessandro said mildly.

'You think I'd hurt her?' he exclaimed with affront. 'You think because of everything that happened in the army I'm a danger to her?'

Alessandro looked sad. 'No,' he said quietly. 'You are the only one who thinks that. I helped Señorita Winner to go home because she's pregnant and because she needs peace now—not the anger you feel for yourself. Until you can accept that you have every right to a future, you have nothing to offer her. You have hurt her,' Alessandro said bluntly, 'and now it's up to you to make the first approach.'

'She didn't tell me she was pregnant.'

'Did you give her a chance?'

'I didn't know—'

'You didn't want to know. *I* knew,' Alessandro said quietly.

Kruz stood rigid for a moment, and then followed Alessandro to the stable, where he found the old *gaucho* preparing to groom his favourite horse.

'You drove her to the airport,' he said, still tight with indignation. '*Dios*, Alessandro, what were you thinking?'

When Alessandro didn't speak he was forced

to master himself, and when he had done so he had to admit Alessandro was right. His old friend had done nothing wrong. This entire mess was of Kruz and Romy's making—mostly his.

'So she didn't tell you she was leaving?' Alessandro commented, still sweeping the grooming brush down his horse's side in rhythmical strokes.

'No, she didn't tell me,' he admitted. And why would she? He hadn't listened. He hadn't seen this coming. So the mother of his child had just upped and left the country without a word.

What now?

She wasn't *all* to blame for this, but one thing was certain. Romy might have pleased herself in the past, but now she was expecting his baby she would listen to *him*.

'No,' Romy said flatly, preparing to cut the line having refused Kruz's offer of financial help. 'And please don't call me at the office again.'

'Where the hell else am I supposed to call you?' he thundered. 'You never pick up. You can't keep on avoiding me, Romy.'

The irony of it, she thought. She knew they should meet to discuss the baby, but things had happened since she'd come back to England—

big things—and now she was sick with loss and just didn't think she could take any more. Her mother had died. There—it was said…thought… so it must be true. It *was* true. She had arrived at the nursing home too late to see her mother alive. Somehow she had always imagined she would be there when the time came. The fact that her mother had slipped away peacefully in her sleep had done nothing to help ease her sense of guilt.

And none of it was Kruz's fault.

'Okay, let's meet,' she agreed, choosing an anonymous café on an anonymous road in the heart of the bustling metropolis. The café was close by both their offices, and with Kruz back in London the last thing she wanted was for them to bump into each other on the street.

'I could meet you at the house,' he said, 'if that's easier for you.'

There *was* no house. The lease was up. The house had gone. She was sleeping on a girlfriend's sofa until she found somewhere permanent.

'This can't be rushed, Romy,' Kruz remarked as she was thinking things through. 'Five minutes of your time in a crowded café won't be enough.'

He was right. In a few months' time they would be parents. It still seemed incredible. It made her heart ache to be talking to him about such a monumental event that should affect them both equally while knowing they would never be closer than this. 'I'll make it a long lunch,' she offered.

She guessed she must have sounded patronising as Kruz repeated the address and cut the line.

Without him asking her to do so she had taken a DNA test to prove that the baby was his. She had had to do it before a solicitor would represent her. Putting everything in the hands of a stranger had felt like the final nail in the coffin containing their non-existent relationship. This meeting in the café with Kruz to sort out some of the practical aspects of parental custody was not much more.

Not much more? Did she really believe that? Just catching sight of Kruz through the steamed-up windows of the chic city centre café was enough to make her heart lurch. He'd already got a table, and was sipping coffee as he read the financial papers. He'd moved on with his life and so had she, Romy persuaded herself. She had suffered the loss of her mother while he'd been away—a fact she'd shared with no one. Kruz, of all people, would probably understand, but she wouldn't burden him with it. They weren't part of each other's lives in that way.

'Hey,' she murmured, dropping her bag on the seat by his side. 'Watch that for me, will you, while I get something to drink?'

Putting the newspaper down, he stood up. He stared at her without speaking for a moment. 'Let me,' he said at last, brushing past.

'No caffeine,' she called. 'And just an almond croissant, please.'

Just an almond croissant? Was that a craving or lack of funds?

He should have prepared himself for seeing Romy so obviously pregnant. He knew how far on she was, after all. He should have realised that the swell of her stomach would be more pronounced because she was so slender. If he had been prepared he might be able to control this feeling of being a frustrated protector who had effectively robbed himself of the chance to do his job.

Taking Romy's sparse lunch back to the table, he sat down. She played with the food and toyed with mint tea. *I hope you're eating properly,* he thought, watching her. There were dark circles beneath her eyes. She looked as if she wasn't sleeping. That made two of them.

'Let's get this over with,' he said, when she seemed lost in thought.

She glanced up and the focus of her navy blue eyes sharpened. 'Yes, let's get it over with,' she agreed. 'I've appointed a lawyer. I thought you'd find that easier than dealing with me directly—I know I will. I'm busy,' she said, as if that explained it.

'Business is good?' he asked carefully.

'You should know it is.' She glanced up, but her gaze quickly flickered away. 'Grace keeps me busy with the charity, and my work for that has led me on to all sorts of things.'

'That's good, isn't it?'

She smiled thinly.

'Are you still living at the same place?'

'Why do you ask?' she said defensively.

He should have remembered how combative Romy could be. He should have taken into account the fact that pregnancy hormones would accentuate this trait. But Romy's wellbeing and that of his child was his only concern now. He didn't want to fight with her. 'Just interested,' he said with a shrug.

'I don't need your money,' she said quickly. 'With money comes control, and I'm a free agent, Kruz.'

'Whoah…' He held his hands up. She was bristling to the point where he knew he had to pull her back somehow.

'I'd do anything for my child,' she went on, flashing him a warning look, 'but I won't be governed by your money and your influence. I don't need you, Kruz. I am completely capable of taking care of this.'

And completely hormonal, he supplied silently as Romy's raised voice travelled, causing people to turn and stare.

'I'm not challenging your rights,' he said gently. 'This child has changed everything for both of us. Neither of us can remain isolated in own private world any longer, Romy.'

She had expected this meeting with Kruz to be difficult, but she hadn't expected to feel quite so emotional. This was torture. If only she could reach out instead of pushing him away.

The past was a merciless taskmaster, Romy concluded, for each time she thought about the possibility of a family unit, however loosely structured, she was catapulted back into that house where her mother had been little more than a slave to her father's much stronger will.

'You don't know anything about this,' she said

distractedly, not even realising she was nursing her baby bump.

'I know quite a lot about it,' Kruz argued, which only made the ache of need inside her grow. 'I grew up on an *estancia* the size of a small city. I saw birth and death as part of the natural cycle of life. I saw the effect of pregnancy on women. So I do understand what you're going through now. And I know about your mother, Romy, and I'm very sorry for your loss.'

Kruz knew everything about everything. Of course he did. It was his business to know. 'Well, thank you for your insight,' she snapped, like a frightened little girl instead of the woman she had become.

Not all men were as principled as Kruz, but he would leave her to pick up the pieces eventually. Better she pushed him away now. It wasn't much of a plan, but it was all she'd got. She just hadn't expected it to be so hard to pull off.

'When the baby's born,' she said, straightening her back as she took refuge in practical matters, 'you will have full visiting rights.'

'That's very good of you,' Kruz remarked coldly.

She was being ridiculous. Kruz had the means to fight her through the courts until the end of time, while *her* resources were strictly limited. She might like to think she was in control, but that was a fantasy he was just humouring. 'Independence is important to me—'

'And to me too,' he assured her. 'But not at the expense of everyone around me.'

She was glad when he fell silent, because it stopped her retaliating and driving another wedge between them. 'I hope we can remain friends.'

'I'd say that's up to you,' he said, reaching for his jacket.

She wanted to say something—to reach out and touch him—but it had all gone wrong. 'I'll get the bill,' she offered, feeling she must do something.

Ignoring her, Kruz called the waitress over.

She wanted him in her life, but she couldn't live with the control that came with that. She felt like crying and banging her fists on the table with frustration. Only very reluctantly she accepted that those feelings were due to hormones. Her emotions were all over the place. She ached to share her hopes and fears about the baby with Kruz, and yet she was doing everything she could to drive him away.

'Ready to go?' he said, standing. 'My lawyers will be in touch with yours.'

'Great.'

This was it. This was the end. Everything was being brought to a close with a brusque statement that twisted in her heart like a knife. She got up too, and started to leave the table. But her belly got stuck. Kruz had to move the table for her. She felt so vulnerable. She couldn't pretend she didn't want to confide in him, share her fears with him. He stood back as she walked to the door. Somehow she managed to bang into someone's tray on one of the tables, and then she nearly sent a child flying when she turned around to see what she'd done.

'It's okay, I've got it,' Kruz said calmly, making sure everything was set to rights in his deft way, with his charisma and his smile.

'Sorry,' she said, feeling her cheeks fire up as she made her apologies to the people involved. They hardly seemed to notice her. They were so taken with Kruz. 'Sorry,' she said again when he joined her at the door. 'I'm so clumsy these days. When the baby's born we'll have another chat.'

He raised a brow at this and made no reply. Now he'd seen her he must think her ungainly and clumsy.

'I'll be in touch,' he said.

This was all happening too fast. The words wouldn't come out of her mouth quickly enough to stop him.

Pulling up the collar on his heavy jacket, he scanned the traffic and when he saw a gap dodged across the road.

Her heart was in shreds as her gaze followed him. She stayed where she was in the doorway of the café, sheltering in blasts of warm, coffee-scented air as customers arrived and left. When the door was opened and the chatter washed over her she began to wonder if a heart could break in public, while people were calling for their coffee or more ketchup on their chips.

Grace had taken her in, insisting Romy couldn't expect to keep healthy and look after her unborn child while she was sleeping on a friend's sofa. There was plenty of room in the penthouse, Grace had explained. Romy hadn't wanted to impose, but when Grace insisted that she'd welcome the company while Nacho was away on a polo tour Romy had given in. They could work together on the charity features while Romy waited for the birth of her child, Grace pointed out.

Romy had worked out that if she budgeted carefully she would have enough money to buy most of the things she needed for the baby in advance. She searched online to find bargains, and hunted tirelessly through thrift shops for the bigger items, but even with her spirit of make do and mend she couldn't resist a visit to Khalifa's department store when she noticed there was a sale on. She bought one adorable little suit at half-price but would have loved a dozen more, along with a soft blanket and a mobile to hang above the cot. But those, like the cuddly toys, were luxuries she had to pass up. The midwife at the hospital had given her a long list of essentials to buy before she gave birth.

Get over it, Romy told herself impatiently as her hormones got to work on her tear glands as she walked around the baby department. This baby was going to be born to a mother who adored it already and who would do anything for it.

A baby who would never know its grandmother and rarely see its father.

'Thanks a lot for that helpful comment,' she muttered out loud.

She could do without her inner pessimist. Emotional incontinence at this stage of pregnancy needed no encouragement. Leaning on the nearest cot, she foraged in her cluttered bag for a tissue to stem the flow of tears and ended up looking like a panda. Why did department stores have to have quite so many mirrors? So much for the cool, hard-edged photographer—she was a mess.

It had not been long since her mother's funeral, Romy reasoned as she took some steadying breaths. It had been a quiet affair, with just a few people from the care home. There was nothing sadder than an empty church, and she had felt bad because there had been no one else to invite. She felt bad now—*about everything.* Her ankles were swollen, her feet hurt, and her belly was weighing her down.

But she had a career she loved and prospects going forward, Romy told herself firmly as an assistant, noticing the state she was in, came over with a box of tissues.

'We see a lot of this in here,' the girl explained kindly. 'Don't worry about it.'

Romy took comfort from the fact that she wasn't the only pregnant woman falling to pieces during pregnancy—right up to the moment when the assistant added, 'Does the daddy know you're here? Shall I call him for you?' Only then did she notice Romy's ring-free hands. 'Oh, I'm sorry!' she exclaimed, slapping her hand over her mouth. 'I really didn't mean to make things worse for you.'

'You haven't,' Romy reassured her as a fresh flood of tears followed the first. She just wanted to be on her own so she could howl freely.

'Here—have some more tissues,' the girl insisted, thrusting a wad into Romy's hands. 'Would you like me to call you a cab?'

'Would you?' Romy managed to choke out.

'Of course. And I'll take you through the staff entrance,' the girl offered, leading the way.

Thank goodness Kruz couldn't see her like this—all bloated and blotchy, tear-stained and swollen, with her hair hanging in lank straggles round her face. Gone were the super-gelled spikes and kick-ass attitude, and in their place was…a baby.

He'd kept away from Romy, respecting her insistence that she was capable of handling things her way and that she would let him know when the baby was born. They lived in different countries, she had told him, and she didn't need his help. He was in London most of the time now, getting the new office up to speed, but he had learned not to argue with a pregnant woman. Thank goodness for Grace, who was still in London while Nacho was on a polo tour. At least she could reassure him that Romy was okay—though Grace had recently become unusually cagey about the details.

The irony of their situation wasn't lost on him, he accepted as he reversed into a space outside Khalifa's department store. He had pushed Romy away and now she was refusing to see him. She was about to give birth and he missed her. It was as simple as that.

But even though she refused his help there was nothing to say he couldn't buy a few things for their baby. Grace had said this was the best place to come—that Khalifa's carried a great range of baby goods.

The store also boasted the most enthusiastic assistants in London town, Kruz reflected wryly as they flocked around him. How the hell did he know what he wanted? He stood, thumbing his stubble, in the midst of a bewildering assortment of luxury goods for the child who must have everything.

'Just wrap it all up,' he said, eager to be gone from a place seemingly awash with happy couples.

'Everything, sir?' an assistant asked him.

'You know what a baby needs better than I do,' he pointed out. 'I'll take it all. Just charge it to my account.'

'And send it where, sir?'

He thought about the Acosta family's fabulous penthouse, and then his heart sank when he remembered Romy's tiny terrace on the wrong side of the tracks. He would respect her wish to say there for now, but after the birth…

The store manager, hurrying up at the sight of an important customer, distracted him briefly—but not enough to stop Kruz remembering that the only births he had attended so far were of the foals he owned, all of which had been born in the fabulous custom-built facility on the *estancia.*

No one owned Romy, he reflected as the manager continued to reassure him that Khalifa's could supply anything he might need. Romy was her own woman, and he had Grace's word for the fact that she would have the best of care during the birth of their baby at a renowned teaching hospital in the centre of London. But after the birth he suspected Romy would want to make her nest in that tiny terraced house.

Another idea occurred to him. 'Gift-wrap everything you think a newborn baby might need,' he instructed the manager, 'and have it made ready for collection.'

'Collection by van, sir?' The manager glanced around the vast, well-stocked floor.

'Yes,' Kruz confirmed. 'How long will that take?'

'At least two hours, plus loading time—'

He shrugged. 'Then I will return in two hours.'

Brilliant. Women loved surprises. He'd hire a van, load it up and deliver it himself.

The thought of seeing Romy again made him smile for the first time in too long. It would be good to see her shock when he rolled up with a van full of baby supplies. She would definitely unwind. Maybe they could even make a fresh start—as friends this time. Whatever the future held for them, he suspected they could both do with some down-time before the birth of their baby threw up a whole new raft of problems.

CHAPTER TWELVE

THAT WAS NOT a phantom pain.

Bent over double in the small guest cloakroom in the penthouse while Grace was at the shops buying something for their supper was not a good place to be…

Romy sighed with relief as the pain subsided. There was no cause for panic. If it got any worse she'd call an ambulance.

For once he didn't even mind the traffic because he was in such a good mood, and by the time he pulled the hired van outside the terraced house he was feeling better than positive. They would work something out. They both had issues and they both had to get over them. They had a baby to consider now.

Springing down from the van, he stowed the keys. Relying on Grace for snippets of information about Romy wasn't nearly good enough, but he was half to blame for allowing the situation to get this bad. Both he and Romy were always on the defensive, always expecting to be let down. Raising his fist, he hammered on the door. Now he just had to hope she was in.

Oh, oh, oh... She had managed to crawl into the bathroom. *Emergency!*

They'd mentioned pressure at the antenatal classes, so she was hoping this was just a bit of pressure—

Pressure everywhere.

And no sign of Grace.

'Grace…' she called out weakly, only to have the silence of an empty apartment mock her. 'Grace, I need you,' she whimpered, knowing there was no one to hear her. 'Grace, I don't know what to do.'

Oh, for goodness' sake, pull yourself together! Of course you know what to do.

Now the pain had faded enough for her to think straight, maybe she did. Scrabbling about in her pockets, she hunted for her phone. All she had to do was dial the emergency number and tell them she was having a baby. What was so hard about that?

'Grace!' she exclaimed with relief, hearing the front door open. 'Grace? Is that you?'

'Romy?' Grace sounded as panicked as Romy felt. 'Romy, where are you?'

'On the floor in the bathroom.'

'On the floor—? Goodness—'

She heard Grace shutting her big old guide dog, Buddy, in the kitchen before moving cautiously down the hall with her stick. 'Grace, I'm in here.' There were several bathrooms in the penthouse, and Grace would find her more easily if she followed the sound of Romy's voice.

'Are you okay?' Grace called out anxiously, trying to get her bearings.

That was a matter of opinion. 'I'm fine,' Romy managed, and then the door opened and Grace was standing there. Just having someone to share this with was a help.

Grace felt around with her stick. 'What on earth are you doing under the sink?'

'I had a little accident,' Romy admitted, chucking the towel she'd been using in the bath. 'Can't move,' she managed to grind out as another contraction hit her out of nowhere. 'Stay where you are, Grace. I don't want you slipping, or tripping over me—I'll be fine in a minute.'

'I'm calling for an ambulance,' Grace said decisively, pulling out her phone.

'Tell them my waters have broken and the baby's coming—and this baby isn't waiting for anything.'

'Okay, keep calm!' Grace exclaimed, sounding more panicked than Romy had ever heard her.

He had thoughts of reconciliation and an armful of Romy firmly fixed in his head as he hammered a second time on the door of the small terraced house. Like before, the sound echoed and fell away. Shading his eyes, he peered through the window. It was hard to see anything through the voile the girls had hung to give them some privacy from the street. His spirits sank. His best guess…? The tenants of this house were long gone.

How could he not have known? He should have kept up surveillance—but if Romy had found out he was having her followed he would have lost her for good.

There was nothing more pitiful than a man standing outside an empty house with a heart full of hope and a van full of baby equipment. But he had to be sure. Glancing over his shoulder to check the street was deserted, he delved into the pocket of his jeans to pull out the everyday items that allowed him entry into most places. This, at least, was one thing he was good at.

The house was empty. Romy and her friends had packed up and gone for good. There were a few dead flowers in a milk bottle, as if the last person to turn out the lights hadn't been able to bear to throw them away and had given them one last drink of water.

That would be Romy. So where the hell was she?

Grace would know.

Grace had called the emergency services, and Romy was reassured to hear her friend's succinct instructions on how to access the penthouse with the code at the door so she wouldn't have to leave Romy's side. But the ambulance would have to negotiate the rush hour traffic, Romy realised, starting to worry again as her baby grew ever more insistent to enter the world. Even with sirens blaring the driver would face gridlock in this part of town.

She jumped as Grace's telephone rang. The sight of Grace's face was enough to tell her that the news was not good. 'Grace, what is it?'

'Nothing…'

But Grace's nervous laugh was less than reassuring. 'It must be something,' Romy insisted.

'What's happened, Grace?' She really hoped it wasn't bad news. She wasn't at her most comfortable with her head lodged beneath the sink.

'Seems the first ambulance can't get here for some reason,' Grace admitted. 'But they've told me not to worry as they're sending another—'

'Don't worry?' Romy exclaimed, then felt immediately guilty. Grace was doing everything she could. 'Can you ring them back and tell them I need someone right away? This baby won't wait.'

'I'll do that now,' Grace agreed, but the instant she started to dial her phone rang. 'Kruz?'

'No!' Romy exclaimed in dismay. 'I don't want to speak to him—there's no time to speak to him—' A contraction cut her off, leaving her panting for breath. By the time it had subsided Grace was off the phone. 'You'd better not have told him!' Romy exclaimed. 'Please tell me you didn't tell him. I couldn't bear for him to see me like this.'

'Too late. He's on his way.'

Romy groaned, and then wailed, 'I need to push!'

'Hold on—not yet,' Grace pleaded.

'I can't hold on!' She added a few colourful

expletives. 'Sorry, Grace—didn't mean to shout at you—'

Kruz had heard some of this before Grace cut the line. He had called an ambulance too, but the streets were all blocked. It was rush hour, they'd told him—as if he didn't know that. Even using bus lanes and sirens the ambulance driver could only do the best he could.

'Well, for God's sake, *do* your best!' he yelled in desperation. And he never yelled. He had never lost his cool with anyone. *Other than where Romy and his child were concerned.*

The traffic was backed up half a mile away from where he needed to be. Pulling the van onto the pavement, he climbed out and began to run. Bursting into the penthouse, he followed the sound of Grace's voice to the guest cloakroom, where he found Romy wedged at an awkward angle between the sink and the door.

'Get off me,' she sobbed as he came to pick her up. 'I'm going to have a baby—'

As if he didn't know that! 'You're as weak as a kitten and you need to be strong for me, Romy,' he said firmly as he drew her limp, exhausted body into his arms. 'Grace, can you bring me all the clean towels you've got, some warm water and a cover for the baby. Do we have a cradle? Something to sponge Romy down? Ice if you've got it. Soft cloths and some water for her to sip.'

By this time he had shouldered his way into a bedroom, stripped the duvet away and laid Romy down across the width of the bed. He found a chair to support her legs. This was no time for niceties. He'd seen plenty of mares in labour and he knew the final stages. Romy's waters had broken in the cloakroom and now she was well past getting to the hospital in time.

'What are you doing?' she moaned as he started stripping off her clothes.

'You're planning to have a baby with your underwear on?'

'Stop it… Not you… I don't want you undressing me.'

'Well, Grace is busy collecting the stuff we're going to need,' he said reasonably. 'So if not me, who else do you suggest?'

'I don't want you seeing me like this—'

'Hard luck,' he said as she whimpered, carrying on with his job. 'Strong, Romy. I need strong, Romy. Don't go all floppy on me. I need you in fighting mode,' he said firmly, in a tone she couldn't ignore. 'This baby is ready to enter the world and it needs you to fight for it. This isn't about you and me any longer, Romy.'

As he was speaking he was making Romy as comfortable as he could.

'Are you listening to me, Romy?' Tenderly taking her tear-stained face between his hands, he watched with relief as her eyes cleared and the latest contraction subsided. 'That's better,' he whispered. And then, because he could, he brushed a kiss across her lips. 'We're going to do this together, Romy. You and me together,' he said, staring into her eyes. 'We're going to have a baby.'

'Mostly me,' she pointed out belligerently, and with a certain degree of sense.

'Yes, mostly you,' he confirmed. Then, seeing her eyes fill with apprehension again, he knelt on the floor at the side of the bed. 'But remember this,' he added, bringing her into his arms so he could will his strength into her, 'the harder you work, the sooner you'll be holding that baby in your arms. You've got to help him, Romy.'

'Him?'

'Or her,' he said, feeling a stab of guilt at the fact that he hadn't attended any of the scans or check-ups Romy had been to.

Yes, she'd asked him not to—but since when

had he ever done anything he was told? Had she tamed the rebel? If she had, her timing was appalling. He should have been with her from the start. But this was not the best time to be analysing where their stubbornness had led them.

'Whether this baby is a boy or a girl,' he said, talking to Romy in the same calm voice he used with the horses, 'this is your first job as a mother. It's the first time your baby has asked you for help, so you have to get on it, Romy. You have to believe in your strength. And remember I'm going to be with you every step of the way.'

She pulled a funny face at that, and then she was lost to the next contraction. They were coming thick and fast now.

'How long in between?' he asked. 'Have you been keeping a check on things, Grace?' he asked Grace as she entered the room.

'Not really,' Grace admitted.

'Don't worry—you've brought everything I asked for. Could you put a cool cloth on Romy's head for me?'

'Of course,' Grace said, sounding relieved to be doing something useful as she felt her way around the situation in a hurry to do as he asked. 'I didn't realise it would all happen so quickly.'

'Neither did I,' Romy confessed ruefully, her voice muffled as she pressed her face into his chest.

'This is going really well,' he said, hoping he was right. 'It's not always this fast,' he guessed, 'but this is better for the baby.'

At least Romy seemed reassured as she braced herself against him, which was all that mattered. The speed of this baby's arrival had surprised everyone—not least him.

'Grace, could you stay here with Romy while I scrub up?'

'No, don't leave me,' Romy moaned, clinging to him.

'You're going to be all right,' he said, gently detaching himself. 'Here, Grace—I'll pull up a chair for you.' Having made Romy comfortable on the bed, he steered Grace to the chair. 'Just talk to her,' he instructed quietly. 'Hold her hand until I get back.'

'Don't go,' Romy begged him again.

'Thirty seconds,' he promised.

'Too long,' she managed, before losing herself in panting again.

'My sentiments entirely,' he called back wryly from the bathroom door.

He was back in half that time. 'I'm going to take a look now.'

'You can't look!' Romy protested, sounding shocked.

Bearing in mind the intimacy they had shared, he found her protest endearing. 'I need to,' he explained. 'So please stop arguing with me and let's all concentrate on getting this baby safely into the world.'

'How many births have you attended?' Romy ground out as he got on with the job.

'More than you can imagine—and this one is going to be a piece of cake.'

'How can you know that?' she howled.

'Just two legs, and one hell of a lot smaller than my usual deliveries? Easy,' he promised, pulling back.

'How many human births?' she ground out.

'You'll be the first to benefit from my extensive experience,' he admitted, 'so you have the additional reassurance of knowing I'm fresh to the task.'

She wailed again at this.

'Just lie back and enjoy it,' he suggested. 'There's nowhere else we have to be. And with the next contraction I need you to push. Grace, this is where you come in. Let Romy grip your hands.'

'Right,' Grace said, sounding ready for action.

'I can see the head!' he confirmed, unable keep the excitement from his voice. 'Keep pushing, Romy. Push like you've never pushed before. Give me a slow count to ten, Grace. And, Romy? You push all the time Grace is counting. I'm going to deliver the shoulders now, so I need you to pant while I'm turning the baby slightly. That's it,' he said. 'One more push and you've got a baby.'

'*We've* got a baby,' Romy argued, puce with effort as she went for broke.

Romy's baby burst into the world with the same enthusiasm with which her parents embraced life. The infant girl didn't care if her parents were cool, or independent, or stubborn. All she asked for was life and food and love.

The paramedics walked in just as she was born. A scene of joy greeted them. Grace was standing back, clasping her hands in awe as the baby gave the first of many lusty screams, while Kruz was kneeling at the side of the bed, holding his daughter safely wrapped in a blanket as he passed her over to Romy. Grace had the presence of mind to ask one of the paramedics to record the moment on Romy's phone, and from then on it was all bustle and action as the medical professionals took over.

He could hardly believe it. They had a perfect little girl. A daughter. *His* daughter. His and Romy's daughter. He didn't need to wonder if he had ever felt like this before, because he knew he never had. Nothing he had experienced came close to the first sight of his baby daughter in Romy's arms, or the look on Romy's face as she stared into the pink screwed-up face of their infant child. The baby had a real pair of lungs on her, and could make as much noise as her mother and father combined. She would probably be just as stubborn and argumentative, he concluded, feeling elated. All thoughts of him and Romy not being ready for parenthood had vanished. Of course they were ready. He would defend this child with his life—as he would defend Romy.

Once the paramedics were sure that both mother and baby were in good health, they offered him a pair of scissors to cut the cord. It was another indescribable moment, and he was deeply conscious of introducing another treasured life into the world.

'You've done well, sir,' one of the health professionals told him. 'You handled the birth beautifully.'

'Romy did that,' he said, unable to drag his gaze away from her face.

Reaching for his hand, she squeezed it tightly. 'I couldn't have done any of this without you,' she murmured.

'The first part, maybe,' he agreed wryly. 'But after that I think you should get most of the praise.'

'Don't leave me!' she exclaimed, her stare fearful and anxious on his face as they brought in a stretcher to take Romy and their baby to hospital.

As soon as the paramedics had her settled he put the baby in her arms. 'You don't get rid of me that easily,' he whispered.

And for the first time in a long time she smiled.

CHAPTER THIRTEEN

SHE WOKE TO a new day, a new life. A life with her daughter in it, and—

'Kruz?'

She felt her anxiety mount as she stared around. *Where was he?* He must have slipped out for a moment. He must have been here all night while she'd been sleeping. She'd only fallen asleep on the understanding that Kruz stayed by her side.

Expecting to feel instantly recovered, she was alarmed to find her emotions were in a worse state than ever. She couldn't bear to lose him now. She couldn't bear to be parted from him for a moment. Especially now, after all he'd done for her. He'd been incredible, and she wanted to tell him so. She wanted to hold his hand and stare into his eyes and tell him with a look, with her heart, how much he meant to her. Kruz had delivered their baby. What closer bond could they have?

Hearing their daughter making suckling sounds in her sleep, she swung cautiously out of bed. Just picking up the warm little bundle was an incredible experience. The bump was now a real person. Staring down, she scrutinised every millimetre of the baby's adorable face. She had her father's olive skin, and right now dark blue eyes, though they might change to a compelling sepia like his in time. The tiny scrap even had a frosting of jet-black hair, with some adorable kiss curls softening her tiny face. The baby hair felt downy soft against her lips, and the scent of new baby was delicious—fresh and clean and powdered after the sponge-down she had been given in the hospital.

'And you have amazing eyelashes,' Romy murmured, 'exactly like your father.'

She looked up as a nurse entered the room. 'Have you seen Señor Acosta?' she asked.

'Mr Acosta left before dawn with the instruction that you were to have everything you wanted,' the nurse explained, with the type of dreamy look in her eyes Romy was used to where Kruz was concerned.

'He left?' she said, trying and failing to hide her unease. 'Did he say when he would be back?'

'All I've been told is that Mr Acosta's sister-in-law, Grace Acosta, will be along shortly to pick you up,' the nurse informed her.

Romy frowned. 'Are you *sure* he said that?'

'I believe your sister-in-law will be driven here.'

'Ah…' Romy breathed a sigh of relief, knowing Grace would laugh if she knew Romy's churning emotions had envisaged Grace trying to walk home with Romy at her side, carrying a newly delivered baby, and with a guide dog in tow.

A chauffeur-driven car!

This was another world, one Romy had tried so hard not to become caught up in—though she could hardly blame Grace for travelling in style. She should have thought this through properly long before now. She should have realised that having Kruz's baby would have repercussions far beyond the outline for going it alone she had sketched in her mind.

'The car will soon be here to take you and the baby back to the penthouse,' the nurse was explaining to her.

'Of course,' Romy said, acting as if she were reassured. She would have felt better if Kruz had been coming to pick them up, but that wouldn't happen because she had drawn up the rules to exclude him, so she could prove her independence and go it alone with her baby.

But he couldn't just walk away.

Could he?

She shook herself as the nurse walked back in.

'It was a wonderful birth—thanks to your partner. I bet you can't wait to start your new life together as a family.' The nurse stopped and looked at her, and then passed her some tissues without a word.

Like the assistant in the department store, the nurse must have seen a lot of this, Romy guessed, scrubbing impatiently at her eyes. She was still trying to tell herself that Kruz had only gone to take a shower and grab a change of clothes when the nurse added some more information to her pot of woe.

'Mr Acosta said he had to fly as he had some urgent business to complete.'

'Fly?' Romy repeated. 'He actually said that? He said he had to *fly*?'

'Yes, that's exactly what he said,' the nurse confirmed gently. 'Get back into bed,' she added firmly as Romy started hunting for her clothes. 'You should be taking it easy. You've just given birth and the doctor hasn't discharged you yet.'

'I need my phone,' Romy insisted, padding barefoot round the room, collecting up her things.

So Kruz was just going to fly back to Argentina after delivering their baby? He was going to fly *somewhere*, anyway; the nurse had just said so. And she'd thought Kruz might have changed. The overload to her hormones could only be described as nuclear force meeting solar storm. She might just catch him before he took off, Romy concluded, trying to calm down when she found her phone.

'Mr Acosta did say you might want to take some pictures, so he had your camera couriered over.'

Of course he did, Romy thought, refusing to be placated.

The nurse gave her a shrewd and slightly amused look as a frowning Romy began to stab numbers into her phone. 'I'll leave you to it,' she mouthed.

'Kruz?' Romy was speaking in a dangerously soft voice as the call connected. 'Is that you?'

'Of course it's me. Is something wrong?'

'Where are you? If you're still on the ground get back here right away—we need to talk.'

'Romy?'

She'd cut the line. He rang back. She'd turned her phone off.

With a vicious curse he slammed his fist down on the wheel. Starting the engine, he thrust the gears into Reverse and swung the Jeep round, heading back to the hospital at speed, with his world splintering into little pieces at the thought that something might have happened to Romy or their child.

'You were going to leave us!' Romy exclaimed the moment he walked back into the room.

'Don't you *ever* do that to me again,' he said. Ignoring her protests, he took Romy in his arms and hugged her tight.

'Do what?' she said in a muffled voice.

'Don't ever frighten me like that. I thought something had happened to you or the baby. Do you have any idea how much you mean to me?'

She stared into his eyes, disbelieving, until the force of his stare convinced her.

'If they hadn't told me at Reception that you were both well I don't know what I would have done.'

'Flown to Argentina?' she suggested.

'You can't seriously think I'd do that now?'

'The nurse said you had to fly.' Romy's mouth set in a stubborn line.

'I did have to fly—I had an appointment.'

'What were you doing? I know,' she said, stopping herself. 'Sorry—none of my business.'

'It's a long story,' Kruz agreed. 'Why don't I ring Grace and give her some warning before I take you back?'

'Good idea.' It was hard to be angry with Kruz when he looked like this, as he stared down at their child, but nothing had changed. This man was still Kruz Acosta—elusive, hard and driven. A man who did what he liked, when he liked. While she was still Romy Winner—self-proclaimed battle-axe and single mother.

'Well, that's settled,' Kruz said as he cut the line. 'Grace is going back to Argentina. Nacho is coming to collect her now, so you'll have the penthouse to yourself.'

She should be grateful for the short-term loan of such a beautiful home. 'Okay,' she said brightly, worrying about how she and the baby would rattle round the vast space.

'There's plenty of staff to help you,' Kruz pointed out.

'Great,' she agreed. The company of strangers was just what she needed in her present mood. 'I'll get my things together.'

'Grace has organised everything for you, so there's nothing to worry about,' Kruz remarked as he leaned over the cradle.

She loved the way he cared about their baby, but she felt the first stirring of unease. Now the drama was over, would Kruz claim their daughter? He could provide so much more than she could for their child. Would it be selfish of her to cling on?

Of course not. There was no conflict. She kicked the rogue thought into touch. No one would part her from her baby. But would she be in constant conflict with Kruz for ever?

'You can't buy her,' she whispered, thinking out loud.

'*Buy* her?' Kruz queried with surprise. 'She's already mine.'

'Ours.'

'Romy, are you guilty of overreacting to every little comment I make, by any chance?' Before she could answer, Kruz pointed out that she *had* just given birth. 'Give yourself a break, Romy. I know how much your independence means to you, and I respect that. No one's going to take your baby away from you—least of all me.'

Biting her lip, she forced the tears back. Why did everything seem like a mountain to climb? 'I don't know what to think,' she admitted.

'Is this what I've been missing over the past few months?' Kruz asked wryly.

'I'm glad you think it's funny,' she said, knowing she *was* overreacting, but somehow unable to stop herself. 'Do you think you can house me in your glamorous penthouse and pull my strings from a distance?'

'Romy,' Kruz said with a patient sigh, 'I could never think of you as a puppet. Your strings would be permanently tangled. And if we're going to sort out arrangements for the future I don't want to be doing it in a hospital. Do you?'

She flashed a look at him. Kruz's gaze was steady, but those arrangements for the future he was talking about meant they would part.

Count to ten, she counselled herself. *Right now you're viewing everything through a baby-lens.*

She slowly calmed down—enough to pick up her camera. 'Just one shot of you and the baby,' she said.

'Why don't we ask the nurse if she'll take one of all three of us together?' Kruz suggested. 'There will never be another moment like this as we celebrate the birth of our beautiful daughter.'

'You're right,' Romy agreed quietly. 'I feel like such a fool.'

'No,' Kruz argued. 'You feel like every new mother—full of hope and fear and excitement and doubt. You're exhausted and wondering if you can cope. And I'm telling you as a close observer of Romy Winner that you can. And what's more you look pretty good to me,' he added, sending her a look that made her breath hitch.

She hesitated, not knowing whether to believe him as the nurse came in to take the shot. 'Do I look okay?' she asked, suddenly filled with horror at the thought of ruining the photo of gorgeous Kruz and his beautiful daughter—and her.

'Take the baby,' he said, putting their little girl in her arms. 'You look great. I like your hair silky and floppy,' he insisted, 'and I like your unmade-up face. But if you want gel spikes and red tips, along with tattoos in unusual places and big, black Goth eyes, that's fine by me too.'

'You're being unusually understanding,' Romy commented, trying to make a joke of it. Once a judgement was made regarding their daughter's future they would be parents, not partners, and she should never get the two mixed up.

'I'm undergoing something of an emotional upheaval myself,' Kruz confessed, putting his arm loosely around her shoulders for the happy family shot. 'I guess having a child changes you…' His voice trailed off, but his tender look spoke volumes as he glanced down at their daughter, sleeping soundly in Romy's arms.

'I've never seen you like this before,' Romy commented as Kruz straightened up.

Kruz said nothing.

'So, will you be going back to Argentina as soon as everything's settled here?' she pressed as the nurse took the baby from her and handed her to Kruz.

'I'm in no hurry,' Kruz murmured, staring intently at his daughter.

This was a *very* different side of Kruz, Romy realised, deeply conscious of his depth of feeling as she checked she had packed everything ready for leaving. He was oblivious to everything but his daughter, and that frightened her. *Would* he try to take her baby from her?

His overriding concern was that his child should grow up as part of a strong family unit as he had—thanks to Nacho. But Romy must make her own decisions and he would give her time.

'Are we ready?' he said briskly, once Romy was seated in the wheelchair in which hospital policy insisted she must be taken outside.

'Yes, I'm ready,' Romy confirmed, her gaze instantly locking onto their baby as he placed their daughter in her arms.

'Then let's go.' He was surprised by his eagerness to leave the hospital so he could begin his new life as a father. He couldn't wait to leave this sterile environment where no expressions of intimacy or emotion were possible. He longed to relax, so he could express his feelings openly.

'Kruz—'

'What?' he said, wondering if there was any more affecting sight than a woman holding her newborn child.

Romy shook her head and dropped her gaze. 'Nothing,' she said.

'It must be something.' She was exhausted, he realised, coming to kneel by her side. 'What is it?' he prompted as the nurse discreetly left the room.

'I'm just…' She shook her head, as new to the expression of emotion as he was, he guessed. And then she firmed her jaw and looked straight at him. 'I'm just worrying about the effect of you walking in and out of our baby's life.'

'Don't look for trouble, Romy.'

Why not? her look seemed to say. He blamed the past for Romy's concerns. He blamed the past for his inability to form close relationships outside his immediate family. He guessed that the birth of this child had been a revelation for both of them. It wasn't a case of daring to love, but trying not to—if you dared. Hostage for life, he thought, staring into his daughter's eyes, and a willing one. This wealth of feeling was something both he and Romy would have to get used to and it would take time.

'Don't push me away just yet,' he said, sounding light whilst inwardly he was painfully aware of how much they both stood to lose if they handled this badly. 'I've done as you asked so far, Romy. I've kept my distance for the whole of your pregnancy, so grant me a little credit. But please don't ask me to keep my distance from my child, because that's one thing I can't do.'

'I thought you didn't want commitment,' she said.

He wanted to say, *That was then and this is now,* but he wasn't going to say anything before he was ready. He wouldn't mislead Romy in any way. He had to be sure. From a life of self-imposed isolation to this was quite a leap, and the feelings were all new to him. He wanted them to settle, so he could be cool and detached like in the old days, when he'd been able to think clearly and had always known the right thing to do.

'Grace said you've never shared your life with anyone,' she went on, still fretting.

'People change, Romy. Life changes them.'

He sprang up as the nurse returned. This wasn't the time for deep discussions. Romy had just had a baby. Her hormones were raging and her feelings were all over the place.

'Time to go,' the nurse announced with practised cheerfulness, taking charge of Romy's chair.

While the nurse was wrapping a blanket around Romy's knees and making sure the baby was warmly covered, Romy turned to him. Grabbing hold of his wrist, she made him look at her. 'So what do you want?' she asked him.

'I want to forget,' he said, so quietly it was almost a thought spoken out loud.

CHAPTER FOURTEEN

ROMY REMAINED SILENT during the journey to the penthouse. She was thinking about Kruz's words.

What did he want to forget? His time in the Special Forces, obviously. Charlie had given her the clue there. Charlie had said Kruz was a hero, but Kruz clearly didn't believe his actions could be validated by the opinion of his peers. Medals were probably just pieces of metal to him, while painful memories were all too vivid and real. She couldn't imagine there was much Kruz couldn't handle—but then she hadn't been there, hadn't seen what he'd seen or been compelled to do what he had done. She only knew him as a source of solid strength, as his men must have known him, and her heart ached to think of him in torment.

'Are you okay?' he said, glancing at her through the mirror.

'Yes,' she said softly. *But I'm worried about you...so worried about you.*

Everything had been centred around her and the

baby, and that was understandable given the circumstances, but who was caring for Kruz? She wanted to…so badly; if only he'd let her. There were times for being a warrior woman and times when just staring into the face of their baby daughter and knowing Kruz was close by, like a sentinel protecting them, was enough. Knowing they were both safe because of him had given her the sort of freedom she had never had before—odd when she had always imagined close relationships must be confining. He'd given her that freedom. He'd given her so much and now she wanted to help him.

He wasn't hers to help, she realised as Kruz glanced at her again through the driving mirror. She mustn't be greedy. But that was easier said than done when his eyes were so warm and so full of concern for her.

'My driving okay for you?'

As he asked the question she laughed. Kruz was driving like a chauffeur—smoothly and avoiding all the bumps. The impatient, fiery polo-player was nowhere to be seen.

'You're doing just fine,' she said, teasing him in a mock-serious tone. 'I'll let you know if anything changes.'

'You do that,' he said, his eyes crinkling in the mirror. 'You must be tired,' he added.

'And elated.' And worried about the future… and most worried of all about Kruz. They had no future together—none they'd talked about, anyway—and what would happen to him in the future? Would he spend his whole life denying himself the chance of happiness because of what had happened in the past?

She pulled herself together, knowing she couldn't let anything spoil this homecoming when Grace and Kruz had gone to so much trouble for her.

'I'm looking forward so much to seeing Grace,' she said, 'and being on familiar ground instead of in the hospital. It makes everything seem…' She really was lost for words.

'Exciting,' Kruz supplied.

Her eyes cleared as she stared into his through the mirror. 'Yes, exciting,' she agreed softly.

'I can understand that. Grace has been rushing around like crazy to get things ready in time. She's as excited as we are.'

We? He made them sound like a couple…

It was just a figure of speech, Romy reminded herself, though Kruz was right about life changing people. They had both been cold and afraid to show their feelings until the baby arrived, but now it was hard to hide their feelings. She'd been utterly determined to go it alone after the birth of their child. The baby had changed her. The baby had changed them both. She couldn't be more thrilled that Kruz would be sharing this home-coming with her.

She gazed at the back of his head, loving every inch of him—his thick dark hair, waving in dis-order, and those shoulders broad enough to hoist an ox. She loved this man. She loved him with every fibre in her being and only wanted him to be happy. But first Kruz had to relearn how to enjoy life without feeling guilty because so many of his comrades were dead. She understood that now.

She had so much to be grateful for, Romy re-flected as Kruz drove smoothly on. As well as meeting Kruz, and the birth of their beautiful daughter, these past few months had brought her some incredible friendships. Charlie and Alessan-dro—and Grace, who was more of a sister than a friend.

And Kruz.

Always Kruz.

Her heart ached with longing for him.

'Grace has been working flat out with the housekeeper to get the nursery ready,' he revealed, bringing her back to full attention.

'But I won't be staying long,' she blurted, suddenly frightened of falling into this seductive way of life when it wasn't truly hers. And Kruz wasn't her man—not really.

'We both wanted to do this for you,' Kruz insisted. 'The penthouse is your home for as long as you want it to be, Romy. You do know that, don't you?'

'Yes.' Like a lodger.

She couldn't say anything more. Her feelings were so mixed up. She was grateful—of course she was grateful—but she was still clinging to the illusion that somehow, some day, they could be a proper family. And that was just foolish. Now tears were stabbing the backs of her eyes again. Pressing her lips together, she willed herself to stop the flow. Kruz had enough on his plate without her blubbing all the time.

'I really appreciate everything you've done,' she said when she was calmer. 'It's just—'

'You don't want to feel caged,' he supplied.

'You're proud and you want to do things your way. I think I get that, Romy.'

There was an edge to his voice that told her he felt shut out. Maybe there was no solution to this—maybe she just had to accept that and move on. She could see she was pushing him away, but it was only because she didn't know what else to do without appearing to take too much for granted.

'You're very kind to let me stay at the penthouse,' she said, realising even as she spoke that she had made herself sound more like a grateful lodger thanking her landlord than ever.

Kruz didn't appear to notice, thank goodness, and as he pulled the limousine into the driveway of the Acosta family's Palladian mansion he said, 'And now you can get some well-earned rest. I'm determined you're going to be spoiled a little, so enjoy it while you can. Stay there—I'm coming round to help you out.'

She gazed out of the window as she waited for Kruz to open the door. The Acosta family owned the whole of this stately building, which was to be her home for the next few weeks. Divided into gracious apartments, it was the sort of house she would never quite get used to entering by the front door, she realised with amusement.

'This isn't a time for independence, Romy,' Kruz said, seeing her looking as he opened the door. 'You'll be happy here—and safe. And I want you to promise me that you'll let Grace look after you while she's here. It might only be for a few more days, but it's important for Grace too. She's proving something to herself—I think you know that.'

That her blind friend could have children and care for them as well as any other mother? Yes, she knew that. The fact that Kruz knew too proved how much they'd both changed.

'Grace has been longing for this moment,' he went on. 'Everyone has been longing for this moment,' he added, taking their tiny daughter out of her arms with the utmost care.

She would have to get used to this, Romy told herself wryly as Kruz closed her door and moved round to the back of the vehicle. But not too much, she thought, gazing up at the grand old white building in front of them. This sort of life—this sort of house—was the polar opposite of what she could afford.

Every doubt she had was swept away the moment she walked inside the penthouse and saw Grace and the staff waiting to welcome her, and when she saw what they'd done, all the trouble Grace had gone to, she was instantly overwhelmed and tearful. They had transformed one of the larger bedroom suites into the most beautiful nursery, with a bathroom off.

'Thank you,' she said softly, walking back to Grace, who was standing in the doorway with her guide dog, Buddy. Touching Grace's arm, Romy whispered, 'I can't believe you've done all this for me.'

'It's for Kruz as well as for you,' Grace said gently. 'And for your baby,' she added, reaching out to find Romy and give her a hug. 'I wanted you to come home to something special for you and your new family, Romy.'

If only, Romy thought, glancing at Kruz. They weren't a proper family—not really. Kruz was doing this because he felt he should—because he was a highly principled man of duty and always had been.

Kruz caught her looking at him and stared back, so she nodded her head, smiling in a way she hoped would show him how much she appreciated everything he and Grace had done for her, whilst at the same time reassuring him that she didn't expect him to devote the rest of his life to looking out for her.

She felt even more emotional when she put their tiny daughter into the beautifully carved wooden crib. Grace had dressed it with the finest Swiss lace, and the lace was so delicate she could imagine Grace selecting this particular fabric by touch. The thought moved her immeasurably. She wanted to hug Grace so hard neither of them could breathe. She wanted to tell Grace that having friends like her made her glad to be alive. She wanted to tell her that, having been so determined to go it alone, she was happy to be wrong. She wanted to be able to express her true feelings for Kruz, to let him know how much he meant to her. But she had to remind herself that they had agreed to do this as individuals, each of them taking a full part in their daughter's life, but separately, and she couldn't go back on her word.

Damn those pregnancy hormones!

The tears were back.

How could anyone who had been such a fearless reporter, a fearless woman, be reduced to this snivelling mess? When it came to being a woman in love, she was lost, Romy realised as Grace explained that the housekeeper had helped her to put everything in place. Romy was only too glad to be called back from the brink by practical matters as Grace went on to explain that she had also hired a night nurse, so that Romy could get some rest.

'I hope you don't mind me interfering?'

'Of course not,' Romy said quickly. 'It isn't interfering. It's kindness. I can't thank you enough for all you've done.'

'You're crying?' Grace asked her with surprise when she broke off.

Grace could hear everything in a voice, Romy remembered, knowing how Grace's other senses had leapt in to compensate for her sight loss. 'Everything makes me cry right now,' she admitted. 'Hormones,' she added ruefully, conscious that Kruz was listening. 'I've been an emotional train wreck since the birth.'

She seemed to have got away with it, Romy thought as Grace and the nurse took over. Or maybe Grace was just too savvy to probe deeper into her words, and the nurse was too polite. Kruz seemed unconcerned—though he did suggest she take a break. Remembering his words about Grace wanting to help, she was quick to agree.

'Champagne?' he suggested, leading the way

into the kitchen. Her heart felt too big for her chest just watching him finding glasses, opening bottles, squeezing oranges.

'What you've done for me—' Knowing if she went on she'd start crying again, she steeled herself, because there were some things that had to be said. 'What you've done for our baby—the way you helped me during the birth—'

'It was a privilege,' Kruz said quietly.

Her cheeks fired red as he stared at her. She didn't know what he expected of her. There was so much she wanted to say to him, but he had turned away.

'Drink your vitamins,' he said, handing her the perfect Buck's Fizz.

'Thanks…' She didn't look at him. Was she supposed to act as if they were just friends? How was she supposed to act like a rational human being where Kruz was involved? How could she close her heart to this man? Having Kruz deliver their baby had brought them closer than ever.

'You're very thoughtful,' he said as he topped up her glass with the freshly squeezed juice.

'I was just thinking we almost had something…' Her face took on a look of horror as she realised what she'd said. Her wistful thoughts had poured out in words.

'And now it's over?' he said.

'And now it can never be the same,' she said, making a dismissive gesture with her hand, as if all those feelings inside her had been nothing more than a passing whim.

Kruz made no comment on this. Instead he said, 'Shall we raise a glass to our daughter?'

Yes, that was something they could both do safely. And they *should* rejoice. This was a special day. 'Our daughter, who really should have a name,' she said.

'Well, you've had a few months to think about it,' Kruz pointed out. 'What ideas have you had?'

'I didn't want to decide without—' She stopped, and then settled for the truth. 'I didn't want to decide without consulting you, but I thought Elizabeth...after my mother.'

Kruz's lips pressed down with approval. 'Good idea. I've always liked the name Beth. But what about you, Romy?' he said, coming to sit beside her.

'What about me?'

She stared into her glass as if the secret of life was locked in there. There was only one place she wanted to be, and that was right here with this man. There was only one person she wanted to be, and that was Romy Winner—mother, photographer and one half of this team.

'Come on,' Kruz prompted her. 'What do you want for the future? Or is it too early to ask?'

A horrible feeling swept over her—a suspicion, really, that Kruz was about to offer to fund whatever business venture she had in mind. 'I can't see further than now.'

'That's understandable,' he agreed. 'I just wondered if you had any ideas?'

She looked at him in bewilderment as he moved to take the glass out of her hand, and only then realised that she'd been twisting it and twisting it. She gave it up to him, and asked, 'What about you? What do *you* want, Kruz?'

'Me?' He paused and gave a long sigh, rounded off with one of those careless half-smiles he was so good at when he wanted to hide his true feelings. 'I have things to work through, Romy,' he said, his eyes turning cold.

Was this Kruz's way of saying goodbye? A chill ran through her at the thought that it might be.

For what seemed like an eternity neither of them spoke. She clung to the silence like a friend, because when he wasn't speaking and they were still sitting together like this she could pretend that nothing would change and they would always be close.

'I've seen a lot of things, Romy.'

She jerked alert as he spoke, wondering if maybe, just maybe, Kruz was going to give her the chance to help him break out of his self-imposed prison of silence. 'When you were in the army?' she guessed, prompting him.

'Let's just say I'm not the best of sleeping partners.'

He was already closing off. 'Do you have nightmares?' she pressed, feeling it was now or never if she was going to get through to him.

'I have nightmares,' Kruz confirmed.

They hadn't done a lot of sleeping together, so she wouldn't know about them, Romy realised, cursing her lust for him. She should have spent more time getting to know him. It was easy to be wise after the event, she thought as Kruz started to tell her something else—something that surprised her.

'I'm going to move in downstairs,' he said. 'There's an apartment going begging and I want to see my daughter every day.'

Part of her rejoiced at this, while another part

of her felt cut out—cut off. To have Kruz living so close by—to see him every day and yet know they would never be together…

'It's better this way,' he said, drawing her full attention again. 'I'm hard to live with, Romy, and impossible to sleep with. And you need your rest, so this is the perfect solution.'

'Yes,' she said, struggling to convince herself. If Kruz was suffering she had to help him. 'Maybe if you could confide in someone—'

'You?'

She realised how ridiculous that must sound to him and her face flamed red. Romy Winner, hard-nosed photojournalist, reduced not just to a sappy, hormonal mess but to a woman who couldn't even step up to the plate and say: *Yes, me. I'm going to do it.* 'I'll try, if you'll give me the chance,' she said instead.

Pressing his lips together, Kruz shook his head. 'It's not that easy, Romy.'

'I didn't expect it would be. I just think that when you've saved so many lives—'

'Someone should save *me*?' He gave a laugh without much humour in it. 'It doesn't work that way.'

'Why not?' she asked fiercely.

'Because I've done things I'll never be able to forget,' he said quietly, and when he looked at her this time there was an expression in his eyes that said: *Just drop it.*

But she never could take good advice. 'Healing is a long process.'

'A lifetime?'

Kruz's face had turned hard, but it changed just as suddenly and gentled, as if he was remembering that she had recently given birth. 'You shouldn't be thinking about any of this, Romy. Today is a happy day and I don't want to spoil it for you.'

'Nothing you could say would spoil it,' she protested, wanting to add that she could never be truly happy until Kruz was too. But that would put unfair pressure on him. She sipped her drink to keep her mouth busy, wondering how two such prickly, complicated people had ever found each other.

'Believe me, you should be glad I'm keeping my distance,' Kruz said as he freshened their drinks. 'But if you need me I'm only downstairs.'

And that was a fact rather than an invitation, she thought—a thought borne out as Kruz stood up and moved towards the door. 'I have to go now.'

'Go?' The shock in her voice was all too obvious.

'I have business to attend to,' he explained.

'Of course.' And Kruz's business wasn't her business. What had she imagined? That he was going to pull her into his arms and tell her that everything would be all right—that the past could be brushed aside, just like that?

He stopped with his hand on the door. 'You believe in the absolution of time, Romy, but I'm still looking for answers.'

She couldn't stop him leaving, and she knew that Kruz could only replace his nightmares when something that made him truly happy had taken their place.

'It's good that you'll be living close by so you can see Beth,' she said. Perhaps that would be the answer. She really hoped so.

Kruz didn't answer. He didn't turn to look at her. He didn't say another word. He just opened the door and walked through it, shutting it quietly behind him, leaving her alone in the kitchen, wondering where life went from here. One step at a time, she thought, one step at a time.

She couldn't fault him as a devoted father. Kruz spent every spare moment he had with Beth. But where Romy was concerned he was distant and enigmatic. This had been going on for weeks now, and she missed him. She missed his company. She missed his warm gaze on her face. She missed his solid presence and his little kindnesses that gave her an opening to reach in to his world and pay him back with some small, silly thing of her own.

Grace had returned to Argentina with Nacho—though they were expected back in London any day soon. This was a concern for Romy, as she knew Grace had hoped a relationship might develop between Romy and Kruz. It was going to be a little bit awkward, explaining why Romy's new routine involved Beth, mother and baby groups, and learning to live life as a single mother, while the father of her baby lived downstairs.

Kruz had issues to work through, and she understood that, but she wished he'd let her help him. She had broached the subject on a few occasions, but he'd brushed her off and she'd drawn back, knowing there was nothing she could say if he wouldn't open up.

The day after Nacho and Grace arrived back in London, Kruz dropped by with some flowers he'd picked up from the market. 'I got up early and I felt like buying all you girls some flowers,' he said, before breezing out again.

This was nice—this was good, Romy told herself firmly as she arranged the colourful spray in a glittering crystal vase. She felt good about herself, and about her life here in Acosta heaven. She was already taking photographs with thoughts of compiling a book. She treasured every moment she spent with her baby. And watching Kruz with Beth was the best.

Crossing to the window, she smiled as she watched him pace up and down the garden, apparently deep in conversation with their daughter. She longed to be part of it—part of them—part of a family that was three instead of two. But she had to stick to the unofficial rules she'd drawn up—rules that allowed Romy to get on with her life independently of Kruz. They both knew that at some point she would leave and move into rented accommodation, and when she did that Kruz had promised to set up an allowance for Beth, knowing very well that Romy would never take money for herself.

As if the money mattered. Her eyes welled up at the thought of parting from Kruz. What if she moved to the other side of London and never saw him again except when he came to collect Beth? When had such independence held any allure? She couldn't remember when, or what that fierce determination to go it alone had felt like. Independence at all costs was no freedom at all.

This wasn't nice—this wasn't good. Sitting down, she buried her face in her hands, wishing her mother were still alive so they could talk things through as they'd used to before her father had damaged her mother's mind beyond repair. Angry with herself, she sprang up again. She was a mother, and this was no time for self-indulgence. It was all about Beth now.

She was used to getting out there and looking after herself. No wonder she was frustrated, Romy reasoned. In fairness, Kruz had suggested that a babysitter should come in now and then, so Romy could gradually return to doing more of the work she loved. She had resigned from *ROCK!*, of course, but even Ronald, her picture editor, had said she shouldn't waste her talent.

She started as the phone rang and went to answer it.

'I'm bringing Beth up.'

'Oh, okay.' She sounded casual, but in her present mood she might just cling to him like an idiot when he arrived, and burst into tears.

No. She would reassure him by pulling herself together and carrying on alone with Beth as she had always planned to do; anything less than that would be an insult to her love for Kruz.

He bumped into Nacho and Grace on his way back into the house. They were staying in the garden apartment on the ground floor, to ensure they had some privacy. It was a good arrangement, this house in London. Big enough for the whole Acosta family, it had been designed so each of them had their own space.

Nacho asked him in for a drink. Grace declined to join them, saying she would rather play with Beth while she had the chance, but he got the feeling, as Grace took charge of the stroller, that his brother's wife was giving them some time alone.

'You've made a great marriage,' he observed as Grace, her guide dog, Buddy, and baby Beth made their way along the hallway to the master suite.

'Don't I know it?' his brother murmured, gazing after his bride.

As he followed Nacho's stare he realised that for the first time in a long time he felt like a full member of the family again, rather than a ghost at the feast. It was great to see Nacho and to be able to share all his news about Romy and their daughter, and how being present at the birth of Beth had made him feel.

'Like there's hope for me,' he said, when Nacho pressed him for more.

'You've always been too hard on yourself,' Nacho observed, leading the way into the drawing room. 'And a lifetime of self-denial changes nothing, my brother.'

Coming from someone whose thoughts he respected, those straight-talking words from his brother hit home. It made him want to draw Romy and Beth together into a family—*his* family.

'Have you told Romy how you feel about her?' Nacho said.

'How I…?' Years of denying his feelings prompted him to deny it, but Nacho knew him too well, so he shrugged instead, admitting, 'I bought her some flowers today.'

'Instead of talking to her?'

'I talk.'

Nacho looked up from the newspaper he'd been scanning on the table.

'You talk?' he said. 'Hello? Goodbye?'

They exchanged a look.

'I'm going to find my wife,' Nacho told him, and on his way across the room he added, 'Babies change quickly, Kruz.'

'In five minutes, brother?'

'You know what I mean. Romy will move out soon. We both know it. She's not the type of woman to wait and see what's going to happen next. She'll make the move.'

'She won't take Beth away from me.'

'You have to make sure of that.'

'We live cheek by jowl already.'

'What?' Nacho scoffed, pausing by the door. 'You live downstairs—she lives upstairs with the baby. Is that what you want out of life?'

'It seems to be what Romy wants.'

'Then if you love her change her mind. Or I'll tell you what will happen in the future. You'll pass Beth between you like a ping-pong ball because both of you stood on your pride. You're not in the army now, Kruz. You're not part of that tight world. *You* make the rules.'

Kruz was still reeling when Nacho left the room. His brother had made him face the truth. He had returned to civilian life afraid to love in case he jinxed that person. He had discarded his feelings in order to protect others as he had tried to protect his men. By the time Romy turned his world on its head he hadn't even been in recovery. But she had started the process, he realised now, and there was no turning back.

The birth of Beth had accelerated everything. The nightmares had stopped. He looked forward to every day. Every moment of every day was precious and worthwhile now Romy and Beth were part of his life. That was what Romy had given him. She had given him love to a degree where not allowing himself to love her back was a bigger risk to his sanity than remembering everything in the past that had brought him to this point.

Nacho was right. He should tell Romy what she'd done for him and how he felt about her. Better still, he should show her.

CHAPTER FIFTEEN

WHEN KRUZ CALLED to explain to Romy that he and Beth were down with Grace and Nacho, so she didn't worry about Beth, he added that he wanted to take her somewhere and show her something.

She fell apart. Not crying. She was over that. Her hormones seemed to have settled at last. It was at Kruz's suggestion that Nacho and Grace should look after Beth while he took Romy out. Take her out without Beth as a buffer between them? She wasn't ready for that.

She would never be ready for that.

Her heart started racing as she heard the strand of tension in his voice that said Kruz was fired up about something. Whatever this something was, it had to be big. There was only one thing she could think of that fired the Acosta boys outside the bedroom. And the bedroom was definitely off the agenda today. In fact the bedroom hadn't been on the agenda for quite some time.

And whose fault was that?

Okay, so she'd been confused—and sore for a while after Beth's birth.

And now?

Not so sore. But still confused.

'Is it a new polo pony you want me to see?' she asked, her heart flapping wildly in her chest at the thought of being one to one with him.

'No,' Kruz said impatiently, as if that was the furthest thing from his mind. 'I just need your opinion on something. Why all the questions, Romy? Do you want to come or not?'

'Wellies, jeans and mac?' she said patiently. 'Or smart office wear?'

'You have some?'

'Stop laughing at me,' she warned.

'Those leggings and flat boots you used wear around *ROCK!* will do just fine. Ten minutes?'

'Do you want a coffee before we go—?' Kruz was in a rush, she concluded as the line was disconnected.

Ten minutes and counting and she had discarded as many outfits before reverting reluctantly to Kruz's suggestion. It was the best idea, but that didn't mean that following anyone's suggestions but her own came easily to her. Her hair had grown much longer, so she tied it back. She didn't want to look as if she was trying too hard.

What would they talk about…?

Beth, of course, Romy concluded, adding some lips gloss to her stubborn mouth. And a touch of grey eyeshadow… And just a flick of mascara… Oh, and a spritz of scent. That really was it now. She'd make coffee to take her mind off his arrival—and when he did arrive she would sip demurely, as if she didn't have a care in the world.

While she was waiting for the coffee to brew she studied some pictures that had been taken of Kruz at a recent polo match. *She* would have done better. She would have taken him in warrior mode—restless, energetic and frustratingly sexy.

While she was restless, energetic and *frustrated*, Romy concluded wryly, leaning back in her chair.

She leapt to her feet when the doorbell rang, feeling flushed and guilty, with her head full of erotic thoughts. Kruz had his own key, but while she was staying at the penthouse he always rang first. It was a little gesture that said Kruz respected her privacy. She liked that. Why pretend? She liked everything about him.

She had to force herself to take tiny little steps on her way to the door.

Would she ever get used to the sight of this man?

As Kruz walked past her into the room he filled the space with an explosion of light. It was like having an energy source standing in front of her. Even dressed in heavy London clothes—jeans, boots, jacket with the collar pulled up—he was all muscle and tan: an incredible sight. *You look amazing,* she thought as he swept her into his arms for a disappointingly chaste kiss. Was it possible to die of frustration? If so, she was well on her way.

'I've missed you,' he said, pulling her by the hand into the kitchen. 'Do I smell coffee? Are you free for the rest of the day?'

'So many questions,' she teased him, exhaling with shock as he swung her in front of him. 'I have *some* free time,' she admitted cautiously, suddenly feeling unaccountably shy. 'Why?'

'Because I'm excited,' Kruz admitted. 'Can't you tell?'

Pressing her lips down, she pretended she couldn't.

He laughed.

Her heart was going crazy. Were they teasing each other now?

'There's something I really want to show you,' he said, turning serious.

'Okay…' She kept her expression neutral as Kruz dropped his hands from her arms. She still didn't know what to think. He was giving her no clues. 'Did you tell Nacho and Grace where we're going?' She dropped this in casually, but Kruz wasn't fooled.

'You don't get it out of me that way,' he said. 'Don't look so worried. We'll only be a few minutes away.'

All out of excuses, she poured the coffee.

'Smells good.'

Not half as good as Kruz, she thought, sipping demurely as wild, erotic thoughts raged through her head. Kruz smelled amazing—warm, clean and musky man—and he was just so damn sexy in those snug-fitting jeans, with a day's worth of stubble and that bone-melting look in his eyes.

'I could go away again if you prefer,' he said, slanting her a dangerous grin to remind her just how risky it was to let her mind wander while Kruz was around. 'Come on,' he said, easing away from the counter. 'I'm an impatient man.' Dumping the rest of his coffee down the sink, he grabbed her hand.

'Shall I bring my camera?' she said, rattling her brain cells into line.

'No,' he said. 'If you can't live without recording every moment, I'll take some shots for you.'

He said this good-humouredly, but she realised Kruz had a point. She would relax more without her camera and take more in. Whatever Kruz wanted to show her was clearly important to him, and focusing a camera lens was in itself selective. She didn't want to miss a thing.

If she could concentrate on anything but Kruz, that was, Romy concluded as he helped her into her coat. It wasn't easy to shrug off the seductive warmth as his hands brushed her neck, her shoulders and her back. Kruz was one powerful opiate—and one she mustn't succumb to until she knew what this was about.

'So what now?' she said briskly as she locked up the penthouse.

'Now you have to be patient,' he warned, holding the door.

'I have to be *patient*?' she said.

Kruz was already heading for the stairs.

'Remember the benefits of delay.'

She stopped at the top of the stairs, telling herself that it was just a careless remark. It wasn't enough to stop fireworks going off inside her, but that was only because she hadn't thought about sex in a long time.

Today it occupied all her thoughts.

She was thrilled when Kruz drove them to the area of London she loved. 'You remembered,' she said.

He had drawn to a halt outside a gorgeous little mews house in a quaint cobbled square. It was just a short walk from the picturesque canal she had told him about.

'You haven't made any secret of your preferred area,' he said, 'so I thought you might like to take a look at this.'

'Do you own it?' she asked, staring up at the perfectly proportioned red brick house.

'I've been looking it over for a friend and I'd value your opinion.'

'I'd be more than happy to give it,' she said, smiling with anticipation.

And happy to dream a little, Romy thought as Kruz opened the car door for her. There was nothing better than snooping around gorgeous houses—though she usually did it between the covers of a glossy magazine or on the internet. This was so much better. This was a dream come true. She paused for a moment to take in the cute wrought-iron Juliet balconies, with their pots of pink and white geraniums spilling over the smart brickwork. The property was south-facing, and definitely enjoyed the best position on the square.

She hadn't seen anything yet, Romy realised when Kruz opened the front door and she walked inside. 'This is gorgeous!' she gasped, struck immediately by the understated décor and abundance of light.

'The bedrooms are all on the ground floor,' he explained, 'so the upper floor can take advantage of a double aspect view over the cobbled square, and over the gardens behind the building. You don't think having bedrooms downstairs is a problem?'

'Not at all,' she said, gazing round. The floor was pale oak strip, and the bedrooms opened off a central hallway.

'There are four bedrooms and four bathrooms on this level,' Kruz explained, 'and the property opens onto a large private garden. Plus there's a garage, and off-street parking—which is a real bonus in the centre of London.'

'Your friend must be very wealthy,' Romy observed, increasingly impressed as she looked around. 'It's been beautifully furnished. I love the Scandinavian style.'

'My friend can afford it. Why don't we take a look upstairs? It's a large, open-plan space, with a kitchen and an office as well as a studio.'

'The studio must be fabulous,' she said. 'There's so much light in the house—and it feels like a happy house,' she added, following Kruz upstairs.

She gave a great sigh of pleasure when they reached the top of the stairs and the open-plan living room opened out in front of them. There were white-painted shutters on either side of the floor-to-ceiling windows, and the windows overlooked the cobbled square at one end of the room and the gardens at the other. Everywhere was decorated in clean Scandinavian shades: white, ivory and taupe, with highlights of ice-blue and a pop of colour played out in the raspberry-pink cushions on the plump, inviting sofa. Even the ornaments had been carefully chosen—a sparkling crystal clock and a cherry-red horse, even a loving couple entwined in an embrace.

'And there's a rocking horse!' she exclaimed with pleasure, catching sight of the beautifully carved dapple grey. 'Your friends are very lucky.

The people who own this house have thought of everything for a family home.'

'And even if someone wanted to work from home here, they could,' Kruz pointed out, showing her the studio. 'Well?' he said. 'What do you think? Shall I tell my friend to go ahead and buy it?'

'He'd be mad not to.'

'Do you think we had better check the nursery before I tell him to close the deal?'

'Yes, perhaps we better had,' Romy agreed. 'At least I have some idea of what's needed in a nursery now.' She laughed. 'So I can offer my opinion with confidence.'

'Goodness,' she said as Kruz opened the door on a wonderland. 'Your friend must have bought out Khalifa's!' she exclaimed. Then, quite suddenly, her expression changed.

'Romy?'

Mutely, she shook her head.

'What is it?' Kruz pressed. 'What's wrong?'

'What's wrong,' she said quietly, 'is that it took me so long to work this out. But I got there eventually.'

'Got where? What do you mean?' Kruz said, frowning.

She lifted her chin. 'I mean, you got *me* wrong,' she said coldly. 'So wrong.'

'What are you talking about, Romy?'

'You bring me to a fabulous mews house in my favourite area of London because you think I can be bought—'

'No,' Kruz protested fiercely.

'No?' she said. 'You're the friend in question, aren't you? Why couldn't you just be honest with me from the start?'

'Because I knew what you'd say,' Kruz admitted tersely. '*Dios*, Romy! I already know how pig-headed you are.'

'*I'm* pig-headed?' she said. 'You'll stop at nothing to get your own way.'

All he could offer was a shrug. 'I wanted this to be a surprise for you,' he admitted. 'I've never done this sort of thing before, so I just went ahead and did what felt right to me. I'm sorry if I got it wrong—got *you* wrong,' he amended curtly.

'Tell me you haven't bought it,' she said.

'I bought it some time ago. I bought it on the day I brought you home from hospital—which is why I had to leave you. I bought it so you and Beth would always have somewhere nice to live—whatever you decide about the future. This is your independence, Romy. This is my gift to you and to our daughter. If you feel you can't take it, I'll put it in Beth's name. It really is that simple.'

For you, she thought. 'But I still don't understand. What are you saying, Kruz?'

'What I'm saying is that I'm still not sure what you want, but I know what *I* want. I've known for a long time.'

'But you don't say anything to me—'

'Because you're never listening,' he said. 'Because you haven't been ready to hear me. And because big emotional statements aren't my style.'

'Then change your style,' she said heatedly.

'We've both got a lot to learn, Romy—about loving and giving and expressing emotion, and about each other. We must start somewhere. For Beth's sake.'

'And that somewhere's here?' she demanded, opening her arms wide as she swung around to encompass the beautiful room.

'If you want it to be.'

'It's too much,' she protested.

'It isn't nearly enough,' Kruz argued quietly. Putting his big warm hands on her shoulders, he kept her still. 'Listen to me, Romy. For God's sake, listen to me. You have no idea what you and Beth have done for me. My nightmares have gone—'

'They've gone?' She stopped, knowing that nothing meant more than this. This meant they had a chance—Kruz had a chance to start living again.

'Baby-meds,' he said. 'Who'd have thought it?'

'So you can sleep at last?' she exclaimed.

'Through the night,' he confirmed.

It was a miracle. If she had nothing more in all her life this was enough. She could have kicked herself. She'd had baby-brain while Kruz had been nothing but considerate for her. The way he'd removed himself to give her space—the way he was always considerate with the keys, with Beth, with everything—the way he never hassled her in any way, or pushed her to make a decision. And had she listened to him? Had she noticed what was going on in his world?

'I'm so sorry—'

'Don't be,' he said. 'You should be glad—*we* should be glad. All I want is for us to be a proper family. I want it for Beth and I want it for you and me. I want us to have a proper home where we can live together and make a happy mess—not a showpiece to rattle round in like the penthouse.

I don't think you want that either, Romy. I think, like me, you want to carry on what we started. I think you want us to go on healing each other. And I know I want you. I love you, and I hope you love me. I want us to give our baby the type of home you and I have always dreamed of.'

'And how will we make it work?' she asked, afraid of so much joy.

'I have no idea,' Kruz admitted honestly. 'I just know that if we give it everything we've got we'll make it work. And if you love me as much as I love you—'

'Hang on,' she said, her face softening as she dared to believe. 'What's all this talk of love?'

'I love you,' Kruz said, frowning. 'Surely you've worked that out for yourself by now?'

'It's nice to be told. I agree you're not the best when it comes to big emotional declarations, but you should have worked that out. Try telling me again,' she said, biting back a smile.

'Okay…' Pretending concentration, Kruz held her close so he stared into her eyes.

'I've loved you since that first encounter on the grassy bank—I just didn't know it then. I've loved you since you went all cold on me and had to be heated up again. I loved you very much by then.'

'Sex-fiend.'

'You bet,' he agreed, but then he turned serious again. 'And now I love you to the point where I can't imagine life without you. And whatever you want to call these feelings—' he touched his heart '—they don't go away. They get stronger each day. You're a vital part of my life now—the *most* vital part, since you're the part I can't live without.'

'And Beth?' she whispered.

'She's part of you,' Kruz said simply. 'And she's part of me too. I want you both for life, Señorita Winner. And I want you to be happy. Which is why I bought you the house—walking distance to the shops—great transport links…'

'You'd make an excellent sales agent,' she said over the thunder of her happy heart hammering.

'I must remember to add that to my CV,' Kruz teased with a curving grin. 'Plus there's an excellent nursery for Beth across the road.'

'Where you've already put her name down?' Romy guessed with amusement.

Kruz shrugged. 'I thought we'd live part of the year here and part on the pampas in Argentina. Whatever you decide the house is yours—

or Beth's. But I won't let you make a final decision yet.'

'Oh?' Romy queried with concern.

'Not until you test the beds.'

'All of them?' She started to smile.

'I think we'd better,' Kruz commented as he swung her into his arms.

'Ah, well.' Romy sighed. 'I guess I'll just have to do whatever it takes…'

'I'm depending on it,' Kruz assured her as he shouldered open the door into the first bedroom.

'Let the bed trials begin,' she suggested when he joined her on the massive bed. 'But be gentle with me.'

'Do you think I've forgotten you've just had a baby?'

Taking her into his arms, Kruz made her feel so safe.

'What?' she said, when he continued to stare at her.

'I was just thinking,' he said, stretching out his powerful limbs. 'We kicked off on a mossy bank on the pampas beside a gravel path, and we've ended up on a firm mattress in your favourite part of London town. That's not so bad, is it?'

Trying to put off the warm honey flowing

through her veins for a few moments was a pointless exercise, Romy concluded, exhaling shakily with anticipation. 'Are you suggesting we work our way back to the start?'

'If none of the beds here suit, I'm sure we can find a grassy bank somewhere in the heart of London…'

'So what are you saying?' she whispered, shuddering with acute sexual excitement as Kruz ran his fingertips in a very leisurely and provocative way over her breasts and down over her belly, where they showed no sign of stopping…

'I'm saying that if you can put up with me,' he murmured as she exclaimed with delight and relief when his hand finally reached its destination, 'I can put up with you. I'm suggesting we get to know each other really, really well all over again—starting at the very beginning.'

'Now?' she said hopefully, surreptitiously easing her thighs apart.

'Maybe we should start dating first,' Kruz said, pausing just to provoke her.

'Later,' she agreed, shivering uncontrollably with lust.

'Yes, maybe we should try the beds out first, as we agreed…' Covering her hand with his, he held her off for a moment. 'I'm being serious about us living together,' he said. 'But I don't want to rush you, Romy. I don't want to make you into something you're not. I don't want to spoil you.'

'This house isn't spoiling me?' she said.

'Pocket change,' Kruz whispered, slanting her a bad-boy smile. 'But, seriously, I don't want to change anything about you, Romy Winner.'

'No. You just want to kill me with frustration,' she said. 'I can't believe you're suggesting we go out on dates.'

'Amongst other things,' he said.

'Then I'll consider your proposition,' she agreed, smiling against his mouth as Kruz moved on top of her.

'You'll do better than that,' he promised, in his most deliciously commanding voice.

'Just one thing,' she warned, holding him off briefly.

'Tell me…'

She frowned. 'I need time.'

'Does for ever suit you?' Kruz murmured, touching her in the way she liked.

'For ever doesn't really sound long enough to me,' she whispered against the mouth of the man she had been born to love.

EPILOGUE

IT WAS THE wedding of the year. Eventually.

It took five years for Kruz to persuade Romy that their daughter was longing to be a bridesmaid and that she shouldn't deny Beth that chance.

'So, for your sake,' she told her adorable quirky daughter, who was never happier than when she had straw in her hair and was wearing shredded jeans with a ripped top covered in hoof oil and horse hair, 'we're going to have that wedding you keep nagging me about, and you are going to be our chief bridesmaid.'

'Great,' Beth said, too busy taking in the intricacies of the latest bridle her father had bought her to pay much attention.

Kruz had finally managed to convince Romy that a wedding would be a wonderful chance to affirm their love, when to Romy's way of thinking she and Kruz already shared everything—with or without that piece of paper.

'But no frills,' Beth insisted, glancing up.

So she *was* listening, Romy thought with amusement. 'No frills,' she agreed—not if she wanted Beth for her bridesmaid.

And a slinky column wedding dress was out of the question for the bride as Romy was heavily pregnant for the third time. Kruz was insatiable, and so was she—more than ever now she was pregnant again. The sex-mad phase again. How lovely.

She felt that same mad rush of heat and lust when he strode into the bedroom now. Pumped from riding, in a pair of banged-up jeans and a top that had seen better times, he looked amazing—rugged and dangerous, just the way she liked him.

Who knew how many children they would have? Romy mused happily as Kruz swung Beth into the air. A polo team, at least, she decided as Kruz reminded their daughter that she was supposed to be going swimming with friends, and had better get a move on if she wasn't going to be late.

Leaving them to plan the wedding…or not, Romy concluded when he finally looked her way.

'The baby?'

She flashed a glance at the door of the nursery where their baby son was sleeping. 'With his nanny.'

She turned as Beth came by for a hug, before racing out of the room, slamming the door behind her. A glance at Kruz confirmed that he thought this was working out just fine. She did too, Romy concluded, taking in the power in his muscular forearms as Kruz propped a hip against her desk.

'Is this the guest list?' he asked, picking up the sheaf of papers Romy had been working on. 'You *do* know we only need two people and a couple of witnesses?'

'You have a big family—'

'And getting bigger all the time,' Kruz observed, hunkering down at her side.

'Who would have thought it?' Romy mused out loud.

'I would,' Kruz murmured wickedly. 'With your appeal and my super-sperm, what else did you expect?' He caressed the swell of her belly and then buried his head a little deeper still.

'I think you should lock the door,' she said, feeling the familiar heat rising.

'I think I should,' Kruz agreed, springing up.

He smiled as he looked down at her. 'I'm glad you lost those red-tipped gel spikes.'

'She frowned. 'What makes you bring those up?'

'Just saying,' Kruz commented with amusement, drawing her into the familiar shelter of his arms.

She had almost forgotten the red-tipped gel spikes. She didn't feel the need to present that hard, *stay-away-from-me* person to the world any more. And now she came to think about it losing the spikes hadn't been a conscious decision; it had been more a case of have baby, have man I love and have *so* much less time for me. And she wouldn't have it any other way.

'So, you like my natural look?' she teased as Kruz undressed her.

'I love you any way,' he said as she tugged off his top and started on his belt. 'Though the closer to nature you get, the more I like it…'

'Back to nature is best,' Romy agreed, reaching for her big, naked man as he tipped her back on the bed.

'Will I ever get enough of you?' Kruz murmured against her mouth as he trespassed at leisure on familiar territory.

'I sincerely hope not,' Romy whispered, groaning with pleasure as her nerve-endings tightened and prepared for the oh, so inevitable outcome.

'Spoon?' he suggested, moving behind her. 'So I can touch you…?'

Her favourite position—especially now she was so heavily pregnant. Arching her back, she offered herself for pleasure.

'Tell me again,' she told him much, much later, when they were lying replete on the bed.

'Tell you what again?' Kruz queried lazily, reaching for her.

'Do you *never* get enough?'

'Of you?' He laughed softly against her back. 'Never. So what do you want me to tell you?'

'Tell me that you love me.'

Shifting position, he moved so that he could see her face, and, holding her against the warmth of his body, he stared into her eyes. 'I love you, Romy Winner. I will always love you. This is for ever. You and me—we're for ever.'

'And I love you,' she said, holding Kruz's dark, compelling gaze. 'I love you more than I thought it possible to love anyone.'

'I especially love making babies with you.'

'You're bad,' she said gratefully as Kruz settled back into position behind her. 'You don't think…?'

'I don't think what?' he murmured, touching her in the way she loved.

'I'm expecting twins this time. Do you think it will be triplets next?'

'Does that worry you?'

She shrugged. 'We both love babies—just thinking we might need a bigger house.'

'Maybe…' he agreed. 'If we practise enough.'

She was going to say something, but Kruz had a sure-fire way of stopping her talking. And—*oh*… He was doing it now.

'No more questions?' he queried.

'No more questions,' she confirmed shakily as Kruz set up a steady beat.

'Then just enjoy me, use me. Have pleasure, baby,' he suggested as he gradually upped the tempo. 'And love me as I love you,' he added as she fell.

'That's easy,' she murmured when she was calmer, and could watch Kruz in the grip of pleasure as he found his own violent release. 'For ever,' she whispered as he held her close.

* * * * *

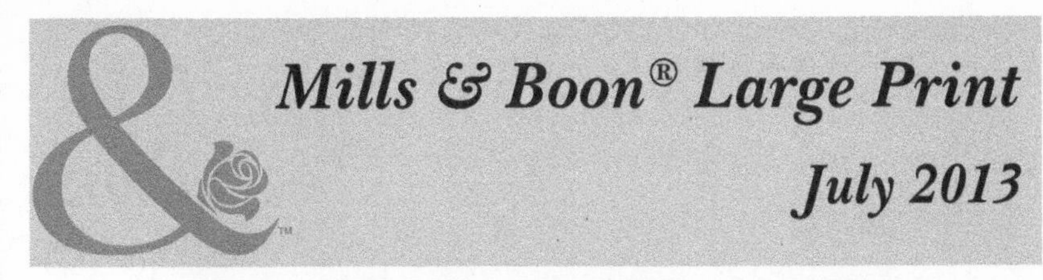

PLAYING THE DUTIFUL WIFE
Carol Marinelli

THE FALLEN GREEK BRIDE
Jane Porter

A SCANDAL, A SECRET, A BABY
Sharon Kendrick

THE NOTORIOUS GABRIEL DIAZ
Cathy Williams

A REPUTATION FOR REVENGE
Jennie Lucas

CAPTIVE IN THE SPOTLIGHT
Annie West

TAMING THE LAST ACOSTA
Susan Stephens

GUARDIAN TO THE HEIRESS
Margaret Way

LITTLE COWGIRL ON HIS DOORSTEP
Donna Alward

MISSION: SOLDIER TO DADDY
Soraya Lane

WINNING BACK HIS WIFE
Melissa McClone

Mills & Boon® Large Print

August 2013

MASTER OF HER VIRTUE
Miranda Lee

THE COST OF HER INNOCENCE
Jacqueline Baird

A TASTE OF THE FORBIDDEN
Carole Mortimer

COUNT VALIERI'S PRISONER
Sara Craven

THE MERCILESS TRAVIS WILDE
Sandra Marton

A GAME WITH ONE WINNER
Lynn Raye Harris

HEIR TO A DESERT LEGACY
Maisey Yates

SPARKS FLY WITH THE BILLIONAIRE
Marion Lennox

A DADDY FOR HER SONS
Raye Morgan

ALONG CAME TWINS...
Rebecca Winters

AN ACCIDENTAL FAMILY
Ami Weaver

0713 Rom LP